FA
AND

"What a memory you have," she said.

"I remember everything about you," he answered. It was spoken as simple fact . . .

Faythe felt herself pulled toward him, but she forced her body to stay motionless. It was Ray who moved toward her, so slowly it seemed to take ages. His hands came up and framed her face, gently forcing her to look up at him. Then his lips were on hers, soft and questing, and his hands had moved up and were buried in her hair.

She felt herself sink against him, her breasts against the hardness of his chest, and his hands moved to her back, caressing the length of it as if they'd never been apart. She felt the old familiar warmth spread through her and wanted to moan his name. Her lips parted under his and she felt his tongue in her mouth, thrusting and imparting some desperate message.

They were both trembling. She felt the tremors in his back, and her legs seemed unsteady, as if with one more caress she would fall to the floor. Nothing had changed. She longed for his weight and plunged her fingers into his soft hair, drawing him closer . . .

IT'S NEVER TOO LATE FOR LOVE AND ROMANCE

JUST IN TIME (4188, $4.50/$5.50)
by Peggy Roberts

Constantly taking care of everyone around her has earned Remy Dupre the affectionate nickname "Ma." Then, with Remy's husband gone and oil discovered on her Louisiana farm, her sons and their wives decide it's time to take care of her. But Remy knows how to take care of herself. She starts by checking into a beauty spa, buying some classy new clothes and shoes, discovering an antique vase, and moving on to a fine plantation. Next, not one, but two men attempt to sweep her off her well-shod feet. The right man offers her the opportunity to love again.

LOVE AT LAST (4158, $4.50/$5.50)
by Garda Parker

Fifty, slim, and attractive, Gail Bricker still hadn't found the love of her life. Friends convince her to take an Adventure Tour during the summer vacation she enjoys as an English teacher. At a Cheyenne Indian school in need of teachers, Gail finds her calling. In rancher Slater Kincaid, she finds her match. Gail discovers that it's never too late to fall in love . . . for the very first time.

LOVE LESSONS (3959, $4.50/$5.50)
by Marian Oaks

After almost forty years of marriage, Carolyn Ames certainly hadn't been looking for a divorce. But the ink is barely dry, and here she is already living an exhilarating life as a single woman. First, she lands an exciting and challenging job. Now Jason, the handsome architect, offers her a fairy-tale romance. Carolyn doesn't care that her ultra-conservative neighbors gossip about her and Jason, but she is afraid to give up her independent life-style. She struggles with the balance while she learns to love again.

A KISS TO REMEMBER (4129, $4.50/$5.50)
by Helen Playfair

For the past ten years Lucia Morgan hasn't had time for love or romance. Since her husband's death, she has been raising her two sons, working at a dead-end office job, and designing boutique clothes to make ends meet. Then one night, Mitch Colton comes looking for his daughter, out late with one of her sons. The look in Mitch's eye brings back a host of long-forgotten feelings. When the kids come home and spoil the enchantment, Lucia wonders if she will get the chance to love again.

COME HOME TO LOVE (3930, $4.50/$5.50)
by Jane Bierce

Julia Delaine says good-bye to her skirt-chasing husband Phillip and hello to a whole new life. Julia capably rises to the challenges of her reawakened sexuality, the young man who comes courting, and her new position as the head of her local television station. Her new independence teaches Julia that maybe her time-tested values were right all along and maybe Phillip does belong in her life, with her new terms.

NOW'S THE TIME
KATE HANFORD

ZEBRA BOOKS
KENSINGTON PUBLISHING CORP.

ZEBRA BOOKS are published by

Kensington Publishing Corp.
850 Third Avenue
New York, NY 10022

First Printing: January, 1995

Printed in the United States of America

One

It was going to take every ounce of her considerable ability to seem calm and cool. To a stranger, Faythe McBain would seem in total control of her emotions— a lovely woman, impeccably dressed and groomed, probably not a day over thirty-five, listening politely to a proposal in an office in Hollywood.

Except, she told herself, she was forty-six and her heart was beating so rapidly she was afraid Ray Parnell would be able to see it pulsing away beneath her demure silk blouse.

"You haven't said anything," Ray prompted her, his hazel eyes reminding her, as if she could ever forget, that he was very far from being a stranger.

She tried to sound light and amused. "Perhaps your offer has made me speechless, Ray."

"Speechlessness was never one of your

traits," he said, matching her bantering tone. His eyes told a different story though, and she remembered how intense he could be.

She forced herself to remain still by a supreme act of will. She wouldn't allow her hands to flutter at her collar or twirl a strand of hair; they remained gracefully folded to deflect attention from the emotions warring in her. Twenty years of playing the perfect hostess for a demanding husband were not about to fail her now. She'd put in her time, and at least she was well versed in looking and acting one way while feeling another.

She permitted herself a smile, the gracious kind she'd give to any respected director, warm but not too intimate. "Of course I'm flattered by your offer, Ray, but I'm compelled to be realistic, too. I haven't acted in twenty years. It's not something you just take up again, like riding a bicycle."

"Isn't it, Faythe?" He was teasing now, a softness in his deep voice that she remembered too well. She was suddenly aware of the white band on her tanned finger, the place where her wedding ring had been, and turned her hand inward.

"There's something else," she said, and then wished she hadn't spoken. Wildly, she cast about for something to say other than what she'd been thinking, but he was a step ahead of her.

"Why you? Why Faythe McBain in the role of Carlotta Fitzgerald?" He grinned and picked up a trade paper, pretending to read a hot scoop. "In an unprecedented move, Ray Parnell has drafted Faythe McBain to play the pivotal role of Carlotta in the upcoming mini-series based on the best selling novel *The Senator's Daughter*. Insiders are stunned that Parnell has picked a relative unknown and are wondering if the director has lost his savvy."

"Lost his marbles," she said, relieved that he was avoiding the real issue. She decided to play along. "Miss McBain is best known for cavorting on the beach in an undistinguished series of teen movies made two decades ago."

"Hey, undistinguished? Careful, lady. I seem to remember that I had something to do with those bikini epics."

She laughed with genuine pleasure. He had always been able to laugh at himself, and that was a rare trait in Hollywood.

"Really, how can you justify casting me in such an important role? I know it's just an expanded cameo, but from what I've heard . . ." Her voice trailed off as she entered a new minefield. She hadn't read the book, but her daughter Casey had and she didn't want to bring Casey or any reminder of her broken marriage into Ray Parnell's office.

"I can justify it for two reasons," he said with a touch of arrogance. "Number one, I'm the director and I get to make the call. Number two, you started out as a real actress. You had great potential and a gift that doesn't come along very often. It may not be like riding a bicycle, Faythe, but that gift doesn't just disappear. No matter how long you've left it alone, it's there, and I think this role will bring it back like no other I can imagine."

She was silent, wondering what it was in the part of Carlotta that made him have such extravagant feelings. "I'll have to read the book," she said.

Instantly he was on his feet, striding across the room to a large bookcase. It was crammed full of bound scripts and hardcover books. Like no other director's office she had ever seen, Ray's was cluttered and almost homey. There were no priceless art works on the wall and no eighteenth century French furniture to proclaim his affluence and accent his success. Framed posters of his favorite movies were about all he had in the way of decor, and she was glad to see that *Bikini Prom Night* and *Horror Boardwalk* were not among them.

"Here," he said, handing her a copy of *The Senator's Daughter.* "Read the novel first, and then I'll give you the screenplay. I think Jerry Nagle and Len Brock did a remarkable job of converting it."

She took the book and for a moment his fingers brushed hers. He had large hands, the kind that could so easily be clumsy and almost brutish, but Ray Parnell's hands had always been graceful as they accompanied his thoughts, and gentle when— *Stop it!* Faythe took the book firmly and stood up.

"I'll have to give this a lot of thought," she said.

"Too much thought is a dangerous thing," he replied. "You can think yourself right out of something if you're not careful."

She met his eyes suspiciously, but he seemed to imply no double meaning. The hazelnut color had darkened to a foresty green, and she remembered how, and why, his eyes darkened like that. It was when he wanted something very much and was afraid he might not get it. *Careful, Faythe,* she told herself. *No need to imagine drama where none exists.*

"I'll be in touch," she said breezily, and it wasn't until she was back in the parking lot that she realized who she'd sounded like. She'd reverted to the role of Mrs. Cal Caruso when she and Ray parted, while she'd been Faythe McBain in his office.

Who was she, anyway? Certainly not Mrs. Cal Caruso anymore, and thank God for that, but who was Faythe McBain? Faith McBain had been a Midwestern girl, a heartland beauty who'd shown a talent in university theater. That same girl had been persuaded by a talent scout to come to Hollywood, and then she'd become Faythe. She wasn't a young girl, she was no one's wife, and she'd been feeling pleased at the prospect of living on her own after twenty years. Why did someone from her past have to materialize in a puff of devilish smoke and suggest something so audacious?

She swung out into traffic and found herself stalled almost immediately in the great Los Angeles migration. Next to her a young man was speaking urgently into his car phone, his brows furrowed as if he were considering a declaration of war. Faythe took the opportunity to study herself in the rearview mirror. She was ruthless, pulling off her sunglasses and scrutinizing her face in the harsh sunlight. She saw and approved of the high cheekbones, the heart-shaped face and smoky brown eyes. Her nose had always been good and had required no surgery, but the firmness of her chin had been helped along by a cosmetic surgeon five years ago. Miraculously, her lips were still full and free of mummy-like pucker lines, and that was natural, too. No collagen injections necessary. Her heavy auburn hair was colored to an exact approximation of its once natural color and hung in a glossy bell curve that terminated just above her shoulders.

Yes, she told herself, *no need for false modesty. You are still a good-looking woman. In any other place you'd be a beautiful woman, but the beauty stakes are jacked up here. Youth is worshipped and the one thing you'll never be again is young.* Traffic moved forward again and she clapped her glasses back on with an impatient gesture. She hated all this insecurity about her looks. Especially now, when she was through with all that expensive maintenance. Why did Ray have to reenter her life and make her think about how she'd look in extreme close-up on a screen?

At the turn off to Santa Monica she allowed herself to address the real problem, the one she'd nearly voiced in Ray's office. The Hollywood gossips would be quick to pick up on his use of an actress who hadn't acted in two decades. *They had a thing going years ago, didn't they? Wasn't she going to marry him before she married Cal? Isn't there a statute of limitations on the casting couch? Apparently not, dear.*

It was late afternoon by the time she pulled into the drive of her rented house in Santa Monica. Casey laughed at her mother's new quarters, frequently pointing out that the whole house could fit into the kitchen of the Pacific Palisades place she'd called home for twenty years. There was no jacuzzi, no pool, no apartment for a chauffeur over the garage. All of this was more than made up for by the fact that there was no Cal Caruso, either.

Faythe went into the kitchen, slipping out of her heels and feeling the delicious coolness of the blue Spanish tiles against the soles of her feet. There were two winking red lights on her answering machine and she played her messages while she poured out a glass of white wine.

"Hi, sweetie, long time, huh? Are you

free for lunch Friday? I have so much to catch up on with you!"

The voice was that of a woman who hadn't made any attempt to see Faythe since the divorce. Amanda wouldn't be calling now if she didn't have a good reason. Shaken, Faythe poured her wine into the sink. The mill was grinding already. Somehow word had slipped out that she was being wooed for a part in a hot miniseries, and the Amandas of this world were eager to chew the rumor like a juicy plum. Faythe poured herself a pineapple juice. Everything you ate or drank showed up in your face on screen. If that had been true twenty years ago, how much more careful she'd have to be at forty-six.

The second message was from Casey. "Mom, I think we need to talk. Call me as soon as you can." As usual, Casey sounded like a stern mother talking to a recalcitrant daughter, as if *she* were the middle-aged woman and Faythe the recent college graduate.

"After I've had a long hot bath, darling," she said to the empty room. She needed some form of pampering before she addressed her daughter, and if she couldn't sip a glass of cold chablis, she'd take her pineapple juice and her copy of *The Senator's Daughter* upstairs for an hour.

Even the act of taking a bath was fraught with perils now that she had Ray's offer. Just as she'd studied her face on the freeway, she forced herself to appraise her naked body in a full-length mirror. Good, very good for a woman over forty. But did she really want to find herself on a set with lean, gorgeously toned women half her age? Faythe had been called long-legged in her youth, but now that females all seemed to grow to six feet, she felt puny and stunted at five-six.

What did they call them, the girls who exercised as if they were preparing for the Olympics? Hardbodies. She ran her hands over the swelling curve of her hips before immersing herself in the scented water. A hardbody she was not.

She opened the book and then immediately put it aside, postponing the revelations it would bring about the character of Carlotta. A drowsiness came over her and she lay back, letting the warmth of the water relax limbs she hadn't known were so tense. Unbidden, an image of Ray as he'd been twenty years ago emerged: a tall young man, with those endearingly large hands and feet and a long, tapering torso that just missed being skinny and was lean instead. His dark blond hair was untouched by gray and had a habit of falling over his forehead in a sweet, floppy way. The eyes were the same as she'd seen them today, luminous and changeable, capable of growing dark with passion.

They were on the beach, and it was sunset and improbably romantic and beautiful, the way so many memories are. "Faythe," he was saying, "there's only one thing in this world that terrifies me."

And she, teasing, "The thought that you'll never get to be John Huston?"

"Be serious," he warned, and something in his voice made her stand very still, alert. He drew her into his arms and held her lightly, one hand sifting through her long hair as he whispered, "The only thing that frightens me is the thought of having to live without you. Promise me I'll never have to. Promise."

She lifted her lips to his, feeling radiant with love and as strong as a woman could be in the knowledge that she was loved.

"Mom! Are you upstairs?"

Casey's voice shattered her reverie and she sat up, heart pounding again as it had in Ray's office. "I'll be right down," she called. As she wrapped herself in a thick towel she shook the false memory from her consciousness. It had happened, oh yes, Ray had assured her he couldn't live without her all those years ago, but he'd been lying. It was the old lie, the one for which she'd finally left Cal—the illusion of love that contained only betrayal.

She could see Casey's red BMW from the window and hear her daughter pacing on the tiles. Casey was always impatient about something. Faythe descended the stairs, trying to look bright and lively, and hugged Casey in greeting.

"Why haven't you called, Mom? I left a message for you to call."

"I was going to call you tonight."

Casey strode into the living room and sank down on the couch, turning an accusing look on Faythe. She was wearing linen pants and a severe blouse of handpainted silk. Her hair was cut even shorter than Faythe remembered.

"I'm having dinner with Dad tonight," she said in a defiant tone. Why, Faythe couldn't imagine, since she'd never tried to discourage Casey from a warm relationship with Cal. She'd never so much as allowed herself to say anything bad about him. As far as she was concerned, every child had a right to illusions about her parents.

"That's nice, honey," she said. "Is that what we had to discuss so urgently?"

"You know perfectly well what I need to know."

"I'm afraid I don't," Faythe said, but even as the words left her she had a sinking feeling. The rumor had reached Casey, too, and through her, Cal.

"I hate it when you play innocent, Mom. You know what I'm talking about. There's a rumor that you're going to take a part in that miniseries. Is it true?"

"It is, as you say, only a rumor at this stage. I have a lot of thinking to do before I make up my mind. I haven't even read the novel yet."

Casey got up and paced around the room. She really did look, Faythe thought, like a trial attorney preparing to grill a witness. "Let me tell you," she said. "I think you'd be making a big mistake, Mom. The part, Carlotta . . . well, she's a real siren type. She's older, but she's *gorgeous*. Like Catherine Deneuve." Her pale face colored. Casey had always been prone to blushes; it was one of the few things she'd carried with her from childhood. Still, her words had been stinging.

"They can do wonders with makeup and soft lights," she said tartly.

"Oh, Mom, I didn't mean it like that. You're great looking, but you're not a kid anymore."

"Neither, apparently, is Carlotta Fitzgerald. That's the whole point."

"But you haven't acted for *ages*," Casey wailed. "Do you think you can just step in and pick up where you left off— "

"In the Dark Ages?" Faythe smiled at her flustered daughter. "What you and your father want to know is this: am I going to make a fool out of myself?"

Casey made a protesting sound.

"It's too early to discuss this," Faythe said. "I need time to think it through. I will promise you one thing, though. If I do take the part, I will try very hard not to make a fool of myself. Does that answer your question?"

Casey turned a mutinous look on her mother. Faythe knew there were a dozen things she wanted answered, but for now she would have to be satisfied with a pledge.

"Now," said Faythe. "Do you have time for some iced tea?"

Round one to Faythe, she told herself, and suddenly felt exhausted. If she did choose to reactivate her long-dead career, she'd be in for a battle.

The daughters of major Hollywood agents lead lives as charmed as the children of stars, and Casey Caruso was no exception. From the time she was old enough to speak, her father had given her anything she wanted. Faythe sometimes thought that if she hadn't been there to lend a note of reality, Casey might have grown up to be a monster. And she had been there— that was the point. Faythe had waited until her daughter was college age to leave Cal.

Her persevering in an unhappy marriage for her daughter's sake was utterly lost on Casey. "But why now?" she'd asked over and over. "Everything's been great between you two all these years. Why leave now, when you're over forty?"

The implication was that Faythe was foolish to leave when she clearly had no life worth speaking of to lead anymore. She had to grit her teeth when Casey stated that everything had been great between her parents, but she wasn't going to be the one to reveal how wretched things had been.

There was a woman she knew slightly who took pleasure in telling her son what a brute his famous father had been. She would never forget how shocked she'd been when the woman, bending over her Bloody Mary at a charity brunch, had outlined her methods.

"Every time Jack hit me I took a polaroid. I framed each and every one— all my black eyes and cut lips and swollen noses— and I had them framed. I sent them to my son and told him to look at them every time he was tempted to think what a great guy dear old dad was."

Not that Cal had ever raised a hand to her. He wasn't a violent man and would never dream of damaging what he thought of as his property. No, Cal's cruelty had been a different kind, and its most striking property was that he never thought he was cruel at all. The suggestion would stun him. Hadn't he given her a life most women could only pine for? Hadn't he adored their daughter and been loving and affectionate to Faythe herself?

Cal's trouble was that he felt loving and affectionate toward so many women— or wanted to make love to them—that his affection became devalued. An "I love you" from Cal was about as meaningful as a "Have a nice day."

Casey's brief visit had started an unwanted chain of thoughts. Faythe kept them at bay as long as it took her to finish the novel and pop a Lean Cuisine into the microwave for her solitary dinner, but after a long, relaxing bath that was intended to make her sleepy she found herself tense and wakeful. She lay in her bed, the window open so she could smell the night blooming stock from her garden, and instead of sleep came memories.

Here was Cal in the early days of their marriage. She saw him so clearly—the young Cal, before his tar black hair had become streaked with gray, his powerful body wrapped in a monogrammed white terry robe. His eyes so dark they almost had a grape-like tinge of dusty purple when his passions were roused. Now, in this particular memory, Cal was staring straight at her as he always did when he was lying.

"Faythe, baby, it didn't mean a thing to me. I'd forgotten her five minutes after it was over."

She'd been repelled by the coldness of

the words. "Why bother, then?" The tone was cold, but inwardly she'd been howling. They'd been married less than half a year, and already he'd cheated on her with a soap opera actress, a client of his firm.

"You don't know what it's like, Faythe. These little chicks come on so strong, you wouldn't *believe* some of their tactics. I'm human, I get aroused. We do the deed, and then it's over. End of story. It's not like when we make love, sweetheart— it's not even making love. You're the only woman I make love to."

Had she really fallen for that? A part of her had wanted to believe that Cal was merely weak, that women took advantage of his passionate nature in the hopes of sleeping themselves to success. Above all, she'd needed to believe his assertions about making love to her alone. It was true that he'd lavished erotic attention on her. Cal was nothing if not an ardent lover, and he'd worshipped her body so thoroughly she walked around in a perpetual glow of fulfillment in those early days.

What she'd wanted to do was cry out "Aren't I enough for you?" but pride and a sudden sense that she was behaving childishly prevented her. Where she came from, men and women married and stayed faithful to each other, or if they didn't, it was a very big deal that more than likely ended up in divorce. She couldn't imagine any errant husband in her hometown excusing his cheating by saying, "It was nothing." But that was then and this was now. She was married to a successful Hollywood agent who could make or break the dreams of girls who'd come to the coast as she had done. She saw him, briefly, as an outsider might: a ruthless man who didn't care much about his clients' feelings. A bottom line kind of guy who cared only for power, money, and success.

"Now Sybil will think you owe her something," she'd said. "It may have meant nothing to you, but how about her?"

"Baby, that Sybil has been with half a dozen guys since me. It didn't mean anything to her, either."

Faythe had felt her insides clench fastidiously. Did that mean Cal had been, or would be, with half a dozen Sybil-like women?

He seemed to read her thoughts and was across the room and kneeling by her side in a flash. "It's not going to happen again, Faythe," he said, looking deeply into her eyes. "I swear it. You're all I need, all I'll ever need. I love you so much, baby. I'd rather cut my right hand off than ever hurt you again.''

It had crossed her mind that it wasn't his hand that needed to be excised, and then, despite her unhappiness, she'd giggled. Still, she'd turned a cool profile to him when he'd tried to make love to her that night. It was three days before she allowed herself to be wooed by his warm lips and caressing hands, and although their love-making brought her as much pleasure as ever, things were never quite the same. She'd lost her trust in him.

When she was pregnant with Casey, Cal treated her like a fragile princess. He brought her flowers every day and rubbed her back and lay with his face against her swollen belly. They shared a closeness and she almost believed in a new start. She forgave him his fling with Sybil, telling herself that the birth of their child would make them a family. A family, she thought, was much harder to cheat on than a wife.

Remembering, Faythe felt her head grinding against the pillow. She was amazed that Cal's endless capacity to deceive her could still bring so much pain. She'd never been more wide awake, so she got out of bed and knelt at the window, pillowing her head on her arms. What hurt the most was that second deception, because it made her feel like a fool for imagining Cal could change.

Giving birth to Casey had made her feel ten feet tall. She held the tiny scrap in her arms, marvelling at the little rust-colored spirals of hair on her infant daughter's head, thrilling at the unexpected strength in the baby's fingers when she clutched her mother's thumb. Like all young mothers, she'd thought no other woman had ever felt this exultation, and Cal, too, was euphoric. There were tears in his fine, dark eyes when he first saw them together.

"You've made me the happiest man in the world," he whispered. "I have all I'll ever want."

Her elation came to an abrupt end the day after she came back to the house in Pacific Palisades. The end was heralded by the ringing of the phone, just as a phone call had alerted her to Cal's dalliance with Sybil. It was always some woman she knew socially through Cal. Never a friend of hers, because she didn't seem to have any friends. By marrying Cal, she'd inherited a vast number of acquaintances and lost the people she'd counted as friends before.

"Just wanted to congratulate you, Faythe.

I'm sure your daughter is the most gorgeous little thing. I'm dying to see her. And I've never seen Cal looking happier. We saw him at Chasen's the other night with that new girl from the office. The one with the long black hair, like Vampira? It was strictly business, of course, no need to even say it, but Cal was on top of the world."

Strictly business. Of course. She'd had the Vampira girl to dinner and noticed the way she looked at Cal, but in the last months of her pregnancy she'd been self-absorbed, and lustful, burning looks had seemed beside the point, something from another, trivial world.

Cal had denied carnal knowledge of Vampira most convincingly, but there'd been a time when she picked up the phone and heard a fragment of conversation.

"I told you not to call me at home, Rita. Don't let it happen again."

"My roommate's going to San Diego tomorrow. We can have the place to ourselves."

"Fine, babe. That's just fine, but don't call me here. Not ever. I don't care if your roommate is going to Saturn."

Faythe had put the receiver back quietly, tasting ashes on her tongue. While she'd been experiencing the natural high of a lifetime and imagining that her marriage was about to begin anew, Cal had been sleeping with one of his employees. Rita. Rita, whose roommate would be in San Diego tomorrow. She pictured him in Rita's apartment in Studio City or West Hollywood.

He'd be removing his clothes in that way she knew so well— impatiently, letting his shirt fall to the floor, kicking his shoes to the far corners of the room, baring his muscular body for the act of love. His eyes would be clouded with that grapey look that appeared when he was excited, and he would murmur "I love you" as he caught her up in his arms and pushed her down on to a Murphy bed.

The Murphy bed was sheer spite. For all she knew Rita had an elegant apartment full of antiques and graced with an eighteenth century four poster. Rita didn't matter, her quarrel was with Cal, who couldn't even keep his pants zipped while Faythe was bringing their daughter into the world.

From that moment on, her relationship with Cal had formed a pattern. Trust and mutual respect had no part in it. For a few years he repeated the meaningless phrases— he loved only her, his current infidelity had meant nothing, he would never do it again— until the pretense became ridiculous. Faythe stopped wanting to cry. She stopped wanting to ask "Aren't I enough for you?" Clearly, she wasn't.

She settled into her role as Cal Caruso's wife: the perfect hostess, the tasteful decorator, the beautifully maintained showpiece who accompanied him in public. Cal grew less circumspect about his affairs, and she had actually walked in on him once, during a party in their house, and found him in the arms of one of her so-called friends. She walked right out, shutting the door quietly, knowing that he hadn't even noticed.

She tried to see him merely as a friend with whom she happened to live, a friend who had many good qualities but was hopelessly flawed. Cal continued to make love to her once or twice a week, and this too she thought of as something necessary but unromantic, a healthy release of tensions. For Casey's sake she never reproached him, but she did ask him to stop saying that he loved her.

She had almost forgotten what it was like to be truly loved by a man, and that suited her fine. It would be too painful to remember powerful emotions that were no longer available to her. She got up from her position by the window and noticed that her legs were slightly stiff. She was too old, as Casey would remind her, to kneel by a window in the moonlight. She got back into her bed and tried to compose herself for sleep, but something was nagging at the edge of her consciousness. It had to do with the hypocritical voice that had invaded her kitchen hours before. *I never knew you were an actress!*

Hell, yes, she was an actress. Forget her youthful triumphs in college, and especially forget her time served in a bikini in those B movies. She'd been an actress for twenty years of marriage, playing a role to such perfection she thought she deserved an Academy Award.

"Not to worry, Casey," she breathed in the dark room. "I'm not going to make a fool out of myself."

Two

She was cutting through the water like a sleek pleasure vessel, like a porpoise or a mermaid or . . . like a forty-six year old woman who was feeling the strain as she approached her thirtieth lap in Juanita Grace's swimming pool. She could see Juanita coming out onto the patio with a tray in her hands, grinning.

"Give it a rest, Faythe," Juanita called. She sat down at a patio table and poured herself a drink from a glass pitcher.

Faythe turned, pushing off powerfully with her feet against the tiles, and completed her last lap. Water streamed from her body as she hitched herself over the edge of the pool and sat still until her breathing was absolutely calm again.

"Honey, you're welcome to use my pool anytime you want," said Juanita, "but don't you think thirty laps is overdoing it a little?"

"Not," said Faythe, "if I don't want to have Chuckie reenter my life."

Juanita arched one eyebrow politely. She had the very blue eyes of her Irish father, which were startling in her caramel colored face. "Who's this Chuckie?" she asked. "Do you mean to tell me there's a man in your life I don't know about?"

Faythe towelled herself off and went to sit beneath the umbrella. She sniffed at the contents of the pitcher, and finding nothing more sinister than Juanita's special lemongrass iced tea, poured herself a glass. "Chuckie," she said, "was my personal trainer. He came to the house four days a week at seven in the morning and worked me for ninety minutes. He was a sadist. I used to have fantasies of pushing him over the cliffs."

"Mmmm," said Juanita. "The view from that house was spectacular."

"I don't miss it at all. The whole time Casey was little I was worried sick. The way that lawn sloped down, it would have been so easy for her to fall."

"Faythe, you had a fence put up, don't you remember? That fence didn't come down until Casey was in her teens."

"Even so." Faythe knew it was unreasonable, but the dizzying chasm between her back garden and the Pacific below had always frightened her. If it had been up to her, the Caruso family would have lived in a house much like the one she rented now. Except, of course, her rented house didn't have a pool, which was why she was using Nita's. "You're sure you don't mind?" she asked.

"Mind what?"

"My using the pool. I could go to the club, of course, but I'd like to get in shape in private." She looked at Juanita and smiled. "Semi-private."

"Of course I don't mind, but if you're not in shape, who is?"

Juanita didn't know about the miniseries, and she certainly didn't know about the insecurities a middle-aged woman could feel when confronted with the terrors of appearing on camera. Juanita was a year older than Faythe, but she ate whatever she wanted, wore baggy old jeans and shapeless T-shirts, and didn't care how deeply the sun etched laugh lines in around her eyes. Today she wore her heavy black hair in a single braid down her back and no makeup. Faythe thought she was beautiful. Juanita was the closest thing she had to a friend in Hollywood, and it was only possible because they hadn't started out on an equal footing. Juanita was incapable of the petty jealousy of an Amanda because she moved in an entirely different world. She would never resent any success of Faythe's or try to denigrate her talent. Juanita would never have slipped, oh so casually, into a conversation the fact that she'd seen Cal at a restaurant with one of his young employees. No kiss-kiss, stab-stab techniques were in Juanita's repertoire.

"A penny for them," Juanita said. "You're smiling in a very secretive way, Faythe."

"I was just thinking that you're my only friend in this whole ridiculous town."

"Ironic, isn't it?" Juanita pantomimed holding a tray and said in an exaggeratedly servile way, "I thought a salmon mousse would be nice for starters, Miz Caruso."

"Oh, no," said Faythe. "It wasn't that way at all. You had me terrorized, not the other way around. It was so clear you were going to be a star."

Juanita had been one of the catering staff Cal had hired on a hot tip from one of his clients. She'd first come to the house in Pacific Palisades when Casey was five years old, and in her neat black dress and frilly white apron she had seemed to be just one of the crew, one of the unit known as "Mario's Epicurians, Ltd." Mario himself had been a bad-tempered young man who sucked up to celebrities and underpaid his staff. Cal had adored him, Faythe remembered, because it was rumored that Steven Spielberg prized his grapefruit sorbet with cilantro as a palate cleanser between courses. She could still remember the taste of the sorbet— like ice cream mixed with salsa— and shuddered.

"I'm happy not being a star," said Juanita, pouring more lemongrass tea into Faythe's glass. "It means I can live the way I want to and do what I do best. It's all I ever wanted."

Faythe said a silent amen, but beneath it was the knowledge that she did not occupy this enviable position. Juanita was now one of Hollywood's most successful business-women, owner of her own catering outfit and possessor of a pool almost as large as the one Mrs. Cal Caruso had barely noticed in the days of her marriage.

"Did you teach your son to swim?" she asked Juanita.

The blue eyes contracted and Juanita snorted. "Carlos?" she said incredulously. "He'd run a mile from water. He's right where he wants to be, in Bloomington, In-diana, studying computer science." She studied Faythe for a moment, unsmiling. "What's this all about, honey? Your mind's all over the place this morning."

"I'm sorry. I guess I sound kind of scatterbrained." Faythe didn't want to mention the miniseries or the possibility of her return to acting. Juanita might be the only person in town who hadn't heard the rumors, and it was comforting to be in the presence of someone who cared so little about the business. Instead of confessing her doubts and fears about acting again, she chose another topic of concern.

"I'm worried about Casey," she said truthfully.

"What's to worry about there? She has a job, she has her own apartment, she drives a BMW, she isn't into drugs, and she's not pregnant. As far as I know."

Faythe laughed. "You're too much, Nita. I'm worried about less dramatic things. Intangible things."

"That's a luxury. I say worry about the big things and the little ones will take care of themselves."

"You sound so sure of everything," Faythe said, and then promptly felt ashamed. What would Juanita think of her—a woman who had had everything money could buy, who had not known a moment of poverty or want. Nita had wrenched herself out of a disastrous marriage, raised a son on her own, and made her business wildly successful. And what had she, Faythe, done? Stayed in a loveless marriage, abandoned a once-promising career, and accepted all the perks of being a rich agent's wife.

"Call me an overprivileged twit," she said, taking a deep breath. "Call me old-fashioned, out of touch, whatever you like, but I'm worried about Casey's set of values. She's bright, she's beautiful, and I love her as much as I did when she was a baby, but sometimes I don't . . . I don't know how to say this . . ."

"You don't like her," Juanita said.

"Well, that's putting it a little strongly, but yes. I don't feel I have anything in common with her anymore. She used to want to be a veterinarian when she was twelve, and before that she wanted to be a mountain climber. I'm relieved she didn't follow up on that one, but the last thing I ever thought she'd want to do was be an agent. I'm proud that she's taking her work so seriously, but I'm scared to death she's going to be like—" She broke off, feeling guilty.

"Let me guess," Nita said, pretending to

find it difficult. "Could you possibly mean that Casey might be like . . . her father?"

"It's not so far-fetched, is it? She's always worshipped Cal, and I've tried not to disillusion her. I don't want her adopting his values. She's so cold and judgmental, so in charge all the time."

Juanita looked off at her prize avocado tree and spoke as if to herself. "I wouldn't have thought being cold was one of Mr. Caruso's bad points."

Faythe felt heat rise up from her throat and bathe her face. Juanita knew Cal's reputation, everybody did, but something in her manner indicated personal knowledge of Cal's ways. Had he put a move on her, back when she was delighting their guests with her duck molé and salmon mousse?

"I'm sure you must have things to do," she said stiffly, retrieving her handbag and shrugging into her oversized shirt. Her one piece tank suit was still damp and she shivered a little in spite of the warmth of the day and the blush suffusing her face.

Juanita reached for her hands and held on tight. "Whooaah, there," she said. "I didn't mean anything deep, honey. I only meant that whatever else went wrong be-

tween you two, I didn't figure you were . . .
neglected."

Oh, but I was, Faythe thought. *In every way
but the one you meant.* "No offense taken,"
she said, kissing the other woman's cheek.

"Come by tomorrow for another swim.
And don't be so prickly."

Is that how she seemed to Juanita? Prickly?
Faythe backed out of the drive and headed
toward Topanga Canyon. "I am not prickly,"
she said, putting a vintage Bob Dylan tape
into the deck, "only scared to death."

On the rare days when traffic wasn't
hopelessly snarled, she liked to drive aimlessly around, sometimes down to the Coast
Road, as she was doing now, and others to
communities like Sherman Oaks and Encino in the Valley. The Valley was distinctly
downscale to people like her ex-husband,
but she liked to drive past the ordinary
houses and imagine the lives being led
there. Once she'd caught herself weaving a
scenario around a stranger, a woman who
was getting into a Toyota with her toddler
daughter. Mother and child had curly, red,
short hairdos, and in the glimpse she'd had
both were laughing.

What would it have been like if she'd
married a nice, ordinary man and settled

into a little three-bedroom house in the Valley? She pictured the woman's husband: he was a college professor who brought home a salary in the mid-five-figure range. She was temporarily staying home to raise her little girl— maybe she was even now in the early stages of another pregnancy— but she dreamed of going back to college one day and completing her degree in, say, child psychology. Faythe calculated what she would have to do without if she were that woman: designer clothes, extravagant entertaining, large-scale travel, good jewelry, a personal trainer, plastic surgery when and if she needed it, and everything that had distinguished her marriage to Cal. She'd told herself she could gladly do without any of it if only her husband were an ordinary, loving man. A man who adored his wife and found her, even after they'd been married for years, more desirable than a twenty-five year old with endless legs and a shiny, unused face. A husband who might look at other women with lust occasionally, even one who might contemplate an affair, but a man who wouldn't feel the need to make love to every female who crossed his path and showed a smidgin of interest.

She knew her scenario was ridiculous.

Nothing guaranteed that a man like her imagined college professor would be a good husband, the laughing woman she'd glimpsed could be married to an alcoholic, a wife-beater, a compulsive gambler, or a philanderer like Cal— only the scale of his infidelities would be different, and the degree of power he wielded. She was a rational woman, but her little fantasies helped to shield her from the pain in those days when she knew she had to leave Cal.

Now, driving along the Pacific Coast Highway, she was immune to the dizzying sweep of the ocean as she negotiated hairpin curves. As a child of the landlocked Midwest, she'd once found the ocean such a marvel she thought she could never have enough of it, but her years in the house at Pacific Palisades had made her all too familiar with it. Too often she'd stared out at those blue billows, her eyes blurred with unshed tears, and by the time she'd stopped wanting to cry the ocean had become just another backdrop.

She drove because it helped her to think, and she wanted to examine what Juanita had said about Cal. *I wouldn't have thought being cold was one of Mr. Caruso's bad points. You weren't . . . neglected.* Nita had meant that Cal was still a passionate man— he wore his sensuality on his sleeve— and she was right, but what use was passion when it could be so easily transferred to other women? How could you listen to a man lie and lie— *it will never happen again*— and still respect him? How could you believe he loved you when he was out with another woman on the night of his only child's birth?

Faythe thought she'd been right to use the word "cold" in connection to Cal and his effect on Casey. Cal was cold, would always be. It didn't matter that he could make love like a man half his age or that he responded to beautiful women with the ardor of a teenager. He was hot in bed, to put it crudely, and cold in the heart. He cared only for immediate gratification and appearances. Beyond that, he cared for making a deal and being considered the best at what he did. Period. Cal could move himself to tears by swearing undying love for her, and the next day he would be considering how to steal a hot property from another agent. The day after, he'd be plotting how to seduce her.

He was like a big-game hunter who kept trophies in his library. She laughed as she thought of the library in their old house—

the yards of leather-bound books he never read, the medieval maps he had framed on the walls because a dealer had told him they would be priceless one day, the roaring fire in the man-sized fireplace he kept lit even in the summer with the air-cool system going full-blast. She stripped away the maps and planted Cal's conquests on the walls, mounted tastefully and arranged in order of their importance. Secretaries and other functionaries at the agency occupied a humble position, with starlets ranked over them and full-fledged stars at the highest point. Oddities, like the lady novelist he'd bedded the summer Casey turned ten, were in a small alcove together with other women not associated directly with the business. But the biggest trophy, mounted over the fireplace, her glass eyes flickering in the endless firelight, was his wife. Faythe McBain Caruso, her hair styled in the casual ringlets she'd worn twenty years ago, was the biggest trophy of all.

She wasn't the most beautiful, and she certainly wasn't the most famous, but she'd lasted longer than any of them. The others had come and gone, but Faythe McBain Caruso had hung in there for more than two decades.

She was the biggest sap, the fool, and the knowledge of her wasted years cut her to the quick, even now.

"Don't waste time, Faith, because it's a commodity you can never get back again."

That had been her father's favorite advice, and there were many things that Gerry McBain considered a waste of time. Dancing lessons, because "any girl can pick it up on her own," and sleeping late on the weekends when there was no school because "you'll be a long time dead." Yet he wasn't a morbid man or even a stern one. There wasn't anything he wouldn't do to please his wife or only child, and he was always affectionate and fairly cheerful— a popular man in their Midwestern town and a leading citizen.

McBain Retail Lumber was the business handed down to him by his own father, and Gerry McBain's one sadness was that he had no son to pass the business on to; to give him credit, he never tried to interest Faith in running the company, because it was clear to him she was destined for greater things. He was a tall man with dark, burning eyes that could give him a fanatic look, but the moment he smiled or made a joke you could see that the eyes were misleading. Tollie, Faith's mother, had pale brown eyes that shaded to amber, and the two gene pools had produced a radiant girl who looked like neither of her parents. The golden light in her dark eyes came from her mother, but she had inherited some of her father's more dramatic look, and the result had been startlingly pretty from infancy on. What was off-putting in the father became softened and pleasing in the child, and what might have seemed too meek and placid in the mother was transformed, in Faith, to a vibrancy that made people turn to look at her in the streets.

Tollie McBain delighted in dressing her little girl in colors that complemented the natural palette of her beauty. She could sit for hours at her sewing machine and produce garments in colors no other child in Sayerville, Wisconsin, had ever thought to wear. Mrs. McBain turned out dresses and blouses in dusty rose hues and golds, and Faith would protest that she wanted an outfit in navy and bright red, like her best friend Glenda's, only to grow silent when her mirror told her how original her mother's vision had been.

If her parents had been richer, or Faith a

less nice child, she might have become unbearably spoiled, but fate had conspired to
plant the McBains in a small town in central
Wisconsin. It was too far north to have a cosmopolitan flavor and not northerly enough
to be in the region of lakes and forests that
drew wealthy tourists from Chicago every
summer. No one saw Faith as a show off or
as conceited— the cardinal sin in the days
when she was growing up— because Faith
wore her beauty carelessly and didn't rub it
in. She would share her lunch, help you with
your homework, and refuse a date with the
high school hunk because she knew another
girl wanted him desperately.

"That's going too far," her friend Glenda
Mosley told her when she passed up the date
with Bob Boxer. "What does it get you? Just
because you won't go out with him doesn't
mean he'll ask Cathy to the dance."

"True," Faith said, "but I'm not giving
up anything I want. Why hurt Cathy when
I don't even have a crush on Bob?"

"He's the cutest you'll find in Sayerville,
Faithy. What are you waiting for— one of
those guys from Liverpool?"

Faith wouldn't say what she was waiting
for, because she didn't want to sound conceited, but she knew, and it wasn't Bob

Boxer. The man who would one day claim her would come from a wider world than that of central Wisconsin. Vaguely, she imagined a dark stranger with exquisite manners. He would be from Paris or maybe Rome. Then that began to seem too alien, and she decided he would be from New York. He would have a rugged physique, like Bob Boxer's, true, but there all resemblance halted. Her dream man would wear his hair slightly long, and he would have a voice that was somehow soft and rough at the same time.

When it was time to choose a homecoming queen Faith was the natural selection, but in the end the students thought it more appropriate to choose a senior girl who was engaged to marry one of the football players. Faith was relieved, because it was her senior year and she was looking forward to college. She felt she was already gone from Sayerville and lived only for the future.

She'd been so afraid her father would pronounce college a waste of time, but Mr. McBain surprised her. College was essential, he said, because if she didn't plan to serve behind the counter at the lumber company, she'd better equip herself to take her rightful place in the world. Her mother also thought college was important, but

Faith knew that Tollie saw it as a fertile ground for husband hunting.

"A lovely girl like you, Faith— the sky's the limit," said her mother.

"In college," said her father, "you won't have a minute to yourself. The time's very structured there."

And so, between her father's obsession with using time to her advantage and her mother's determination to see her well-married, Faith was soon to be on her own for the first time. Ironwood College, in neighboring Michigan, would be her proving ground.

Her father thought she was going to become a teacher. Her mother thought she was going to become a wife. Only Faith knew her true destiny. She was going to find love, and not the safe and familiar love her parents offered. In Ironwood, she would find the man she could love with her whole heart and soul, and it would be the kind of love— elemental and thrilling— that had never been available in Sayerville.

Something else, too. She was sad to leave her parents, but there was something she planned to leave behind with relief, something that had haunted her in all the years she was growing up. It was the knowledge, never stated but always understood by her, that her mother and father had wanted other children, a whole host of them. All the caring they had lavished on her had been meant to extend to half a dozen more kids. Without ever being told, she understood that Tollie had never been able to have more babies after she was born. She felt somehow greedy for taking up the excess.

Perhaps, after all, it was what had kept her so nice.

"Mother. Give me a call. I have some very important news for you."

Sighing, Faythe turned off the answering machine and prepared to call her daughter at work. It was always jarring to hear the familiar "Caruso Creative" greeting at the other end of the line. By her calculations, Cal had known most of his receptionists in the Biblical sense, and she was sure this dulcet-voiced one was no exception.

"This is Faythe McBain," she said. "I'd like to talk to Casey Caruso, please."

"Oh, Mrs. Caruso, I think she's in conference at the moment."

"It's not Caruso, actually. It's Ms. McBain."

"Oh, right. Sorry. Can I have her get back to you?"

Faythe said that would be fine and went to resume her reading of *The Senator's Daughter.* She was only about a quarter of the way through the fat novel and hadn't met the character she was to play yet. She supposed she could cheat and go straight to the climactic scene with Carlotta Fitzgerald, but she was forcing herself to read straight through for the sense and flavor of the thing.

The senator's daughter was named Rosie Madigan, and she was already in deep trouble on page 183. Her father was a U.S. senator, a Jack Kennedy type. He was handsome, charismatic, and destined for greatness, but he was also a self-centered son of a bitch, a man who ignored his patrician wife and bedded everyone in sight. Kind of like Cal, except the senator went beyond Cal in his need for approval and love and to be numero uno in little Rosie's life, too. Although Cal basked in Casey's love and admiration, he had never behaved in any way Faythe thought of as inappropriate toward his little girl.

The senator was another matter. Although he never actually abused her, physically, he was so jealous of any young man Rosie looked at that he made sure to humiliate the luckless kid. There was a harrowing scene where the senator, Big Tom Madigan, taunted a goodlooking Cheyenne boy— the Madigan constituency was in Montana— into riding an unbroken and dangerous horse. Poor Rosie had to see her prospective lover thrown into the dust while her father looked on knowingly. *See, baby? He's not man enough for you.*

By the time Rosie was eighteen, she couldn't even consider a boy her age as a possible love interest. Daddy had seen to that, because no one could measure up to him. Rosie was a mess for all her beauty— shy, withdrawn, and miserable.

Faythe knew from the prologue that the senator would be murdered by his mistress when Rosie was nineteen, and she was just approaching the pages wherein the poor child would undergo the most severe trauma of her young life. Bad enough when an adored daddy is murdered, but calamitous when his daughter has always been half in love with him, and even worse when she doesn't acknowledge it.

She took a sip of Pellegrino water, wishing it could be white wine, and opened the book where she'd left off. Here was Rosie, out on a date with a nice young man who doesn't interest her at all. They are dining at a chic New York restaurant, and the reader knows that this is the night when the senator will come to the end of his chaotic and tempestuous life, stabbed to death by a voluptuous blonde called Jolie. Rosie will always remember that she was eating osso bucho when the knife first pierced Daddy's chest and that when he breathed his last she was engaged in her raspberry sorbet.

For all the timely references and glitz, the novel was essentially a psychological one. Faythe understood that the meat of the story would be in the healing of Rose Madigan's fractured psyche. Only when she could love a man who wasn't Daddy-like would she be cured. Faythe was rooting for her, but she couldn't concentrate today as she had the day before. Too many things were shrieking for attention. If she were honest, she'd have to admit that what she'd said to Juanita was only partially true. She didn't want Casey to inherit Cal's values, and she'd never thought it was a problem until Casey had gone to work for Caruso Creative.

There had been an ill-fated partnership for a while when she had allowed Casey to act as her own agent. It was the last thing she'd wanted, but Casey had been so persuasive, so ardent in her desire to represent her mother.

"It'll be so great, Mom. I know just the sort of properties for you, the ones you'd shine in. Nobody else in this town can know you like I do, no one can just know in their bones what's right for you."

"Isn't it what they call a conflict of interest?"

"Grow up, Mom. I'm working for Dad, for heaven's sake. Nepotism is what it's all about."

"Really," Faythe had said, trying to sound neutral and suppressing laughter.

"I know what bums you, Ma," Casey said, reverting to the teenager who had been so maddeningly lovable and annoying. "You're afraid you'll have to see Dad if you sign with me. Nothing can be further from the truth. We're a huge agency, in case you hadn't noticed. I could go a week without seeing him if I wanted to."

"That's good to know, dear."

"You sound so superior. I hate it when you sound like that. What's the big deal, even if you did see him? I know he has your best interests in mind and always will. He's not like you, Mom. He's not bitter or vindictive. He cares, he really cares."

Bitter? Vindictive? When had she shown Casey either of these qualities? "Was this his idea, then?"

A long-suffering sigh had come down the wire. "Of course not. He encourages independent thinking and movement. That's what the agency is all about. This is my idea, Mom, my masterplan! What could be more brilliant than Faythe McBain reclaiming her career through the acumen and business sense of her very own daughter?"

How could she refuse such a pitch? She had pretended to need time to think about it, but she knew she'd say yes. The truth was that she'd half believed her daughter could be the instrument of her return to acting. It was so seductive, the idea that Casey could somehow reclaim for her the career she'd given up so long ago. It had a circular beauty to it, and she had always been a sucker for plans and schemes that seemed to promise unity and rebirth.

After two days' deliberation, she'd signed on the dotted line, feeling that she and Casey had somehow switched positions in the world. It was a matter of days before she realized how far apart their visions really were. She'd read in the trades that casting was about to begin for a film based on a historical novel. Kevin Costner and Rachel Ward were cast for the leads, and Faythe had her eye on a small but juicy role: a fortyish widow who finds a new life in the Pacific Northwest at the turn of the century.

Casey listened with an ominous silence when Faythe suggested that she'd like a shot at the part. Then she sighed.

"Mother, that's impossible. They want someone like Julia Roberts for that part."

"But she's much too young," Faythe had replied after the initial shock wore off.

"They're making the widow lots younger."

"It's such a small part. Julia Roberts would never agree to such a minor role, would she?"

"Honestly, Mom, where have you been? I said someone *like* Julia Roberts, and anyway, they're expanding the role." Casey laughed as if dealing with an unrealistic child. "There is a part for you, though. I'd like you to read for Lucinda."

"Lucinda?" She knew of no casting director named Lucinda. "I thought Margo was casting for this one."

"Get a grip, Mom. Lucinda is the part. She's the woman who gets killed in a log-

ging accident." A pause, presumably to allow her mother to recall the novel.

Faythe recalled and felt a wave of humiliation wash over her. "Darling, that Lucinda
is an old woman who is raising her grand-
son. As I recall."

"Right. I think you could make something of that part."

"Casey, I will say this only once. I don't
expect to play glamorous, young women.
I'm quite prepared to act my age, both on
and off the screen, but I did not decide to
return to acting to play a grandma with a
clay pipe. Do I make myself clear?"

"God, I just love it when you get all
haughty. Okay, no Lucinda then, but you've
got to be more realistic, Mom. You're—
what?— forty-nine years old, and— "

"Forty-six."

"Whatever. You can't expect to get plum
roles at your age. Now if you were twenty
years older, I could cast you as the matri-
arch, the grand old woman of Washington
territory. Ideally, they'd love to get Jessica
Tandy."

And so it went. They were eternally at
cross-purposes. Faythe readjusted her sights
and expressed interest in modest, plain
parts, but it seemed she could not be hum-

ble enough. Every time Casey informed her that she was being unrealistic and suggested the kind of part that made Faythe shudder. It crossed her mind that her daughter was doing it purposely, but she couldn't imagine Casey behaving so spitefully.

Three months ago, she'd taken Casey to Starbuck's and explained that it wasn't working out. "I'm sure you have my best interests at heart, honey, but we'll never see eye to eye on this. I think it would be better for both of us if I get an agent who isn't related to me."

That was the first time she'd seen Casey's new, stern face. The chin went up, the eyes narrowed, and Casey's pretty lips compressed into a grim line. "It's no use arguing with you, Mother. When you make your mind up about something you lose perspective. You're not being rational, but if you don't want me working for you, so be it. I have plenty of other clients who accept my guidance."

Uncomfortably, they had finished their cups of the world's best coffee and gone their separate ways. Casey wouldn't allow Faythe to pay the small check, and she had only one question.

"Do you have an agent in mind?"

"Not really." But of course she did, and

within the week she was signed with Barney Glasser, a deceptively avuncular man who was known for the uniqueness of his vision. At least he had the grace to roar with laughter when she told him about Casey's casting plans for her. "No, sweetheart, I see no withered crone before me. It'll be slow going at first, but I guarantee you'll be working steadily before very long."

Even Barney could not have predicted the rapidity with which his new client was catapulted back into the business. When Ray Parnell called him about the Carlotta Fitzgerald role, he confessed to amazement.

"Has Parnell ever seen you act?" he asked Faythe.

"Oh, I knew him way back when," she replied, keeping her voice light and casual.

"He's got a terrific memory," Barney said.

Faythe realized she'd read several pages of *The Senator's Daughter* without absorbing a word. She put the book down and massaged her temples, trying to banish old memories. The world would surely come to a halt if people told the whole truth all the time. What would Barney have said if she'd told the truth: "Ray Parnell was my lover, the man I thought I'd be with forever. I only married Cal because he was there when Ray and I broke up . . . no, we didn't break up. I left him when I realized he didn't really love me. I left him when I found him with another woman."

The phone rang and she breathed deeply. She didn't want whoever was calling her to hear the agitation in her voice. Strange, there was still more pain in that memory of faithless Ray than in anything to do with Cal.

"Hi, Mom, it's me." Casey sounded artless and very young, more like the Casey of five years ago than the workaholic agent.

"You sound pleased about something," Faythe said.

"Oh, yeah, but that's not why I called. I thought you'd want to know that Tara Johanson is going up for Rosie."

"Sorry? Rosie?"

"Rosie. The senator's daughter. Were you taking a nap or something? You sound dazed."

"I was reading, actually."

"Tara's not my client, but she is with the agency. I just wanted to warn you. I think she's going to get it."

"I've never heard of her."

"Think in terms of the new Kim Basinger. She's gorgeous."

"Why are you warning me? Isn't she a good actress?"

"She's plenty good, Mom, but she's pure poison. You wouldn't like working with her."

Was this another attempt to discourage her from accepting Ray's offer?

"Tara's unbelievably self-destructive," Casey went on in a cheerful voice. "Talk about abuse! It doesn't show on her yet, but it will in a few years."

"Maybe she'll straighten out," Faythe said, hearing how silly her words would seem to Casey.

"She'd better work all she can, Mom. She'll be lucky to live to twenty-five."

"I wish you wouldn't exaggerate so much, Casey. I'm sure she can't be as bad as you say."

"Well, maybe you'll see for yourself." Casey's voice was brisk now. "Gotta go, Mom. I'm having dinner with Dad."

Three

The child lay on her stomach on the deck of the boat, feeling the sea lift and swell beneath her. The sun was hot on her back, and Daddy had thoughtfully covered her with one of his shirts so she wouldn't burn. They were moored off the coast of Sardinia on this graceful white yacht that belonged to one of her father's friends.

She was deliciously tired and moved in and out of a state of sleep, hearing the grown-ups laughing and the tinkle of ice in their glasses. Daddy had played a game with her earlier that afternoon, and once the initial fear wore off she had loved it and begged for more. He would stand at the edge of the ship's deck, holding her tight in his arms, the sea boiling against the faraway rocks but purple and placid where they were anchored. "Ready?" he would inquire, and she would nod in terror and delight against his chest, and then he would jump into the sea, clasping her tightly, and they would plunge beneath the surface, down and down, and just when she began to grow afraid he would thrust powerfully upward until their heads broke water and they were in the comforting sunlight again.

When she'd become overexcited, he had massaged her back with his strong hands, gentling her as he would one of his horses back home on the ranch, and she had calmed down. Or she seemed calm, but the combination of the sun and the pressure on her belly where she lay against the deck— that and his soothing hands— made her feel warm and itchy. She knew it was a sensation that was somehow not right, though she couldn't put a name to it, and so she had lain still, feigning sleep, and then sleep had actually come.

The grown-ups had grown silent now, and she wondered if they had all gone below for naps or to the galley, where the cook might be preparing a delicious snack. There was no sound but the steady lapping of the waves against the bow of the ship and the occasional scream of a sea bird. Daddy had shown her in an atlas exactly where they were— in the Tyrrhenian Sea, off the coast of Sardinia, miles from Washington or Montana, her two homes.

She heard a low sound, musical and so faint she thought she might be dreaming, but there it came again. She thought it might be like the Song of the Sirens she'd read about in mythology during fifth grade, and she allowed her eyes to open slowly. She saw nothing but the teak boards of the deck, which appeared white to her sun-starved eyes, but gradually she made out the little table that held glasses and an ice bucket. She moved her head around on the pillow of her arms and saw them so suddenly her breath caught in her throat.

Terror! But they hadn't heard her pathetic gasp. Daddy and the lady called Carlotta would not have noticed anything. Daddy's lips were pressed to the arched, white neck and his eyes were closed. Carlotta's eyes were closed, too, and the hood of her caftan had fallen away, leaving her long, wild hair free to lift and ripple in the sea breeze. Daddy's hands were beneath the caftan. She could see them, wriggling like kittens in a sack, and she knew she ought to look away but couldn't.

Suddenly the game she had played with

her father, the jumping into the sea in his arms, seemed unbearably childish and stupid. *Aren't I enough?* she thought, and then immediately, in a new and scornful voice, *Of course I'm not enough!*

Even as she watched, paralyzed with fascination and dread, Carlotta's eyes opened and seemed to stare straight at her. They were golden eyes, like the eyes of a witch or a goddess, but they meant no harm to her. She stared back at Carlotta, unable to look away, and then the witch-goddess disentangled herself and stood up, leading Daddy away, below decks.

What she would remember later, and for the rest of her life, was the expression in those golden eyes. It was neither angry nor triumphant. The eyes held an expression of sadness so profound they might have stood for all the heartbreak and betrayal in the history of the world.

Carlotta Fitzgerald had the saddest eyes she had ever seen . . .

It never fails, Faythe thought. *When you want to impress someone, that person will somehow manage to catch you at your worst.* She had put the book down after reading the scene about Carlotta Fitzgerald and gone straight to the shower to wash her hair. Now someone was at the door. Ray Parnell. And she would be forced to answer wearing a terry robe and with a towel turban-style on her wet hair. No makeup, of course.

She felt angry at Ray for barging in un-announced, but she tried not to show it. "I wasn't expecting you, Ray," she said.

"I apologize. This is obviously a bad time."

"Only," she said, "if you were expecting to see Carlotta Fitzgerald. Today you're only getting Faythe McBain."

"She's all I wanted," he said, and then they were both struck speechless by the double en-tendre. He recovered first. "There's some-thing I wanted you to see. I was coming to your neighborhood anyway, so I thought I'd drop it by."

Faythe stood back and motioned for him to come in.

"I won't stay," he promised, looking around her small living room. "This is nice, Faythe."

"Quite a come-down most people would say. I suspect Casey barely restrained herself from saying 'What a dump'."

"Not at all. It suits you, I think."

Ray sat on the couch, his long legs doubled

up. It was definitely not a room built for a
big man's comfort. Faythe noticed the gray
in his dark blond hair was more pronounced
than she'd thought, but it was attractive. He
wore jeans and a tweed jacket, and in a certain light she could almost think he was that
boy she'd known so long ago. It wasn't fair,
because she knew no light would ever make
her seem twenty-two again, especially with a
towel around her head.

Ray handed her an envelope. "Open it
after I leave," he said. "It's something that
might make you decide to be my Carlotta."

"It doesn't feel heavy enough to be a
bribe." She felt restless and self-conscious
with Ray's eyes taking her in so frankly.
"Can I get you a drink?"

"No, I have to be somewhere in a few
minutes. Faythe, I meant it when I told you
not to think about it too long. I expect a
decision from you soon."

"I haven't even finished reading the book
yet. Honestly, Ray, you'd think I'd been sitting on this for a month." A shaft of late
afternoon sunlight moved across his face,
lighting up the green eyes, but he refused
to smile. "I'm serious," he said.

The phone rang and they both listened
while a woman Faythe knew slightly said she

hoped Faythe would be coming to her party that evening.

Ray said, "Sherry Brooks."

"I forgot to send my regrets."

"Busy tonight?"

She shrugged. "I don't feel like seeing those people, the ones who didn't call when I divorced Cal. They're only calling now because my name's been in the trades." She did not add that she tried not to go where she might meet Cal.

"The hell with them, Faythe. What do you care? You ought to go out more often."

Easy enough for him to say. And how did he know how often she went out? She held the envelope, consumed with curiosity about its contents. "I've been thinking," she said. "I just read the section where Rosie sees her father with Carlotta on the yacht. Up to that point Carlotta's been a fairly sympathetic character. She's the senator's mistress, we know that, but Rosie doesn't until that moment. Carlotta has been kind to her. She's the only other adult on the boat besides the senator, who even seems to notice the kid."

"What are you getting at?" Ray's words were impatient but his expression was anything but.

"Well, Carlotta goes from being a sympathetic person to a villain almost. What kind of woman lets her lover— well, you know— when his daughter is a few feet away?"

"A careless woman, or maybe one who has a hidden agenda."

Faythe turned the envelope in her hands, studying it to avoid Ray's gaze. It felt odd to talk to him about such matters, and she was uncomfortable. "The only agenda would have to be wising Rosie up."

Ray nodded, as if she were a pupil performing well. "To what?" he asked.

"Obviously to the fact that she's not an appropriate love object for her daddy, but what a cruel way to do it."

"Maybe she honestly thought the girl was asleep. It's an enigmatic moment, and Carlotta is an enigmatic woman. The novel is about love and betrayal."

Betrayal! I know all about that. Maybe that's why he'd wanted her to play Carlotta?

"I know what it's about," she said. "I'm just not sure I can handle the part."

"You can. Trust me."

The irony of Ray Parnell's saying "trust me" to her was staggering. She had trusted him all those years ago, and her trust had not been warranted. "The least you could do is allow me to finish the book," she said. "I'll call you when I have."

She hadn't meant to sound so dismissive, but he was already on his feet, restless as always. She walked with him to the door, and he stood for a moment, framed in her doorway, his eyes darkening in the way she knew so well. He spoke her name once, lifted a hand as if to touch her, and then became brisk. "Thanks," he said. "I'll wait to hear from you, dear."

Then he was gone. The "dear" smarted, because it had once been a joke between them. Just as Faythe's parents had called each other "dear" while she was growing up, so, too, had Ray's parents, Tommy and Maureen Parnell, in darkest Brooklyn. She and Ray had agreed that "dear" was what you called someone when you didn't want to call them "darling" anymore. It was an affectionate term for the elderly, sexless and prim, and it sounded like a nurse talking to a bedridden patient.

"Get a grip," she told herself, parroting Casey. Why would Ray remember a conversation from over twenty years ago? She dragged the towel from her head impatiently and plunged her fingers through the damp mass of her hair. The envelope he had given her had fallen on the carpet, and she picked it up with a sensation of dread. She slit it open and encountered a single sheet of xeroxed paper. It was a review from the *San Rafael Times* written in March of 1971, and the title read: *Bell, Book, and Candle: Sheer Sorcery.* She read on, able to remember the exact feel of the costumes she had worn in the Van Druten play and the feel of the small stage at the now defunct Venice Players' Theater.

In the role of Gillian, Faith McBain shines in an other-wordly way. Playing a modern witch with a familiar called Pyewacket, Miss McBain manages to suggest both a flesh and blood woman and an eternal sorceress. Her beauty is of the timeless variety, but it is her remarkable skill as an actress that persuades and seduces the audience. Her magic is partly acquired through study and the perfection of her craft, but it cannot be explained in such mundane terms alone. Faith McBain has the elusive quality that used to be known as 'it.' What she makes of it remains to be seen.

She sat for a long time, the review in her hands, unseeing. The phrase "What she makes of it remains to be seen" was particularly painful. She knew that Ray had not meant to mock her by giving her this review, but why on earth had he saved it? He hadn't directed the play, wasn't involved in it in any way, yet he'd been able to xerox a crumbling piece of paper and hand it to her as easily as a dozen roses.

She'd played Gillian at the height of her love for Ray, when everything seemed possible, magic included. Her marriage to Cal was still in the future, after Ray had betrayed her. She was still that girl from Sayerville who believed she could accomplish anything, and only a part of that belief had stemmed from confidence in herself. The greater part had come from Ray himself, who believed in her and gave her that extra adrenaline which made her feel invincible. They would never die, never call each other "dear," and never admit defeat under any circumstances.

Didn't he know that she was not the same woman?

Sherry Brooks lived in a spectacular house built on three levels in Laurel Canyon. The pool was on the second level, but it was covered over for dancing and surrounded by three dozen jack o'lanterns she'd had specially carved at Party Emporium for the occasion. Faythe had forgotten it was Halloween— you did tend to forget in California— and was wearing a cashmere dress with the new, shorter skirt and a wide belt to emphasize her slender waist. Her dress was pale gray and the belt gold, and on impulse, to accommodate the season, she plucked three nasturtiums from a flower arrangement and wound them in her hair. The colors clashed, but as Ray had said, what the hell!

Sherry was coming toward her, wearing a Betsey Johnson dress that was all layered ruffles and more appropriate to a woman Casey's age.

"Faythe, you look stunning!" She put too much surprise in it, as if she'd expected Faythe to look like the undead. She kissed the air next to Faythe's cheek and murmured, "I especially wanted you to come to meet a man I know you'll adore."

Faythe smiled but didn't even ask who it was Sherry had in mind. The woman was famous for thinking she could bring people together and frequently pointed to happy couples as if she'd been the matchmaker. Usually she'd had nothing to do with it, but in her own mind Sherry Brooks was at the center of everything. Mainly, Sherry was known for marrying very rich men and managing to get whopping divorce settlements. She'd had a brief career as an actress and abandoned it for more lucrative work.

Sherry took Faythe's arm in her hard, muscular one and drew her toward a group of revellers standing in the flickering, jack o'lantern light. "Everyone," she called, "I want you to meet Fabulous Faythe. She's back in circulation, so watch out!"

Half a dozen pairs of middle-aged male eyes lit up as they turned to her. Introductions were made: Hal, Richard, Greg, Gordie, Martin, and Doug were delighted to meet her, and for a moment she panicked. Where were all the women at this party? She could hear female voices on other levels and inside, but now Sherry had disappeared and she was left with six men who were apparently all in real estate. "Just breaking into the business?" Gordie asked her, and she shook her head no, feeling as gauche as a high school girl at her first mixer.

"Sherry's done right well for herself," said the one called Doug, who was obviously a Texan. "Business is on its way up again, and don't let no one tell you different."

"We're all learning how to be politically correct," said Gordie, "so I hope you won't slap my face if I say that a woman as lovely as yourself has a natural advantage."

She smiled, realizing that this was no ordinary party but something known as networking. It wasn't an A-list party, like one of Cal's, nor even a B-list. It was business. She'd always despised the ranking of guests that went on in Hollywood, but she'd hoped to get back in the swing of things, see a few people she knew, and generally reacclimate herself to going out in public. What she had not expected was that Sherry would assume she would be getting her real estate license like every other ex-wife in town.

She refused a canape from a passing waiter but grabbed a glass of champagne. "I haven't seen Sherry for weeks," she told the men. "I didn't realize she was in real estate now."

She drank her champagne too quickly and saw a familiar face pass a window inside—Amanda, whose calls she had not returned. Murmuring her excuses, she fled indoors and found Amanda guiltily smoking a cigarette on the stairs. She, like Sherry, had a hard, desperately honed body shown to best advantage in the silken equivalent of a muscle shirt.

"It's Faythe McBain," Amanda said in a tight voice. "Reclusive divorcee, fair-weather friend, and non-returner of calls."

"Thanks for sharing," Faythe said. It had been what Casey always said whenever their old dog, Nathaniel, passed air.

"Look who's talking," Amanda said, brushing smoke away with an angry gesture. "I can't even give up smoking, and suddenly Mrs. Speak-no-evil has developed a lively repartee. I can't stand it."

Faythe knew hostility when she saw it, and Amanda was more wounded than angry. How had she misread things so drastically? Sherry and Amanda didn't read the trades anymore; they had invited her out because she was one of their select sorority, a woman once married to money who was now on her own. It didn't matter that they were secure and didn't have to work. For women like Sherry and Amanda there was no rest, no time of peace. Their husbands had been their careers, and between husbands they'd developed alternative careers. Sherry had once been an art dealer; Amanda had owned a shop that imported exotic birds. Now they were apparently both in real estate.

"Look," she said. "I only came to this party because I knew I wouldn't run into Cal. He and my daughter are at some screening. I felt shaky just walking in."

Amanda relented a little. "You look wonderful," she said. "Really wonderful, not good the way I do. You look like you don't have to work at it."

"Thirty laps a day. My new regimen."

"You know," said Amanda, stubbing out her cigarette in a champagne flute, "I'm glad you're rid of Cal. He was a real bastard, first class. He never appreciated you."

People always seemed to think it would make you feel better to know that the man you'd spent twenty years with was a snake. Didn't they know it only cast you as a fool?

"I think I'd better leave now," she said. "I'm not ready to be out with the grown-ups yet."

"Wait," said Amanda. "Before you go you've got to see the statue of Sherry in Carerra marble. It says it all."

Up they went, to the third level, passing through people on the stairs, to what had once been the master bedroom. She tried not to look at the elaborate Venetian bed or the rococco bath and sauna beyond— proofs of the hopefulness of Sherry's last marriage— and followed Amanda onto the small balcony that looked down on the pool.

"Voila," said Sherry.

There, in the corner of the balcony, a life-like nude was poised at the low railing. It was most unclassical in its slenderness, its Sherry-like, worked-for fitness. The legs were taut and the buttocks small, the waist no more than twenty-three inches. Only the breasts were large and perfect. The sculptor had idealized Sherry's face, giving it a youthfulness it no longer possessed, but the cleft chin and wide-set eyes were definitely that of their hostess.

Faythe found herself giggling. "When was that done?" she asked.

"About nine years ago, for her fortieth birthday."

"Why haven't I ever seen it?"

"Well, you know Arthur was always jealous. I guess he was afraid if anyone saw it, any man, he'd fall hopelessly in love and never rest until he got into Sherry's pants."

"I guess that's what Sherry's hoping now."

"It was a tug of war during the divorce. Arthur wanted it, but Sherry's lawyer claimed that since it was a gift to her, she ought to keep it." Amanda placed a hand on one of the statue's large, round breasts. "These were the deciding factor. Sherry only had the augmentation done because Arthur wanted it. She liked her boobs the way they were. Under the circumstances, even Arthur saw that she was the rightful owner."

"A custody battle," said Faythe. "Hollywood style."

More guests were arriving when they descended the stairs, much younger guests. Some looked no more than Casey's age. Faythe decided they would be friends of Felice, Sherry's daughter by her first marriage, and wondered how they would contribute to the networking. A few of them were dancing out by the pool, hurling themselves about to the strains of "An American Werewolf in London." One of the jack o'lanterns had already fallen into the pool. She felt tired and a bit depressed. She was too old to dance the way they did and too young to want to talk to Hal, Richard, Greg, Gordie, Martin, or Doug.

She thanked Sherry and was at the door when a tall man she hadn't seen before came up to her with a sheepish smile. "Sherry said I had to introduce myself to you," he said apologetically. "I'm Tim Brady, from New York."

She gave him her hand and a bright, social smile. "I'm Faythe McBain," she said.

Tim looked uncomfortable, as if he were harboring a secret. "I know," he said. "I've had a crush on you for more than twenty years."

"Have we met?" He was an attractive man with a sensitive and winning smile; she felt sure she'd remember him.

"In a manner of speaking. I was in the darkened theater, and you were up on the screen in a bikini."

Faythe started to laugh, afraid she wouldn't be able to stop. *"Horror Boardwalk?"* she sputtered. "Is that where we met?"

He nodded solemnly. "There and subsequently at *Bikini Prom Night.* I hoped there would be more, but you just disappeared."

"Any more movies like that might have done me in," she said. "I didn't think anybody ever got a crush on those characters. They were so silly. All I did was pose and scream."

"Oh, but I didn't have a crush on the character," he said. "I had a crush on Faythe McBain, the actress." He gave her a level look. "I had good taste. Time has borne me out."

Faythe was used to compliments, many of which were insincere, but Tim Brady was pleasing her. Some men might have taken this line and seemed sleazy and dumb, but his manner was just right: sincere without being overearnest.

"Thank you, Tim," she said. He had very clear blue eyes and hair that seemed a close match to her own. She'd never been attracted to redheaded men, but Tim's curly hair looked auburn in the dim light. She reckoned he was about eight years younger than she was. He'd have to have been a teenager to sit through one of her old movies.

"I'll walk you to your car," he said, and took her arm on the steeply pitched street. "I never thought I'd meet my idol at my cousin Sherry's," he said.

"Is this your first trip to California?"

"No, I've been here half a dozen times. My ex-wife lives in Orange County with my son and daughter."

"Are you in real estate?"

He looked at her oddly. "No . . . should I be?"

"I only thought, because of Sherry . . ."

"Oh, good old Sher," he said fondly.

"She's something different every time I come out here. I teach history at NYU."

Well, here he was, the college professor she'd fantasized about. She felt no quickening of the breath, no surge of blood in his presence, but he was so unlike the men she knew, so refreshingly up front, she liked being with him.

"I don't suppose you'd have dinner with me?" He sounded tentative but not sure of her refusal. Sherry must have told him she was a free woman.

"How would you like to go to a house-warming brunch with me? My daughter is having people over Sunday." She'd spoken impulsively and was half beginning to regret it, but the eager look in his eyes reassured her. He took her address and said he'd pick her up at noon, and she drove off feeling the evening hadn't been a total waste after all. Now she could face Cal and Casey with a man at her side. It didn't matter that he was a nobody by their lights, and it didn't matter that he wasn't her lover. He was just a very nice man who didn't judge her by the harsh standards of Hollywood, and he was on her side. It would be the first time she'd seen Cal in a social situation since the divorce, and she needed an ally.

Coward, she thought as she braked in her drive. *You shouldn't need to have a man with you to face Cal.*

The Senator's Daughter mutely reproached her from the kitchen counter, so she took it to bed with her. She'd read until sleep came and feel virtuous. *How ironic,* she thought, settling against her pillows, *that Ray wants me to play Carlotta Fitzgerald.* She had none of the qualities of that mysterious and powerful woman. She was as insecure as a teenager. In fact more so than she had actually been in her teens. She'd only gone to the party because of Ray. She'd thought he might show up, but of course his admonition that she should go out more was merely idle, social talk. A cliché.

If Tim Brady hadn't shown up to save the evening, she'd be feeling like a girl who'd been stood up.

Casey's condo was in Santa Monica, too, but in the posh part, north of Montana. Casey would never say she lived in Santa Monica without adding "North of Montana," because her address was very important to her.

Tim cast a jaundiced eye on the overpriced shops and cute boutiques as they crossed Montana in his rented car. "Reminds me of Columbus Avenue in New York," he said. "Practically overnight, in the eighties, all the old stores were closed. They were replaced with tasteful little places where you could buy overpriced soap or cheese. They used to joke that the old funeral home would reopen as 'Dead 'n Things'."

Faythe laughed and then said that her daughter loved Montana Avenue and her condo. "She hasn't let anyone see it in all the time she's lived here. She wanted to get it perfect before she had a housewarming. It's been four months."

A brightly wrapped, awkwardly shaped parcel lay on her knees— Casey's housewarming present. Since she already had everything up to and including an espresso machine Cal had bought for her, Faythe had chosen something purely ornamental for her daughter. The delicately woven Indian basket, smelling of sweet grasses, was a work of art, and it had set her back three hundred dollars. Tim had surprised her by arriving with a gift for Casey, too.

"It's just . . . um . . . guest towels," he'd

said uncomfortably. "I thought they were kind of nice."

Faythe had protested. Tim wasn't meant to bring anything but himself. He was doing her a favor, she'd said, but he maintained it was bad luck to go to a housewarming without a gift.

North of Montana were mainly big houses set in spacious grounds, but there were a few tasteful blocks of condos, no more than two or three stories high, and she spotted Casey's by the number of cars lining the street. Certainly Tim's would be the only Pontiac in a sea of Range Rovers, BMWs, Jags, and the odd Rolls or Bentley, but that was fine with her.

Tim helped her from the car, holding his gift-wrapped guest towels, and she hoped he wouldn't feel out of place. Casey, the new Casey, was quite capable of freezing people out if they didn't meet her expectations, but she was also still young enough, Faythe hoped, to be charmed by Tim's good looks and evident nice instincts.

The brunch had been set for noon. Casey was an early riser. Faythe wanted to arrive early enough to have some time with her daughter, but not so early that she'd encounter Cal in an underpopulated room. She saw there was no danger of that; she could hear the many voices in the lobby, and Casey's apartment was on the top floor.

The door stood open and she could spot five people she knew before she'd even passed inside with Tim: two Caruso Creative agents, an actress who'd just landed a part opposite Tom Cruise, a hot young screenwriter, and Beckie Berens, Casey's best friend from Beverly Hills High days. The sixth was Casey herself, looking ravishing in white leggings and a tight black jacket with a double row of buttons.

"Isn't that Julia Roberts?" Tim blurted, and then looked ashamed for behaving like a hick.

Faythe squeezed his arm. "No, it's just Beckie Berens. I knew her when she had braces."

Casey saw her immediately, as if she'd been alerting herself for Faythe's arrival. She was flushed and happy looking and held what looked like a Bloody Mary.

"Mom!" she cried. "I thought you'd never get here."

All eyes turned to Faythe, and belatedly she saw Cal, who had just emerged from the kitchen with an enormous pitcher of margaritas. He hadn't seen her yet, and she was able to study him briefly before going to her daughter. No doubt about it, Cal was eye-catching. He seemed larger than life in his jeans and old flannel shirt. Everything about his dress screamed a message, and it was that Cal Caruso was so important he didn't have to dress up for his little girl's housewarming. His black hair, his grapey eyes, dark, shading to purple, were as dramatic as they had ever been. His hand, curved around the pitcher, was a study in contrasts. The hand itself was huge and rough looking, but the nails were so beautifully manicured it was clear he'd done no manual labor for years.

Casey hugged her warmly and regarded Tim with friendly interest. Then she grabbed Faythe's hand and took her on a tour of her new apartment with as much puppy-like need for approval as the old Casey had once exhibited. The apartment consisted of a large living and dining room, a modern, gleaming kitchen, two bedrooms, and two baths. The second bedroom was Casey's office, and contained only a desk with a computer, a chair, and several file cabinets.

The whole apartment, if stripped of its many guests, seemed rather bare to Faythe, and she wondered what her daughter had been doing to make it perfect. She said nothing and made cooing noises of admiration at the space, the hardwood floors, and the many closets. As far as she could see, Casey had brought nothing with her from the house in Pacific Palisades, but perhaps that was as it should be. Casey was beginning life as an adult and could call her own shots.

"Well?" Casey demanded. "Isn't it a great space?"

"Wonderful," said Faythe. "I hope you'll be happy here, honey."

"Why shouldn't I?"

"No reason whatsoever. I just said it to be traditional."

"I seem to remember," said the forgotten Tim, "that you're supposed to throw salt around for luck."

"Not on these floors," Casey said, but she smiled at him and seemed to take a second look. "Be right back."

"She's a lovely girl," Tim said, "but I expected her to be."

Casey was back in a flash, beckoning them to the long table where the drinks and brunch food were laid out. "Old tradition!" she called to the room at large, and then she ran her finger around the rim of one of the glasses near the margarita pitcher, scooping up salt. She let the grains trickle down harmlessly on the tablecloth and made a mock bow to Tim, who applauded. Faythe thought it was almost as if her daughter was flirting with him, but then she was surrounded by people, introducing them to Tim, making small talk, uneasily aware of Cal at every moment. He had on a look she knew very well, a little half smile that was indulgent and dismissive at the same time. She would have to talk to him, at least say hello, but every time she tried to will herself to cross the room she found an excuse not to.

There was Al Bloom to say hello to, and of course Beckie, who wanted a hug, and Casey's hottest client, a sultry young woman from Latin America who'd made a big splash playing a Salvadoran rebel in last year's sleeper.

"So," said Milagros Rivera, "you are my agent's mother."

There was no point in denying it, so she said she was. The girl wore ripped jeans and a velvet vest, so secure in her beauty she hadn't bothered to wear makeup. Her eyes were as black as ripe olives, and about as expressive. "You look a bit young," she said.

Faythe didn't know if it was the language barrier or malice, so she excused herself and went to rescue Tim, who was trapped in conversation with Don Olphant, a screenwriter who had dated Casey in her last year at college. Don was singleminded and very boring, as Casey had said when they'd broken up. All he could talk about was how writers were always shafted, how Hollywood couldn't live without its writers but paradoxically treated them like dirt. He was as gorgeous as a movie star—the initial attraction for Casey—but Faythe secretly believed he could be dangerous and nearly cheered when Casey broke things off with him.

His eyes were glittering, and she wondered again if Don had a habit of some kind. Drugs, which had become passé for a time, were enjoying a resurgence.

"Hello, stranger." Cal had intercepted her, still wearing his indulgent look. *Like a heat-seeking missile,* she thought, and now she was drawn into that hot aura of his. She checked herself for signs of his power over her and found none. She was experiencing only the natural nervousness of the encounter. It would be unpleasant to her but not devastating. The fact that he'd used the old "hello, stranger" line was comforting, reminding her that for all of Cal's many attractions, verbal brilliance had not been one of them. She said hello and smiled. It was the smile she'd give someone she'd known for a long time and didn't see much anymore.

"Do you approve of the place?" he asked. Implicit in his question was the fact that he had bought the condo for Casey. It was Daddy's choice for his brilliant young daughter, but even at the salary he was paying her she could never have afforded it on her own.

"You chose well," she said lightly, and repeated her hopes that Casey would be happy there.

"You look like the proverbial million bucks," he said. "You're still the loveliest woman in the room."

Oh, please. "I thought that accolade should be reserved for our daughter," she said.

"Case is a doll, but you were always special. Not like other women."

"I'm just like other women," she said briskly. "I'm monumentally just like other women, Cal dear, and don't you forget it."

"Not every woman your age gets a chance to make a comeback," he said. "I hope you'll give it a lot of thought, Faythe. Success can be a double-edged sword, and I wouldn't want you to be hurt.''

"Of course not," she said. There was a lot more she could say, but Cal's fatuous charade of looking out for her interests was sickening to her, and the only way to win was not to play.

Suddenly Tim was at her side, and she felt weak with gratitude. She made the introductions.

"Casey is our daughter," Cal said, suddenly enveloping her shoulder in a possessive way. It was one of a number of poses he'd developed over the years: The Doting Husband, The Penitent Husband, The Loving Husband, The Loving Father, The Brilliant Agent.

Tim looked confused but recovered himself. He realized that Faythe didn't enjoy being clamped to the body of her ex-husband and was considering what to do when they were saved by a huge commotion.

The sound of a Harley down below filled the room with its powerful, stuttering chaos, and most of the guests flocked to the windows to see who'd arrived.

"Tara!" someone shouted. "All right."

Halfway across the room, Casey's radiant face became shut down and aloof. She was wearing her stern look.

Four

The sky was cerise and golden as the sun began its descent into the ocean. Faythe and Tim sat on a bench watching the sunset, something she hadn't done for years. He'd brought her to Santa Monica Beach after Casey's brunch, and that was something else unfamiliar to her. The aristocracy of Hollywood never went to democratic Santa Monica Beach with its crowds of roller bladers and humble beach houses, but Tim was gloriously unconcerned with status.

"My marriage didn't so much break up as fall apart slowly, by degrees, so we didn't know it was over until it was, if that makes sense." He glanced at her and continued. "Jeannie and I met in college and married when I was in graduate school. She's a wonderful woman and a great mother, but we discovered we didn't have that much in common. It sounds like a trivial reason to divorce, but believe me, it wasn't."

Faythe knew he wanted her to part with some of her history, but she felt it was too ugly. In some ways she thought of Tim as an innocent. She considered what she might say that wouldn't reveal too much.

"I did the conventional thing. I waited until my daughter was grown. Now I'm not so sure I was right."

"She seems fine," he said. "As long as kids remain close to both parents they seem to emerge undamaged."

"You saw my former husband," she said softly. "What do you suppose he does for a living?"

"No fair. I already know. That guy Don told me he was the most important agent in Hollywood."

"One of them, anyway. He's a flesh peddler."

"You surprise me, Faythe. You make him sound like a white slave trader." Tim laughed and ran his hands through his hair. She knew he wanted to say something about Cal but was too honorable to bad-mouth a man he'd barely met.

"There's nothing wrong with being an agent," she said. "There are some quite nice ones, but Cal passed the point of no return a long time ago."

He looked at her almost shyly and said nothing.

"It was a case," she said, "of too much mixing business and pleasure."

"I'm about to utter a cliché, and then I'm going to take you to dinner at a little place I discovered up the coast. You didn't eat anything at brunch."

"I'm in training, and eggs benedict is on the forbidden list. I had some fruit."

"Are you ready for the cliché?"

She nodded, knowing what was coming.

"What you said about Caruso, I can't understand it when he had a wife like you."

"Funny you should say that. I used to think the same thing."

The horizon was rimmed with a band of gold now, and she turned her face to the mauve light and shut her eyes. It felt good to be there, where no one she knew would ever find her, and where she could talk to a man without wondering if he was merely currying favor with Cal through her.

When the gold rim faded, they drove up the coast and ate at an unpretentious little seafood restaurant. Faythe ate scallops and took a bite of Tim's dessert, peach pie. She allowed herself a glass of wine and felt a glow of well-being spread through her as she relaxed. "What did you think of Tara?" she asked as they were sipping espresso.

"The girl on the Harley? Well, she's a looker of course, but you expect that here. I got the impression your daughter wasn't exactly thrilled to see her."

Casey had been cool to Tara, thanking her for the bottle of good champagne she'd brought. Faythe remembered Casey's harsh words about the girl's bad habits, but she had seen nothing but a glowing beauty who had an almost touching need to be noticed. She and Tim had been leaving as the girl came in, so she hadn't had much time to form an opinion, but if someone had asked her to describe Tara Johanson in one word, it would be "sweet."

She told Tim a little about *The Senator's Daughter* and Tara's possible role in it. "That beautiful wheat-colored hair will have to be dyed red," she said.

Tara was easily five feet ten, with the long legs and supple torso of a dancer. Her mane of tousled fair hair was not dyed; it was the good Scandinavian hair she remembered from girls in Sayerville. She had the almond-shaped eyes of a Slav, but they were a very pale blue, almost silvery. She was very beautiful, and Faythe wondered if Casey's animosity might not be fuelled by envy.

She had a sudden thought that caused a pain in her temple, but she pushed it away, not wanting to ruin this pleasant evening. It had to do with some rivalry between Tara and her daughter, but over what, and whom, she didn't want to dwell.

The evening was still young when he brought her home, but he said he had a long drive to Tustin and wouldn't come in. She could tell that he wanted to and was refusing himself.

"I'd like to see you again," he said ruefully, "but I'm spending tomorrow with the kids, and then I fly home the day after. Do you see any trips to New York in the future? It's wonderful at Christmastime."

"I won't know until I get the shooting schedule," she said. And then, "Listen to me! I don't even know if I'm going to take the part."

"I think you do, Faythe. You've made up your mind without knowing it."

He cupped her chin in his hand and brushed her lips with his so lightly it was almost reverent. She put her hands on his shoulders and felt herself tremble slightly. It had been a long time since anyone had kissed her, and she couldn't deny that he was attractive to her. But it wouldn't be fair to him to imply a passion she didn't feel.

"I'll write to you," he murmured against her cheek. "I'm one of the last people who writes letters left in the Western world."

It didn't occur to her to ask for his address in New York, but as she watched him drive off she felt bereft and physically lonely. She went into the house and turned on more lights than she usually did. She put on a tape of classical Spanish guitar, but within minutes she realized it was the wrong choice to soothe her. The music was so sensual, throbbing like a woman in pleasure, and she turned it off, regretting that she hadn't let Tim make love to her. The drive to Tustin wasn't that long, it had simply been a pretext to give her an out.

She knew women who would have thought her crazy to turn away a man like Tim. They thought of sex as something healthy and therapeutic, like a facial or sauna. It was their right to grab pleasure whenever they wanted it, just as men had been doing for centuries. These women were usually ten years younger than she was. The women her own age tended to marry too often, as if to put an official seal on their coupling. And the ones

Casey's and Tara's age? They were infinitely more sophisticated about sex than their mothers had been, but sex was no big deal with them. It was one of a variety of pleasant activities they might choose to indulge in, and they didn't have to be "in love" to make love.

In spite of young Faith McBain's dreams of a dark man from New York, her first lover had been a southerner with pale, straw-like hair. With his sweet, slurry accent and aristocratic looks, Graham Leeson had been an exotic in Ironwood, Michigan. His North Carolina voice pronounced her first name as if it had two syllables— *Fay-uth*— and he seemed to her the sexiest, most desirable man she'd ever seen. Unlike some of the men she'd dated, Graham courted her slowly. It would have been unthinkable of Graham to say, as cruder boys did, "What are you saving it for?" or "Don't you like guys?" Faith was a virgin throughout her first year, not because she wanted to be, and not because her body didn't respond to ardent lips and fumbling hands, but because she'd never met a man she thought she could love. It was necessary for her to love the one who helped her lose her virginity, or so she believed, and she'd earned the title "ice queen" by the time

Graham transferred up from North Carolina.

By degrees, she convinced herself that she was in love. He went from being adorable to broodingly handsome, from someone she liked very much to someone she thought she could love.

She was following her body's dictates, because when Graham kissed her and touched her breasts he created an ache that couldn't be ignored. Her body told her that she must "love" Graham, and it was a short step from that permission to the actual act. And what a disappointment that first time had been! The steady pulse of pleasure he'd built up in her was stopped dead when she let him inside her sacred temple. It was all pain and a kind of relentless battering, and then embarrassing wetness and specks of blood on his sheets.

"Oh, mah luvly Fay-uth," Graham panted when it was over, and all she could think was "Is that all? Is that *it?*" Even so, she told him that she loved him, because to deny it would mean that she was just another slutty, promiscuous girl from a small town.

The lovemaking grew better with practice, and although she never could achieve an orgasm with Graham inside her, he could always stroke her into a paroxysm of abandoned pleasure. No one had ever suggested to her that sex was as much a matter of the mind as of the body, and it never occurred to her that she might suggest ways that he might please her. It would be unromantic, for example, to ask him to move in a certain way or not to move at all for a moment. All of her concepts of romantic passion came from movies and novels, and she believed ecstasy arrived on the scene effortlessly or not at all.

She didn't know how it would have ended if Graham's father hadn't suffered a stroke during their second year. He made the trip home, stayed for two weeks, and returned to her, only to have his father die the next day. In his grief he looked very young to her for the first time. She saw him as a boy her age, nineteen, who was in pain, and she took his head on her breasts and smoothed his hair, feeling maternal.

He skipped a whole semester, staying in Winston-Salem with his family, helping to sort things out as the oldest son. He called her every night at first, telling her how he missed her, how he didn't feel whole without her. Faith would stand in the dorm corridor, hunching against the phone booth, whispering endearments back to him even as his image grew unclear to her. By the time he returned to Ironwood, she was involved in theater productions and feeling more passion for acting than she had ever felt for Graham. All the inhibitions she'd known with him in bed were gone when she was on a stage. She felt strong and vivid and in control, as if she'd finally discovered what she wanted to do in life. She was an actress, and learning how to become a good one took up all her time. She begrudged time spent away from the college theater, and her grades began to suffer.

She'd always been an A student, with Bs in geology and French, and here she was pulling Cs and, once, a shameful D. It was useless to explain to her parents that she'd nearly failed geology because she'd been working so hard on her role in *The Crucible* or learning her lines for *Our Town*.

"I didn't send you to college to fool around on a stage," her father said, sounding more hurt than angry.

"Pretty girls are a dime a dozen," her mother told her. "I don't want you to break your heart."

They just didn't get it, Faith thought. It wasn't about looks, or ambition. She didn't want to set the world on fire— she only wanted to be allowed to act. She thought she'd be happy in a place like England, where actors were respected and nurtured. She'd read about the repertory system, where young actors were never out of work; they traveled around in the provinces, sometimes for years before they settled down and became famous in London.

Only now, years later, could she appreciate how naive she had been, but she wasn't alone. Hollywood was full of women who had once dreamed of a life on the stage but settled for brief or aborted careers in the movies. She wondered if she were just part of a dreary pattern after all. Her happiest years had been when she still believed she would become an actress, even though her only work on film was more like a joke than the real thing.

"Now I've come full circle," she said out loud in her over-lit living room. It all fit together like a well-crafted puzzle. Two things had made her happy in those days: having someone who believed in her future and the man she loved. Both Ray Parnell. All her happiness had been predicated on a falsehood, and here she was, ready to let him lead her back into the fray.

With Ray she'd known what had only been hinted at in her lovemaking with Graham. The nineteen-year-old Faith had equated great sex with true love; the forty-six-year-old was sure she was through with love, but acknowledged that her body was not ready to give it up for good. That was the trouble with being an old-fashioned woman. She had never cheated on Cal, which would have astounded many people if they knew, and now that he was no longer in her life she couldn't manage to have a friendly affair.

Neglected. That had been Juanita's word, and it was accurate. She was feeling neglected.

"Mom!" Casey managed to sound buoyant at eight-thirty in the morning, when Faythe was still in bed sipping orange juice. Her voice came down the wire as if she were in the room, urging her mother to get out of bed and engage in strenuous activities.

"Have you read *Variety* yet?"

"I haven't done anything yet."

"Vincent Coleman is out of *Senator's Daughter*. Career conflicts. I bet Ray Parnell is plenty pissed off."

Faythe wasn't. She'd never liked Vince as

an actor. He was mannered and always seemed to play the same part. He was, however, a big star, and Ray would have to find someone of equal magnitude to take his place. "That's not the end of the world," she observed mildly.

"You don't get it, do you? Without an actor like Vincent Coleman, Parnell will have to look for someone more famous to play the daughter. He can't possibly use Tara. She's not exactly bankable material."

"None of it affects me," Faythe said. "My part doesn't require a star."

There was a silence, as if Casey were restraining herself from saying what the part required— something her mother didn't have, no doubt— and then she said: "I won't say another word about what I think, but I wanted you to know that it's not all smooth sailing over at Parnell Productions."

"Thank you, dear. You do keep me informed."

"Now you can return the favor. Who was that cute guy who brought you to my place?"

Faythe explained, and Casey snorted when Sherry Brooks's name was mentioned. "He's awfully young for you, isn't he? I never thought I'd see you robbing the cradle." She said it teasingly, but Faythe knew she was serious.

"Tim is just a new friend, Casey. Period. Friend. He's going back to New York tomorrow, and I might not ever see him again."

"New York! What does he do?"

"He's a history professor."

Casey promptly lost interest in Tim and asked her second question. "What did you think of Tara? What a bimbo, right?"

This would require diplomacy. Casey so clearly loathed Tara that anything Faythe said in the girl's defense would be like a declaration of war. "I only saw her for a moment," she said. "Not long enough to form an opinion. No doubt when I have time to savor her horrible qualities, I'll be able to agree that she's a bimbo."

"She's from some nonstate like South Dakota. I heard she never even finished high school. A talent scout discovered her, if you can believe that. I didn't even know they had talent scouts anymore."

"Yes, it happens to the best of us," Faythe said.

"Oh, I know all about how you were plucked from the bosom of some school in

Michigan, but that was back in the days of silent films."

Faythe laughed. Sometimes Casey seemed to realize that she was harsh and chose to parody herself. "But seriously, Mom, if you do decide to take the part, you can be very glad that Tara isn't on board."

Faythe braced herself for some comment from Cal relayed by her daughter, but Casey seemed to have exhausted her conversational supply for the moment. Just before she hung up, as an after-thought, Casey thanked her for the Indian basket. "It's really beautiful, Mom. You always did have good taste."

Faythe got out of bed and into her tank suit, averting her gaze from the mirror. In certain lights she could persuade herself that her body was as firm and resilient as ever, but early morning wasn't one of them. She had a brief flash of Tara's legs, endless in the spandex bicycle shorts she'd been wearing, and wondered why Tara had never finished high school.

She was in her car, preparing to drive to Nita's, when she decided. She'd finished *The Senator's Daughter* last night, reading until 2:00 A.M., and she had no excuse for putting Ray off any longer. The changes in casting meant nothing to her, representing Casey's dire take on the situation more than anything in the real world. She liked the book and she thought she would be able to understand Carlotta and make her memorable. Any procrastination beyond this point would be simply dithering.

She slid out of the car and went back inside, picking up the kitchen phone and squaring her shoulders with resolve.

The receptionist told her Mr. Parnell was in a meeting, but when she heard Faythe's name she abruptly rang through.

"Hello, Faythe," he said in the deep, soft voice that still made her think of things better forgotten.

"How did you know it was me?" she asked stupidly, as if she really were new in town. The "hello, Faythe" had sounded so intimate.

"I told the receptionist I wasn't to be disturbed unless it was you," he said, sounding pleased with himself. "Do I have myself a Carlotta?"

"You do," she said.

"I'll call your agent. All hell's breaking loose here, but everything is going to be fine. I'm glad you're going to be with us. It means a lot to me."

She was halfway to Nita's before she realized she'd broken a cardinal rule. She'd called the director, when she should have called her agent. She was behaving like a rank beginner, and all because Ray Parnell was mixed into the equation. She vowed to expect no special favor from him, to be treated like just another member of the cast.

When she got to Nita's she shucked out of her robe and sandals and took a running dive into the pool. Swimming her laps seemed much more important now, and she knifed through the water with real purpose.

For better or worse, she had turned a corner. Things were going to change.

Barney Glasser looked like a Disney owl with his bushy, winging brows, but he was as good an agent now as he'd been thirty-five years ago, in Hollywood's so-called golden years. He had come out west originally to study photography at U.C.L.A., and southern California had agreed with him. He'd become an agent when his first wife's brother needed a partner in his fledgling business. Barney was a natural. He made a habit of schmoozing with writers, because, he said, they may be on the low end of the totem pole, but they know everything. Writers knew about grudges that never got reported in *Variety*, and they knew about potential trouble spots weeks, or even years, before a picture went into production. When other agents prided themselves on how often they were seen lunching with famous faces, Barney prided himself on being a true insider. In the gentler days, when theatrical agents, like their literary counterparts, took care of everything for their clients, Barney throve. He liked the psychology of agenting much more than the glamor, and many a star was wooed by Barney's civilized and intimate manner.

He stuck out like the proverbial sore thumb now, in the age of the super agencies whose owners were reckoned among the most powerful players in Hollywood. He was no longer a player like a Michael Ovitz or a Cal Caruso, but he was respected and well liked. He was old enough to carry the residual glitz of the old Hollywood and savvy enough to cope with the corporate world of the new.

Faythe sat in his office and listened to him explain the probable time frame of the miniseries: shooting to begin as soon as final casting was completed, a period of six weeks to finish it, maximum, and one week's work for her. He was toying with the idea of her credit, wanting it to call attention to the fact that she was something special.

"How about 'Re-Introducing Faythe McBain After a Period of Twenty Years'?" she asked.

Barney chuckled but he shook his head at her. "You're not taking yourself seriously enough," he said. "That's refreshing in this business, but this is not a game. You have a chance to revitalize your career in a very dramatic way, and I intend to do everything I can to see that it happens."

"Yes, Barney," she said meekly. "You're right. I'm an actress. I can pretend to take myself seriously. It's the least I can do."

She had a sudden memory of Cal giving her the same advice, to take herself more seriously. It played itself out in Barney's office so clearly that she could remember their actual words.

"I don't need a new dress to entertain the Pastorinis, Cal. I've got a closetful of beautiful things. Do you honestly want me to go out and spend another thousand bucks to have dinner with an eighty-year-old film director and his wife?"

"Maurizio Pastorini is a legend, a great,

great director. He won't be the only one looking at you, in case you've forgotten. We've asked thirty for dinner, or had you forgotten?"

"I've spent two weeks planning it. It's not likely to slip my mind."

"I want you to buy a new dress and look like a million bucks, because how you look reflects on me. People judge a successful man by many things, Faythe, and his wife is one of them."

"Do you even hear what you're saying?"

"Yes. I'm telling you to take yourself more seriously, and if you can't do it for me, do it for yourself."

Faythe grimaced as the words chased themselves around Barney's office. "Did you ever meet Maurizio Pastorini?" she asked him.

"Several times, once in Rome on the set of *Una Vecchia*. He was very likable, and geniuses often aren't."

"We had him to dinner once, when I was married to Cal. He was wearing old gray trousers and a cardigan sweater."

"He was the least pretentious of men, and his wife was a real sweetheart." He cocked a bushy eyebrow at her. "What brings up the great Pastorini, he should rest in peace?"

"Nothing, really." She shrugged apologetically. "Just a sudden memory."

As she was leaving, Barney came from behind his desk and took her hands in his. "This miniseries," he said. "It's a beginning, and you can make it what you want. It's not easy to crash back into the business after so many years, but I think you have a good chance at building a real career. One you can be proud of. It's up to you, Faythe, and if you decide to make this a one-shot thing, fine. But if you go for something bigger, I'm prepared to help you every step of the way."

She planted a kiss on his cheek, touched by his evident sincerity. This was why she had wanted him to be her agent. Barney would never use words like Casey's, to the effect that her clients were willing to be guided by her decision. Where did a girl her age get the chutzpah to make such pronouncements? Certainly not from her. Casey, at any rate, had no trouble in taking herself seriously.

She allowed herself a lazy day, doing errands and catching up on what passed for domestic work. The little house was easily cleaned, but she reminded herself to engage someone for the time when she'd be working. At the Farmer's Market she bought a lush bunch of dahlias and left them on Juanita's doorstep with a card. She stocked up on fruit and other wholesome foods, passing up the fatty avocados she loved. She made an appointment to have her hair and nails done— the time had passed, for now at least, when she could do her own. Too many eyes would be on her now, and she knew it was a part of her new job to look as glamorous as possible. No more driving to Juanita's with a robe slung over her bathing suit in the mornings, and no more jeans if she slipped down to Starbucks for a cup of fresh-brewed coffee. *In fact,* she told herself ruefully, *no more coffee for the duration of the shooting. Tea, juice, and mineral water.*

Her mind would not turn loose the image of that night when Maurizio Pastorini and his wife had come to dine at the house in Pacific Palisades. She'd been smarting over the charge to "take herself seriously," since Cal meant to take him seriously and to reflect his glory as best she could.

She would always be, by nature, a girl from the Midwest who secretly bridled at spending fantastic amounts on clothes and who preferred to wash her own hair. Left to her own devices, she might even have let the gray creep in to her chestnut hair and stay, but in this town that simply wasn't a possibility, unless, like Nita, you were not a part of the dream business.

It had been fun, at first, to wear beautiful clothes that cost more than the combined dress allowances of every woman in Sayerville, Wisconsin, but the fun had its limit. Cal's desire to acquire and display, she soon saw, would never be satisfied, would never seek a level and stay there. If his wife looked lovely in a $750 cocktail dress, why wouldn't she be even lovelier in a $2,000 Ungaro? If his daughter expressed a mild desire to have a playhouse, why not hire an architect to build her a small replica of an Italian villa, and why shouldn't the teacups she passed to her small friends when they played at grown-up entertaining be genuine Spode?

It was all a part of Cal's unappeasable hunger, and she'd spent half a lifetime trying to understand where it had come from. His parents had been quite old when she met them and were long since dead. They had been pleasant, middle-class people from Sacramento, two generations removed from the Abruzzi mountains in central Italy. Mr. Caruso had been a lawyer and his wife, Anna, a schoolteacher. They had raised three children, of whom Cal was the youngest. His sister, Maryanne, lived in Canada with her industrialist husband, and she had been so much older than Cal that the two did little more than exchange Christmas cards.

They had known one tragedy, and this was the death of their middle child, Michael. Cal would never say much about Michael except that he'd been four years older and had died in Vietnam.

The Carusos had come to Pacific Palisades several times before their deaths, and had welcomed Faythe into the family with no hint of displeasure that she was neither Italian nor Catholic. They dutifully smiled and made big eyes at the many luxuries Cal pointed out to them: "Look, Ma, real gold taps on the faucets in the guest room! Hey, Pa, want to take a turn in the Lamborghini?"

His eagerness to impress them had touched her at first— it was the first time she had seen him as vulnerable— but gradually it had become embarrassing. It was so clear that the elder Carusos, like Faythe, had limits. Yes, luxury was very nice, very nice indeed, but after a while one had seen enough of it. Mrs. Caruso was bewildered by the state-of-the-art kitchen, and intimidated by Mrs. Steinhoff, the cook.

The more Cal tried to impress, the more he seemed a surly child. All of the things he was good at, the qualities that had made him so successful, were alien to his parents. If Mr. Caruso had been a different kind of lawyer, an entertainment lawyer for example, he might have appreciated the art of the deal at which his son excelled, but Cal's father was the kind of advocate who defended young men and women who were down on their luck, for next to no money. He earned a living as a family lawyer, did some pro bono work, and collected stamps. That was the sort of man her father-in-law had been.

Both the Carusos seemed sad, and she thought it was the death of Michael that had permanently subdued them. "You should have seen them before," Cal said to her. "They had so much life. They were always joking and fooling around, and Dad used to whistle all the time."

Before what? she'd wanted to ask. Before the natural aging process had set in, or before Michael had died?

There had to be an explanation for a man like Cal, a man who could never have

enough women, enough toys, enough respect, enough proof that he was a success.
Children who had been abused required
the sort of pacification Cal seemed to require, but she would stake her life that he
had never been beaten. She believed his
parents had loved all their children and
provided for them with affection and good
sense, but something had happened to Cal
that created this bottomless pit that could
never be filled.

The answer had to lie with Michael. She
had seen a photograph of Michael, and he
was darkly handsome like his brother, but
there was a special quality, even in an old
black and white snapshot, that made him
seem a god to Cal's human male. Michael
had a charisma only granted to the dead;
you looked at the photo and thought: "Oh,
what if he had lived?" It was all that promise cut short so early that made Michael
seem larger than life.

The Carusos were only human, and she
thought Michael had been their favorite.
Try as they might to conceal it, their par-
tiality for their older son would have been
sensed by his brother. Children always knew
such things. If Michael had lived, Cal might
have dealt with feeling the lesser of the two,

but Michael had died, and Cal was forever left behind, feeling that his parents would have preferred that he had been blown to pieces in a town halfway around the world.

It was only a theory, but it was the one she used to forgive him time after time. If he had ever talked to her about his feelings, his grief, her forgiveness might have been more genuine, but Cal would not talk about anything that went beyond the immediate. He regarded her interest in his past as prying, or "back story" as they said in the business.

Cal was no longer her business but Casey was. She hoped she had given her daughter enough unconditional love so that Casey would never know the hunger that could never be satisfied.

Five

The word through the grapevine was that, having lost its star Vince Coleman, *The Senator's Daughter* was going for quality rather than star power. The network had battled Ray Parnell over the central role of Rosie. They wanted to go with a big name, a proven commodity, while Ray wanted an unknown. A truly young actress, he argued, would be able to play Rosie both as young teenager and young adult— all she wouldn't be able to do was play the role in the scenes where Rosie was a child.

The network agreed to screentest unknown actresses, the term itself an insult to many of them. They had all worked in film and on the stage, many of them far from unknown in the circles they cared about, but to the network they were nobodies who couldn't hope to rope in millions of viewers.

The network went courting a young, waiflike model whose face was known around the world, but she couldn't act at all.

In the end it didn't matter, because a star more incandescent than Vince Coleman signed on to play the senator. Parnell had flown to London and consummated the deal with a British agent, and everyone at Caruso Creative and the other major agencies viewed it as an act of treason.

Desmond O'Connell was an actor who had never worked for television and had once said he never would. He was a stage actor of distinction and a movie star who'd won the Academy Award fifteen years ago for his astounding performance in *Silverton,* a film about an alcoholic priest who became a freedom fighter in an unnamed country very like South Africa. He was an Irishman with many of the qualities of his American counterpart, Senator Tom Madigan, but he had never let any of his peccadillos prevent him from turning in stellar performances. He was adored by women everywhere, because they saw in him the glorious man who could be redeemed by the love of a good woman. His name alone was enough to ensure an audience for *The Senator's Daughter,* so once again the part of Rosie was up for grabs. With Des O'Connell on board, Rosie could be played by almost anyone who wasn't embarrassingly bad on screen.

How had Parnell managed to snare O'Connell, who had never worked on television? The *Hollywood Reporter* hinted that the famous actor needed money and was being offered a gargantuan salary. O'Connell had squandered his vast holdings on gambling and unwise investments and general profligacy, went the gossip, and the only remedy was an infusion of good old American money.

The truth was somewhat different, as Ray Parnell told Faythe McBain. O'Connell was a reading man, a man who enjoyed literature as much as he valued Irish thoroughbred horses, high-stakes gaming, beautiful women, and aged malt whiskey.

Unlike almost anyone in Hollywood, he had actually read the novel, and he had been moved. In the future he would appear on talk shows and confide that the character of Tom Madigan appealed to him because he had known so many men like the senator. In private, he told Ray that the character challenged him because "the old son of a bitch is just like my old man."

Faythe could hardly believe her good luck when she heard that Des O'Connell would be playing the senator, her paramour. It delighted her and then sent waves of uncertainty through her perilously balanced system. Would she ever be able to hold her own on screen coupled with an actor like the mighty O'Connell? She had worshipped him back in Sayerville, when she and Glenda took in the beauty of his black hair and cornflower eyes, and then, at Ironwood College, she had begun to see what a fine actor he was. He matured along with her, always a few years older, but always somehow familiar, and by the time his beauty had begun to be eroded by too much drinking and hard living, he was one of the most celebrated actors in the world. He was still handsome in a way that shot you to the heart, and if, at fifty-two, he was no longer the pretty boy who had turned down the role of James Bond, he offered something more: he was legend.

She was surprised when Ray asked her to come to his office in Century City. She had signed her contracts and nothing further was required of her for now, but he hinted that he wanted her advice on something important. "I hope and pray you're not going to tell me Desmond O'Connell has backed out?" she said, as he whisked her off to his screening room.

Ray shook his head. "He's signed, sealed, and delivered. He'll be in California in a week." He shot her a teasing look. "You always had the hots for him, didn't you?"

"I had a dignified crush on him," she said, "like every other woman in the world."

They settled in comfortable, padded chairs. Nothing had changed in screening rooms over the years, except for the ashtrays. They'd all been removed now that nobody smoked.

The lights were lowered and Ray murmured, "Just watch and tell me what you think. I'm interested in your opinion."

The first screen test showed a girl she'd never seen, a tall, somewhat rangy girl with lovely cheekbones and a sensual mouth. The camera followed her as she walked through a field somewhere, wearing jeans and cowboy boots. She sat on a fence and looked pensive. Next she appeared in a mini-dress, '60s version, looking tense and not sure that she belonged wherever it was she was supposed to be. These emotions came through loud and clear, and in the next scene she had lines to speak. The actor with her was a journeyman type Faythe recognized, Chris Anders. The scene was one she recognized from the book: Rosie has fled to Europe after the murder of her father. She has changed her name and imagines that nobody knows who she is. She is lost and frightened and masking it with a pretended arrogance and hauteur. In short, she is behaving like a first-class bitch, but the reader knows what's really going on inside. Chris Anders was standing in for whoever would play the unhappy young English nobleman who falls in love with Rosie. The girl was leaning against a tree, watching with an unreadable look as a man walked toward her.

He: Are you Aurora?

She: No. I'm Caroline.

He: Aurora is the Goddess of the dawn. I mistook you for her.

She: That's a terrible mistake. I'm no one's goddess.

He: How do you know? You might be mine.

She: (dismissively) Do you have insomnia? What brings you out so early in the morning?

He: I like to write before anyone else is up. I looked out my window and

saw you emerging through the
mists. Are you one of those born-
again Druids?

She: If you must know, I had a nightmare. I thought the garden might
have a soothing effect.

He: A nightmare? How distressing. What
was it about?

She: (mocking him) It was distressing. I
don't remember, really. It's not important.

He: (gently) Do you often have night-
mares?

She: Dreams are something everyone has.
It's boring to discuss them.

He: As it happens, I agree with you, but
I find that anything to do with you,
any slightest thing, is of interest to
me.

She: (languidly) It's also boring when
men are interested in me.

He: Of course, because it happens so
often. Beautiful women must have
a terrible time of it, all those men
trying to think up original techniques to seduce them. But I'm not
trying to seduce you, Caroline. I'm
engaged to be married, you know.

I'm determined to become your
friend because I want to help you.

She: Do I look like a person who needs
help? (Long, defiant pause). I'm
going back to bed. The garden was
much nicer when I had it to myself.

It was significant that the man had more
lines than the subject of the screen test,
but Faythe understood that it was
Rosie/Caroline's reactions that were important. In the novel you understood that
Rosie had come to a decision in the middle of her dawn encounter. She would let
the man make love to her and ruin his
engagement, because at this stage of her
bereavement she could only react with cruelty. The actress telegraphed the message
too obviously, throwing her head back
against the tree to reveal the length of her
neck, letting her tongue protrude in a kit-
tenish way. She might as well be auditioning for a porn flick. Her voice was also
not right for Rosie. She spoke in a modified twang; probably she knew that Rosie
came from Montana and didn't understand that the senator's daughter had
grown up in international circles.

The next actress was much better, more

subtle and intelligent, but she was so wholesome and untroubled looking that she
might have pitched cornflakes.

Faythe slanted her eyes in Ray's direction,
but he was looking straight ahead in a neutral way. He didn't seem to realize she was
there beside him, so close in the darkened
room. If she moved a fraction of an inch,
her arm would brush against his. She drew
away slightly and redirected all her attention to the screen.

Next came a New York ingenue who had
won praise for her part in a revival of *The
Glass Menagerie* but who had never acted on
film. When she came to the line "It's boring when men are interested in me," she
spoke with conscious irony, as if she'd been
analyzed for so long she knew her every
motivation. Faythe sighed impatiently at this
one. The whole point to poor Rosie was
that she hadn't a clue to what was going on
in her bruised psyche. What was the point
of this, anyway? What had she to do with
Ray's casting?

The next screen test made her sit forward
with interest, because the girl was Tara Johanson. She walked toward them, the wind
lifting her wheat-colored hair and whipping
it across her face. She didn't pull it back with

an extravagant gesture, like a model, but shook her head like someone accustomed to strolling along the Great Plains. The camera loved her, and she was even more stunning on film than in real life. But could she act? Faythe found herself holding her breath for the first sound of Tara's voice in the garden scene. "I'm Caroline," Tara said, and it was perfect. You knew she wasn't Caroline, but you wondered if the lost young girl knew it anymore. Beneath her arrogant words, you detected something childish, but the dazzling quality of her beauty overruled the childishness. Tara played the moment when she decided to let the man make love to her with a mere flicker of her expressive eyes. She looked almost pitying, as if she knew how fatal her consequences might be for the man who stood before her, yet she couldn't stop herself.

There was no doubt about it: Tara was perfect for the part. She looked at Ray expectantly, but it seemed there were two more screen tests to watch. They passed by in a blur. When the lights came up he turned to her. "Anyone strike you?" he asked.

"Of course," she said, wondering how he could even ask. "Number four. Head and shoulders above the others. I think she's truly gifted."

Ray nodded. "We agree," he said. "I'd cast her in a minute, but I wanted some outside input. I wanted to hear from someone who's been out of it for a while."

"Out of it . . . that's me, I guess."

"Oh, come, Faythe, you know what I mean. People in the industry bring all sorts of baggage to their decisions. Either they want someone else as a favor to their Uncle Al or they've heard this actress can be difficult or . . ." He shrugged. "You remember, I'm sure."

"I have a confession. I know who she is. I met her, briefly, at Casey's. She came in on a Harley."

His eyes narrowed slightly. For once she'd surprised him. "So are you prejudiced for or against her as a result of this meeting?"

"No, I don't think so. Although . . ." she smiled, knowing how silly this would make her, "my daughter seems to think Tara is the epitome of all evil. I don't always listen to my daughter."

Again, the shift of light in his eyes. This time she knew he was keeping something from her. Maybe he knew why Casey had such a low opinion of Tara, but she wasn't going to ask him. Instead, she had another question for him, one which she was trying to frame tactfully.

Back in his office, she asked it. "You said you wanted my input. What if I hadn't liked Tara as much as I do? As an actress, that is."

He put his head to one side and studied her in a way that made her feel like screaming. Was he noticing that her skin was more radiant than it had been a week ago, thanks to a strict diet and several facials? Was he comparing her to the glowing youthful Tara Johanson? But no, of course not, she remembered now— whenever she'd asked Ray Parnell a question, he had always tried to answer as honestly as possible. He cupped his hands behind his head and leaned back. "I would have listened with interest to everything you had to say on the subject, and then I would probably have cast her anyway."

"That's honest," Faythe said, "but why bother then? I want to understand, Ray."

"It shouldn't be difficult," he said. "I respect your opinion. I always did. You knew a lot about what made an actor magic back then, and I assume you still do." He got up and went to the windows, where blinds

were half drawn against the powerful mid-
day sun. When he turned around, she could
read displeasure in his mobile face.

"What's wrong with you?" he asked. His
voice was soft but there was rising anger un-
derneath. He spoke in measured tones, as if
to a wayward child. "For God's sake, Faythe,
I've known you for twenty-three years.
Doesn't that mean anything? Does it seem so
odd to you that a man might ask for your
opinion? That your opinion might carry
some weight? Why do you read strange motives into the simplest things I say or do?"

She felt as if he'd knocked the breath
from her. Where had all this emotion come
from?

"I didn't mean to offend you," she said.
"I don't think your motives are strange, Ray,
but I still don't see why my input should interest you." No reply. He was looking at her
as if she were the most obtuse woman he'd
ever encountered, and suddenly it made her
angry.

"And what's all this about knowing me for
twenty-three years?" she said scornfully. "We
knew each other for three years, Ray— three
measly little years— and then there were
twenty years where you didn't know me at
all. Twenty years is a long time. Oh, we may

have glimpsed each other now and then. As I recall you even came to our house several times, but that hardly qualifies as knowing me. What do you know about those two decades? For all you know I have as much sense of what makes people magic," she spat the word out, "as that malachite paperweight on your desk!"

She'd risen somewhere during her outburst and was now confronting him, hands on her hips, ready for a fight. The audacity of it took the wind out of her sails, and she lapsed into silence.

"Quite a speech, Faythe," he said in an almost inaudible voice. "More words than I've heard from you in that famous two decades."

He was mocking her now, and she felt the anger return with a vengeance. "Oh, stuff it, Ray. Don't make it seem you've been missing me for twenty years. I thought you were more honest than that."

"As I seem to recall," he said, still in that voice that withheld so much, "my honesty was called into question. I'm so flattered that you've revised history, Faythe."

They were saved by the buzzer on his desk, the voice informing him that he had a meeting. She instantly scooped up her handbag and headed for the door. At the last moment she turned. "Let's forget we had this conversation," she said.

Silently, he nodded.

She managed to get out of the building and onto the carlot with a purposeful step, but her hands shook so badly she had to sit for a moment before she could start the car. It seemed amazing that she could be having a quarrel with Ray Parnell after all these years, amazing that both of them could experience such a pitch of anger. How could he dare to say "my honesty was called into question," to her, of all people, as if she had wronged him!

Was he such a hypocrite that he'd managed to forget how he'd betrayed her? Or, worse, could she have been so unimportant to him that he'd rewritten their personal history in his favor? The most wounding thing was that it was something she could never bring up to him, and she would have to ignore it. Oh, it was a bitter thing to have Ray make it seem that she willfully mistrusted him, and for no reason!

The only thing that frightens me is the thought of having to live without you. He had spoken those words passionately, and she had believed him because she felt the same way.

He was the first to speak of love, to say I love you, to make, as they said now, a commitment. They hadn't spoken of marriage then, because it was implicit in everything he said: *We'll go to Europe together one day. . . . We'll have a house by the ocean. . . . We'll be at the top of our careers . . .*

Less than a week after he'd made her promise never to leave him, she had discovered him with an extra, a girl called Jo Ann. In the ordinary course of events, she would have forgotten Jo Ann, who'd been just another body in a bikini on the set, but Ray had seen to it she'd remember Jo Ann forever. Jo Ann Kluger, who had changed her name to Joanna Kane. She had the requisite, curvy figure and bleached, platinum hair, which she wore in a high ponytail. She had never been heard to utter one intelligent or witty word and was entirely forgettable except for her giggling vivacity whenever she was around the director, Ray Parnell.

Faythe was to have dinner with Ray that evening, and she came early to his funky little house in Venice to surprise him and bring him good news, that Cal Caruso, the agent, was interested in signing her. The surprise, however, had been entirely hers.

She'd heard a familiar giggle even before she made her way back to the cluttered bedroom (She could still see that bedroom: the king-size mattress taking up almost the whole room, the Indian bedspread tacked up instead of real curtains, the way the late afternoon sunlight crept around the edges and made little golden stripes on the half-clothed bodies.)

Ray and Jo Ann had obviously just made love, and she lay with one leg drawn up over his flank, her bleached hair wild on the pillow and her mouth all soft and loose looking. Her panties were on the floor, but she still wore a t-shirt, as if they'd been so eager they hadn't bothered to undress. Ray's floppy hair was in his eyes, and the toes of his beautiful feet were still slightly curled, as if in the aftermath of pleasure. Neither of them saw Faythe, standing in the doorway, her mouth stretched wide in pain and disbelief . . .

He refused to believe she was through with him and said over and over that it hadn't meant a thing— the unfaithful man's refrain— and that she was the love of his life. He made things worse by claiming that Jo Ann had come to the house uninvited and had practically steamrolled him into bed. She felt such contempt for his rationalization. No one could have steamrolled her into bed, and if that was the difference between men and women, she thought a life of celibacy might be looking attractive.

She had hardened her heart against him and accepted the suffering it brought her with one thought: Nothing could ever hurt this much again. And she'd been right. Ray had done her one favor, because as much as Cal's compulsive infidelities had pained her, she never again felt as she had in that doorway. When Rod Stewart's song "The First Cut is the Deepest" became popular, she thought it might have been written for her.

Hands steady now, she started the car and headed out of Century City on the Avenue of the Stars. She waved to a pretty young woman getting out of a limo and belatedly realized she didn't know her at all. With her pale brown hair and distinctive, laugh-crinkled eyes, she had seemed to be Betsy London, the woman Ray had married ten years ago. Betsy was a set designer of great talent, and Faythe was sure she might have liked her if circumstances had been different. She was always extra nice to Betsy whenever their paths crossed, because it would be unbearable to let the other woman think she was jealous.

"Get a grip," she told herself, feeling afraid. If words with Ray could make her see a ghost, then she was in worse trouble than she knew. Betsy had died of Lou Gehrig's disease five years ago, and everyone had mourned the abrupt end of such a promising life. Faythe had felt a pang so deep she knew it came from guilt. She had never wished Betsy harm, yet she had always secretly resented her.

On Hollywood Boulevard the hookers and runaways and panhandlers were out in force, as if for them there was no difference between night and day. She saw a girl in a long black wig and a tiny rubber dress crying inconsolably, her mascara running in black rivulets down her cheeks, and she knew it was probably drugs but wondered if the girl had come to Hollywood to be a star.

Everything seemed terribly sad— the ruined girls and Betsy's early death and her own inability to learn from her mistakes. She thought she'd like a good cry, but crying was something she had abandoned when she lived with Cal. She wasn't sure she still knew how to cry. *Maybe,* she thought, *my tear ducts are drying up along with the rest of me.*

In addition to the *Hollywood Reporter* and *Variety,* agents Casey's age devoured a new publication called *Deep Dish.* It was a small-scale scandal sheet that came out weekly, and it avoided libel suits by employing only rumor and innuendo. *Deep Dish* wasn't interested in things that everyone already knew about— mean divorces and plastic surgery and outrageous affairs— but preferred to do what Casey called "stirring the shit." It looked for what might be possible between people and in situations of interest to the movie community. Could it be that a certain actress hadn't done very well in such and such a movie because she was unrequitedly in love with the leading man? Was it possible that Kenny Roche was overdoing the testosterone bit— a rumored brawl in a club— to overshadow the fact that he was coming up effeminate in the rushes of his new picture?

It was mean-spirited stuff, everybody agreed, but they all read it. *Deep Dish* was supposedly the work of two screenwriters who had an informant in one of the agencies, but nobody knew for sure who wrote the venomous little articles. It was considered a temporary blot on the landscape, and most people thought it would last another six weeks or so before folding its tents.

Faythe had never seen it, so she was unprepared when Casey rattled the current issue in her face at Prospero's. She had returned home to find a message on her machine: "Meet me at Prospero's at six, okay, Mother?" It was a typical Casey command, the kind that didn't acknowledge that her mother might have had other plans.

Prospero's was a small espresso parlor on the less chic side of Montana. It had become less popular as the neighborhood to the north was gentrified, and Faythe understood her daughter had chosen it because no one important would see them. The place had an air of abandonment, but she thought it looked nice, like something from New York's Little Italy transplanted on the West Coast. Black and white tile floors, overhead fans lazily rotating, small tables with little wire-backed chairs, it wasn't much different from any other espresso place, except that "people of importance" no longer frequented it.

"What are you waving at me?" she asked, trying for a light note. She noticed that Casey had already demolished a sherbet glass full of coffee granita and wished that she herself could order a cup of cappuccino with whipped cream. She ordered a plain espresso and addressed herself to the ratty looking paper Casey was clutching. It looked like a supermarket tabloid minus the photos.

"This is *Deep Dish*, the magazine— well, really it's more a paper— anyway, Mother, it doesn't much matter what it is. It's what it says."

Faythe felt a wave of exasperation pass over her. What could possibly be so important that her daughter had summoned her to a clandestine meeting? "Why don't you just tell me?" she suggested.

"Better yet, you can read it yourself." Casey folded the paper back and stabbed at an item with one beautifully manicured nail. (Even in the midst of a sense of foreboding, Faythe admired those nails. She could remember all too well when Casey had bitten her nails to the quick.)

Now there was a new humiliation. She couldn't possibly read the small, inky print thrust in front of her. Her vision, always excellent, was beginning to give her trouble. She needed her reading glasses, but she'd left them at home. She tried holding the paper out at arm's length, but it was no go. She started to explain, but she became aware that Casey was not merely in her bullying mode today. She was white around the mouth, a sign of real distress.

"Honey, what is it? You read it to me. It can't be all that bad."

Casey bent forward and began to read in a breathy undertone. "Insiders are asking why big-time director Ray Parnell has cast the former Mrs. Cal Caruso in his upcoming miniseries *The Senator's Daughter,* based on the best-selling novel by. . . . Faythe McBain, best known as Caruso's wife for twenty years, would not seem the logical choice for the glamorous role of Carlotta Fitzgerald. Although the superagent's ex-wife has glamor to spare, careful research turns up only two film credits— "

"Yes, I know," Faythe said wearily, "spare me the snickers over *Horror Boardwalk.*" She'd been prepared for this; it was nothing she couldn't handle, and she was surprised that Casey was making such a big deal of it. As Casey continued to read, though, Faythe felt her fingertips grow cold.

"At first the common wisdom held that a director was paying back a favor to an agent, but *Deep Dish* has discovered something much more interesting. Before she married Cal Caruso, the lovely Faythe was linked to Parnell romantically. According to sources, the youthful pair were 'inseparable' and 'mad for each other.' Now that Parnell is a widower and McBain is a free woman, what better way to fan the embers of a fire that has been dead for more than twenty years? Never let it be said that Romance is dead in Hollywood."

Casey slammed the paper down on the table. "Well?" she asked between gritted teeth. "How much of this is true?"

Faythe stirred her espresso and deliberated. "None of it," she said, "about fires springing back to life. None of that romantic garbage."

"And the rest?" Casey was twirling a piece of her hair manically. "Were you and Parnell really lovers?"

"He was my . . . boyfriend, yes, before I met Daddy. We didn't use the word lover then."

"Jesus!" Casey drummed her nails on the marble tabletop as if seeking inspiration. "This is just so incredibly embarrassing. No wonder you wouldn't take my advice about this project. No wonder you went over to Barney Glasser. He doesn't care if you make a fool of yourself. What's it to him?"

Faythe caught her daughter's hands and stilled them. "What's so embarrassing, Case?" she asked quietly. "I was about your age, I had a boyfriend, and it happened to be Ray Parnell. What's so awful about it?"

"You really don't see?" Casey turned a pitying look on her. "You can't understand that this is ridiculous? Parnell is just doing you a favor, for old time's sake. I thought he was smarter than that, but never mind him. How could you? How could you allow yourself to embarrass Daddy like this?"

A flush of real anger suffused her. "Your father does not embarrass easily," she said tartly. "He is hardly a frail flower, my dear, in case you hadn't noticed."

"Oh, right, bad-mouth him. That's such a cheap shot, Mom. He never says bad things about you. He thinks you're a wonderful woman who was never meant to live out here. He has compassion for you, which is more than I can say— "

"Hold it, Casey. Let's get something straight. I am doing nothing to make your father uncomfortable. Believe it or not, this is not about him, it has precisely zero to do with him, and I won't have you accuse me like this."

Casey subsided a bit under her firm words, but a rebellious nerve twitched along her right eye and she'd become even paler.

"Okay," she said at last. "Let's suppose you don't understand what's going on. I'm willing to believe you're innocent about Parnell's motives, but why didn't I know about this? You've been dishonest with me."

There was that word again, "dishonest." Her honesty was being called into question. "You never asked," she said. "It's ancient history and has nothing to do with my playing Carlotta."

"Right." said Casey, drawing the word out to indicate her disbelief. "You're playing that part because you're this wonderful actress who's been knocking 'em dead all these years. He cast you because of all the middle-aged actresses in the world you had the highest profile. Not."

She put so much poison into the last word that Faythe recoiled.

"Try to understand. Ray and I started out together when we were young. I always knew he'd be a great director one day, and he . . . well, he thought I'd be an important actress. He believed in me."

"You sound like some spacy seventeen year old," Casey said. "That's what every man says to every girl: 'I believe in you'."

"Ray meant it," Faythe said quietly, more to herself than to the outraged girl she had trouble recognizing as her daughter.

"I can't handle this," Casey slapped some bills on the table and stood up. Faythe made no move to stop her. She was tired of defending herself when she'd done nothing wrong. Much as she hated knowing that Casey was upset and misinformed and letting her imagination run amok, she had no strength at present to smooth things over.

She finished her espresso and thought it was time to go home, but the lonely little house held no appeal for her just now. Briefly, before she left Prospero's and Casey's tantrum behind her, she thought it might be nice to move away from Hollywood for good. She could go up to Oregon, maybe, and buy a little house in the woods or on the coast. She'd meditate and learn the secrets of inner peace, let the gray grow back into her hair, eat and drink what she liked, and grow plump and complacent. Casey would like this new, nonthreatening Mom and visit frequently, all her hard-driving ambition and judgmental ways left behind in southern California. Faythe would find a circle of supportive women friends and forget all about men, except as friendly wood-choppers or fishermen. Life would be dull; life would be bliss.

Six

Katherine Iverson's house in the Hollywood Hills was as timeless and lovely as Katherine herself. It was decorated with English country furniture and plenty of chintz and looked more like a cottage in Devonshire than a movie star's house. Unless you looked very carefully, you might fail to notice that the small painting on the stair landing was a real Renoir, and that was like Katherine, too, because her very essence was understated beauty and elegance.

Katherine was only five years older than Faythe, but she had been prominent in films since she was nineteen. She'd begun her career playing classy, aristocratic women who acted second-fiddle to the star. Hollywood had decreed that she was a character actress and not a leading lady, because in the days of Katherine's youth stars were busty, preferably blonde, and always bubbly.

Faythe admired her from the doorway as

she made her own entrance, hoping to feel less nervous. Katherine was dressed in cream-colored silk trousers and matching shirt, and her dark blond hair was scraped back in the signature topknot that emphasized her classic features. Her earrings were yellow diamonds, and she wore no other jewelry except for the wedding band on her left hand.

Compared to her, Faythe thought, *I look like a Christmas tree.* She had deliberated long on what to wear, and it was too late to regret her choice now. She'd finally selected a dress with a black velvet bodice and a square-cut neck that revealed her still creamy skin but displayed no cleavage. The skirt of the dress was made of many-colored panels of Venetian silk, and she wore a pretty collar of amethysts and sapphires that Cal had given her many birthdays ago. She felt delicate and ornamental and thought she'd hit on the perfect ensemble for this first gathering of the principals in the miniseries. Katherine had volunteered to play hostess at this party, just as she was so often the hostess of parties in her pictures. Faythe advanced into the room, thinking of the irony of Hollywood's typecasting. Katherine played society women because she looked like an aristocrat, but she was in fact the daughter of a poor farmer from Alabama. Legend had it that Kate Iverson had been forced to train her voice for a year before it became the voice they all knew now— cool, precise, and without any discernible accent.

"Faythe! How good to see you." Katherine gave her a cool hand and studied her with wise, dark eyes. "I think you've made a marvelous decision," she said in a lower voice. "Welcome back."

As if Faythe had ever worked with her! As if, in fact, Faythe had merely taken a few years off from the business of acting! She felt grateful for the older woman's tact and smiled her thanks. She was dying to know why Ray had not thrown this party himself. He had a nice house in Bel Air, and it would have been natural for the director to make the effort. But Ray seemed to be staying in the background. The invitation had come from Katherine herself, delivered by hand at the beginning of the week, and Faythe didn't even know if Ray would be present.

She looked around and saw a few familiar faces: Beverly Redfox, a Native American actress who would be playing Lee Rainwater, Rosie's best friend, and Ty Gardner, a comic actor who was cast against type as the man Rosie finally learns to love. Katherine, of course, was playing the Senator's long-suffering wife— another part in which she would embody the virtues of aristocratic stoicism.

By his accent, the cute young man who was chatting up Beverly had to be the English actor who was playing the part from Tara's screen test. The rest were strangers.

"Let me introduce you to some of our guests," Katherine said. The "our" was strictly rhetorical, since Katherine's husband lived in New York most of the year. "May I present Faythe McBain," she said grandly, addressing a knot of people who were grouped around Ty Gardner. All eyes were on her, appraising coolly even as everyone smiled.

"Well," said Ty gallantly, "a woman lovely in her bones."

"Where's Tara?" someone else asked.

They were all disappointed that Des O'Connell would not be coming. He was still in New York, having decided to see everything on Broadway before he came to California. "So like Des," Katherine said. "He always refers to Hollywood as a 'Cultural Dessert.' Not desert, but dessert. He maintains that the main course is elsewhere, and we're the banana split— totally without nutritional value but delicious."

"That's so snobbish," said a young woman Faythe hadn't noticed before. "It's passé and totally without foundation."

"This is Lisbet Adkin," Katherine said, introducing the disapproving girl to Faythe. "Lisbet is a young woman with views." She smiled to soften her sarcasm. "Never mind, Lizzie dear, I think it sounds snobbish, too, but I assure you Des is anything but a snob. You're going to adore him."

"Katherine played his wife in *The Capitol*," said Ty, proving that he'd been boning up on old movies. *The Capitol* had been made before he was born.

Faythe remembered, though. It had been a typical Kate Iverson role. She'd played the wife of an idealistic Washington lawyer who fell in love with one of his clients. She contracted a fatal disease so he was free to marry . . . who?

"I lost him to Rhonda Fleming in that one," Katherine said.

Lisbet Adkin was still frowning, and now Faythe remembered where she'd seen her. Lisbet had been on a long-running sitcom as a child and had vanished in everything but reruns. She couldn't imagine what role the girl was playing and asked Katherine.

"Bless you, dear, she's not in the thing at all. She's a very talented make-up artist now, and she'll be making us all beautiful."

"She likes to look at what she's got to work with," Bev Redfox whispered in Faythe's ear. "Sort of like a cook checking out the vegetables."

She followed Beverly into a second living room, where a man was playing Gershwin tunes on a piano and white-coated waiters were circulating. It was like a recreation of a fashionable party of the 1940s, one she might have seen in an old movie as a child in Sayerville. Most parties in Hollywood were either much noisier or much, much quieter. She'd been stunned to discover how early dinner parties ended here, with guests heading for home well before eleven. This was, Cal had explained, because people had to be up so early the next day.

"This is what I imagined a sophisticated party would be like when I was ten," she told Beverly.

Bev raised one perfect black eyebrow.

"I'm not complaining," Faythe said. "I like it here." She had meant she liked the hothouse atmosphere at Katherine Iverson's, but her companion took her literally.

"I hate California," she said. "I'm only here until I make enough money to go home and buy a place."

"Where's home?"

"Washington state. I was sitting around one afternoon, reading a movie magazine. I saw where Native American movies were gonna be the next big thing and said to myself 'Bev Cotter, your ma is half Chinook and you ain't half bad looking, so just change your name to Redfox and get your ass on down to California.' I haven't been out of work since."

Faythe laughed. "Your instinct was certainly right," she said. "I remember when you came to the house. It was around the time when they were making all the movies about Geronimo. Your agent represented you as a full-blooded Apache."

"Well, whatever works," Bev said.

"What happened to that agent? Bill something?"

"He's still around. He's just not with your ex's agency." She looked annoyed with herself for having said too much. Her dark eyes closed down, and she bent and took a curried prawn from a tray, her silver earrings brushing her bare shoulders. "Anyway," she said, moving off, "I wish you luck."

Faythe spoke to an old character actor called Wally Fowler, who treated her like a little girl.

"Well, it's that pretty Faythe," he said, and she could see that he'd already had too much to drink. Wally was said to have been a cowboy, a real one, who'd left the rodeo life to make a living in the movies years ago. He had a face as seamed as a walnut and incongruous, baby blue eyes. He bent close to her, breathing bourbon fumes. His words came out haltingly, and he spoke with emotion. "I'm glad you escaped from that house up at the Palisades," he said melodramatically, as if she'd been a princess locked away in a tower. "There's plenty of people around this town who are rejoicing to see you free, and don't you believe anything you hear to the contrary."

She thanked him, at a loss for words, and wondered what he could be doing here at Kate Iverson's.

"I bet you're playing the senator's ranch manager," she said, coming up with the only part an aging ex-cowboy could possibly play. He looked pleased.

"That's exactly right," he said. "I know

this get-together is supposed to be for the principals, but Miss Kate asked me specially. I don't get out much anymore."

He kissed her hand gallantly and then went off to get a refill. Faythe wondered if she couldn't be part of some charitable scheme of Ray's, a plan to employ a few has-beens. *Let's see,* she had Ray musing, *there's a part in it for old Wally, and come to think of it, I can squeeze good old Faythe in, too.*

Ty Gardner's wife, a beautiful, feline model wearing a dress that showed off her midriff and its pierced navel, was looking alertly over Faythe's shoulder. Someone important had arrived.

She turned and saw Ray silhouetted in the doorway, holding Kate Iverson's hand. There was someone with him. He held his arm protectively around that someone's shoulders, but she couldn't see who it was. Then Ray dropped his arm and presented his companion to Kate.

It was Tara. Tara Johanson, dressed all in black. Black jeans, black clunky lace-up boots, and a black leather jacket. Her long, pale hair lay wildly, any which way, as if it hadn't been combed in recent memory. Her face was dead white, and she looked terrified, as if she'd come to this party to meet her death.

Katherine said something, and Tara smiled wanly, as if she'd had a reprieve. Even such a faint smile lit the exquisite face up with a radiance granted only to the very young, and Faythe felt the familiar pang. Ray moved off, leaving Tara on her own, and soon Katherine was summoning their attention, ringing a dessert spoon against her champagne flute.

"Attention, all," cried Katherine, holding Tara's hand in her own and looking very proud. The noise leveled off, and throats were cleared. The rooms became silent, and everyone formed a circle around the hostess and the young actress, who seemed to be her hostage. Tara looked wildly around her and then composed herself.

"Our director has arrived," said Katherine in her thrilling voice, "and that's reason enough for a toast. But first I'd like to introduce you all to Miss Tara Johanson, who will be playing the senator's daughter. This is an historic occasion, because I believe Tara will become an actress of great distinction. Raise your glasses now, because someday you will be able to say 'I knew her at the beginning'."

Everyone applauded and the English actor said, "Here, here!"

Tara turned even paler, if possible, and murmured a thank you. Her eyes were glittering, and Faythe wondered again if she could be on some drug. What else could Casey mean when she said that Tara was self-destructive, that she wouldn't live past twenty-five? Even discounting her daughter's propensity to exaggerate, there was something wrong with Tara Johanson. Ray had brought her in almost as if she were an invalid. If he had been Cal, she was sure there'd be a proprietary, sexual reason for such conduct, but Ray had never been one to prey on young girls. At least, she thought, he confined his bed-hopping to grown-up women.

Sipping her white wine slowly, she took herself off to the pretty conservatory at the back of the house. Here Kate cultivated rare orchids, one of which had actually been named for her. The flowers were delicately beautiful, fragile, and even in California's balmy climate they required special care. She admired a pale green bloom, wondering if it could be the one that bore Kate's name. Someone had once explained to her that the word "orchid" came originally from the Greek word "orkhis," which meant testicle. The shape of the roots was sexual, like the male organ, and she shrugged in irritation. Did everything have to come down to sex?

Nothing was as it seemed. Ray, once her anchor, was as movable as the tides and about as stable. Casey, her sweet baby girl, behaved like a nagging mother. And Tara, the actress of such promise and purity, was probably shoving coke up her nose in the bathroom at this very moment. No, correction: cocaine was out, and something called Ecstasy was in. That, or the deadly crank, a homebrewed methamphetamine. She knew very little about drugs and wondered which ones made the eyes glitter and which dulled them.

For all his faults, Cal had never abused drugs or alcohol as far as she knew, nor had Casey. They were both too much the control freak type to surrender to illicit pleasures of the chemical variety. Cal had been a social drinker; Casey rarely drank. Occasionally, when Casey had been closeted in her bedroom with Beckie Berens or other friends, Faythe had smelled the sweet, slightly stalish odor of marijuana, but every parent she knew agreed that if marijuana were the only drug your child tried out, you were doing well.

Through the door of the conservatory she could glimpse Ray, deep in conversation with Ty Gardner and the English actor. As she watched, Bev joined them, and Ray put his arm around her casually. It was a friendly gesture, she thought, the kind he could not allow himself with her. As he talked, his floppy hair slipped down over his forehead in the old familiar way, and she felt a faint ache of memory.

"Hello. Mind if I join you?" Coming down the path between two ranks of orchids was Tara, looking like a lovely Darth Vader among the fragile blooms. She held a bottle of Stoli in one hand, a glass in the other. She looked half defiant, half shy, if such a combination were possible.

"Please do." Faythe sat on a broad stone ledge and made way for Tara to sit beside her. She wanted to say something encouraging to the girl, but it wouldn't do to let her know she'd seen her screen test. It would only make Tara feel uncomfortable.

"Those were high words of praise from Katherine," she said. "I feel privileged to be working with someone so promising."

Tara looked at her, as if going for a reality check. "Are you kidding?" she said. "Katherine doesn't know what she's talking about."

Faythe tried again. "We're probably equally nervous about this," she said. "I guess you know I haven't acted for twenty years."

"You'll do fine," Tara said breezily. "And for the record, I'm not nervous."

"Lucky you." She watched while Tara drank an inch of Stoli and refilled her glass. "We do have one thing in common," she said "We're both Midwesterners. I'm from Wisconsin."

"It's a shitpile out there, in the Midwest. Everyone always judging everyone else. Nobody has anything to say except about the weather, or gossip about the neighbors. I'm never going back." She tossed her hair back and looked at Faythe intently. "You don't go back, do you?"

"No," said Faythe, "but not because I hated it. My parents died in an accident years ago, and I was an only child. I don't really know anyone in Wisconsin anymore."

"How'd they die?" Tara asked the question in a matter-of-fact tone, as if they'd been discussing a movie that hadn't done well at the box office.

When Faythe didn't reply immediately, she lowered her head and mumbled an apology. "It's none of my business," she said. "It's only. . . . mine are dead, too. It's a coincidence."

"It was a freak accident," Faythe said. "They were driving over the train tracks at the edge of town. The gate didn't work anymore, and you were supposed to stop if there was a red light. Some farmer's corn was high that year, and my father didn't see it."

"Did you sue?" Tara looked fierce.

"No. No, I didn't sue. My father had a thing about time, wasting time. He was impatient about certain things, and he probably whizzed across those tracks without a second thought." As always, she felt sad when she contemplated her parents' violent death, but at least it had been swift. She was not going to ask Tara how her parents had died, but she would listen if the girl chose to tell her.

Tara brought one knee up to her chest and rested her chin on it, seemingly far away. "Yeah," she said at last, "that would be the way to go— quick, clean, over— pow!" She sounded drunk, and Faythe wondered if it was hundred proof vodka.

"Tara? Are you all right, honey?" She

was, after all, the mother of a young woman not much older than Tara. Somebody had to look after her.

"Who's all right? Who wants to be all right?" Tara regarded her with hostile eyes, and then she laughed. "I'm fine, Mrs. McBain. Don't mind me. In actual fact, I think you're very cool. The thing about me is, I'm a liar. I lie all the time, just can't seem to help it. F'rinstance, my parents aren't dead. I just made that up."

"I see," said Faythe. "I wonder why?"

"I could see I'd been rude, so I covered up by saying my folks were dead, too." She took a sip of her vodka and sneaked a look at Faythe, gauging her reaction.

"I'm glad they're not dead."

"Brrrr— I'm not. I'm not"

Faythe was familiar with the melodramatics of the young, the overstatements for effect, the shocking pronouncements made to provoke a reaction, so she remained silent. In any case, Tara seemed to forget all about the subject of her parents, because the next thing she said was: "I gotta apologize. I crashed your daughter's party."

"Not to me do you have to apologize. I enjoyed your entrance. I suppose you could apologize to Casey, but why bother?" She felt disloyal to her daughter, but she wanted to make Tara smile. Tara did not.

"Casey," she said succinctly, "does not like me. She's probably right. Not to like me. I'm trouble."

This last was said so self-importantly Faythe restrained an impulse to laugh. "We're all trouble, honey," she said. "If I'd had as much to drink as you've had, I'd probably be weeping in my cups."

"In your cups?" Tara giggled.

"It's an old-fashioned expression, before your time. Come to think of it, even before my time."

Tara giggled again. "I only crashed at Casey's because I wanted to get a look at you. I was afraid you might be like her . . . older version of Casey, I mean." She looked distressed. "No offense. I'm not dissing your daughter. It's just . . ."

Faythe reached out and touched Tara's hand, surprised at how icy it felt. "You don't have to explain anything to me," she said.

"But I want to. Your part is so important, even though it doesn't last very long. Carlotta is the first adult to ever treat Rosie decently, with honesty and affection, and then comes the let-down. In the end her meeting with Carlotta is seen as a turning point, don't you think?"

Faythe nodded gravely. It was exactly what she thought.

"I just had to see if you were the kind of woman . . ." she faltered.

"You wanted to see if I was the kind of woman who could bring Carlotta to life?"

"Exactly. Among my other faults, I get kind of inarticulate when I'm not on stage." She grinned, and this time she seemed a normal, likable young woman who knew her limitations.

"Well, did I pass?"

"Yeah. Oh, yeah." She stood up a trifle unsteadily, then squared her shoulders and took a long breath. "I better get back and show Ray I'm not a nut-case," she said. "He took a big gamble when he hired me, and I don't want to disappoint him."

"We're in very similar positions," Faythe said softly, but Tara hadn't heard her. She was walking away between the aisle of orchids, her heavy boots ringing on the stone floor, when she turned back.

"I lied to you some more," she said. "When I said Katherine didn't know what she was talking about. You can forget that.

I didn't mean it. Katherine's been wonderful to me."

"It's forgotten," Faythe said. She wanted to say something more to Tara but didn't want to sound bossy or superior. She bit back pleas for Tara to quit hitting the vodka, to be a little easier on herself. She turned to look out on the darkened garden beyond the conservatory, but when she looked up Tara was still standing there.

"Another lie," she said. "I told you I wasn't nervous."

"But you are, of course."

"No, I'm not just nervous," Tara said. "I'm scared to death."

Toward the end of the evening, Faythe found herself longing to ask questions. In what way had Katherine Iverson been "wonderful" to Tara, and how had they ever met? Did Tara have a drinking problem, a drug problem, or both? Why had Ray cast poor old Wally in his miniseries when it was becoming clear Wally'd become a drunk? There was no polite way to ask any of these questions, so she sipped her wine, talked conscientiously to these people she'd be working with, and was constantly aware of

Ray, whether they were in the same room or not.

Her jaw began to ache from smiling so much. She was used to being a hostess, not a guest. A hostess had to smile, too, but there were dozens of things a hostess could do to get away for a spell. She could disappear to the kitchen, pretending to supervise the caterers, or to her daughter's room, despite the presence of a nanny, or to any locale in her huge house, once things were under way. She remembered once when she had disliked their guests and excused herself on the pretext of having to take an important call. She had gone to the little room adjoining the bedroom, her "dressing room" as the architect had called it, and sat blissfully in an armchair for almost half an hour, the sounds of the party coming to her from far away.

Now she sat eating a plate of canapés to soak up the wine she had drunk, nodding while Ty's wife spoke of the luncheon she was giving to benefit endangered marine life.

"I hope you'll be able to come," Valerie Gardner said. "It's so important to support the cause."

"I'll try," Faythe said. "I'll have to check with my book."

She knew she would be giving Valerie's lunch a miss, not because she didn't want marine life to be protected, but because she wasn't ready to slip into another rigorous social scene yet. She wanted to work, to do well by Ray in the part of Carlotta, and to prove that she was still viable as an actress.

Here came Ty and the English actor—Derek?— Merrick?— each taking one of her hands and drawing her into the room with the piano. The hired player had taken a break, and Ty slid onto the bench with a grin. He began to play a medley of show tunes, and Derek-Merrick grinned at her encouragingly. "What'll it be?" he asked her. She stared at him, uncomprehending, and he asked his question again, rephrasing it. "What would you like to sing?"

"Excuse me," she said, "I don't sing. Not well enough to do it in public."

She could see the look of incomprehension on Ty's face.

"I told you so," said the unpleasant Lisbet Adkin. "She's not that Faythe."

"Well, somebody'd better sing," said a woman she hadn't met yet.

"I'm so sorry," said Derek-Merrick, coming to her side. "I mistook you for Fay Crawley."

"Nobody's ever heard of this Fay Crawley," said Lisbet.

The Englishman blushed, his fair skin pinking to the roots of his hair. "I saw her sing at a supper club in New York," he told Faythe. "It was my first time over the pond. She sang 'Send in the Clowns,' and I thought she was so marvelous."

She had never heard of Fay Crawley, supper club singer, but she took pity on the English actor and murmured that people had often mistaken them for one another. He looked relieved.

Back she went for a turn around the conservatory, glad that Ray hadn't heard the last interchange. Here she was, thinking that everyone was chewing over her private life, munching the morsels of venom from *Deep Dish*. The truth was that most people had never heard of her. Faythe McBain was not a name to conjure with, unlike Faythe Caruso. She'd always been able to see the humor in things, but her ego was a bit too fragile to sustain any more embarrassment. She thought she'd repair her face and then head for home, but someone was in the downstairs powder room. She climbed up to the second floor, passing the Renoir on the stairs, and headed for an empty bathroom. She wasn't afraid of encountering anything intimate on the second floor of Katherine Iverson's house. Nobody would be shut away in one of the bedrooms furtively making love or snorting a line. If she did encounter anyone, it wouldn't be her husband, pretending to show a woman one of his collections.

Oh, hi, Faythie. Come join us. I was just showing Charlene, here, my jade bowl. The T'ang Dynasty one.

Hi, Charlene. Thought, but not spoken: *I notice you're half out of your dress, couple buttons undone there. Guess you really dig Chinese art the most, hmmm?*

And yet, there in the gloom of what must be Katherine's bedroom, she saw a wild tumble of pale hair. Tara was sitting on Katherine's bed, regarding an oil painting lit by a tiny sconce.

"It's incredible," she said, without turning around. "Come and look, Faythe."

Faythe joined her in the shadowy bedroom. "How did you know it was me?" she asked.

"It was your footstep on the stairs. I have fantastically good ears."

Faythe sat beside her on the thick brocade

that covered her hostess's bed. The room was perfumed in the scent Kate always wore. It was a special blend she had made that hinted at lily-of-the-valley, but a deluxe version of that humble odor. She looked up at the painting and saw that it was a portrait of Katherine, painted soon after she had acted in her first film. She was dressed in a period costume, English, Edwardian by the hairstyle.

Clad in purest white, her hair piled atop her head in a Gibson Girl, the young Kate Iverson looked out across the decades with a serenity that was matchless. She had been playing a part from an era she had never known, yet she seemed totally at home, tranquil and happy.

"She belongs back there," Tara said. "Back when things were simple and, like . . . decent."

"Things were never simple," Faythe said. "Not since the world began." She felt a maternal need to comfort Tara, but at the same time she knew it would be a mistake to hold her as she'd once rocked Casey.

"I know that," Tara said impatiently. "Christ, I know that." She turned an accusing look on Faythe. "Don't patronize me," she said. "I thought you'd understand."

Tara stood up suddenly and stretched, cat like. " 'I'm so tired," she said. "I think I'll crash."

"You can't sleep here, honey. I'll be glad to drive you home. I'm ready to leave."

"Oh, but I can sleep here," Tara said craftily. "I have a room here. Katherine lets me crash now and then, you know. Say goodnight for me, will you? Say goodnight to Ray. I've had enough of this."

Faythe followed her down the hall. Tara was already peeling off her leather jacket, revealing a skimpy black garment that looked like the top half of a teddy. She dropped the jacket on the hallway carpet, a priceless Oriental, and then bent to pick it up.

"Mustn't litter," she said. "Must learn to live like a human being. A civilized human being."

She turned into a room and stood in the doorway, waggling her fingers. Faythe glimpsed a four-poster bed, a dusky rose carpet, and a pretty chaise longue piled with satin pillows. It looked rather like Casey's old room in Pacific Palisades minus the menagerie of stuffed animals.

"Like I said, I think you're cool," Tara told her, adding, "I just don't trust you yet."

Then she closed the door in Faythe's face.

* * *

It was close to midnight before she had a chance to speak to Ray. People were beginning to leave and Ray caught her eye in a way that clearly meant: Wait, I want to talk to you. With a face as expressive as his, it was a wonder he hadn't gone in for acting. "Tell the truth," she'd said to him when they had known each other for two weeks. "Didn't you ever want to be on the other side of the camera?"

"Nope." He'd smiled the lazy smile that belied his intense nature. "Never. I always wanted to be the boss man." It was said as a joke, of course. Ray wanted to direct because his talent was for coaxing amazing performances out of ordinary acting students, and out of gifted ones he'd pulled miracles. Even on a project as silly as the horror beach movies, Ray was always able to convince them that they were working toward something honorable, building the mortar that would one day cement their careers.

She'd known he would become an important director, and after her marriage to Cal she'd seen it happening from the sidelines. At first some people had compared him to Scorsese, but in the end they had to ac-

knowledge that Ray Parnell was very much
an original. When she'd been married for
five years, Ray was nominated for an Academy Award. He didn't win, but insiders said
it was too early, and Ray too young, for the
Academy to allow him that supreme triumph. *The Eye of the Peacock* had produced
an Oscar for its leading lady, Meredith
Carver, and ever after Ray was known as a
director who worked very well with women,
especially women who had been somewhat
overlooked.

Meredith Carver had been a popular actress in the 50s, and then, when her star had
begun to fade, she'd joined the cast of a soap
opera and spent the next ten years playing
the bitch you love to hate in a style so over-
wrought it came close to parody. He had
wanted Meredith for *Peacock* and had fought
hard to get her. It was generally predicted
that she'd fall flat on her famous face, but
instead she'd surprised them all with a performance so poignant and powerful it was
all people could talk about for months. How
had Parnell intuited that Meredith could
truly act? How had he known that a former
sex symbol turned soap actress could be such
a presence on the screen? Faythe knew. It was
very simple, really. Ray knew women. He

liked them and he knew what made them tick, divined what they really wanted and then set about to make it happen.

It was a wonderful quality in a man you loved, but an unsettling one, too. It was the old problem of not being enough . . . how could one woman satisfy Ray's boundless desire to give? Once in love with a giver, and married to a taker, Faythe had despaired of the human condition.

He'd never been nominated for another Oscar, and directing a miniseries for television represented a small step down the scale, but Ray didn't seem to feel slighted. He was doing what he did best, directing, and he had spent this evening watching the ingredients in his stew interacting.

He caught up with her in the foyer, where she was saying goodnight to Bev and the Englishman, whose name turned out to be Dirk. He steered her to a corner of the now empty living room and sat beside her on a chintz-covered couch.

"I just wanted to say I was sorry for the other day."

"I thought we were never going to mention it again," she said.

"I know. I told myself I wouldn't, but then I thought of how harsh I must have seemed. I was going to send you flowers, but that seemed too easy. Facile."

"I wasn't exactly blameless," she told him. "All's forgiven, Ray."

He turned to her and looked almost anguished. "There's a lot I want to say to you, but I feel I'm walking on eggs. You're so proud, and you might take it the wrong way."

"Try me," she said, thinking that she might regret it.

"I know how scary this must be for you. It's no small feat for a woman to return to acting after such a long time. You'll just have to trust me, Faythe, because I know you can do it. I'll be there to help in any way I can."

She nodded, not trusting herself to speak. He seemed so much the Ray she remembered at this moment, and that was the trouble. She was no longer the same Faythe.

"I was glad to see you talking to Tara, because she's scared, too. She's played some parts in studio theater productions, but as far as film goes she's only done bit parts. It's a huge leap for her, and I think she's petrified."

"I know she is. I feel protective about her,

but she scares me, too. She's not . . . entirely stable, is she?"

He smiled, acknowledging her tactful choice of words. "No," he said. "Stable is not the word I'd choose for Miss Johanson. I think this project will be a stabilizing factor if all goes well. She needs a dose of unmitigated success to calm her down."

"How did she and Katherine become friends? They seem such an unlikely duo."

"I put them together," he said vaguely. "I introduced them. Katherine needs a daughter and Tara needs a mother. Believe it or not, they're more alike than you think."

She felt impatient at this easy puzzle-solving, but intrigued, too. Ray was seldom wrong about women, as she'd just been thinking. Suddenly she felt tired beyond exhaustion. The effort of being on display had taken more out of her than she'd imagined.

"You're sleepy," Ray said. "Let me drive you home. Kate can have your car returned in the morning."

She wanted very much to lay her head on his shoulder and allow him to take charge of her, at least for this one evening. She felt drawn to him magnetically and might have succumbed if there hadn't been a terrible commotion in the hall. She heard shrieks of panic and the low moan of a man in pain.

When they reached the foyer, Wally was lying on the parquet floor, his leg bent at an unnatural angle. It was obvious that he'd taken a drunken fall and that he was suddenly, and terrifyingly, sober.

"I've broken my damn leg," he groaned.

Katherine immediately took charge. "I'll call an ambulance," she said, striding off.

Faythe got to her knees and took his hand. He was an unsavory old coot, but he was afraid and in pain. "Maybe it's just a sprain, Wally," she said. "Take it easy." Fumes of bourbon scrolled up into her face as the old man wailed, "It's the damn pills! Bourbon never hurt nobody, it's those pills."

He scrabbled at his breast pocket ineffectually, and Faythe removed a small phial of prescription pills. They were made out to Wallis Fowler, and they were valium.

"Throw 'em out," Wally commanded between gritted teeth.

When the ambulance arrived, Ray said he'd better accompany Wally to the emergency room and left with the attendants.

Faythe drove home wearily, thinking of her pledge to Casey: not to make a fool of herself. She certainly hoped she could keep it, because so far *The Senator's Daughter*— a film of high psychological drama— was shaping up into low farce.

Seven

The principals of the miniseries sat around a polished table in Century City, deep in the heart of the network's bailiwick. They had been summoned by Brant Pooley, a network executive, to read selected scenes from *The Senator's Daughter.* This was a custom seldom employed, and Faythe knew it was because of Tara: the network needed to be reassured that Tara was not a losing proposition.

Pooley hadn't entered the room yet, but a secretary had shown them in to the conference room and equipped them with coffee, tea, and a plate of bran and whole-wheat muffins. No bagels and no cream cheese. Pooley was rumored to be extremely health conscious. Besides the people she had seen at Katherine's a few nights ago, Faythe counted two unknown to her. One was Heather Lewison, a slight ten year old who was to play Rosie as a child, and the other was her mother Sylvia, a large, fierce looking woman who was overdressed for the occasion.

Heather was a pretty child with ash blonde hair. She seemed quiet and withdrawn and did not respond to Ty Gardner's friendly teasing. Although Desmond O'Connell had finally reached Los Angeles, he was not present. A star of his magnitude could not be asked to read, so Ray would enact the senator.

"Good news about poor old Wally," Dirk said to the table at large. "No bones broken, just a bad bruise."

"Mr. Fowler had apparently never heard that one doesn't mix valium and alcohol," Katherine said indulgently. "He'll be fine, won't he Ray?"

"Sure he will," Ray said, but Faythe could see that his mind was not on Wally Fowler. He sat with his chin in his hand, doodling on a memo pad.

Tara was directly across from her, and the transformation was astounding. Today Tara looked like a schoolgirl. Her thick hair was in a neat plait, and she wore a denim skirt and a shirt of white cotton, the cuffs turned neatly back on her slender wrists. Her face appeared to be bare of makeup, but Faythe

knew she had used pencil around her eyes
and then wiped it off. It was an old trick,
and enough of the dark smudge remained
to highlight the extraordinary eyes. She was
as pale as she'd been at Katherine's, and
that at least was natural. Tara was still terrified, and it was her terror that was disturbing Ray.

Beverly had gone whole hog today and
was wearing quantities of silver Indian jewelry and feather earrings. She winked at
Faythe when Mrs. Lewison asked if she were
a full-blooded Apache.

"Heather has a good friend who is a
Sioux," Sylvia Lewison said, and the remark
hung heavily in the air, especially since
Heather shot her a look of contempt.

Brant Pooley strode into the room, grinning at everybody with that false bonhomie
Faythe remembered so well. His every move
was meant to show you how vigorous he
was, how in control and attuned to the business at hand. This might have been reassuring if he had not looked, to Faythe, to
be about fifteen years old.

He wore a peach-colored sweater and
faded jeans, and sported a gold Rolex.
Brant Pooley was the new breed of entertainment executive: he had a good degree

from an ivy league college and never read
a book. To him a project only existed if it
could be compared to another, already
proven, successful project. Faythe waited to
see what he could possibly find to button-
hole *The Senator's Daughter.*

"Sorry to be late," he said. "I think we
have something genuinely exciting here,
and I have every faith in Ray Parnell's abilities, but we thought it might be fruitful to
hear some of you read together. It's very
gracious of you to agree." Here he nodded
at Katherine, who was still a big name, and
repeated, "very gracious." As if they had a
choice!

"I see no reason why this miniseries
shouldn't capture a large share. We're
thinking in terms of the huge audience for
Daughters of Silence."

Faythe bit her lip. Better than she could
have imagined. *Daughters of Silence* had
been a turgid made-for-TV movie about
women whose mothers had been raped.
They were the product of that rape, and
some of them didn't know until they were
full-grown women. It had been badly written, atrociously acted, and had captured an
enormous audience. It had also spiked appearances on "Oprah" and "Donohue" by

Women Who Discover They are the Result of Rape. Faythe wondered if Brant Pooley's underdeveloped mind had hit on the comparison because the word "daughter" appeared in both titles. She shot a quick look at Ray, but his face was professionally impassive, unreadable. Katherine's imperious nostrils were dilated somewhat, as if she'd caught a bad smell, but no one else seemed to react.

Before her, Faythe had a schedule of the scenes to be read. Hers, with Rosie, was number seven. They would dispense with the scenes requiring Heather Lewison first. She had never worked with a child before and wondered how someone Heather's age could possibly grasp the implications in anything as subtle as *The Senator's Daughter.*

"Let's start with the second scene," Pooley said, grinning at Heather. He wasn't going to make her go first, after all. Scene 2 was between the senator and Margaret, his wife. Ray leaned forward, preparing to feed Katherine her lines, and an amazing transformation rippled over Kate's face. She had been looking radiantly patrician, her usual look, and now in an instant she did something with her facial muscles that produced a look of chronic pain. Her lips assumed a downward trajectory— the expression of a woman who is perpetually disappointed— and her lively eyes grew dull.

The scene was one between the flamboyant man and his falsely meek, withdrawn wife, the princess from the East who has married a big, crude stud from Montana and is determined that he will never forget their social differences. Kate slid easily into the role, as if to the manor born, and the scene was over in less than four minutes.

"Superb," breathed Pooley. "Thank you again, Miss Iverson. You're free to go."

"Oh," said Katherine, "I think I'll stay." It was not a request. Faythe saw that she was as apprehensive about Tara as Ray, and as protective.

Next came Heather, playing a scene with Daddy in which she begged to be allowed to accompany him on a trip to Paris. Ray tried to give her something to play off. He was the glamorous daddy who adored his daughter but was able to cut her off without a second thought. He enjoyed the power he had over her. On the written page, it was chilling, and Faythe wondered how Heather could understand the subtext, but the child gave a moving and thoroughly professional performance. Sitting very straight in her conference chair, Heather Lewison embodied every little girl who has ever been betrayed by a beloved parent. She got the innocence down perfectly, but she also seemed to understand that relations between the senator and his little daughter were . . . unwholesome. Her voice flirted with Daddy and then gave it up, seeing that she was basically powerless in his world.

When the scene was over, Ty Gardner applauded and Sylvia Lewison smiled with relief, as if her artistry had been complimented. She and Heather departed immediately in a cloud of triumph.

Faythe saw Tara surreptitiously picking at her cuticles, her blunt fingernails vicious and compulsive in their assault, yet when she was asked to read two scenes, the first with Ray and the second with Beverly, a great calm seemed to settle over her. Faythe could almost see the tension leave her face as she spoke her first line. She didn't need to consult her script even once, and she became the overprivileged teenager who loved and hated her father, who knew of the love and repressed the hate. Her voice became Rosie's, a cultured yet uncertain voice that was flirtatious and hiding much pain.

The emotions that chased across her face were so subtle, so right for the camera, that Faythe could hardly believe she hadn't acted in film before.

When she read with Beverly she was the Rosie who could unwind with her only friend; with heartbreaking art she let you see how Rosie might have developed if her parents had not been monsters, the mother a monster of indifference, the father one of loverlike possessiveness. Faythe thought she understood something about Tara, and it was that the girl's terror vanished only when she could submerge herself in another character. Right up until the moment she began to read, Tara had been suffering the agonies of stage fright, but the moment she became Rosie she was liberated. When the scene came to an end, the relief in the air was palpable. Tara went back to picking at her nails, but secretly, under the table. Faythe knew without seeing that Tara was inflicting pain on herself as a distraction from the pain of living in the real world.

"Super," said Brant Pooley, consulting his watch. "Let's go on to the next scene, shall we?"

It was the scene with Dirk, the one she had done for her screen test. Up came her hands from beneath the table, and onto her lovely face there stole a more knowing look, the look of the Rosie who has seen her father's murder played over and over in the world press, who has changed her name and run off to Europe, believing that nobody knows who she is.

Dirk read well, giving the young aristocrat the perfect blend of arrogance by birth and humility at the hands of ruthless beauty. Tara was now the Rosie who understood her own sexual power and the suffering she could bring to men who fell in love with her. When she came to the line "Do you think I need help?" Faythe heard Beverly whisper "Wow."

Tara's schoolgirl clothing only intensified the power of her sexuality, and it was a power that every man in the room felt keenly, even Brant Pooley.

When the scene was over, Dirk looked dazed, as if he really had fallen for Tara and couldn't remember he was in a conference room in Century City.

Katherine actually applauded, and a little color crept into Tara's cheeks.

"I don't think we need to prolong this," Pooley said. "I've seen all I need to see, and it's very reassuring. I'll be giving an extremely positive report to the network, and, barring acts of God, we should be able to get a shooting schedule underway."

Ty Gardner and Faythe were not to read, it seemed. Ty's popularity was a foregone conclusion, and all Pooley had needed to see of Faythe was her face. He had apparently judged her to be sufficiently unravaged to portray a great beauty in middle age.

She was grateful but disturbed. It was obvious to everyone that Tara could not play Rosie in the scene on the yacht in Sardinia. Faythe would be playing it with the child Heather. Why then had Tara gone to such lengths to meet her, crashing Casey's party? The only reason she could come up with was Tara's intensity about the role. It was possible that she needed to know that Faythe, as Carlotta, had the necessary depth to impress Rosie. This confusion of real life and dramatic characters was unsettling. She had never been one to think it desirable that an actor "become" her character, losing herself so utterly in it that her real self was reeling somewhere out in the ether, ready to possess her body again as soon as the lights dimmed and the curtain fell.

Pooley was circling the room, shaking hands with everyone and spreading a few words of good cheer. He was obviously

overdue for another meeting, and even as
he approached Faythe a chime-like telephone was heard in the room. He took
her hand briefly and narrowed his eyes in
what she could only see as a parody of
young-man-savoring-the-autumn-charms-of
-an-older-woman.

"Give your daughter my warmest re-
gards," he said to her, and then left the
room at a trot.

The principals were free to go and obviously delighted at the good showing they
had made.

"You were fantastic," Dirk said to Tara.
"Absolutely fantastic."

"Lunch is on me," said Ray. "We'll drive
in a cavalcade to Orsa, shall we?"

"Pizza with lobster," said Bev. "White
man's haute cuisine."

"I'm sorry, I can't join you," said Faythe.
"I have a lunch date with my daughter."

Traffic was heavy, as usual, and Faythe
tried not to fume as she sat in a motionless
line of cars all headed for Beverly Hills. She
was surrounded by people talking into car
phones; at least she didn't have to resort to
doing business in a traffic jam. It had always

struck her as ironic that the most powerful movers and shakers in Hollywood were as powerless in traffic as nonplayers. Traffic was democratic; it inconvenienced everybody.

She and Casey had taken to lunching every Wednesday, alternating choices of restaurants. Faythe always tried to select homey places where noise was at a minimum, but Casey favored power restaurants. Lunch to her was successful only if she saw and was seen by celebrities. Today was her Wednesday to choose and she'd opted for The Grill in Beverly Hills. Faythe didn't like The Grill, finding it excessively masculine and clubby, and now she was going to be late. Casey would be sipping a Pellegrino water and thinking that her mother was an unreliable type.

The stream of cars inched forward and then began to flow steadily for a block or two until the next jam forced them to halt again. She slipped a tape of Scottish folk music into the deck and tried to relax as a high, pure female voice lamented the sad fate of fair Jeannie, whose father would not let her marry the man she loved. Instead, the cruel father insisted she marry a laird of the land, a man Jeannie could never love if she lived to be a hundred. As was often the case in these sad songs, Jeannie died of a broken heart on her wedding night, and her true love returned just in time to see her body borne away.

Do people ever die of a broken heart these days? She doubted it and thought it was just as well, but something in her rejoiced at the mere concept of a love that was so potent it was a matter of life and death. She was a part of the last generation to take love seriously, she thought. When she'd been Casey's age love was the great objective. To find a man you could love for the rest of your life, to have him feel the same about you, to marry him and keep the love alive as long as you both had breath in your bodies. It had been an unrealistic goal, but at least, as a myth, it was beautiful.

She had wanted her daughter to be more realistic and had been glad when Casey showed every sign of being practical, but there was such a thing as going too far. She'd once overheard Casey and a friend discussing Michael J. Fox, debating his pros and cons.

"He's really cute, he's got that great smile, but I think he's pretty short," the friend had said.

"Well," Casey had rejoined without missing a beat, "he'd be fine for a first husband."

She'd been fifteen at the time, and since then she'd become even less romantic. If she and a friend were to discuss the impending marriage of two stars today, Faythe assumed they'd be most interested in the terms of the prenuptial agreement.

It was ten after one when she arrived at The Grill and surrendered her car to the valet. She entered the familiar restaurant, with its white tiles and green leather booths, and there was Casey, just as she'd imagined her, lifting a glass of mineral water to her lips and looking impatient. The only thing that she hadn't anticipated was a second party, a man sitting in the booth across from her daughter. The edge of the booth blocked him from her view, but she saw a masculine hand break off a bread stick, and then Casey made a comment to the owner of the hand, losing her impatient look for a moment.

Faythe approached the booth, aware of the many eyes that appraised her. She was glad she'd worn the flattering silk gabardine coat dress to the reading as she walked the gauntlet. The maitre d' had greeted her by name— a pleasant surprise— and she was feeling pleased with herself right up to the moment she saw who Casey's companion was.

"Hi, sweetheart," said Cal.

She felt icy cold and then burning with rage. How could Casey have done this to her? Casey was looking sly and pleased as she blew her a kiss.

"Hello, Cal," Faythe said in barely civil tones. She slid into the booth on Casey's side and clutched her handbag to keep her hands from trembling visibly.

"You look gorgeous," Cal said. "Getting this part has done more for you than a week at a health spa."

"I love that dress, Ma," Casey said. "Is it new?"

"Not particularly." She turned to Cal. "Nice to see you," she said, "but shouldn't you be getting back to your own table?"

Cal's eyes narrowed for a moment, but then he decided to take it as a joke. "This is my table, Faythie," he said. "Our daughter thought it would be a nice idea if we lunched together."

It was a horrible idea, but Faythe realized that Casey hadn't tried to make her angry. She was simply trying to sustain the illusion that the Carusos were still a family. Casey didn't admit defeat gracefully. If her mother wanted a divorce, fine, but she'd take every opportunity to make it seem that her parents were still together, still married. Perhaps, Faythe thought, all Casey's romanticism had been subverted away from herself and into a false and rosy picture of her parents' life together. Cal, however, knew better, and she felt pure rage that he had accepted Casey's invitation.

Cal asked her about the miniseries. Had she met Des O'Connell yet? Was the network treating her right? She replied in brief sentences, not willing to act out a charade even for Casey's sake.

"You seem to be in a rotten mood, Mom," Casey said. "Lighten up, okay?" She studied the menu and announced that she would have the crab. "Don't look now, but Nicole Kidman just came in. She's lunching with her agent."

"He's a loser," said Cal.

Faythe hated Cal's vocabulary, with its roster of "losers" and "players," and she declined to join them as they gossiped and picked away at other people's private lives. Her grilled chicken arrived, but she wasn't hungry. Two producers and a director came by to shake Cal's hand. In the days when they'd been married, she would have smiled and greeted them with feigned pleasure, but she kept herself aloof. She wanted no speculation about a reconciliation between the Carusos to enter anybody's mind.

"You may not believe this," he said to Casey, "but when I first married your mother she had a healthy appetite. Come on, Faythie, eat your nice chicken. It's not fattening, and you look terrific. You don't have to worry."

She smiled icily. "Perhaps it's the company," she said.

Casey hooted. "Oh, come on, Mom, don't be so bitchy to Dad. Can't we have a nice lunch without you acting like injured royalty?"

Cal was speaking into his cellular phone now, and Faythe turned to her daughter, speaking in low but urgent tones. "Casey," she said, "I am always happy to see you. Any time, any place. I love our Wednesday lunches, but I do not appreciate your bringing your father here without asking for my approval."

"Your approval! For God's sake, Ma, you were married to the man for twenty years. It's not like I brought some gigolo to lunch."

"I like to choose the people I eat lunch with, and your father is a companion I would not choose. I'm sorry if that hurts you, but it's a fact. I divorced him, Casey. I wish him well, but I don't want to find myself in a booth with him at The Grill. Especially not without warning. Do I make myself clear?"

"As crystal Pepsi. As sparkling mineral water. As clear as your real reasons for not wanting to see him. You are so transparent it's unreal."

"Girls," said Cal when he'd put away his phone, "duty calls. I regret to say I must cut short this lunch." He turned to Casey, excluding Faythe. "That was Mel Marco," he said. "They're jerking him around at Paramount." He bent to kiss her ostentatiously. "Later, Princess. I'll let you know what happens." He blew a kiss to Faythe, knowing he couldn't get away with kissing her hand, and had started off when he turned abruptly and came back to the green booth.

"I forgot to say congratulations," he said to Casey. "Your mother should only know what miracles her little girl is capable of working."

Casey watched him go and then turned to Faythe, her face wearing its stern look. "You had to go and spoil everything," she said bitterly. "This happens to be a red-letter day for me, which is why I invited Dad along, and then you have to act like I'd done something wrong."

There was genuine pain in Casey's voice, and Faythe felt the pang that always accompanied any action that might have inadvertently hurt her daughter. "What were the congratulations for?" she asked, trying to lighten her voice. "Why is it a red-letter day, honey?"

Casey was sulky and silent, needing more coaxing.

Faythe began to eat her excellent grilled chicken, even though she had no appetite. Being a mother never ended, she thought, although now the tables were turned. She remembered Casey in her high chair, adamant about not eating her spinach until Mommy turned the spoon into an airplane that gradually circled around until it found its target— Casey's mouth. Now Casey needed her to surrender and eat her chicken and pretend that she'd been the recalcitrant one.

"I signed my first big client," Casey said. "She would like to have gone with Dad or Art or Milly, but she went with me. With me. I laid the groundwork, got her interested in Caruso Creative, and it paid off. She's going to be famous, and I'm the one who'll get her to the top."

"Who is she?" Faythe knew she wouldn't know the name, and tried to think of ways to insulate Casey against her ignorance.

"Inida Campbell," said Casey. "She's this incredibly gorgeous black model from Martinique. She's no relation to Naomi Campbell, but she's going to be just as big. She makes Naomi look like the girl next door. Scorsese is interested in casting her in a project he has in mind, and I've got her."

"That's wonderful news." She saw a handsome young man heading in their direction, his eyes on Casey, his expression one of deep admiration. He was wearing a beautifully cut suit, which meant, Casey had once told her, that he wasn't a top level person. Top level people wore jeans.

"Hi, Casey," he said, looking awkward.

"Oh, hello, Spencer," Casey said in tones so casual she might have been addressing a waiter. "Meet my Mom. This is Spencer Blum."

Faythe gave him her hand and a smile. He was really very nice looking and obviously had a crush on her daughter.

"Nice to meet you, Mrs. Caruso," he said.

"She doesn't use that name," said Casey wickedly. "My mother is an actress. Faythe McBain."

He brightened. "You're going to be in *The Senator's Daughter,*" he said, and then looked embarrassed. He probably read *Deep Dish.*

Casey gave him no encouragement, and he repeated that it had been nice to meet Mrs. McBain and withdrew.

"You were awfully rude to him," Faythe said. "He seems so nice, and he's clearly interested in you."

"Give me a break. Spencer Blum? He's a writer, Mom. You know the joke about the bimbo who was so new in town she . . . ah . . . slept with the writer?"

Faythe knew that Casey had not used the "F word" on her account, but she was disturbed anyway. "Honey," she said, "I wasn't suggesting that you sleep with Spencer, just that you could have been nicer to him. I don't like to think that you're only pleasant to people who're important. That's not how I raised you."

"Let me explain something to you. If I'd been nicer to that guy I'd be encouraging him, and then he'd be calling and I'd have to reject him. See? It's easier to cut him off early. I don't have much of a love life. I'm too busy. When I get to where I want to be, there'll be time enough to look around. And when I do, it won't be anyone like Spencer. He's a nice guy with a middling talent, but he's never going to amount to much. When I get serious with a man, he'll have to be at least as successful as I am."

"I see," said Faythe. "Well, at least I don't have to worry about my little girl getting her heart broken."

"Meaning I don't have one? Come on, Ma. I'm just being realistic. I notice you didn't marry a struggling screen writer."

Yes, and look how that turned out, she thought. "I didn't marry your father for his position," she said. "I never judged men by how successful they were. I judged them as you ought to, as human beings with individual faults and virtues."

Casey laughed. "Virtues," she said. "You sound practically biblical. Don't worry about me. I know what I'm doing."

Faythe put her American Express card down when it became apparent that lunch was over, but Casey shoved it back at her. "It's on me today," she said, grinning. "Inida Campbell is quite an investment."

As they stood in front of The Grill, waiting for their cars to be delivered, Faythe studied her daughter covertly. Beneath the severe hairdo Casey's face was still heartbreakingly young to her. She had the glowing skin and bright eyes that came from growing up in luxury, and she was pretty by anyone's standards. She had taken trouble with her appearance, dressing in the casual but expensive style she favored. Her Larry Mahan cowboy boots were bright red, and made her legs look even longer in her suede mini. Did she go to the trouble to look attractive and stylish only for business reasons?

"You told Spencer I didn't use the name 'Caruso' because I was an actress," she said.

"Uh-huh." Casey fiddled with one long silver earring, and her face tightened. She knew what was coming.

"That's not why I don't use your father's name. You know that, honey. We're divorced. Divorced women don't use their ex-husband's names."

"Ivana Trump does," said Casey, and then they both laughed.

Faythe hugged her daughter, wishing there were a better way to show her love, and wishing that Casey could be more like her, less like Cal.

* * *

Katherine Iverson's voice on the phone had an edge to it. "Something's come up," she said. "I'd like very much to talk to you, Faythe. It's a matter of extreme delicacy, strictly *entre nous.*"

What now? "Of course, Kate. I hope nothing's wrong?"

"I know it's short notice, but could you possibly come to my house at tea time? I'll give you a lovely tea. We'll indulge in scones with double cream and then diet for the rest of the week."

She hadn't been joking. The table was spread with lace and contained a silver tea service, cucumber sandwiches, biscuits from Fortnum & Mason, scones, and the evil double cream.

"I lived in London for a year," Katherine said. "Terrible climate but gorgeous customs. I solace myself with an English tea whenever something troubling happens. Life being what it is, I manage to have tea parties quite often, but I only allow myself the double cream for special occasions."

Faythe nibbled at a cucumber sandwich, admiring Kate's elegant hands as she poured the tea into Spode cups so thin you could see through them.

"It's Tara, of course," Katherine continued. "You are a woman of intelligence and instinct, Faythe, and it can't have escaped your notice that Tara is not emotionally . . . well-equipped."

"Yes, I know Tara's terrified about the prospect of starring in a miniseries. She's told me so, but I think it goes beyond mere stage fright. I like her, Kate, but she makes me nervous."

"As well she might. Tara is the proverbial time bomb. With any luck she'll be diffused, and this film will convince her that she's a person of consequence. But luck is fickle, and we can't bank on it."

"Can you tell me something about her? She's such an enigma."

"She is to me, too, and I've known her far longer than you have. She was brought up in a very strict, religious family in North Dakota. Her family lived in a remote area, which compounded the problem. I gather that there might have been . . . abuse, although she's never told me so."

"Maybe that's why she escapes into her character so totally when she's acting."

"I think you're right. Tara knows that

she's talented, she knows it in her brain, which, incidentally, is a very fine one. But she doesn't know it here." Kate laid her hand on the plum-colored silk covering her heart. "Tara feels utterly worthless. She thinks she deserves nothing good, and she behaves in a manner likely to make that scenario come true."

"How can I help?"

"You can join me in trying to protect her. You know the sort of thing I mean. We'll be buffers against the people who look down on her, and they are many."

Faythe thought of Casey and slathered double cream on a scone.

"I can't do it alone," Katherine said. "I've befriended her, but I'm an old woman."

"No one who looks like you could possibly be described as old, Kate."

"Nevertheless, she needs a younger woman to confide in."

"I'm forty-six years old. I'm twice her age."

Katherine smiled. "You have a youthful outlook, my dear, and a natural sympathy. Tara likes you. She may even try to pattern herself on you if all goes well."

"Dear God, I'd hate to think of my life as exemplary. I've made terrible mistakes."

She saw the other woman's face alter subtly, as if she were withdrawing her confidence.

"Of course I'll help in any way I can," she hastily amended. "I'm on Tara's side. I have been from the first time I saw her. I don't know why, exactly, but it's true. I'll keep the sharks away, Kate, and I'll try to be a friend to her."

This time the smile spread to Katherine Iverson's eyes, and she nodded, pleased. "That's all I want," she said. "A little help in keeping the sharks away. Ray is good with her, but he doesn't know what I do."

Faythe waited. It didn't do to hurry things with Kate.

"When I said something had come up I meant something that could devastate the girl. I hope and pray it won't be made public, but in this town that's an unlikely scenario. Now that Tara is about to be famous I've had calls . . . calls from nasty people sniffing about and trying to pry information from me. I've given them nothing and will continue to be mum, but that's no guarantee it won't come out."

Why did she have to be so elliptical? "You've lost me," she said. "What's going to be made public? The fact that Tara drinks too much? Is she taking drugs?"

"That would hardly be news," Katherine said. "If every actress who behaved excessively were exposed in the papers, there'd be no room for anything else."

Kate rose from the table and went to stand at a window, deliberating. When she turned, it was with a superb sense of timing. Sincere as she was about Tara, and Faythe had no doubts about her sincerity, a lifetime as an actress had left its mark.

"Tara," she said, "is a runaway. When she first came to Los Angeles she was what they call a street kid."

Faythe heard herself gasp in the quiet room, but it was a gasp of recognition, not surprise. Of course Tara was a former street kid.

It made perfect sense.

Eight

Desmond O'Connell was staying at the Malibu house made famous in the late seventies by Jinna Jerrard, an actress who had died of an overdose at a party there. The couple who had lived in the house had sold it soon after the tragedy and moved to Santa Barbara. It had passed through two other owners and now belonged to Franco Cammarada, a fabulously wealthy photographer who was a member of the minor nobility in his native Italy.

Franco and Des were great friends, ever since O'Connell did a Fellini film that stretched on forever, shot in Siena and the surrounding countryside, where the Cammarada family owned an incomparable villa. Since Franco was now on a protracted trip to Indochina, what could be more natural than his old chum O'Connell staying at the Malibu house for the duration of his time in California?

These were the facts, as Faythe got them from her new housekeeper, Milagros Flores. Milagros was from Guatemala, a motherly woman who had been in the US for many years, ever since she was a slender twenty year old. Now, five years younger than Faythe, she had six grandchildren. She was a walking compendium of Hollywood history and informed Faythe that the house in Malibu was famous for two reasons: the death of the *pobrecita* so many years ago and the tiles in the several bathrooms.

"They are special tiles," she told Faythe, "with miraculous properties. The Signore Cammarada imported them from someplace in Italy. They change color with the sea. Whatever color the sea may be, the tiles are that color, too. Blue, green, gray . . ."

She liked Milagros and realized that the Guatemalan woman saw in her a nearly perfect employer. For two days a week, she would be required to clean the little Santa Monica house, stock Faythe's fridge with the modest items she required, and deposit and pick up her employer's dry cleaning. This left her free to see to her other employers three days of the work week, maintain her own home in Las Reyes on Saturdays, and relax with her grandchildren on Sundays. There was an added bonus, and it was that Faythe was glamorous, had access to the world Milagros chronicled, and was unencumbered by a husband. Single women were much easier to work for, she told Faythe. Married women were forever on edge, having to cater for their husbands' whims instead of their own.

She was very discreet and never named names, but Faythe was sure that Milagros had once worked for Sherry Brooks as a live-in cook and nanny. "This particular woman," Milagros told her, "she required three different menus if the family was at home. For the husband, heavy sauces on everything, lots of cream, and the nouvelle look with little vegetables. For herself, the plate must look the same, but the sauce is a fake. Yogurt instead of cream. For the daughter, a little plate of rice and sprouts. Bird food. She starved the daughter, because she was a chubby little thing. Not fat, you understand, just a little extra flesh. This woman saw her little girl as the circus fat lady, and she kept her starved.

"I used to take a plate to her room when no one was looking. I brought her roast beef slices, very thin, and once mashed potatoes. Another time some ice cream. Her mother fired me when she smelled chocolate on her daughter's breath. Can you imagine such cruelty?"

Faythe could. She remembered Casey's stories of Felice Brooks's trials. The child had money deposited to her account at the weekly weighing session if she'd lost weight. If she'd gained, her mother wouldn't speak to her for a week. Polaroid pictures of Felice were tacked up on a special corkboard in her bedroom, showing her at the ideal weight and at the other weights her mother couldn't tolerate.

Sitting in Katherine's limo between Santa Monica Beach and Malibu, she asked, "Is it true the bathroom tiles in this house change with the ocean?"

"I believe it's an optical illusion," Kate said.

"You sounded like a little girl when you asked that question," Tara said. "You reminded me of someone." Then, as if she'd said too much, Tara clammed up and stared out the tinted window. She was again dressed modestly, but today she didn't look like a schoolgirl. Her blouse was silk and brightly striped, and she wore very high heels. She was over six feet in her shoes; Faythe felt almost dwarfish in comparison. Kate was taking them to meet O'Connell, since the three of them comprised his trio of female victims in the film: wife, daughter, and mistress. The network had talked of writing out the character of Jolie, the woman who murders the senator, and assigning the murder to the Carlotta character, but Ray had persuaded them to leave things as they were. Carlotta Fitzgerald was not a murderess. She was the eternal woman the senator always returned to when he tired of his current squeeze.

The limo came to a halt at a plain wall on the Pacific Coast Highway, and the driver spoke into an intercom. The wall drew aside and they rolled down into the private world of the beach colony as the wall closed up again. It was a balmy, golden day for late autumn, and the ocean was gloriously blue, breaking in big creamy combers against the sand.

"This is where I'd live if I could live anywhere," Tara said.

"Someday you will, then," Kate told her.

Tara looked doubtful but said nothing.

O'Connell was waiting for them on the enormous deck of his borrowed house. He'd been sitting with his bare feet propped up on a rail, a glass of amber liquid in one hand,

and now he rose to greet them. He took Katherine in his arms and kissed her forehead.

"You'll have to help me, Kate," he said in the famous, soft voice that still retained the barest hint of brogue. "Which of these lovely women is my daughter and which my mistress?"

Faythe laughed and Tara said, "Hello, Daddy."

"Yes," he said, taking her hand. "Here's a daughter worthy of Senator Thomas Madigan, the son of a bitch."

Then it was Faythe's turn. He looked smaller, of course, as people did when you were used to seeing them ten feet high, but he was still a marvel. The blue eyes were framed in thick, dark lashes any woman would envy, and the gray in his black, Irish hair only served to make him more handsome. Yet it was a lived-in beauty, and there were lines and creases on his weathered face. *No face-lift yet, maybe never,* Faythe thought. *Here is a man who thinks well of himself. Whatever it is, he has it.*

"Welcome to the Cultural Dessert," she said.

"Ah, yes, and isn't it looking its most dessertish today?" He indicated the blue waves and white sand, and just then a woman

walking her dog passed by, dressed in a fuch-
sia jumpsuit. "A tropical dessert," he said,
eyeing the woman. "When I left London it
had been raining for two weeks without
letup."

They sat at a table on the deck, which
was protected from the sun by an enormous, pale green awning. A tray contained
bottles of whiskey, gin, vodka, scotch, mineral water, and soda. White wine was cool-
ing in a bucket, and there was a huge bowl
of macadamia nuts perched on top of
O'Connell's script. He had marked a place
in it, and Faythe approved of this mightily.
O'Connell was taking the miniseries seriously, unlike so many big stars who considered this kind of work an opportunity to
hit their marks, mouth their lines, and take
the money and run.

"I'm drinking Irish whiskey," he told
them, "and you must help yourself to whatever you like."

Faythe regarded the bottle of Stoli nervously, remembering how Tara had poured
it down on the night of Kate's party, but
Tara poured herself a glass of wine and appeared to be perfectly at ease. Kate took a
small amount of Irish whiskey, adding so
much water the liquid was tan compared to

O'Connell's amber, and Faythe allowed herself a gin and tonic.

"Are you Irish, or did your mother love 'Gone With The Wind'?" he asked Tara.

"Neither one," she replied. "My mother didn't go to movies much. I'm Swedish, mostly, with a dash of Norwegian in there. My real name is Karin."

Faythe was amazed. She had heard more from Tara in these few moments than in the days she'd known her.

"And so you named yourself Tara," O'Connell said. "You reinvented yourself."

"Something like that," she said. Again, she seemed to retreat, as she had in the car.

He didn't take it further, sensing her discomfort. "Our director tells me you're returning to acting after an absence," he said to Faythe. "I admire that. Everyone goes on about what marvelous actresses the English are, and it's true, but you Americans are more flexible, it seems to me."

"Not everyone has a chance to be flexible," said Kate. "I've been playing the same part for years."

There was no discontent in her voice, and Faythe wondered if O'Connell had infused their drinks with truth serum. You would think such a gorgeous man would fill the air with tension, but instead women seemed to relax around him.

"This is Paradise," he said. "A weather-less day, a drink in my hand, the whole ocean at my feet, and three lovely women to talk to. Paradise. And yet if I were here for more than six weeks I'd begin to go mad. I'd have to be carted out and put on a plane to Beirut or Belfast."

Katherine shuddered fastidiously. "Not for me," she said. "I can't imagine why any-one would be drawn to danger."

"Of course I exaggerate, dear Kate. I'm a physical coward, but too much comfort can be dangerous, too. That's why I have a house in Donegal, where I can go and be buffeted by icy winds."

"Is that in Ireland?" Tara asked.

"Indeed it is, in the north, although not, you understand, in Northern Ireland. When the Brits carved my country up they took only the six northeast counties and left Donegal for the natives. There is no indus-try in Donegal, just hard, bare rock and a treacherous sea. It is curiously beautiful, as some barren, wild places can be. When I made my first serious money I was living in a flat in London, sharing with two other young actors from the colonies. One was

Australian and one, like myself, Irish. They sensibly gave up the acting game and became successful at grown-up professions. Ralph became a schoolmaster and Liam a solicitor."

"A pimp?" Tara blurted.

O'Connell laughed, thinking she had made a joke, but when it became apparent that she was serious, he leaned toward her and said: "I don't mean to laugh. It's a perfectly natural mistake for an American to make, and now that I think of it, lots of your countrymen would see no difference between a ponce and a lawyer."

"Oh, this Liam became a lawyer," she said slowly, as if to herself, and then blushed to the roots of her pale hair. It was the most color Faythe had ever seen in Tara's face.

"What's a ponce?" Faythe asked.

"A pimp," said O'Connell, his shoulders shaking with unvoiced mirth. As if to put Tara at ease, he told a story about his earliest days in London, when he had nearly got in a fight with an American. The Yank had said to a young woman of O'Connell's acquaintance "Give you a ride when the pub closes?" She'd been a shy girl from the west country, and he couldn't imagine why she wasn't more offended at this monumental rudeness.

"I told the Yank any more language like that and he'd have me to contend with. He looked astounded, poor boy, because he'd been offering her a ride home in his car. Where I grew up 'ride' meant something different, and I thought he'd propositioned her in an unforgivably crude way." He drank some of his whiskey and shook his head, looking out at the ocean. "Well," he said, "those were the days of raging innocence."

Tara looked only partially mollified "That was so stupid of me," she murmured.

"Not a'tall," he said, sounding more Irish by the minute. "What is stupid is people never speaking what's on their minds because it's not the thing to do. People so afraid to offend they confine their conversation to the weather, or so uneasy in themselves they can only gossip about the misfortunes of others."

Faythe remembered Tara's condemnation of the Midwest, or her part of it, in almost exactly the same words. She saw Tara react as if she'd passed an examination at long last.

"Yesss," she whispered. "I agree."

Katherine shot a covert look in Faythe's direction. A potential crisis averted, she seemed to say. She turned to Des O'Connell. "What made you decide to take on this part?" she asked. "I thought the book was very good, but heaven knows the senator is not a very likable man. He's not a hero, or even an antihero."

Des selected a macadamia nut and chewed it while he thought. It was possible to see the thoughts crossing his mobile face, and when he'd finished crunching the nut he folded his hands between his knees and hitched forward in his seat. "I told Ray, and I see no reason not to tell you. I wanted to play Tom Madigan as a sort of salute to my old man. My da was like the senator in many ways, though he hadn't a grand title or a pot to piss in. What he had was what you call 'attitude' over here. He managed to convince us that he was the lord of the manor, even though the manor was a stone farmhouse in County Roscommon.

"My mother lived in terror— not that he would ever lift a hand to her in anger— because she feared she wasn't enough to make him happy. We weren't enough, his wife and five children, to bring the smile to his face. We lived for that smile, that feeling we had managed to please him. Christ! I can still remember what it felt like when the old man smiled at me, approved of something I'd done.

"He was, as they say, a fine figure of a man, and my mother had won him over many competitors. You can be sure he never let her forget it. He had no opportunity to dally with a beauteous Carlotta Fitzgerald." He saluted Faythe with his glass. "Although, come to remember, there was a Carrie Fitzgerald in the county." He laughed, remembering. "She was seventy and had a cast in her eye. The thing of it was, my da would probably have been mortified if a beautiful woman offered herself to him in all seriousness. Painted harlots were not in Paddy O'Connell's game plan. No, he would have denounced her and sat around the kitchen with a face of stone. Bets would be laid as to who could coax out the first smile. Jesus, but his smile was beautiful."

"Like Marlon Brando," Tara said, "at the end of *The Wild One*. When he finally smiled at Mary Murphy it was as if the sun had come out after an endless winter."

"Exactly so," said O'Connell. "Exactly so." He tipped some more whiskey into his glass. "My sister Eileen was the most afflicted by this waiting for the sun. I don't have to tell you she was a bit like Rosie. A gorgeous little girl not understanding why no one measured up to Da, and making herself miserable over it.

"No, the saddest thing about waiting for the sun after such a long winter is that you may not be able to see it when it comes out. You've become partially frozen, like the ground in the Arctic. Permafrost, they call it, because it never entirely melts. We were a family constituted of permafrost, there in our stone farmhouse in County Roscommon."

Faythe felt a wave of sadness wash over her. He hadn't spoken in a self-pitying way, but she was struck by how many ways people could be crippled emotionally. Cal, like O'Connell's father, could never have enough of some indefinable quality to make him happy, and she thought she knew how O'Connell himself had suffered on account of his loveless father. He wasn't really interested in women, which is why Tara felt secure with him. Not that he was gay, but simply a man who might love women, who liked being in their presence, but who no longer wished to make love to them or acquire them like trophies. He knew there was something missing in his emotional core, and he had grown mature enough to spare women the suffering they would surely know if he allowed them to come too close to him. She thought of all the laughing beauties photographed with him and of his two ex-wives and felt a kinship with them. They, too, had known how bitter it was to never be enough, to fail.

Katherine was asking him about his house in Donegal, which he used only in late summer. Why had he opted for such a remote place? Why not a house in Dublin or Galway or Cork?

"When I'm in my country," he said, "I can't permit myself to live where my countrymen don't care to know what's happening in the north. Donegal is border country. They're too close to the war to be indifferent to it. Concepts like peace and justice and equality are spoken of in Donegal."

"I've never been to Ireland," Faythe said. Cal had taken her to Paris, Rome, London, and Madrid. She had been to film festivals in the south of France and the north of Italy with him, but Ireland was not on his agenda of important places.

"Well, you will," O'Connell said. "My house is yours, so long as you give me a week's warning."

Tara excused herself and got up from the table uncertainly.

"I'll go with you," Katherine said, and led her into the house.

"I'm serious about your visiting Ireland," he said to Faythe with an enigmatic smile. "Any woman named McBain must have some curiosity about the mother country."

"I don't even think my parents knew they were Irish in any real way," she said. "My father wore a green tie on St. Patrick's Day, and that was about it. I'd love to see Ireland, but I'll be honest with you. If anyone had told me, back when I was growing up in Wisconsin, that Desmond O'Connell would invite me to his house in Ireland, I would have fainted dead away."

"You have more sense now," he said. "Let's be friends, shall we?"

"Yes," she said. "Definitely."

Katherine returned and began to ask O'Connell about mutual friends scattered throughout the world. Some of them were famous and others were unknown to her, but Faythe was struck by how deeply he seemed to care for them. When she realized that Tara had been gone for a long time, she began to feel uneasy. All this talk of unhappy childhoods would be painful to a girl whose own childhood had been so grim she'd run away.

She slipped away from the table and went inside. The large room on this level was spare and bleached, its seaward looking wall entirely made of glass. Everything was button leather and glass; there were no Cammarada photographs on the walls, but three bead and feather wallhangings brought color and warmth to the room. A large balcony could be reached by stairs in the back, and another stairway led to a lower level. She descended this staircase, feeling like an intruder. She came to a large kitchen with a flagstone floor and a restaurant stove, and beyond it she could see a small suite of rooms intended for a live-in servant. Milagros had said the house contained "many bathrooms" so she pressed on. A pleasant sitting room . . . a bedroom that looked as if it had not been used recently. . . . Faythe tiptoed through the rooms, half afraid of what she might find. The door to the bathroom was ajar, but she could hear nothing inside. She pushed the door and saw Tara sitting on the edge of a bathtub, her arms wrapped tightly around her slender body, rocking back and forth. Tara saw her and shook her head wildly.

"Go away," she said. "I'm fine. Just give me a minute."

Faythe crossed the room and knelt beside her. "You've been gone for a quarter of an hour," she said gently. "Come back out with me, it'll be all right."

Tara shot her a look of pure loathing, but it was only for effect. When she saw Faythe wasn't put off she slumped down and whispered, "Can't a person have cramps in peace?"

"You told me you were a liar," Faythe said brightly. "I don't believe you have cramps. It's something else, and when you're ready to tell me you will. In the meantime, pull yourself together and come back to the world."

There were no tears in Tara's eyes. Whatever pained her went beyond tears, but the pain was real. "Come on, honey," Faythe said. "Do it for me."

"Lady, you have some opinion of yourself. Why on earth should I do anything for you?"

"Because this is supposed to be my big comeback, and you wouldn't want to ruin it for me. You can't let O'Connell think you're a flake."

Tara chose to ignore the subject of O'Connell's opinion.

"I didn't ask you to make a comeback. Why should I care if you fail?" She brushed her hair back and squeezed her eyes shut in exasperation. "In fact, why should I care about you at all?"

"Because I'm cool," Faythe said. "You said so yourself."

Tara's mouth twitched in a hint of a smile. She got up and looked down at Faythe with an unreadable expression. "Jeez," she said. "You are one bossy broad, Mrs. McB." She sauntered off, and Faythe stole a quick look at the bathroom tiles. They were plain black and white, as ordinary as tiles could be.

Milagros had put her mail on the kitchen counter, and Faythe kicked her heels off before running upstairs to run a bath, carrying the envelopes with her. As the scented water filled the tub, she sat on her bed and opened the bills first, putting them in a neat pile, away from where she'd open any personal mail. She took her bills very seriously and thought it strange that she'd reached the age of forty-something before she ever understood about the interest on credit cards.

She had hefty First Card and Am-Ex tabs, but this was only to be expected. She'd bought some new clothes, a necessity once she was sure she'd be returning to the business. She bought good clothes and liked simple natural fabrics, but never again, she hoped, would she drop several thousand on a dress so distinctive she'd wear it only once. She still had a closetful of designer gowns and dresses from the days with Cal, and she'd kept all but the hated Christian LeCroix "puff" dress, which she'd given to a thrift shop when her divorce became final. The hideous LeCroix frocks had been the last word in the mid-eighties, and Cal had got her one in Paris. The whole point to the puffs was that they were decadent, utilizing more precious fabric to create the effect that might have gone into a ballgown. They were short, with skimpy bodices, and then ballooned out into huge balls that made it an Olympian effort just to seat yourself at a dining room table.

Hers had been hot pink, with ribbons and seed pearls adorning the bodice, and she'd felt as if she were wearing something cumbersome and heavy above her knees—a beachball, say, or a wall safe. The puff dress had humiliated her, even as it was meant to make her feel proud and affluent and chic, because it was a joke. She had never met Christian LeCroix, but she would always believe that he had deliberately designed a dress that would make foolish women look ugly. Ugly and proud of their decadence, like Marie Antoinette at her model dairy at the palace.

The very young, who might have looked at least passable in such a fanciful costume, could not afford LeCroix couture, and so it was the starved-looking middle-aged ladies of New York and Hollywood who were made to look ridiculous in the photos that appeared in society pages.

She knew she was supremely lucky not to have to worry about money. She had refused, under community property laws, to take half of the value of the house in Pacific Palisades, and she refused— to Cal's relief— to want to live in it herself. Her divorce settlement was extremely generous, but she had to learn on her own to look after her money.

I'm that old cliché, she thought. *The girl who goes straight from her father to her husband and then winds up having to look after herself in middle age.* There was nothing remotely cute about a woman her age failing to have grasped the principle of interest. *Oh! You mean you pay more than you spent in the first place?*

The trouble, she knew, was that she had not passed directly from her college years to an affluent marriage. There had been that space in between, in her first years in California, when she'd been proud to see herself as an independent spirit.

She'd worked for a time as a waitress and as a receptionist in Burbank, and still later as a doctor's receptionist in Encino. They were part-time jobs, bandaid jobs, meant to pay the rent and see to her needs while she studied and found her place, perfecting her craft as an actress. She'd never been really poor, although when a check was late she would exist on pizza and oranges until it came through.

Everyone in her scene study class was in the same boat. They used to joke about their poverty, doing bits about the phone being cut off and the landlord pounding at the door. They all knew it was strictly temporary, the price they paid until the world recognized their gifts and awarded them their due. She and Ray had once dined on cornflakes and red wine by candlelight, jok-

ing that they'd remember this low point
when they were famous.

That had been in the days of low rents
and infinite possibilities. The days when a
pot of pasta could feed twenty comfortably,
and a jug of red wine could fuel a whole
party. She had somehow been plucked from
those early, hopeful days and set down in a
marriage of almost impossible luxury for
twenty years, only to emerge at the other
end of time in an era when the simplest
things cost so much she could hardly believe
it. The amount of money required to give
her car a full tank of gas would once have
paid for the main course at a Caruso dinner
party. The fees she had saved to pay for
acting classes were now not enough to pay
for Milagros to come in two days a week.
The lunch at The Grill, for which Casey
had paid, would have replenished the
Caruso wine cellars for a week.

If she could only provide for herself without relying solely on the money from Cal,
she would feel a success. Her "comeback"
was important not for reasons of vanity but
because she hoped she'd be working until
she was an old lady. *You have no right to be
dissatisfied,* she told herself. *Thousands of
women would give anything to be independent,*

*financially secure. My daughter is healthy, I'm
healthy (knock on wood) and I'm working. I am
going to play a scene with Desmond O'Connell,
an unforeseen blessing that I never dreamed
could happen . . .*

She went to turn the water off and un-
dressed, pleased by how just two weeks of
daily swimming had tautened her thighs and
behind. Her flesh felt satiny, resilient, and a
small voice told her it was a shame that there
was no one else to appreciate it. She and
O'Connell weren't going to fall in love, not
even for a week or two, and she was old
enough to know that no handsome stranger
was going to appear and sweep her away on
a tide of savage passion. Handsome strangers, the kind women fantasized about, were
plentiful in Hollywood, but they were either
gay or obsessed by their careers. Some were
"users," the kind of men who hooked up
with more successful women to give their
own careers a boost. And then, right on the
bottom of the available pool, there were the
young men who might as well be gigolos—
sleek, well dressed, intelligent men who provided thrills for the lady in question and
always managed to borrow large sums of
money or acquire the car of their dreams.

She would rather never know a man's

touch again than pay for love. Before she got into the tub, she retrieved the last piece of mail from her bed. It was from New York, from Tim Brady. She lowered herself into the deliciously warm water and opened the envelope. Inside were two pages, written in a neat but very masculine hand. He hadn't been making idle chat when he said he was the last letter writer in the Western world.

He described autumn in New York for her, saying that he wished he could make it more appealing, but the truth was that the trees hadn't turned yet. *It must be all the automobile exhaust*, he wrote. Still, New York was exciting as it always was in the season leading up to Christmas. New plays opening, galleries. She read with interest his account of a play he'd seen off-Broadway, one about the perilous matter of sexual harassment and political correctness. He'd thought it much better than *Oleana*, the play that had had audiences baying for blood at the curtain.

She smiled as he went on to describe the backbiting in his department at N.Y.U. He was amusing and informative, and she enjoyed his letter more than she'd imagined she would. On the second page, near the bottom, he told her how much it had meant to him to meet her and spend time with her and how sincerely he hoped he would see her again. He repeated his invitation to her to visit New York "as soon as you've shot your scene" and promised he would make her visit worthwhile. He signed it: *Yours, Tim.*

He was there if she wanted him, in other words. She sank back in the tub and let the letter drift to the floor. She was disappointed, admit it. Yes, she'd hoped something had happened to propel Tim Brady back to Los Angeles in the near future. He didn't understand that she wasn't really free to come to New York anytime soon. It wasn't a matter of "shooting her scene," as he seemed to believe. All of the cast had to be available for reshoots and unexpected calamities. There might even be a hasty rewrite, and shooting schedules were notoriously unpredictable.

Damn! He was so attractive, so nice, but he was three thousand miles away. She hummed a familiar tune and was stunned when she realized how appropriate it was: *Heartbreak Hotel.* "I'm so lonesome I could die." Or was it "cry?" She couldn't remember.

Nobody died of loneliness, and she was being self-indulgent. She imagined what

Casey would say if she knew of her mother's daydreams. *Get beyond that, Mom. In four years you'll fifty.*

Just as she was falling asleep that night she saw the kind of vision that sometimes hovers between sleep and wakefulness. She saw the deck at the Malibu house, swarming with people. She came closer and closer to each of their faces, as if with a zoom lens, but they were all strangers. One man alone was someone she knew, and she thought it was O'Connell. He stood with his back to her, and then he began to turn. She was so happy, so relieved. Someone she knew!

He turned slowly, so slowly, and before she could see his face she knew who he was. She urged herself into sleep, hoping she might dream of him, but instead she dreamed of her agent, Barney, offering Juanita Grace a chance to go on a world cruise. Casey got into the dream, too, and someone very like Katherine, but Ray Parnell was nowhere to be seen.

Nine

She had always wanted to know how Katherine Iverson, grande dame, had met Tara, a runaway, but she hadn't asked. If Kate had wanted her to know she would have said something on the day they'd had tea.

She got a clue quite by accident and determined to follow it up. She was leafing through a *People* magazine in the outer office of the wig and hair department in the Blauer Building. She'd come to have her hair studied and matched so the hairdresser could choose a long wig for Carlotta. Carlotta Fitzgerald had to have long hair, whether it was fashionable or not, because she was the "eternal woman." The "eternal woman" always had long hair, as everyone knew, and Faythe's escaped being long by at least six inches. She hoped they wouldn't put her in some two-ton monstrosity, an early Priscilla Presley look, but of course that wouldn't happen. She chided herself for imagining that things would be as they were a quarter of a century ago. Everything was state-of-the-art.

She flipped the pages, scanning the faces of politicians and celebrities— here a little girl who had been switched at birth with another infant who had died, there a middle-aged woman who claimed to remember satanic ritual abuse carried out on her decades ago. The magazine was months out of date, and she was about to put it aside when Katherine's name flashed out at her from a block of print. She thought she'd seen it but then, scanning, couldn't find it again.

The article was about celebrities who gave their time to charitable causes, actually laying their bodies on the line rather than mailing out hefty checks and forgetting about it until the next time for a tax write-off. Barbara Bush, the former First Lady, was involved in Volunteers for Literacy, as everyone knew, but Faythe was surprised to discover that Franco Cammarada was actively involved in arranging the adoptions of Amerasian children. There were the usual shots of people like Martin Sheen helping out in soup kitchens, juxtaposed with more surprising photos, one of a stunning black model tutoring inner city children. She looked to see if it was

Casey's new client, but the name was unfamiliar.

She had almost forgotten her original reason for reading the story and was thinking that she would like to do something for less fortunate people when she came to the paragraph about Dove House, a home for teenaged girls, runaways, right here in Los Angeles. No runaway was coerced into entering Dove House. It was simply there, a place of refuge for girls who had come to Hollywood in search of adventure and glory and found only brutality, degradation, and disease. Some of the girls had been prostitutes, either to support drug habits or because it was the only way they could avoid starving. Some had AIDS. All had reached the end of their ropes and came to Dove House as to the last refuge available. Girls were not allowed to stay if they did not enter programs for alcohol or drug abuse, if that was the problem, or therapy for problems of an emotional nature. No girl who honestly wanted to be helped was turned away, but the facility only had twenty beds, and not all of the girls were able to live there full-time.

Mrs. Wilma Kinnock, the director, told *People:* "We exist to try to return young

women who have lost their ways to a meaningful place in society. When we lose, it is
heartbreaking, but Dove House has succeeded much, much more often than it's
failed."

Dove House had been the brainchild of
several well-known women, among them the
luminous actress Katherine Iverson, who
declined to be interviewed. These women,
the article said, wished to express their
gratitude to a city that had rewarded them
so richly by trying to make a difference to
those the city had destroyed.

Faythe felt astonished. Never could she
have imagined Kate founding a home for
wayward girls, as they'd called it in Wisconsin. She tried to imagine what had propelled her friend to such a dramatic act of
charity and wondered how Tara fit in. Had
Tara actually lived at Dove House, or was
she one of the unfortunate young women
Kate had met in her secret life as a minis-
tering angel? She ripped the page from *People* and stowed it in her handbag, not sure
what she would do with it.

Five minutes later she was seated in a
padded chair in front of a makeup mirror.
A round young woman called Angie lifted

her hair and complemented her on its texture and volume.

"You've got good hair," Angie said. "A lot of women your age would kill for this hair."

"It doesn't matter, does it, since my hair will be covered up by the wig?"

"Oh, you'd be surprised," said Angie, selecting a chestnut fall and holding it up to Faythe's hair, frowning. "You've got to select the kind of hair that matches most closely. An actress with thin, dry hair, or overbleached hair, she's not gonna look real in a luxuriant piece. It won't go with the rest of her, if you see what I mean. You've got luxuriant hair, you've got the volume, so I've got no problem in matching you up. You're gonna look great, Fay."

None of the swatches seemed to match her exactly. They were either too red or too dark. She supposed she would have to appear in a shade not her own, but here she underestimated Angie.

"Now this is prime Italian hair," Angie said, dangling an auburn fall next to Faythe's cheekbone. "It moves naturally, and it looks wonderful. We don't have a perfect match here, but I'm gonna tint it to get a good effect."

She placed the fall at the back of Faythe's head, and instantly she became the "eternal woman." As Angie adjusted and combed bits of real hair around the piece, Faythe could see herself as Carlotta on that yacht in Sardinia, her hair tossed by breezes off the Tyrrhenian Sea.

"You won't even know you're not wearing your real hair," Angie told her. Then she handed her a card, telling Faythe the date of her final fitting.

"May I speak to Mrs. Kinnock?" Faythe sat beneath the jacaranda tree in her back yard, the L.A. phone book on her knees. She wasn't sure what she was going to do, having acted on impulse.

The soft Hispanic voice that had answered the Dove House line told her to wait a minute, and then she heard the sound of feet walking away on a hardwood floor and the voice calling something. Obviously things were not state-of-the-art at the shelter. No computerized switchboard, and the voice sounded as if it belonged to a runaway. Maybe things were better that way; maybe Dove House had more heart than patina.

"Yes, hello, how may I help you? I'm Wilma Kinnock."

"I'm doing graduate work in sociology at U.S.C.," Faythe lied. "At present I'm researching my thesis, which will be on the long-term effects of life on the street. Particularly as it pertains to very young women."

There was a polite silence at the other end.

"I thought you might permit me to interview you, at your convenience, of course."

"You do realize that anything I tell you about a Dove House resident is strictly confidential?"

"Naturally, Mrs. Kinnock. I can even promise not to mention you or Dove House in my thesis. It's your experience with runaways that's of value to me."

"I have some time this afternoon, after 3:30 . . . make it four? Can you be here? We're on Alameda, you know."

"I'll be there," Faythe said. "I appreciate this."

Mrs. Kinnock sounded slightly miffed when she said, "Hadn't you better tell me your name?"

"Oh, yes, of course. I'm Marie Raymond." The pseudonym slid out as easily as if she'd been calling herself Marie Raymond all her

life. Marie was her middle name, and Raymond was . . . well, Ray's name. *Just like a
teenager,* she thought. She went upstairs to
change her clothes. What did graduate students wear these days? Presumably anything
but her grown-up lady movie star outfits. In
the back of her closet were some casual
things she'd bought when she first moved to
Santa Monica. She selected a pair of oatmeal
colored denim pants, topped them with a
dark blue silk blouse and denim jacket. Then
she shoved her feet into black flats and considered her image in the mirror. Her hair
was too obviously expensively coiffed, simple
as it was, and she found an old felt hat and
gathered her hair up inside. Where had the
hat come from? It was one of Casey's, one
she'd grown tired of on the spur of the moment and left at her mother's house. Faythe
had vaguely thought she could garden in it,
since she had intended to take up gardening.
The gardens at the Palisades had been so
extensive they'd required a full-time man to
maintain them. They'd been daunting to her,
and one of the things she looked forward to
doing was starting from scratch here. She'd
only got as far as buying the seeds, and then
she'd been plunged into the miniseries furor.
     She thought she looked rather dashing in

the hat and reminded herself to pick up a tablet and pen on her way to Dove House. She had a tape recorder, but she didn't think Mrs. Kinnock would take kindly to it.

As she approached the block on Alameda, her props beside her on the car seat, she felt a thrill of purpose. Somehow, without ever mentioning Tara's name, she would manage to find out how best to help her. The block was rundown and seedy. Graffiti blossomed on a few condemned looking buildings, but here and there were intact houses that had once been handsome and still retained a look of blowsy comfort. Dove House was one of them, a big old three-story of the sort usually converted to a rooming house. There was no sign to mark it, only the outline of a dove painted in, white on a bright yellow door. The two tiny plots of grass on either side of the entrance had long ago been worn to nothing, but there was no rubble to be seen, no candy wrappers or cigarette packets, and the windows were sparkling. The frames were old and warped, but the glass was as clean as human labor could make it.

She rang a bell to the side of the door and spoke into the intercom, giving her false name. A buzzer rang her in, and she was standing in a hallway that had been converted into a reception area. An enormous bulletin board covered one whole wall, with dozens of leaflets, flyers, and schedules pinned to it, and behind a desk sat a teenaged girl just hanging up a telephone. She had a small triangular face made even smaller by the explosion of black hair that framed it. "Hi," she said. "I'm Daisy. You got an appointment with Wilma, right?"

Faythe nodded and managed to keep her face impassive when Daisy rose from behind her desk. She was hugely pregnant, and because she was so thin the engorged abdomen made her resemble a serpent who'd swallowed a piglet. Daisy came waddling around the desk and indicated that Faythe was to follow her. They passed a large room with some big, lumpy looking couches and chairs, a television set, and bookcases crammed with everything from glossy bestsellers to the kind of book you could get for a quarter at secondhand stores. A girl with lanky brown hair was sitting on one of the chairs flipping through a magazine.

"That's Tina," Daisy told her. "She just got here last night, so she's a little bit . . ." Daisy waved her hands to show the new arrival's state of mind.

Mrs. Wilma Kinnock was discovered in the kitchen, typing on an old manual at the big wooden table. She thanked Daisy and rose to greet Faythe.

"We're so overcrowded here," she said, "I have to use the kitchen as my office. Please sit down and ask me anything you like, so long as you don't ask me to name names or violate confidentiality."

She was a stylish black woman in her mid-thirties, Faythe reckoned. She exuded warmth, but beneath it was a no-nonsense steeliness that would emerge the moment someone tried to pull a fast one on her.

"Who's your thesis adviser at U.S.C.?" she asked. "Not Jack Wright by any chance?"

"No, it's Dr. Madigan," Faythe said. "Dr. Katherine Madigan."

Mrs. Kinnock's well-shaped eyebrows rose politely. "Not the Katherine Madigan who wrote *Early Sorrow*?"

Faythe wanted to run from the kitchen. Had she inadvertently hit on an actual sociologist at U.S.C.? She felt color flood her face and tried to make the best of it. "No," she said. "What a coincidence."

"Mmm-hmmm. Now what coincidence would that be?"

"That there are two Dr. Katherine Madigans."

Mrs. Kinnock threw back her head and laughed, revealing excellent teeth and making Faythe feel foolish.

"Marie," she said, "it's the oldest trick in the book. People call here all the time saying they're journalists or what have you, all of them trying to find out something. Some of them are mothers of runaways and some of them think there's big money to be made writing about runaways, but not a one of them is who she says she is." Her look was not unkind as she gazed at Faythe from across the table. "My first allegiance is to my girls. I'm sure you can understand that."

"I'm not looking for a runaway, Mrs. Kinnock. I've met one recently, and I want to find out more about her. I don't mean her, specifically, but about what makes her so unhappy and what I can do to help."

"I don't want to know her name, and I don't want to know your real name, whoever you are. You seem like a nice person, but I can't be too careful."

Mrs. Kinnock got up and put water in a saucepan. The kitchen, like the front hall, was festooned with slips of paper on bulletin boards. One of them showed the list of chores allotted to each member of Dove House. Daisy, she could see, was down for vegetable preparation, and the new girl, Tina, didn't have kitchen duty yet.

"Would you like some coffee or a soft drink?" Mrs. Kinnock asked, measuring out instant coffee into a mug that said: "Boss Lady."

"A Diet Pepsi would be fine," she replied. She felt very silly, outfitted in her "costume" and prepared to play a role she'd thought original. The lost look in the lanky-haired girl's eyes and Daisy's huge pregnancy humbled her. Who had fathered Daisy's child, and who would be with her when it was born?

"When is Daisy's child due?" she asked.

"Yesterday," said Wilma Kinnock, chuckling. "She's all set. She's been coached in her Lamaze, and she's got a birthing partner. This baby will have twenty mothers instead of one."

"How old is Daisy?" She hoped she hadn't overstepped the bounds by asking a direct question about an actual person.

"Fifteen," said Wilma, "and a half. She's not the youngest mama we've had here, either." She got a tumbler down from a cupboard and filled it with cola from a food co-op, passing it to Faythe. "Honey," she said, "next time you want to play at being a grad student, try not to wear shoes from Thieves' Market."

Thieves' Market was a very expensive shop on Ventura, specializing in cowboy boots and accessories. It was where Casey had bought her scarlet Larry Mahan's. She felt her toes curl with embarrassment inside the pricey little flats. "Okay," she said, "I'm a rank amateur at impersonation Mrs. Kinnock, but I honestly want to help this girl. Young woman, I should say. She's in her early twenties, but I have good reason to think she lived here for a while."

"Tell me more, and name no names."

Faythe tried to describe Tara as she saw her: afraid all the time, except when she was acting; extravagantly gifted; aware of her talent, confident even, but believing herself to be worthless in all other ways; a liar who admitted that she lied; someone capable of making cruel remarks whenever she sensed that someone else was coming too close; the keeper of a dreadful secret, or one she thought dreadful— correction, probably it was dreadful, but hardly unique.

Wilma listened impassively, nodding at times.

"I know she ran away from a very oppressive family situation in the Midwest," she said. "I don't know the details, but they lived in a remote area and were extremely religious. She once told me her mother didn't see movies, so maybe that was a part of their religion." She was longing to tell Mrs. Kinnock that Tara was about to enter the very world her parents had found sinful, but she felt such an intimate detail might be too much.

"What troubles you about this young woman?"

"I'm afraid she's self-destructive."

"Do you have any evidence?"

She thought of Casey's evaluation of Tara, but Casey wasn't relevant here. "She seems to drink too much. She may be on drugs."

"You've seen her take drugs?"

"No. I've seen her drink too much vodka, though."

"And you? Have you never drunk too much in your life?"

Wilma Kinnock seemed to block her at every turn. Of course Faythe had drunk too much in her life, on certain occasions, but never when so much was at stake.

"So, let me get this straight," said Mrs. Kinnock. "The young lady in question is nervous, seems to lack self-esteem, and has, on one occasion, drunk too much in your presence. She is occasionally hostile, or you perceive her as hostile."

"Yes," said Faythe.

"Let me ask you a question. Do you have children?"

She saw where it was leading and said that she had a daughter who could reasonably be said to answer to all of the above.

"Except," she amended, "for the self-esteem part."

"And is that self-esteem always warranted, in your view?"

She thought of Casey's unassailable self-regard and giggled. "No," she admitted. "My daughter has too much self-esteem at times. She hasn't earned it yet."

Wilma Kinnock spread her hands in a graceful gesture. "You see?" she said. "You could be describing any woman from fifteen to twenty-five."

Tina entered the kitchen apologetically and went to a counter near the sink. There were two mason jars filled with dimes and quarters, and the girl dipped her hand in and took some coins. "Doin' my laundry," she said to Faythe, as if she might be suspected of stealing. Up close Faythe could see the track marks on her scrawny arms.

"Tina, don't forget about the lint on the filter," Wilma said pleasantly to the girl's departing back. "We're going to need a new dryer pretty soon. We need so much. Just when I think we're caught up, something else falls apart."

"What do you need most?" Faythe asked, determined to make a contribution.

"Money, honey. Always money." She stood up with a sigh. "Come on, I'll take you on the tour."

The second floor contained four bedrooms and a single bathroom. The largest room was furnished with two bunkbeds, a single large dresser, and a full-length mirror. The beds were neatly made, each with a different color quilt, and the inhabitants had tried to individualize their tiny space. A poster for a Spike Lee movie hung over one bunk, and on another a pink stuffed rabbit was propped against a pillow.

"We have lots of rules here," Wilma said. "Everyone knows the rules and everyone obeys, or they're out. No drugs, that goes without saying, and no alcohol. You keep your space clean, and you pitch in on the other chores. If you want to listen to music other than in the common room, you wear earphones. Every girl has her own Walkman. You might think my guests here hate the rules, but the truth is, they love them."

Faythe pondered the oddity of girls running away from home to escape rigid lives, only to end up obeying rules that might be more stern than the ones they'd escaped. There might be a kind of relief in conforming to a common good if you'd been on the streets where there were no rules. Chaos and brutality and lawlessness ruled the streets, and by the time a girl came to Dove House she might be grateful for order. She followed Wilma up to the next floor, where the rooms were smaller. One was equipped with a cradle and a stand piled with Pampers, baby powder, and a stack of tiny jumpsuits. "I don't have to ask whose room this is," Faythe said. She felt a kind of despair as she contemplated the room made ready for Daisy's baby. Daisy was a baby herself, and soon she'd be confronted with the joys and horrors of being responsible for another human being. She had had a live-in nurse when Casey had been born, and even with so much help it had seemed overwhelming to be in charge of another life.

How much more difficult it would be for a fifteen-year-old girl. If Daisy had been on drugs, the child might be born addicted and the whole perilous structure of Dove House would be affected.

As if sensing her thoughts, Wilma said, "We have every expectation that Daisy's baby will be just fine. I'm looking forward to having a baby around, and so are most of the girls."

"Where are they?" Faythe asked. "I've only seen two."

"Marty and Joanne are doing the weekly shopping," Wilma said, "and the others have jobs. They're mainly Mickey Mouse, minimum wage jobs, but it's important for them to function in the real world."

They came to a single room whose owner clearly loved the colors in the purple range. The bedspread was lilac, the curtains, made from a queen-size sheet, were mauve, and the girl's name, Deanna, was printed on a card on the door in deep purple marker. Wilma took Faythe's arm and propelled her to the bed, where they both sat down. The sunlight filtering through the mauve curtains turned the room into a fantasy space. Faythe felt as if she were trapped in the heart of a giant, night-blooming flower.

"The child who lives here is dying of AIDS," Wilma said. "She's in the hospital now, and when she comes back— *if* she comes back— it will be to the only place she's ever known where people care for her. She told me these days at Dove House have been the happiest in her life, and that's a crime, isn't it? This purple room is her statement. It's where she expects to die."

Faythe felt she had no words that were adequate. She swallowed hard and met Wilma Kinnock's forceful gaze straight on. She knew the other woman was dosing her with the medicine that was hardest to take— reality in all its ugliness and indifference.

"You see," said Wilma, "when a girl runs away from home and is forced to live on the streets, she becomes an expert at lying to herself. She's not really a prostitute, she's merely using the only tool she has to buy herself a meal. She's not really an addict, she can stop any time she likes, but it makes life so much easier to blur the edges. A girl will come to us for a variety of reasons. You see why this child came, but it doesn't take a death sentence to bring someone to us. It can happen if a man beats up on a girl, or if another street kid out there dies. Anything that wakes them up to the fact that their life is hell, that gets through that protective denial they've built up. We keep them safe for a while, try to build them up to the point where they can face the world. It doesn't always work out, but when it does, there's no better feeling.

"The young lady you were telling me about? This is just a guess, and you're not to take my word as gospel, but from what you've said I imagine she was abused. Sexually, physically, psychologically . . . I don't know just how, but at some point she was a powerless child in an abusive home. She was made to feel wrong, always, and bad, and worthless, and after a while it took.

"When she found herself alone out here, the freedom from that kind of oppression was enough for a while, but gradually she found she'd traded one kind of brutality for another. She lies because she can't stand who she is or where she came from. If she was ever with us, I'd hope she's strong enough now to find her way back."

"What can I do?" Faythe imagined another Tara, a younger Tara, living at Dove House and shoring up enough strength and self-respect to try to become an actress. It seemed a nearly impossible feat.

"What you can do is not feel sorry for her. Treat her as you would any other young woman you like and respect. Don't let her get away with lying to you or she'll despise you secretly. Give her affection by all means, but don't go making allowances. No 'this poor child had it so rough I'll forgive her for being rude or stealing my jewelry.' The moment you make allowances, you're showing her she's not to be judged as other human beings are, and that's fatal."

It was pretty much the way she'd been treating Tara, she thought, and was glad she'd accidentally done something right.

"You said the girl was gifted. I take it she's an artist of some kind. The very fact she still paints, or sings, or dances is hopeful. She hasn't lost track of her gift, and it may be what will save her."

"I think so, too, but I worry that she mixes fantasy with reality too much."

"Honey," said Wilma Kinnock, smiling ruefully, "in her place, wouldn't you?"

They walked back down the stairs together in silence. Daisy was behind her desk again, answering the phone. A round girl wearing pink sweats was coming through the door carrying a carton of groceries, and behind her came several others. The residents of

Dove House were returning to their refuge at the end of the day, and it was time for Faythe to leave.

"Girls," Wilma said, "this is Mrs. Raymond, who came to see our setup. Is there anything you want to tell her?"

The round girl giggled and shook her head, but a tall black teenager shoved her aside. "Yeah," she said. "I got something to say. This is an okay place. The rules are strict but Wilma's fair. The hot water situation sucks with twenty women and only three bathrooms, but you can't have everything. Your hat is slammin'."

"Slammin'?"

"Funky, bad, fresh."

"You like it?" Faythe said, plucking it off. "It's yours."

The girl said no, looking to Wilma for approval, but Faythe explained that it belonged to no one and it might as well belong to someone who appreciated it.

"You know where to reach me," Wilma said to her at the door. "Call me anytime if I can help."

Just as Faythe was halfway to her car she heard Wilma call her name. "Be sure and send me that paper you're writing, Mrs. Raymond," she said, and winked.

* * *

That night, the news carried a horrifying item about an actress who had been robbed at gunpoint when she was retrieving her car at a fashionable restaurant. The newscaster was quick to point out that such crimes had overspilled the borders of the ghetto and were now making their way to the privileged enclaves everyone had previously thought safe.

The stabbing death of a young actress who'd been stalked by a deranged fan was dragged in, as if the two incidents were part of the same crime wave, and the earnest young reporter signed off by saying: "There is a lesson to be learned from these crimes against the rich and famous, and it is this: Nobody is safe in these last years of the twentieth century, when we had all expected civilization to reach its peak. The rage of the have-nots will continue to make itself known to the haves, sometimes with tragic results. In a town where great wealth sleeps behind the most sophisticated systems of security the world has ever known, there is a feeling of unease. No one is safe."

Faythe snapped the remote control button and consigned the evening news to darkness and oblivion. That was all she needed, to start worrying about being mugged or carjacked. This house had good locks on the doors and a timer that put lights on at dusk each day whether she was there or not, and that was it. That and common sense, were all she had thought she'd need.

The security at the house in the Palisades! It gave her a headache just to think about it. Jangling sirens that would be activated if an intruder passed a scanner on the long driveway after the Carusos were in for the night, a house alarm that had to be programmed and deprogrammed, a vault that contained only costume jewelry and the real vault, concealed, in which her best pieces were stored. Cal had even acquired an attack dog, a vicious Doberman called Bingley whom he seemed to love. Odd, that. He used to boast that if Bingley could be trained to talk, he'd make the best agent in town. She'd put her foot down about the dog, saying he frightened her and that it was madness to keep such an unpredictable creature around a small child. Bingley had gone back to his trainer, and Cal had been angry with her for a week.

When the phone rang she jumped, and then laughed at herself.

She was rather hoping it would be Tim, for some reason, but even as she heard her daughter's voice she realized it couldn't have been Tim. It was 2:30 in the morning in New York.

"Mom, have you heard about what happened to Gloria?"

"Just now, on the news. Where are you? Are you all right?"

"Of course I'm all right, relax. I'm at home and I'm about to go to bed. Early appointment tomorrow. I just wanted to warn you about something." She sounded uncertain, which was very un-Casey-like. The last time Casey had "warned" her it had been about Tara, and she'd been very sure of herself then.

"Well, you know the last time I had dinner with Dad, he was very concerned about you. Being alone in that house and all, he said he didn't feel you were safe."

"I hope he's not planning to send me an attack dog," Faythe said. "Do you remember Bingley, honey?"

"Just barely. He was gross, but don't get me sidetracked. He was talking about . . . well, about this thing I wanted to warn you about. I managed to talk him out of it, but now with this new incident . . ."

Faythe waited, not sure she wanted to hear what was coming.

"He wants to get you a gun, Mother. He said a woman living alone had to be able to protect herself."

"What gall! My safety is not his business anymore, and I wouldn't have a gun in my house if you paid me."

"I know. I told him you'd hate the idea, and he listened and said maybe I was right, but now with Gloria Bledsoe getting mugged . . . you know what he's like. He gets an idea and just runs with it and nothing can dissuade him."

"Don't I know it. I'm touched that you'd warn me, honey, I really am. Thanks for trying." A sudden thought rocked her. "He hasn't given you a gun, has he?"

Casey snorted. "No, of course not."

"But you're a woman living alone, aren't you?"

"Please, Ma. I'm north of Montana, and I can take care of myself." She made a smooching sound. "Gotta go. Bye."

Faythe found her heart beating rapidly with rage. How like Cal to grandstand in front of his daughter, and how dare he even think of buying her a gun? He knew she detested them. And then to insinuate that she was unsafe because she no longer inhabited the few neighborhoods he thought of as the right places. She was ready to call him then and there, but she realized she couldn't violate Casey's secret call. She would have to wait until Cal contacted her with his cheesy offer of a gun and then tell him that she would simply turn it in to the police.

And what was this sudden concern for her welfare, anyway? It all boiled down to his self-image. If Faythe were mugged or assaulted it would make him look bad. It would be tacky, and people might say that Cal Caruso had left his former wife in a position not fitting a one-time consort of Hollywood's most powerful agent. "It's all about you," she said bitterly, as if he were in the room with her. "It's always been about you."

She climbed the stairs and got ready to read in bed. A glass of wine would help to relax her, but she thought of the close-ups and went without it. She couldn't keep her mind on the book she was trying to read, even though it was an interesting account of a true crime that had happened in California at the turn of the century. She would read a page only to realize that she hadn't absorbed a word and then she'd ask herself why she was reading about a murder when crime was in the air right here in Hollywood.

She let the book drop to the floor with a thud, feeling a childish pleasure in the loud noise it made. "I'm so tired of this," she said, only half aware of what "this" might be. "You're talking to yourself," she admonished. "This is what happens to elderly ladies who live alone. They may lunch and go to parties and meet people, but when they're all alone in their houses they have no one to talk to but themselves."

She had a sudden memory, and it was as sharp and clear as if it had occurred yesterday instead of nearly thirty years ago.

There she was at the infirmary, in her sophomore year in college. Here's Faith, wearing a matching skirt and sweater and Capezio T-strap shoes. She's just been diagnosed with a very nasty strain of flu and told she must stay in bed for at least the next four days. Here's the prick of a penicillin shot and the nurse's voice telling her to drink plenty of liquids and put a tepid compress on her burning forehead.

But's what this? Faith is crying. Big, self-pitying tears are rolling down her flushed face, and she is trying to tell the nurse that she must audition for *The Playboy of the Western World*. She has memorized all of Pegeen's lines and is a cinch for the part. She has wanted this part so much and worked so hard to secure it, it isn't fair that she should get the flu at this precise moment in time.

The nurse is regarding her with a fair amount of impatience. She can see her clearly: a large woman with tightly permed dark hair and glasses that magnify her cold blue eyes. The nurse is speaking.

"Try to have a sense of proportion," she says. "There are young men dying in Southeast Asia."

Right. The nurse had been right, but somehow it never worked. When you were hurting, it didn't help to tell yourself that you might be a starving child in Ethiopia or a burning monk in Saigon. Human beings weren't constructed in such a way that they could console themselves by saying it could be worse. Much, much worse.

Still, it couldn't hurt to try. Composing herself for sleep, she made herself think of the girls at Dove House, settling in for the night. She thought of Daisy, tossing and trying to find a comfortable position in her advanced stage of pregnancy, her hard, huge tummy making it impossible, and she thought of Daisy's fears for the future and of the childhood she'd never had. Then she considered Tina, the new girl with tracks on her arms, and the black teenager to whom she'd given Casey's hat.

She went further, and forced herself to imagine the girl of the purple room, alone in a hospital tonight, knowing that she hadn't much longer to live.

Things could be worse.

Ten

"Do you remember how intense we used to be about our art?"

Ray bent toward her over the table, smiling with just a hint of self-mockery. Mostly he sounded nostalgic and full of affection for their younger selves.

"I remember all too well," she told him. It was pleasant at this new restaurant just outside Beverly Hills. The Osteria Romana Orsini featured grill work in a grapevine motif and was down a few steps from the street, making it seem intimate. Their meals had been excellent, if highly caloric, and now they were lingering over coffee and a Strega.

"When I was at N.Y.U. film school, just before I came out here, my father sent me an anonymous letter. It was an old quote, maybe from Bernard Shaw. Written in his highly recognizable hand, my old man said: 'An actress is something more than a woman, while an actor is something less than a man'."

Faythe laughed in protest. "You never wanted to be an actor. You always knew you'd direct."

"Acting, directing, it was all the same to him. He thought it was undignified to work in movies. My mother was delighted, but she had to keep it a secret around him."

She felt suddenly shy. She didn't even know if the senior Parnells were still alive.

Ray, who had always been a bit of a mind reader, said: "My mother told me he saw every one of my movies, but he wouldn't admit it. He left the stubs in his jacket pocket for her to find."

"How sad," she said. "Part of being a big success is supposed to be the pleasure you find in your parents' approval. That, and buying them nice things."

"You were deprived of that, too. It must have been hard." As if he sensed that he'd crossed over into forbidden territory, he switched back to his own parents. "I bought them a condo in Florida. It was all they wanted. With their condo in Pompano Beach and my old man's pension from the N.Y.P.D., they were set."

"Des O'Connell calls his father his old man, too."

"It's an Irish thing," Ray said, grinning. "I think it's reserved for dads you love and hate at the same time."

"All these passionate feelings people have for their parents! I loved mine, but they seem very ordinary in retrospect. They were good to me. They tried their best."

"Time is of the essence, Faythe," he said, and when she realized that he was mimicking her father she felt ravished with emotion. Over all the years, he'd remembered this quirk of her dad's, something she had probably told him as she lay in his arms.

"What a memory you have," she said.

"I remember everything about you," he said. It was neither melodramatic nor a cheap seduction ploy. It was spoken as simple fact.

She was grateful when Norman Mailer walked in with his lovely wife Norris because they created a brief distraction.

"Do you think he's the only writer in the world who'd be known by sight in Hollywood?" she said.

"Possible." He unwrapped an Amaretto biscuit, dipped it in his brandy, and ate it in one bite. "Normally, I'd wonder what

Mailer's doing here. Normally, in fact, I'd know, but I've been so wrapped up in our project the rest of the world has gone by in a blur."

"It must be wonderful to be so immersed in your work," she said wistfully.

"But that's what I meant about our former intensity. I think you still have it, Faythe. Playing a cameo role in *The Senator's Daughter* might not be your idea of high art, but I think it's going to lead you back to acting. My guess is that you miss that old pure jolt of daring to create something. You miss it without knowing you do."

"Maybe so, but I'm not sure that kind of intensity is becoming in a mature woman. It's one thing to burn with that old hard, gem-like flame when you're a kid, but quite another when you're a few decades down the line."

"Why?" Ray sat back in the booth as if trying to frame her in an imaginary lens. "Don't mistake me, don't imagine I want you to play Chekhov or O'Neill or the *Horror Boardwalk*. Of course you won't behave the way you did when you were so young, but the feeling is the same. That's the great secret, Faythe, the feeling never changes."

"Really." She was so moved she didn't

trust herself, and the word came out in a brittle, ugly way.

"Really," he said. "I promise you. The feeling never changes."

"Is that your mantra, Ray?" She couldn't stop herself. More than anything, she wanted to sit with him forever, but she knew her feeling wasn't to be trusted. Ray had betrayed her, and just because he had more skill at seeming sensitive than Cal, it didn't mean they were different species. The Carusos and Parnells of this world always knew exactly what they were doing. Some of them were transparent and some opaque. Ray was of the opaque variety, but he had no more capability of being steadfast and true than Cal.

Ray let the remark pass and signalled for the check. Their dinner was already over, and she hadn't discovered why he'd asked her to dine with him. Standing up to make an exit, she regretted not wearing the Ungaro. She'd tried on four outfits before deciding on the off-the-shoulder confection in sea foam green, and now she was afraid it was too young for her.

She tensed as Ray's hand hovered lightly at her back and then withdrew as they left the restaurant. At least he didn't treat her as an expensive *objet* he'd added to his collection.

In silence, she got into Ray's car. It was the same as Casey's first car had been, a 1966 Mustang convertible, a collector's item. Ray's was midnight blue and had been totally restored to its original condition.

"I'm the envy of every fourteen-year-old boy on my block," he'd said when he picked her up.

"Want to go for a drive?" he asked her now. "No particular destination."

She nodded and he put a tape of Thelonius Monk on, playing "Round Midnight." There was little traffic at this hour, and she was borne up Melrose and across Sunset and then out along the Pacific Coast Highway. She put her head back against the seat and gave herself up to the pleasure of the music and the beauty of the night. It was possible to believe, at night, that Hollywood was still a paradise— a balmy, fragrant place where pools glowed turquoise at night and people in formal attire sipped champagne beneath the stars.

They didn't speak, but it was a comfortable silence, and she knew Ray was as pleased by their aimless driving as she was. When the road doubled back on itself she could see the ocean far below, phosphorescent where it eddied around the rocks. At last he pulled in at an overlook and killed the motor. Thelonius was now playing a tune she didn't know. It was slightly mournful but full of a life she remembered, a time of that innocent intensity Ray had referred to earlier. Staring straight ahead, Ray began to speak.

"When Betsy died," he said. "I was devastated. There was the natural grief you'd expect, and then something else that took me by surprise. I felt so guilty, Faythe. I was a good husband to Betsy, we loved each other and had everything a couple are supposed to have in marriage, except for children. That was her abiding sadness, that she couldn't have any children.

"But the guilt was so deep and savage I thought it would finish me. I asked myself why I should be guilty, and finally I understood that it wasn't anything I could control. I felt the way I did because I was alive and she was dead— simple and elemental. Primitive, even.

"Betsy was an especially good person. She wasn't afraid to die and had this kind of serene faith that's always eluded me. She was a better person than I was, yet she was six feet under and here was old Ray Parnell, carrying on the same as usual, hustling up work and eating scampi, looking at the rushes and worrying about my hairline. My trivial life was humming along, and there was nothing to do but hum along with it."

Faythe turned to look at him, but his face in the darkness gave away nothing. "Your life isn't trivial just because you survived," she said. "I'm glad you were a good husband to Betsy. I wanted to say something to you when she died, but under the circumstances . . ."

"Does Miss Manners say that a man's first love can't condole with him on the death of his second love?"

"I'm sorry, Ray. Truly sorry about Betsy, but I kind of imagine you've had more than two loves."

"Then you'd be wrong," he said in an uninflected voice, much as he'd inform a cashier that she'd overcharged him on some item. "Many women, two loves."

"Lucky you," she said. "Some people don't even get any."

"Oh, Faythe," he sighed. "Why is it so difficult to talk to you? You seem determined to undermine me at every move. What are you afraid of?"

"Lots of things. I'm afraid I'll fail my daughter in some way, afraid of aging without grace, for starters. I'm afraid I won't pass muster on the miniseries. Is that honest enough for you, or do you want me to rip my heart out right here and now?"

"It's not honest enough for me," he said. "I meant what are you afraid of about me, as you know damn well."

"I wasn't afraid of anything about you in the past, and as it turns out I was a fool. I should have been afraid."

"What was I—twenty-six years old? And for one stupid, horny mistake I made you turn the world upside down. You marry a man you didn't love and I'm deprived of your company forever." He gave a harsh laugh. "That's the kind of justice the Greek gods used to mete out."

"You don't know what I felt for Cal at the time. How could you? As for being deprived of my company forever, here I am, a captive audience in your car."

"You Midwestern girls are such smart-asses. Do you remember your twenty-second birthday, Faythe?"

She shut her eyes. "Don't, Ray." She remembered it so well, had thought of it so often. He had bought her a Raggedy Anne doll, the kind she'd once had as a child, with *I Love You* written on Annie's heart. The doll was holding a tiny box, and inside was a delicate ring made of woven strands of silver and gold. It was an engagement ring, the only kind he could afford, and he promised her a better one in the future. But she'd loved the ring and allowed him to put it on her finger, and then he had kissed her, his lips so warm and adoring, and called her his precious girl.

To this day, after so many years, she could remember the precise feel of his long back under her hands, the way she was conscious of her new ring passing over his skin, the lovely weight of him on her eager body. It was the first time he'd said he wanted to be with her forever, but not the last. She could hear her voice calling out that she loved him, would always love him.

They'd made love all night long, falling into a stunned sleep with each new surge of pleasure, only to awaken and rekindle the heat, groaning and laughing.

This is ridiculous— you're a wild man, Ray!

I can tell how much you hate it, Faythe.

"Don't Ray," she said again. "Don't make me remember. It's over and done with, a long time ago."

He started the car and drove her back to Santa Monica in silence. The tape had come full circle and "Round Midnight" was playing again and she felt unbearably sad. There'd been a popular place called The Carat where she and Ray had gone when they could afford it. They liked to sit behind the latticework at the bar where they couldn't be seen by the diners, and it always seemed to be midnight. They were pretty people in a room full of pretty people, but she always felt she and Ray were different. Alone of all the patrons at The Carat, she and Ray were in love, not on the prowl and looking for a one night stand.

"Do you remember The Carat?" she asked, breaking the silence as they sat in the darkness in her driveway.

For answer he took her hand. She stiffened at first, and then let her hand rest in his. She felt feverish and not in control of her intellect. Here she had begged him not to make her remember, and then the first thing she'd said . . .

What are you afraid of about me?

"You're right," her voice emerged in a whisper. "I wasn't being honest. It should be obvious, though. It's sadistic of you to make me say it."

"Not sadistic. Therapeutic, I'd say."

She turned to face him. By the lights from her house his face was visible, just, and he looked as serious as she'd ever seen him. "I'm afraid of getting hurt again," she said. "If I trusted you again, as my friend, and you betrayed that trust— " She stopped in mid-sentence, aware that she was still not being honest. If she were to find Ray in her life again— in it as anything more than her director— it wasn't as a friend she would want him.

She forced herself to smile. "All this talk of betraying my trust. I sound like a character in a soap. It was a lovely evening, Ray. Thank you."

She expected him to release her hand, perhaps to get out of the Mustang and see her to her door, but he didn't move. "Ask me in for a nightcap," he said. "Pretend I'm directing you in a scene. You're going to ask me in, and then I'll stay for five or ten minutes. All very civilized. Nothing heavy."

She felt the blood thicken in her veins, actually felt her limbs grow heavier. "What's my objective in this scene?" she asked. "What am I meant to find out?"

"That I'm not the big, bad wolf. I'm a man you can be alone with without being angry or embarrassed. My objective is to be that man and not to alarm you."

"All right." She gripped his hand in a friendly way and spoke in as light and normal a voice as she could produce. "Come in for a few minutes, will you Ray? Let me give you a nightcap."

He released her hand now and got out of the car, coming around to open the door on her side. She let herself in with her keys and tossed her handbag on a table. "Make yourself comfortable," she said, going to her kitchen. "What can I get you?" she called over her shoulder.

"A small brandy would be nice," he said. "A very small one, I've got to drive."

Well, that's it, she realized. *The end of this scene, right now.* "I don't have any brandy," she called back. "I don't have anything but juice and one bottle of white wine." The irony of the situation hit her, and she began to laugh. It was a small laugh at first, in keeping with the smallness of the situation, but the laughter grew. Here she was, trying to be virtuous so she'd look good for the cameras, and her good intentions ensured her failure at this scene.

She went to the door and looked at Ray, who was sitting on the couch leafing through *Elle* as if he found it compelling. Her body shook with laughter and he looked up, alarmed. "Oh, Ray," she gasped, "this scene won't work, will it?"

He looked up with injured dignity. "What kind of juice are you offering?"

"Grapefruit," she said, breaking into a fresh seizure, "the nonfattening kind."

"I'll take a grapefruit juice," he said with studied casualness.

She poured two grapefruit juices into crystal goblets and brought them into the living room. "Here's your nightcap," she said, and then subsided into weak laughter.

"Thanks," he said. He put the magazine down and took a sip of his juice. "For years I've been hearing about what a lavish hostess you were, ma'am, and now I find your hospitality is a bit . . . frugal."

She decided to play his game. "Actually, Mr. Parnell, that lavish hostess wasn't really me. That was Mrs. Caruso, who lived in a fancy house on the Palisades. Now, she could have offered you every exotic nightcap known to mankind."

"Hmmm, yes, I see. It's a case of mistaken identity, then. Happens all the time in my profession."

"Sorry to disappoint."

"Oh, but you don't."

"Well, that's a relief."

"Tell me, Faythe with a 'y,' are you looking forward to acting again?"

She set her glass down and sank to the carpet on her knees across from him. "I think so," she said. "I wake up full of purpose, but sometimes, as the day goes on, I lose confidence." A terrible thought assailed her. "Tell me true, Ray. If I'm just awful, a real turkey, promise me you'll fire me. Promise me you won't keep me on for old time's sake."

Ray considered, then smiled in a way that seemed to make the room grow brighter. "I would never have pressured you to be in the movie if I thought there was the remotest possibility you'd fail. I have thought of you as many things over the years, Faythe, but a real turkey has never been one of them."

"All the same, promise," she said.

"Your agent wouldn't allow it. This isn't *Horror Boardwalk,* you know."

"Promise."

"Christ," he groaned. "Do you want it in writing?"

"A verbal assurance will do."

He laid his hand on *Elle* as if on a Bible, and intoned, "I, Raymond Patrick Parnell, do hereby give my assurance that I will relieve the talent, hereafter referred to as Faythe McBain, if she should prove to be a real turkey, a total washout, an untalented, incompetent, or generally nightmarish actress, of any duties in the project known as *The Senator's Daughter*." He paused. "Will you be the witness to this legal document?"

She nodded.

He drained his glass, consulted his watch, and stood up. "Well, I won't keep you," he said. "Thanks for the nightcap."

"Thanks for a lovely dinner," she said, still in character.

She took him to the door and smiled a bright, social smile. "Tonight was really nice, Ray," she said.

"I enjoyed myself, too," was his reply, and it was so wooden, so spoken in the tones of a really bad B-movie actor, that she felt the laughter well up in her again.

"What's so damn funny?" he said.

"It's just . . . just . . . oh, Ray, it's a good

thing you never wanted to be an actor, because you're really terrible."

"Thanks for sharing, ma'am," he said, but his eyes had darkened in the way she knew so well.

Things went very still between them, and both were frozen in their positions. So close. She felt herself pulled toward him on some magnetic corridor, but she forced her body to stay motionless. It was Ray who moved toward her, so slowly it seemed to take ages. His hands came up and framed her face, gently forcing her to look up at him. Then his lips were on hers, soft and questing, barely brushing her cushioned lower lip, and his hands had moved up and were buried in her hair.

She felt herself sink against him, her breasts against the hardness of his chest, and his hands moved to her back, caressing the length of it as if they'd never been apart. She felt the old familiar warmth spread through her and wanted to moan his name. Her lips parted under his and she felt his tongue in her mouth, thrusting and imparting some desperate message.

They were both trembling. She felt the tremors in his back, and her legs seemed unsteady, as if with one more caress she would fall to the floor. Nothing had changed. She might as well be in his room at Venice, wearing her gold and silver ring. She longed for his weight, and plunged her fingers into his soft hair, drawing him closer.

She never knew who pulled away first. He made a moaning sound as their lips parted. They seemed suspended in time, breathing harshly, aware that something dangerous had happened. He was the first to speak.

"I'm sorry, Faythe. That wasn't supposed to be in the scene."

She wasn't sorry, or rather her body wasn't sorry. It knew what it wanted and told her so with painful insistency, but her mind telegraphed a different message. She felt so grateful to Ray for stopping before their kiss led to the natural conclusion. If they were to make love it would be a brief time of pleasure that would be followed by a lifetime of pain. She was too old to take Ray on his terms, enjoying the moment. She knew she would want much more of him than he was prepared to give.

"Temporary insanity," she whispered.

He remained standing in the doorway, inches away. His eyes searched hers, as if he expected her to say something else, and when she didn't he sighed and gave her a rueful smile.

"Goodnight, lovely Faythe. Goodbye for now."

She watched him get into his car and back out of her drive and continued to watch until the tail lights could no longer be seen. Then she closed the door and leaned against it, still trembling.

If the first cut was the deepest, a second of that intensity could prove nearly fatal.

The jade necklace was so beautiful she felt she had to have it, but she also wanted the sea-green Chinese jacket with black frogging. She felt greedy and unlike herself as she strolled around Gump's department store in a fever of acquisitiveness. *If Cal could see me now*, she thought, *he'd be pleased.* Here was the wife he'd always wanted, a woman who flew to San Francisco on the spur of the moment to visit her favorite store and shop till she dropped. Except, of course, she hadn't bought anything yet. She wanted it all, but every time she was on the verge of taking her credit card out she thought of the dryer that was needed at

Dove House and all the things Daisy's baby would need.

She'd passed a sleepless night and watched the dawn come up, feeling like a prisoner. All parts of Los Angeles seemed off limits to her, because she might meet Ray unexpectedly, and she couldn't bear to remain in her house. His presence seemed to linger, and even the sight of the two goblets on the coffee table made her feel weak. San Francisco appeared unbidden in her mind— city of vertiginous streets and views of the sea that suddenly appeared, like blessings, when you least expected them; Gump's, with its deluxe and exotic wares; city where she knew no one and could be on her own utterly. She'd taken the first available flight from L.A.X. and was standing in Union Square before 10:00 in the morning, watching the pigeons doing their absurd mating dance.

She had a room at the St. Francis and planned to stay for the weekend. Every moment was planned out: dinner tonight at the Washington Square Bar & Grill, her favorite restaurant in San Francisco, brunch tomorrow at Fisherman's Wharf, followed by a matinee performance of *Fool for Love* at a small theater near North Beach. Then, if time permitted, she might phone an old friend from college who lived in Marin County and see if she wanted to come in to the city.

"Excuse me, Miss," said a voice quite close. She looked up in confusion and saw a middle-aged man who was trying to get her attention. He was nicely dressed and had owlish eyebrows like her agent Barney.

"I know this will sound odd," he said apologetically, "but I wanted to ask a favor of you. I'm shopping for a birthday present for my wife, and everything's so nice here I can't seem to make up my mind. I might choose something for her, and then she'd pretend to be pleased with it even if she wasn't. See what I mean?"

"Do you want me to make suggestions?" She was pleased. Here was a harmless chore she could accomplish, and her radar told her that the man was sincere. It wasn't an elaborate maneuver to pick her up.

He smiled gratefully. "I'd just about made up my mind, and then I lost my nerve. We're here on vacation, and my plan is to surprise her with it next month. That way it'll be both a present and a reminder of our time in San Francisco."

"You're a very thoughtful husband," she said. "I hope your wife appreciates you."

He backed up a step and she saw that she'd seemed bitter to him. He was probably from a small town like Sayerville and had deliberated a long time before approaching her.

"I'll be glad to help," she said. "What had you almost decided on?"

And then, wouldn't you know it, he indicated the Chinese jacket she'd been admiring. "It's beautiful, to me, but I'd like a woman's perspective."

"I love it. I love it so much I was thinking of buying it myself."

"Well, I wouldn't want to—"

"No, don't worry. I have too many clothes. Does your wife like this color?"

He nodded. "She's about your size," he said, "although the resemblance stops there. I'm wondering about the fit." He extracted a wallet and flipped through it until he came to a photograph. "Here she is," he said fondly. "This is Milly."

Milly was a trim woman with gray hair and a pleasant smile. She wore oversized glasses and a little too much blusher. Of course you could never tell, but Faythe was willing to bet that Milly was a truly happy woman.

She lifted the jacket from the table, feeling the padded silk slip through her fingers

like cool water. Then she slipped out of the
English tweed jacket she was wearing and
asked the man to hold it. A saleswoman was
looking over at them suspiciously.

"You're going to try it on," he said jubilantly. "That's what I wanted to ask you to
do, but I didn't have the nerve."

The jacket settled around her like a puff
of pure magic. She did up the frogs and then
walked away from him, turned, and said,
"What do you think? It feels wonderful."

"It looks like a million bucks on you,
Miss. I'll be frank with you. This is the
most I've ever spent on a piece of clothing,
so I had to be sure."

She got out of the jacket and he handed
her the tweed, thanking her profusely for
being such a good sport. "Of course," he
said, blushing a little, "it'll never look on
her the way it does on you, but I think
every woman deserves something extravagant, don't you?"

"Oh, very definitely. Milly will love it.
Wish her a happy birthday for me."

She left Gump's and decided to wander
through Chinatown. She was exhausted from
her sleepless night, but she had to keep moving. They'd exchanged first names before
parting, the man holding the Chinese jacket

reverently. Bill. Bill and Milly, from Dayton, Ohio, as it turned out.

Milly was a lucky woman to have a husband who plotted so carefully to surprise and delight her, who wanted her to have something extravagant. Here was a man who still loved his wife after many years— they still existed, apparently. She didn't know of any such marriages in Hollywood, but that went without saying. She wondered, if Betsy London had lived, would Ray still love her, and then pushed Ray out of her consciousness and continued on. It was chilly here, further north, and she told herself it was kind of fun to feel cold for a change. It was natural to feel cold in November.

"Mom, where the hell have you been? I've been trying to reach you for two days."

"I'm in San Francisco. Why, what's wrong?"

"You called me," Casey said. "Do you want to tell me why?"

Because I was lonely, she thought. "I just wanted you to know where I was. I'll be back tomorrow," she said. "I felt like being alone for a few days."

"Great. Just when I needed to talk to her, she decides to go to San Francisco."

Casey sounded genuinely disturbed. Beneath her sarcastic manner Faythe could detect a younger Casey, the one who really did turn to her mother when she was in pain.

"Talk to me Case," she said. "Tell me what's got you so upset. I would never have gone away if I thought you needed me." She recalled their conversation of a few nights ago. "God, honey, it's not that hare-brained plan of your father's to get me a gun?"

Casey laughed, but it was a gulping laugh and didn't contain much mirth. "You can forget about the gun," she said. "He has, I promise you. It's a different kind of hare-brained scheme this time, and I don't think I can handle it. Are you sitting down?"

She was, in fact, sitting on the side of her bed at the St. Francis, the curtains at her window open so she could savor the lights of nighttime San Francisco.

"He wants me to have dinner with this woman, this horrible airhead woman. He thinks I should get to know her, and you know what that means. It means he's thinking of getting married again, doesn't it?"

"Not necessarily. How do you know she's horrible?"

"I ran into them at that new place, Drai's, on La Cienaga. They were coming in just as I was leaving. Her name is Renata something, and she was hanging onto his arm like a leech, making big adoring eyes at him, the whole nauseating bit. He introduced me, and that was it, but then later he called and said he wanted me to get to know her." Casey's voice dripped scorn and loathing.

"That doesn't sound so awful," Faythe said. "What was so horrible about this Renata?"

"Do you have a year? For starters, she has thick ankles and dresses like a dweeb. She was wearing a creepy suit from off some rack, and one of those blouses with bows that went out of style years ago. I think she had an image of herself as 'dressing for success,' like some hick who saw a movie with Debra Winger playing a lawyer back in the eighties. She doesn't belong in L.A. at all, in fact she had an accent like someone from Brooklyn or the Bronx— like a female Al Pacino . . ."

Casey's voice had accelerated as she piled grievance on grievance. Renata was very ethnic looking and her makeup was all wrong. She described her once more for her mother, as if the horrors of Renata had not been adequately detailed. Faythe let her rattle on, but she was appalled at Casey's snobbishness. She, too, was surprised that Cal would be escorting such an unchic woman to a new restaurant, but she thought it might mean something good for him.

"What is it?" Casey was almost shouting now. "Is it some mid-life crisis? Is he trying to go back to his roots and find a Mama Mia? I haven't even told you the worst thing, Mom. She's as old as he is. She's at least fifty."

She told Casey to calm down. She'd be home the next day and they could talk face to face. "If your father wants to get married again, it's really not our business," she said. "You're all grown up, and if he's found a woman who makes him happy, what difference does it make what she looks like? Some of the nicest women in the world look like they don't belong in L.A., honey. I admit she doesn't sound like Daddy's style, but that may be a good thing."

"Can you hear yourself? You were Dad's style. How will you feel if he marries a hideous frump who looks older than you? What would that say about you?"

Faythe covered the receiver and released

a long, shuddering sigh. "It's not about me, honey. Try not to judge people so harshly."

"If he marries her," Casey said dramatically, "my career in this town is over."

By the time she'd mollified Casey, she didn't much feel like going to the restaurant in Chinatown Juanita had told her about. Nevertheless, she freshened her makeup and rode down in the glass elevator that crawled up and down the surface of the St. Francis. In a good mood, the ride seemed exhilarating and the view of the city was superb; in a bad mood one felt like a bug trapped in an ice cube, totally vulnerable. When your life wasn't settled, there was something dreadful about being suspended hundreds of feet above the pavement. The life of the city was so far below, and she thought it a metaphor for her own life, which looked so privileged and fulfilling to a casual observer but was as far from the life she wanted as she was from the reassuring ground.

She got a taxi and settled back, pondering Casey's vitriolic words. Something wasn't right about her scenario. Unless Cal had undergone a spiritual crisis of unimaginable proportions, he was not courting a homey, unfashionable woman with an Al Pacino accent. (She made a mental note to tell Casey that Pacino only used that accent when he was playing certain characters.)

No. What was so disturbing was Casey's values, her assumption that her career would be over if she acquired a stepmother who was not "one of us."

Her eyes closed and she nearly fell asleep on Grant Street. Her sleep the night before had been fragmented and full of dreams she could not recall. San Francisco hadn't been the cure she needed.

She was jolted into complete wakefulness and found herself looking into the window of a shop that featured carp swimming in a tank. Choose your own dinner. Tourists pushed their way through the narrow streets, rubbing shoulders with the Chinese who lived and shopped there. She saw a huge golden Buddha and a lacquered red jewel box and in between the images a thought was struggling for her attention.

When she'd been young, the worst thing that could happen to a girl was her divorced father taking up with a woman only a few years older than his daughter. A sexy, juicy stepmother was something all young women dreaded. The competition! The humiliation! The dirty knowledge that Daddy wanted to sleep with someone just like you!

Casey was horrified because her supposed stepmother might not be up to the standards she'd grown up with, standards she clearly honored as much as Faythe had once honored the concepts of fidelity and decency. Something had gone very wrong along the way. Something she would have to sort out with Casey when she got home. It seemed too late for the sorting out process to occur, and she now felt guilt join the other emotions she was trying to suppress.

"Lady," said the driver. "We're here."

Eleven

Faythe avoided the mirror while Angie pinned her hair back and secured it beneath a mesh skullcap. These were not a woman's most flattering moments. The wig had been magically transformed and was now the precise color of her own hair— a golden-brown with subtle red highlights.

Angie settled it on her head and made some adjustments, combing out long strands with her dexterous fingers. "Looks great, Fay," she said. And it did. Faythe regarded herself in the mirror with pleasure. This was the look of a mythical courtesan, the Carlotta look, and with a professional makeup job she was going to look stunning.

Angie started up the wind machine and studied the effect. Faythe's scene would be shot on location, off Catalina Island, and the winds were often fierce there. The hair blew gracefully when the machine was on medium level and whipped alarmingly at the higher one, but it looked real and it looked gorgeous, and applause came from the chairs where Tara and Katherine were being made up.

They were shooting the first scenes today on the set at Century City. Not, of course, the first chronologically but the first that took place in the Madigan house in George-town, involving the senator's dysfunctional family at a Christmas party. Katherine's face was assuming the enamel perfection that was her trademark, but it was Tara's face that made Faythe stare in wonder.

The makeup man had given her enough color to suggest a kind of innocence neces-sary for the virginal Rosie at this point, and Tara's features were heartbreaking in their loveliness. Her thick, pale hair had been tinted so that she was now a strawberry blonde, and Angie had French-braided it so that Tara now looked like the pampered daughter of Washington royalty.

Ray had closed the set to visitors, but even so Tara was in her usual state of terror. She wouldn't relax until the cameras were on her, and then, Faythe hoped, she would disappear into the role and be brilliant.

She walked over to the makeup chairs and dropped on her knees beside Tara. "I got you a present in San Francisco," she said. "I forgot about your new hair color, but my heart was in the right place." She withdrew a parcel from her carrybag and laid it on Tara's lap. The girl turned wide, uncomprehending eyes on her.

"It's for me?" she said.

"It was for you when you had golden hair."

Tara opened the parcel and made a little sound of pleasure, at the black and crimson Chinese robe inside. She drew it out and held it up admiringly, but then she saw what Faythe had meant. The bright red didn't go well with her strawberry blonde hair; in fact the combination was disastrous. She laughed and said, "If I didn't know better, I'd think you were trying to make me look bad."

"Faythe would never do a thing like that," said Katherine primly.

"Jeez, Kate, I know that." Tara thanked Faythe, forcing a wan smile. "It's beautiful," she said. "I can wear it after this thing is over and I'm back to looking like myself."

Faythe took her hand. "Break a leg," she said, squeezing the slender fingers and wishing she could warm them. Tara's hands were icy, but they, too, were transformed.

False fingernails had been placed over the bitten ones, and Tara now had oval, rosy nails, polished in palest pink.

After she'd surrendered her wig and allowed Angie to repair her flattened hair, it was time to walk the short distance to her ex-husband's agency. She had promised herself to never be alone in Cal's presence again, but she owed it to Casey to confront him. When she'd called him he had sounded surprised and gratified that she needed to talk to him. He'd been gracious and smooth, but as always he'd exacted his price.

"Come to my office," he'd said. "I'll have lunch brought in."

All in all she preferred it to being seen with him in a restaurant; at least there'd be no speculation about the Carusos reconciling.

Des O'Connell was just getting off the elevator and he greeted her warmly, stooping to kiss her cheek. He smelled of extract of peppermint, and that made her worry. It was an old trick to mask the odor of alcohol. It seemed a bad omen that on the first day of shooting the two principals were terrified and quite possibly drunk, respectively.

When she entered the swank reception area of Caruso Creative she felt, as usual, that she was coming into a funeral home. The superthick carpeting that muffled footfalls, the hushed voice of the receptionist, the eggplant-colored walls and soothing lighting all hinted at some recent bereavement, but Cal was very proud of the decor and had paid a fortune to make his agency look tasteful.

Stacey was gone, and there was a new receptionist. Caruso receptionists always looked like high fashion models, and this one was no exception. She regarded Faythe with unflappable calm, her perfect features giving nothing away.

"I have an appointment with Mr. Caruso," Faythe said.

The receptionist consulted her book and nodded. "Oh, yes, Mrs. Caruso. He's expecting you. I'm Georgia."

"Hello, Georgia. I'm not Mrs. Caruso, I'm Faythe McBain."

"Oh, I thought . . . sorry." She made a charming little gesture of confusion. "I'll have someone show you to his office."

"I know the way," Faythe said. She was getting deja vu, confronting someone who was very likely her husband's current sexual partner, except Cal was no longer her husband and she didn't care who he slept with.

Down the long hall, phones twittering from all the offices in polite, cricket-like cadences, past the self-important conference room. Toward the end of her marriage a visit to Cal's office always made her feel she was walking the last mile. He had assured her she wouldn't run into Casey today. Casey was at the Beverly Hills Hotel lunching her new client, and that was a relief. She couldn't imagine quite what she was going to say to Cal about their daughter's hysteria over the Renata woman, but she had to say something. If Cal was really going to marry someone, she had to prepare Casey.

Cal was sitting behind his titan's desk when she entered the office, talking on the phone. He indicated that she should sit, that he'd only be a moment. "I'm not pleased about this, Bernie," he was saying. "Let's talk again when you have something to tell me that will bring a smile to my face."

Faythe looked around to see if anything had changed in his office, but it was much the same— relentlessly male, with big, macho abstracts on the walls, and very lavish. That little figure of a horse on one of his shelves was, as she happened to know, T'ang Dynasty. Her photo was no longer to be seen in the ormolu frame where once she and Casey were featured as proof of his domestic bliss. Now only Casey occupied that place of importance on Cal's desk. It was a new photo Faythe had never seen before, and it showed Casey in her office, feet up on her desk, the phone cradled beneath her chin. She was grinning wickedly. It was a portrait of a baby agent who knew she would swim with the sharks one day.

"Do we have an understanding?" Cal said smoothly into the phone. He hung up and said "Jerk!" Then he turned his attention to Faythe, who was sitting in one of the huge chairs that seemed to have been imported from some gentlemen's club in London.

"Hi, sweetness," he said. "Lunch is coming up shortly. Can I give you a drink? No?" He pushed a button and shouted: "No more calls, Jack."

It made Faythe smile, since his practice of hiring male secretaries had been instituted, originally, to convince her that he wasn't playing around with his employees. All it had done was cut down on the number of possibilities, since the beauteous receptionists, as well as the female agents, remained, not to mention the vast talent pool of his clients.

"Talk to me, Faythe. You look a little tired. Has this crime wave got you down?"

Casey said he'd forgotten about the gun— unlike him to forget anything he'd thought up— but she thought it best to steer the conversation away from carjackings and muggings.

"No," she said, "I spent the weekend in San Francisco and didn't get much sleep."

A glossy black eyebrow lifted itself archly. "Got a fella, huh?"

"Not that I've noticed, Cal. I only meant— " She broke off in irritation. What had she meant? Think before you speak, she instructed herself. "I'm fine, Cal. Shooting starts today, but I won't be needed for a while. I wanted to talk to you about Casey, actually."

"What about her? She's doing great. That's one little girl who knows what her priorities are about."

How like him to select the very quality for praise that she found lacking. He really did look very vital today— black hair fairly gleaming with health, a glow to his smooth, olive skin— and she wondered if he really had found someone he wanted to marry. Something had to account for this smug, radiant Cal, who looked as if he had a secret too delicious to share.

"Casey's got my sense and your class," he said. "She'll always land on her feet."

"She's upset, though," Faythe said. "She seems to think you're rushing into another marriage—"

"Another marriage! Sweetheart, you're not making sense. What's this impending marriage? Who am I supposed to be marrying?"

There was a discreet knock on the door, and Jack came in, wheeling a cart that contained covered dishes. They were silent while he arranged the plates and silver, but the moment he'd gone Cal gave an explosive sound of astonishment and repeated, "Who am I supposed to be marrying? This is ridiculous."

"Then you're not," Faythe said. "I told her she'd misinterpreted something."

Cal dug into his crabmeat salad with a vengeance, stabbing irritably with his fork. "It's like that old game, 'gossip'," he said between mouthfuls. "Somebody whispers something— I don't know, say it's 'he likes green apples'— and by the time it's gone around the circle it ends up 'Jane Doe got knocked up by the family doctor.' You know? Casey says something to you and you worry it around and the next thing I know I'm getting married."

Faythe was used to his brand of logic and waited for him to be spent. "It wasn't like that at all," she said. "Casey most definitely said she believed you were getting married. She based it on a meeting at Drai's, where you and a woman were dining."

"I can't eat out with a woman without being accused of entertaining marriage? I eat out all the time. How am I supposed to remember who I took to Drai's? How long ago was this?"

"Quite recently." She ate a bit of the salad, pondering the situation. Just because Cal said he wasn't thinking of marrying didn't mean it was true. On the other hand, he really did seem to be outraged.

"Casey never said you told her you were going to be married. What you did say was that you wanted her to get to know this woman. In Casey's book, this is tantamount to a declaration of honorable intentions."

Cal drank lustily from a glass of mineral water as if to clear his head of all this female conspiracy.

My poor Casey, she thought. *She makes the mistake of thinking that her father finds her im-*

portant, really important, instead of just his little girl who does him proud. If he says he wants her to get to know someone, she thinks it's something deep, something well thought-out and having to do with her welfare. She doesn't understand he could say it and forget it the next moment. Oh, Casey, honey, it was just something to say, *and you wove this whole drama out of nothing.*

"Try to think," she said. "Who have you been with recently, someone Casey has met, who would prompt you to say such a thing?"

He rubbed a thumb over his lower lip, an old gesture she'd once found sexy. He bent his head, simulating deep thought, but when he raised it again there was true recognition in his lively dark eyes. "Her," he said. "Whatchamacallit."

"Renata," said Faythe.

"You bet. Renata LoCasso." He winced. "Jesus, what would make her think I wanted to marry her?" He turned stricken eyes in her direction. "What's wrong with our daughter that she'd think I'd want to marry Renata LoCasso?"

She explained it again, patiently, without mentioning Casey's distaste for the woman in question.

Cal rose and began to pace around his of-fice, his thumbs hooked in the waistband of his jeans. It was a predatory, stiff-legged walk she remembered. It was vaguely, and unintentionally, humorous, like the mating dance of the pigeons she'd seen in San Francisco, but it was not without real menace. Cal was a man of physical, as well as symbolic, power, and he knew it. He was embarrassed now, and it was up to her to talk him into reason.

"Who is this Renata?" she asked.

He looked at her as if she were pulling a joke on him, and then sank back into his chair, slinging his feet up over the desk as Casey had done in the photograph.

"Don't you read the best seller list?" he asked. "No, of course not. You're beyond all that, aren't you Faythe? Renata LoCasso happens to be right at the top of that list, and she's been there for eighteen weeks. She wrote a book, okay? A book that's hopping off the shelf, called *Surviving The Dysfunctional Family: A Winner's Handbook.*"

"They're making a movie out of a self-help book?"

"Who said anything about a movie? I wasn't seeing her as a client." Cal frowned, and she knew a possibility had occurred to him. Perhaps a lucrative video in which Renata LoCasso dispensed her secrets— only after the book had run its course.

"No," he continued, "I was having lunch with her because I thought maybe I'd see her as a shrink. You could say I was auditioning her. She's a sensible woman, and that's why I suggested Casey might like to get to know her."

Now that she was no longer married to him, Cal's circular thinking amused her. She felt almost fond of him. Here was the man who had resisted marriage counseling because he said only mama's boys went in for that sort of garbage. The very fact that he would even think of letting a woman analyze him would have been unthinkable until recently. The bottom line, though, was simply that Renata was a celebrity, a success in his book, and that made her worthy.

"I didn't think you were interested in therapy," she said.

He shrugged. "In my case, and Casey's, it would be preventive medicine— help us to avoid mistakes in the future. Eighteen months on the best seller list! The woman must know what she's doing. There's a lot of stress in my job, Faythie, something you never seemed to understand."

"You know you love it," she said, teasing. "You couldn't exist without stress."

"True," he said, "very true." He stared

at her with a new expression, one of admiration. "You're a good kid," he said. "You always were. I didn't deserve you, did I?"

"I wouldn't put it like that, Cal." She couldn't bear it if he turned sentimental.

"If I see Dr. LoCasso, and that's a big if, I wouldn't want you to think it had anything to do with you. Your busting up our marriage . . . well, that hurt, but we had years together, sweetheart. They were good years, too. We had good innings."

A nicer person than I would agree with him, just to smooth things over, she thought. But she couldn't lie about those "good innings." She merely smiled.

"You don't hate me, do you Faythie?"

"Of course not," she said. "I wish you well. I'm just happier without you."

"Yeah." He gave her the crooked little grin she'd once found so seductive. "Twenty-two years, and I never figured you out."

He managed to sound proud of it.

Casey ordered a raspberry seltzer at Hugo's, the popular hangout on Santa Monica Boulevard. While Faythe explained the confusion about Renata LoCasso, Casey kept an impassive face. She was wearing what looked like a modified tennis dress, and sported dangling, jokey earrings of red plastic.

"I thought you'd be so relieved," Faythe said when her daughter remained silent. "You were horrified when you thought—"

"Mmmm," said Casey, "true. I was. I should pay more attention to the bestseller list, I guess. Thanks, Mom. Did you notice Georgia, our new receptionist? What a bitch! You should see how she acts around Dad."

"Flirtatious, is she?" *I'm sure it's mutual.*

"She's more like that character on "Saturday Night Live," Mr. Subliminal. She goes, 'Have a nice weekend, Mr. Caruso (rip my blouse off) and don't forget that early appointment Monday (throw me down right here on the carpet and ravish me).' She's outrageous."

Faythe felt herself blushing. Of all the conversations she had never wanted to have with her daughter, Cal and casual sex ranked high. "Well," she said a little primly. "Your father is a very powerful man. Ambitious women will always try to take advantage." They didn't have to try very hard, either.

"I wasn't born yesterday," Casey said. "I know he's no angel. I've heard things. Especially now that I'm in the business. People aren't very careful about what they say to me."

Faythe felt a rush of love for her daughter. She wanted to kill the people who hurt her. Didn't they know she was only twenty-one? A baby.

"You're all red in the face, Ma," Casey said. "Chill out."

"Sometimes I think I'd like to move away from this town. People have no business gossiping about your father in front of you. It's monstrous."

Casey giggled. "Monstrous? I think it's just kind of rude, that's all." She stretched luxuriously. "But living well is the best revenge, and I'm living very, very well." She indicated her dress. "This is an Ivan Sandaval, in case you didn't know. Like it?"

"It looks great on you, honey." She told Casey about Bill in San Francisco, who'd wanted her to try on the Chinese jacket.

"For God's sake, Mom, he was just trying to make a move. You are so childish sometimes!"

"Give me some credit," Faythe said briskly. "I know when a man is 'making a move' as you so charmingly put it, and this man wasn't. He was a perfectly nice guy from Dayton, who— "

"That reminds me— how could I have forgotten to tell you this?— your little friend from the sticks, Tara, has quite a history. She was a runaway, maybe, and you know what that means."

"What?"

"Well, how do most runaways end up? Little Tara was probably a hooker."

Several faces looked up in interest.

"Lower your voice." She felt a knot of nausea in her stomach and wanted to shake Casey. "Where did you hear that?"

"Oh, you know, around. It's in the air."

"Don't repeat it, Casey. Don't help it to get out, do you hear me? I don't believe she was a prostitute, not for a moment, but if she was forced to some rash acts she deserves your compassion, not your contempt."

"She deserves my compassion? Get a grip. She doesn't deserve anything from me. What's she ever done for me?"

"Casey, darling, you sound like a cruel, spoiled brat when you talk like that. I know you're not, but you seem determined to act as unfeeling and cold as you possibly can. Did I ever let you think it was all right to despise people just because they were unfortunate? For heaven's sake, she's a human being, she's your age, and she's trying to make something of herself. If this ugly rumor becomes public, it could ruin her chances."

"Why? She wouldn't be the first whore to star in a miniseries." Casey smiled sweetly. "It may even help her. Think of the publicity."

"It would be devastating, and you know it. She's a fragile girl— "

Casey snorted. "Yeah, right. Fragile little Tara, who's probably sleeping with Ray Parnell."

"Is that another rumor?" Her voice was steady.

"No, but it makes sense, doesn't it? How else did she get the part— a nobody, an actress no one's ever heard of?"

"She happens to be a very good actress."

"Whatever." She consulted her watch. "Gotta run, Mom."

Faythe grabbed her daughter's hands, preventing her from getting up. "I want you to promise me that you won't repeat that rumor. I mean it."

Casey rolled her eyes comically. "That won't keep it from surfacing," she said, as if speaking to a child, "but if it means so much to you, okay, I won't repeat it. Satisfied?"

Faythe nodded, but she was far from satisfied. She watched Casey walk out of Hugo's, her absurd little designer dress twitching as she stalked away, and wondered if she and Cal had created a monster.

She was watching an old Barbara Stanwyck movie when the drone of a motorcycle could be heard, an unusual sound in Santa Monica. It came closer and closer until, making a noise like a chain saw, it seemed about to drive through the walls of her house. She jumped up and immediately there came a tapping at the door, as if whoever was out there didn't understand about doorbells. She went to a window and saw someone with strawberry blond hair, clad entirely in black leather, standing at her door.

"Tara!" she cried, opening her door in a rush. "What a surprise."

"I should have called first." It was a flat statement. She looked very pale without her makeup, but she seemed exhilarated and jumpy. Beyond her, in Faythe's yard, a skinny youth with longish, dirty blond hair sat astride a Harley. Of course, it was the same Harley on which Tara had arrived at Casey's housewarming.

"Come in," said Faythe. "Your friend, too." She wasn't thrilled about the boy on the Harley, but he was much too slight to be an outlaw biker, a Hell's Angel, wasn't he?

"He doesn't want to come in," Tara said. She turned to him. "Come back in fifteen, okay?"

The chain saw noise started up again and Tara stepped into the house. "Oh, Barbara Stanwyck," she said. "Cool." Faythe snapped the remote off.

"If I'm disturbing you . . ." Tara looked uncomfortable now, as if she were regretting this impulse call.

"Not at all, I'm glad to see you." She sat on the couch and told her guest to have a seat. "Want some tea or juice?"

Tara sank to the floor in one graceful motion and grinned. "I notice you're not offering me Stoli," she said. "That's fine, though, I don't want anything to drink. I've got two scenes first thing in the morning."

"I guess everything went well today on the set."

"It did, but how did you know?"

"You seem excited. Beyond that, elated. I remember how that felt, to know you should go to sleep and be fresh for the morning, but instead you wanted to do something wild. Like go for a ride on a motorcycle. I used to dance for hours to get tired enough to go to bed."

"Well, well," Tara said, "you always surprise me, Mrs. McB. Okay, Faythe. That's exactly the way I feel, and I thought I'd have Roger bring me here to thank you for buying me that present. That was a really nice thing to do for someone you hardly know."

"You're very welcome. You didn't have to send Roger away, though. Is he your boyfriend?"

Tara hooted, studying the toe of her Doc Martens. "Nooo," she said, "just a friend. More like a brother. You don't know what it's like getting around this town without a car. I'm getting one with my first paycheck, though."

There was a silence then, but Faythe didn't make small talk. She had an idea that Tara didn't mind silence just now.

"It's nice here," she said. "Homey. Whenever I stay at Kate's I'm always afraid I'll break something, you know? I used to think her bidet was a special place to wash your feet. Dumb? They didn't make them much dumber than yours truly when I first got here.''

''I think I could have given you a run for your money,'' Faythe said. ''I didn't know anything, either.''

Tara began to zip and unzip her leather jacket nervously, and then, aware of how compulsive she seemed, she laced her hands over her knees. ''I want this so much,'' she said. ''I want to be good in this movie. The odds against someone like me landing a role like this are . . . well, it must be a million to one, don't you think?''

Faythe nodded judiciously. ''Yes, it's unusual, but not unheard of. You're extravagantly talented, and that makes all the difference. You're not just some kid, like I was, brought out to Hollywood on the whim of a talent scout.''

Tara looked stricken. ''How do you know?'' she asked.

Faythe remembered then. Casey had said the girl had come here as the result of just such a coincidence. It was when she'd said Tara came from a ''nonstate.''

''However you got here, the point is that you have the ability to become a major actress.''

''I know,'' Tara said in a voice so low it

was nearly inaudible. "That's what makes it so terrifying. If I screw up, if I ruin this, I wouldn't ever be able to forgive myself. You don't understand. You think it's just words, but it's more."

"I know it's more, Tara. You choose your words very carefully. You aren't going to screw up, honey. It may feel like it some days, but believe me, it's going to be all right."

But Tara seemed not to have heard her. "I wouldn't be able to forgive myself," she repeated. "I wouldn't be able to live with it."

Faythe heard *I wouldn't be able to live* and went to sit beside Tara on the floor. Tentatively, she reached out and touched the shoulder beneath the black leather, and found it stiff and unyielding. She stroked the arm of the jacket, refusing to be rebuffed. "Tara," she said. "When you're very young you think the end of the world is coming whenever something terrible happens. Then, somehow, the world goes on until the next terrible thing, and then you believe all over again that it's the end. After a few times, though, you notice that it didn't end, after all, and you're still here."

"Who wants to live like that?" Tara cried.

"Just endless pain but you survive? For what? For what?"

"To see how the story ends. To live your life. Pain gets different as you get older. It's still there, but you've survived it so many times it's not so frightening anymore. And there are all the good things, the happy moments. Sometimes they're so simple, like watching an old Barbara Stanwyck movie, and other times they're more intense, but they do exist. I don't know if anyone is happy anymore, in the old sense, but that was always a lie, anyway. The Constitution guarantees us the right to the pursuit of happiness."

"That's kind of like guaranteeing a carrot to a donkey, when you know the carrot's on a string, and it will always be out of reach."

Faythe laughed in sheer amazement. "How do you know that old expression about the donkey and the carrot?" she asked. "It was an old one when I was your age."

"I've got an inquiring mind," Tara said deadpan. "Only I read *Time* and *Newsweek* instead of the *Enquirer*. Whenever they talk about Congress, they mention the donkey and the carrot."

"I know you think I'm bossy, Tara, but I just have to give you a hug for that. You're

such a smart, funny girl I can't help myself.
I'm sorry, but here it comes."

She put both arms around the black
leather jacket and squeezed gently. She
could smell the residue of the makeup Tara
had washed off and the odor of the hair-
spray in her French braid, but beneath it
she could smell the clean, lemony aroma of
the soap Tara used. It was innocent and
childish— Tara's real essence.

She endured Faythe's embrace without
flinching, but she did not return it. She sat
passively, like an idol on the carpet.

"Thanks," she said. "Thank you, Faythe."

Then the sound of the Harley, a high,
thin whine, filled the room as it came steadily closer on a torrent of ear-splitting noise.
Faythe thought, briefly, of her neighbors.

"Gotta go," Tara said, jumping to her
feet.

Faythe looked at the tumble of hair shield-
ing the fragile skull. She knew she shouldn't
ask but couldn't prevent herself.

"Shouldn't you be wearing a helmet?" she
asked.

Tara looked at her with affection and
laughed as if Faythe had proposed something
truly outlandish. "You're such a mother,"
she said in a stern voice.

It was the only time in their brief acquaintance that Tara had reminded her of Casey.

Twelve

The cast of *The Senator's Daughter* was becoming, in the first week of shooting, like an odd little family. In some cases— Bev Redfox and Dirk had begun "seeing" each other— it was an incestuous family. Faythe often attended the rushes, at Ray's invitation, but except for that gesture toward her, Ray had withdrawn from the cast in any capacity but that of director. He would not socialize with any of them again until the project was wrapped.

The others, though, seemed to crave each other's society and had constant informal parties out at Malibu or at Kate's. Des was the Daddy and Kate the Mommy of their little family, and the younger actors— Tara, Bev, Ty, and Dirk— the children. Faythe was the glamorous young aunt, much in demand, and never left out. By rights, they ought to have been sick of each other, but Katherine explained that when a project was going especially well, as this one was, the actors needed to remain together. If things had been in chaos, she said, they would all flee the set as soon as possible, but success made them want to celebrate.

Soon everyone but Faythe would be going on location to Montana, where they would remain until after Thanksgiving. They were even shooting the English scene in Montana, since all it required was a large tree and the exterior of a house that could look like an English manor. Faythe felt a little lonely, knowing they would all be off in Big Sky country while she cooled her heels in Los Angeles, and the prospect of spending Thanksgiving alone was a little daunting. It would be the first time since she had married Cal that she didn't have to prepare for a huge holiday celebration. Casey was flying down to Puerta Vallarte with two friends from the agency, and it was one of the busiest times of the year for Juanita, so it looked as if Faythe McBain, the Comeback Queen, would spend the day catching up on her reading.

She sat under her jacaranda tree at the beginning of Thanksgiving week, remembering Thanksgivings at the Palisades house, particularly the ones when Casey was old enough to be at the table with them. There was Casey at five, wearing an old-fashioned velvet dress with a lace collar, big-eyed at her first formal dinner with the grown-ups. It was Thanksgiving for twelve, all of them heavies in the industry, and their wives.

"Why aren't they home with their own families?" Casey had wanted to know.

"Well, sometimes it's nice to be invited somewhere else where you don't have to do all the work." A perfectly normal response in most circumstances, but the child could see that her mother wasn't exactly knocking herself out in the kitchen, arms in a turkey up to the elbow. Mommy had a cook and additional staff to do the work. Even the flowers were professionally arranged. Mommy had other tasks, such as making sure she seated everyone without disastrous results. You wouldn't want to place Vi Charteris next to Teddy Stone, for example, because even though they were willing to act civilly in a large room, they hated each other. Vi hated Teddy because he had once behaved inappropriately to her fourteen-year-old daughter, and Teddy hated Vi because she knew.

Or, to take another example, you wouldn't want to put Stella Franks next to Daddy at the head of the table, because Stella was notorious for liking to fool around beneath the table, and Daddy was so very receptive to such games. None of her answers were the kind you could tell a child, and so she had answered Casey with little half-truths and banal clichés. What if her own daughter had known, even at five, that Mommy was a liar? She wouldn't have known why, of course, only that her mother didn't provide truthful answers.

They'd had goose instead of turkey that time, when Casey was in the red velvet and overexcited. "I hate it!" she screamed after her first bite. "I hate this goose."

Faythe had told her there were plenty of other things she could eat, so many her plate couldn't hold them all, but Casey had been inconsolable. "I want turkey," she'd said, her lower lip beginning to tremble. No one paid any attention to the little drama at their end of the table, and eventually Faythe took her away. They assembled a plate of things Casey liked in the kitchen, and then she was allowed to go up and eat them, picnic-style, in her own room.

"Okay, honey? Tomorrow we'll have some turkey, how's that?"

"Sure." She'd nodded happily. Then she'd

spontaneously hugged her mother, planting
something sticky on her St. Laurent dress.

The problem was, she should never have
been expected to dine with them in the first
place. Cal loved to show off his pretty little
daughter, to make much of her when the
drinks and canapés were going round earlier. Casey had fulfilled her obligation long
before they ever sat down at the table, and
wasn't required any longer. She wasn't a
spoiled child who stamped and pouted, not
normally, but Faythe thought her behavior
at the table had come out of her confusion.

They'd compromised in the next few years.
Casey would make an appearance, always
dressed beautifully, and then be whisked off
by a nanny to have her Thanksgiving picnic
upstairs. Often, Faythe had wished she could
go with them.

When Casey grew old enough to join them
at large dinners, she was always seated at her
father's right hand. Even as a slightly sullen
teenager she rose to the occasion, laughing
at Cal's jokes, darting little looks at him to
make sure he appreciated her loyalty. She
was still capable of being affectionate to her
mother, but it was a condescending affection
and had none of the desperate desire to

please she showed in her behavior to her father.

These Thanksgivings had gone on, year
after year, sometimes with many guests and
once or twice just the three of them. Never
once, she realized, had she felt anything but
tense. She, who had so much to be thankful
for, had always dreaded Thanksgiving, and
now she was alone and dreaded that, too.

She had toyed with the idea of taking Tim
up on his invitation, but she needed an excuse to go to New York. It wouldn't be fair
to him to let him think she was coming to
see him; that, alone, could not be her excuse.
Casey accused her of being naive about men,
but even she knew you didn't fly three thousand miles without giving a man ideas.

The more she thought about New York,
the more it appealed to her. It would be
cool and festive in New York, the start of
the holiday season. She had stayed at the
Plaza with Cal, early in their marriage, and
had fond memories of the stately Oak
Room and the breathtaking views of Central Park.

She called the airlines, realizing she'd left
it too late and they'd be fully booked, but
she got a flight on the Tuesday before
Thanksgiving, tomorrow, with no difficulty.

Next the hotels. No luck at the Plaza, but the chic new Paramount had a room for her. She was just in time, there'd been a cancellation.

Now for the excuse. She dragged a big stack of *Variety* papers out from a pile which was waiting to be recycled. She leafed through the ones that were several months old, locating names she knew, and then tracked them to more recent issues. Too bad, she thought when she saw that a revival of a Noel Coward play had closed in late October. Too bad because an old acquaintance, a woman called Marita Gordon, had been playing the lead.

She hit pay dirt when she came to an article about a two character play that was having a limited run at the Helen Hayes. The younger woman was being played by a New York actress whose fame had not yet penetrated to Hollywood, but the older role was filled by no other than Faythe's old pal, Tiger Markowitz. The actress in question was referred to here as Tilda Marks, but she knew it had to be Matilda Markowitz. The age was right, and so was the reference to the actress's characteristic, smoky voice.

Even at the age of nineteen, Tiger had sounded like a woman who'd been smoking three packs of cigarettes for forty years. In fact, she didn't smoke at all but had nodules on her vocal chords, reputedly like those that once turned demure June Allyson into America's baritone sweetheart. She'd been talking like that for so long that the voice remained long after an operation had freed her of the nodules.

She'd been a child of Hollywood, the daughter of a successful entertainment attorney, and she'd hung around with Faythe and the other "serious" young actors of her generation for a lark. They all called her Tiger for her growl, but in fact she had been a very sweet young woman. They'd all known she was not destined to become a serious actress— Tiger herself had known it— and then she'd disappeared to New York, married a television producer, and resurfaced some years later as the star of many TV commercials.

"My God, it's Tiger," Faythe would think whenever the goofy, growling voice complained of odor in her kitty litter box or purred about how warm and toasty she felt in her new fall outfit from the Burlington Coat Factory. And now, apparently, she'd fooled them all, because she was on Broadway.

Faythe called the Helen Hayes in New York and got two tickets for the Friday night performance of *Off Key Duet*.

She had her excuse and called Tim, who said he was grading mid-term papers and seemed bowled over at her news. No, he had no special plans for the holiday, other than the flexible, casual ones that could easily be rearranged. His wife and children would be in Missouri, visiting her mother, and he had resigned himself to a lonely long weekend.

"Are you sure you don't mean a blissful long weekend?" she asked.

"I might have said that before you called, but bliss would have been an overstatement. I can't tell you how happy I am that you're coming."

She could hear the sound of papers being shifted at his end. He really was grading papers. How nice, how refreshing it was, to know that a man was doing exactly what he said he was doing, performing a humble task without feeling the need to glorify it.

"Listen to this," he said, chuckling. "Pinned to this student's paper is a note. It says: 'Dear Professor Brady. This is to explain why I am not following the assignment, which is to analyze the role of for-

eign agents in the American Revolution.
To do so would be, I feel, highly judgmental. Instead I am submitting the en-
closed paper on the Revolution as
experienced by a humble candlemaker in
the Massachusetts Bay Colony'."

Faythe laughed. "Doesn't want to be judgmental," she mused. "That's a good way of
getting out of doing the work."

Again the riffling of papers. "Oh, Christ,"
said Tim, "I don't believe this. It's fiction!
Here's the humble candlemaker, pondering
on sexism in the eighteenth century." He
groaned. "Help, Faythe. Hurry out and prevent me from going round the bend."

"Are you asking someone from Hollywood to come inject you with a dose of reality? Dream on. I'll just bring my own
brand with me and hope it distracts you."

It was fun to banter with him, and she'd
nearly reached the end of the conversation
before she remembered her excuse for coming to New York. She told him about Tiger
and said she couldn't pass up the chance to
see her on Broadway, said she hoped he'd
come with her.

"Oh," he said, sounding a little chastened. "You were coming anyway." She let
it pass. "Bring lots of changes of clothes,"

he warned her. "It was 63 two days ago, but today it's near freezing. They're predicting snow, but you never know."

"You never know," she agreed.

There were purple shadows in Central Park heralding the early dusk, and the trees were bare now, their limbs forming an intricate lacework against the darkening sky. She was walking east on Central Park South, savoring the feeling of being in a place that was utterly foreign to her. She hadn't been in New York as anything but a jumping-off place for somewhere else in years, and the changes saddened her.

Earlier, walking through midtown, she could see that the Great White Way was no longer great. An area of sleaze permeated the theater district, and where once there had been theaters and jazz clubs, X-rated movie houses and nude dancing parlors had sprung up. Everyone seemed to be hustling— playing the old shell game meant to fool the tourists and strip them of their money or selling stolen goods and trying to palm them off as Rolexes. There was no eye contact. People slithered past each other, intent on their own shabby business, and the few legitimate theaters seemed to be showing musicals that had been around for years.

She'd walked past the Helen Hayes to make sure that Tilda Marks was indeed Tiger Markowitz, and the still photos had reassured her. But even here, on the side streets, there were sad beggars dressed in foul layers of clothing who shook Dixie cups in your face to try to coax change.

She had wandered uptown toward her meeting with Tim at the Oak Bar of the Plaza Hotel, and here on Central Park South the decline of New York took on a distinct character. On the south side of the broad street, it was exactly as she had remembered. Beautifully dressed women and men poured out of the Essex House and the St. Moritz, where doormen swiftly summoned taxis if limos weren't already waiting. The women wore silver fox coats and minks, and all the men seemed to have the kind of permanent tan so familiar to her from the West Coast. The only odor in the air was that of the horses who pulled carriages through the park, mixing with the scents of Joy and Poison and Calvin Klein that wafted from the furs and wools and cashmeres of the fortunate few.

Across the street, on the park side, it was a very different story. Drug dealers huddled in shabby knots, calling out their wares in shifty voices, and homeless people shuffled by on feet made huge by layers of cardboard. She had passed on Seventh Avenue what appeared to be a bundle of filthy rags laid out on a subway grating; a closer inspection revealed an ulcerated foot poking up and out of the mass of discarded cloth.

She supposed it was no worse than what you could find along the Strip at home, except for the extremes of temperature, but she was sad to see this evidence of poverty and hopelessness.

In L.A. you passed these human tragedies in your car. Here— unless you were a tourist or Donald Trump— you walked right by them every day. Maybe that fact would be New York's salvation, because if you had to have such horror shoved down your throat every day you might determine to do something about it.

She felt both depressed and exhilarated. New York was still where it all happened, no matter what people like Cal said. In New York you weren't automatically insulated once you became a success. Des O'Connell could spend his whole time in the Cultural

Dessert without ever having to witness any hint of life as the have-nots lived it, but let him come to New York to star in a play on Broadway! The greatest privilege, the sweetest deal, the longest limo— none of them could shield you in New York.

Dressed in long, flat-heeled suede boots, she wore only a heather-colored Scottish cape over her tight pants and cashmere turtleneck, and she was perfectly warm. Those women exiting the posh hotels in their furs wore them for all the world as if they were in the Yukon, preparing to walk through sub-zero temperatures to their waiting cars. It was all for show, and fair enough, Faythe knew about show, but now she was miles from home and didn't have to prove anything to anybody.

She felt years younger and wonderfully free and hurried toward Fifth Avenue in the deepening twilight, her heart lighter than it had been for months. Correction: make that years.

The Tavern on the Green had been closed when she was last in New York and had seemed a dim memory of a bygone era. Now it was a bustling concern again, and it was where Tim had decided to take her for Thanksgiving dinner.

"Not for the food," he'd told her. "For the fun of it. For food I'm going to take you to my special restaurant on Third Avenue."

She thought he'd chosen exactly right. Tens of thousands of tiny lights were woven in the branches of the trees outside the Tavern, and it was constructed in such a way that the trees seemed to be inside. The room was large and festive and packed with other people who'd decided to pass on the traditional turkey at home. "Probably," Tim said, "not a single one is a New Yorker."

He was wearing a Brooks Brothers suit and looked more solid and prosperous than she remembered him. She had dressed for the occasion, sensing that he wanted her to look like a movie star. It didn't offend her, because he wanted it for his own private pleasure and not to score points. It was wonderful to eat in a restaurant and know that every other diner was a stranger. She told him so.

"You mean you can never eat out without seeing someone you know?" he asked.

"Never," she said. "The whole purpose of restaurants in Hollywood is so people can see you. That, and doing business."

"Well," he said uncertainly, "there are places like that here, too. Le Cirque, Mortimer's, the Four Seasons— "

"Spare me," she said. "They'd be just like Spago all over again. If I never dine at Spago again, I won't miss it. This place is just fine, and the one on Third Avenue sounds like heaven."

"Forgive me for getting all gooey, but you look like something from heaven." He lowered his voice. "These women in their expensive dresses and jewels probably spent hours trying to look fantastic, and then you come in in a simple silvery dress and blot them out. You're like a hundred-watt bulb in a room full of sixties."

She smiled and sipped her wine. Her simple silvery dress was in fact a pricey item from the designer floor at Bullocks, but if he wanted to think of her as an artless beauty, why not? From the moment she'd met him at the Oak Bar, the day before, she'd known she'd made the right choice. It felt good to be with a man who offered her unqualified admiration and affection, and if her pleasure was shallow or vain, so be it. She was eating lamb for Thanksgiving, not turkey, and maybe there was a message in that, too. Tim was younger than she was and less experienced in many ways, but he was also the kind of man she'd never known in her adult life. Maybe it was time to start knowing more people like Tim Brady, and if the rest of this long weekend felt as good, she fully expected to know Tim Brady in the Biblical sense.

"How's your daughter?" he asked, pouring a little more of the excellent Valpolicella into her glass.

Loyalty clashed in her with the need to talk to someone about Casey. The need to talk won out, and she found herself describing her encounter with Casey in Hugo's, leaving nothing out but Tara's identity.

"It sounds to me," he said, "as if she's jealous of the other girl. Jealous of your concern for her."

"But she was badmouthing her even before I met the girl. For a time I even thought it might have something to do with Cal, my former husband, but it turns out they've never even met."

"Well," said Tim reasonably, "maybe she was just being catty initially, and then when you met the girl and obviously liked her . . . you see what I mean? Casey's dislike of her grew in proportion to your affection for her. Girls that age, women I should say, very young women, are so self-absorbed. She may even think you've taken up with this woman to spite her, to show you have no faith in her instincts about people."

"Do you mean I owe it to her to cold-shoulder this— let's give her a name." She thought of what Tara had told O'Connell. "Let's call her Karin."

Tim recoiled visibly. "Let's not," he said. "We'll call her Ms. X, shall we?"

"It sounds like a remedy for upset stomach, but why not? Ms. X, then, do I have to pretend to dislike her to please my daughter? I don't think I could do that, not for anyone."

He smiled at her and shook his head. "Of course not," he said. "Just don't rub her nose in it. I'm sure Casey's jealous, and you're the key."

"But how? Why?" She felt impatient, and she also wondered why he'd reacted so strongly to the name Karin.

"I'm a historian, not a psychologist, but I put myself in Casey's place and what do I see? I see that my mother is an artist and my father is a businessman. I go in for his line of work, do well, and get lots of strokes from Daddy. Mom is affectionate and genuinely caring, but she doesn't seem to appreciate how well I'm doing."

Faythe's hands rose to cover her mouth, because the simplicity of it was terrifying.

"Then," he continued, "along comes Ms. X, a 'nobody' by her reckoning, but Ms. X is an artist who apparently is being recognized at a very early age. Mom gives her lots of strokes— even admires her! Here I— I'm still Casey— am, someone who's done everything by the book. I've gone to college, got myself a job, I can take care of myself. But who does Mom go on about all the time? A runaway, someone who, in my eyes, didn't play it by the book, hung out on the Strip, took drugs, maybe. And don't forget the possibility that Ms. X might have been a lady of the night. I'm prudish like many young people— "

"Please go back to the third-person, Tim. It makes me skittish when you assume the role of my daughter."

"Right. You get the point, I'm sure. And the one thing that makes it worse, that makes it really hurt?"

She felt like a student in one of his seminars, but of course she knew the answer, had always known without examining it. "The fact that Casey will never know if she could have succeeded on her own without daddy's agency behind her. The fact that the other girl appears to be succeeding against overwhelming odds."

"Right again," said Tim.

She wanted to talk to Casey right away, to hold her if Casey would allow it, but she was somewhere in Mexico.

They lingered for a while, enjoying the spectacle of no fewer than three birthday cakes emerging from the kitchen, and three sets of people singing "Happy Birthday" to a surprised and flustered diner at their table. One of the birthday girls was sitting near them, and Faythe lifted her glass and smiled at the woman. "Three birthdays in one room," she said to Tim, "and we like to think we're originals."

"You are, anyway," he said.

It had begun to snow when they left Tavern on the Green, tiny flakes with no more substance than a champagne bubble, the swirling drops making dizzying patterns against the myriad lights. She took Tim's arm as they walked west, out of the park. How had she failed to see anything so clear-cut as the situation he had imagined for her? The disapproval she felt for Cal had become so pervasive over the years it was surely crystal clear to Casey, despite the fact that Faythe never permitted herself to speak badly of him.

"When Casey was small, about nine, she wanted to be a ballerina. We'd taken her to see *The Nutcracker*, the usual thing at Christmas, and it didn't do a thing for her." She looked up at Tim and saw that he was listening intently.

"Well, one day I found her watching *Swan Lake* on public television, and she was in tears. 'It's so beautiful, Mommy,' she said. 'That's what I want to do'." Her heart almost stopped, remembering the rapt look on Casey's face, the emotion the ballet had generated in her making her seem both exalted and vulnerable.

"I enrolled her in a class in Beverly Hills, but it became obvious that it wasn't the class for her. Nine is late to start, if you're serious about the dance, and Casey wasn't up to the level of girls her age. Some of them had been studying since they were four.

"I began to look around for other classes, but then Cal stepped in and took over. Before I knew what he was doing, he'd converted one of our rooms to a dance studio. One whole wall was mirrored, and there was a barre for her to do her exercises, or whatever they call it in ballet. He hired an old Russian woman, Natalia, one of those amazing creatures with black hair pulled back so tightly it made her eyes disappear. Madame Natalia might have been forty or a hundred, it was impossible to tell. She claimed to have danced with the Ballet Russe de Monte Carlo, and she moved in with us and vowed to make a dancer out of Casey even if it killed her. She didn't actually say that, but when she murmured 'it vill take much vork' my blood ran cold.

"Casey was willing. More than willing. Cal bought a grand piano for the dance studio, and I could hear it thumping out these punishing cadences while Casey was at the barre. She got so thin and drawn and intense, but every time I tried to tell her it wasn't a matter of life or death she got insulted to the marrow of her bones."

They were walking uptown along Central Park West. The streets seemed deserted on this holiday evening, although it wasn't very late. She could feel the snow in her hair and the warmth of Tim's body where they were joined.

"Well?" he spoke in outraged tones. "What happened? Don't just leave me hanging, ma'am."

"Well, the usual, I guess. Casey wasn't cut out to be a ballerina, or even a very competent *corps de ballet* girl. Madame Natalia made it very clear to me. 'The child has no talent,' she told me one day, after she'd been teaching her for months. 'The heart is there, and she is villing to vork, but without the God-given gift there is no possibility. Cassandra vill never be a dancer'."

"Casey is short for Cassandra?" Tim asked.

"No, she was christened Casey. Madame Natalia called her Cassandra, insisted on it. Anyway, I was heartbroken for her and relieved, all at the same time. You must understand, no one ever told her she had no talent. We all made excuses, said maybe she'd started too late, but she knew. She seemed to take it very well. Too well. Whenever I'd try to comfort her she'd get embarrassed. Madame Natalia vanished, with a fat severance check, and was never heard from again. To my knowledge, my daughter has never gone to the ballet from that day to this."

"And the dance studio? The grand piano?"

"Cal turned it into a video room with lots of those horrible games that burble and shriek. Entertainment from Hell. Casey loved it when she got to be a teenager, or she said she did. We auctioned off the piano for some charity, since we already had one. Some out-of-towner paid a bomb for it, and the proceeds went to a home for indigent actors."

Tim laughed, plumes of frosty air issuing from his mouth. "Tales of Hollywood," he crowed. "I love it."

"We're real people, too," Faythe said, feeling the irritation reserved for the impossibly privileged.

"I know," he said, bending to plant a kiss on her cold nose. "Don't I know it."

On 67th Street they went into the Cafe Des Artistes for a nightcap. In the mellow light the famous murals from the 1920s were both innocent and erotic. The gamboling nymphs presided over the rooms like mythic objects of desire, their perfect breasts and rosy nipples always in evidence, waiting to be noticed.

She felt warm and a little sleepy as they sat at a table near the windows, watching the snow swirl harmlessly over 67th Street. Everything was advancing exactly as she had hoped it would. Tim hadn't tried to see her up to her hotel room or invited her to his apartment. He had been the "perfect gentleman" of legend, but there was a warmth between them that went beyond affection, and she could sense that it was coming to a boil.

Tomorrow they would go to the play and afterward to his favorite restaurant. It would happen the next day, Saturday, she thought. He had wanted to make her a meal, claiming to be an excellent cook, and so Faythe McBain would go to the Village apartment of Timothy Brady, ten years her junior, and that was where she might embark on her first affair since the birth, and death, of her marriage.

"You seem very far away," he said, and she nearly jumped at the sound of his voice. She grasped for something to say and came up with the name Karin.

"You were so affronted when I said the name," she said. "I guess there was a Karin in your past."

Tim buried his face in his hands dramatically and moaned. "Oh God," he said. "Karin. She put me through more agony than any woman I've ever known. I can't stand to hear her name, even now."

She felt a little pique, since the last thing she'd expected was a ghost from his past to wander into Cafe Des Artistes and cast her shadow on an affair that hadn't even begun yet.

"Do you want to tell me about her?" She hoped he didn't, but he uncovered his face and looked at her with real zeal.

"What can I say about Karin? She was so splendid, so beautiful and unique. When I let go of her a part of my life went with her. Not a day passes that I don't remember her in some way. She's like a phantom limb. She's gone, but I still feel the pain."

She tried not to let her eyes widen under this barrage of B-movie dialogue. The warmth she'd been feeling for him was receding fast, but she tried to hold onto it. She composed her face in sympathetic lines and waited to see if he'd say more. Slowly, he sat up straight again and crinkled his eyes in a wry smile. He tossed his head back and forth as if trying to exorcise a demon and then bent forward again.

"Karin," he said in a confidential murmur, "was the title of my novel. My one and only. I was so sure I was writing the great American novel of my generation. I'd planned to be the kind of novelist who quietly teaches history and then, every two years or so, rocks the world on its heels with fiction that just won't let go. I used to sit up late and imagine reviews in the *New York Times* and clever things I'd say on talk shows."

She bit her lip to repress a gust of laughter. "What happened?" she asked gently. "What happened to *Karin?*"

"Simple," he said "Nobody wanted her. She was rejected by twenty publishers. It was a little like your daughter and her ballet lessons. I had the heart and the will, but I just didn't seem to have the talent."

She slid her hands over his and worked her fingers up under the sleeves of his jacket to stroke his wrists. "Who says so?" she asked loyally. "Everybody knows publishers just want to make a mint. Maybe they couldn't take a chance on your Karin because she wasn't commercial enough?"

"It's nice of you to say so, but the truth is that the novel wasn't very good. It was your typical young man's jabbering. The publishers were right."

"Can I read it?"

"Thank God you can't," he said. "I burned *Karin* ten years ago. I don't want to be a novelist anymore, but I don't regret giving it a try."

His eyes clouded over, as if he sensed they shouldn't be discussing his youthful failure.

* * *

The apartment was on Perry Street, in the heart of the West Village. Tim said he kept it instead of looking for something better because he could walk to work, and he said it apologetically, as if to excuse the lack of what he called "creature comforts."

Faythe was enchanted by the four rooms and felt transported back in time. No sauna. No ice-maker. No walk-in closets. The living room seemed miniature to her, even by her new, Santa Monica standards, but it was nicely furnished and had a wood-burning fireplace. The floors were old, with wideboards sanded and polished so that they gleamed around the edges of a Peruvian rug.

In the room he used for a study he'd built floor-to-ceiling bookcases, and they were crammed with books that she knew were well-read and not bought by the yard. She did not go into the bedroom but exclaimed over the kitchen, which alone of all the rooms had been modernized. It was larger than the living room and had a big butcher block table and workspace and a Welsh dresser.

He'd lit a fire that smelled deliciously of

pine cones and smiled at her delight with his rent-stabilized and far too small apartment. She was, he told her, like a princess exclaiming over a model cottage.

"That looks like a real Bonnard," she said, indicating the painting that hung near the fireplace.

"Not on a teacher's salary," he said. "It's by Denis Binet." He handed her a glass of wine and watched intently as she sat in the best chair, curling her legs up under her. "On a certain level," he said, "I can't believe you're really here."

"Come on," she said. "It's not as if you were having Elizabeth Taylor over for dinner."

"A thousand times better, Faythe."

"After that disaster yesterday I'm surprised you're willing to cook for me," she said. They both laughed, remembering how awful *Duet Off Key* had been— a watered down version of *'Night, Mother.* A blatant ripoff. To make matters worse, a slip of paper in their programs informed them that the role of Madge would be performed by the understudy. Tilda Marks, it seemed, had the flu. They'd wanted to leave at the intermission, but a professional courtesy kept Faythe in her seat to the bitter end.

Tim's little restaurant had saved the evening, serving up the best paella she had ever tasted, and they'd laughed themselves weak trashing *Duet Off Key,* improvising further terrible lines the playwright might have added.

Tim selected a CD and suddenly the room was flooded with the haunting sounds of High Andes music. Ghostly pipes and flutes combined to create a music she had never heard before.

"Funny thing," he said. "There are some guys who play this exact same music at the Columbus Circle stop on the subway. They're street musicians. They play for coins."

She had never felt further away from home, not even in Italy or the West Indies. Wherever she had gone with Cal, it was always in luxury, all first-class and five-star, so that after a while every place seemed the same. "I feel so happy today," she told him, and then, seeing the look on his face, she adopted a brisk tone and asked, "What's for dinner?"

"The only thing I know how to cook well," he said. "Chinese. Tonight's menu features shrimp with black bean sauce and stir-fried vegetables. I'll be serving you tonight, and my name is Tim."

"Aren't you going to tell me to enjoy my meal?"

She could hear him moving about in the kitchen, taking down the wok and lining up utensils. Then came the sound of a knife rapidly slicing something on a board. She liked a man who wasn't afraid to be efficient in a kitchen. Cal had been proud of the fact that he'd never prepared a meal in his life. Soon the apartment was redolent of a smell so delicious she felt her mouth water. It would be a week of deprivation for her when she returned to L.A. to make up for her indulgences here, but Catalina Island and the shoot seemed far away in time as well as distance.

They ate by candlelight in the kitchen, and the succulent shrimp in pungent sauce was so good she said it was what she would order as a last meal if she were ever to be executed.

"High praise," Tim said, "but remember, Chinese is the only food I can do. I acquired a taste for it when I was a graduate student, it was about all I ever ate. It was cheap and I was poor. Just as I was getting sick of it, when I thought I'd rather die than contemplate another pork lo mein or beef with broccoli, my thesis advisor invited me to dinner.

"His wife, Xuan, was Chinese, and she served the most amazing duck I'd ever eaten. Upshot was, I would babysit for them in return for cooking lessons from Xuan. Now there was a tough lady! She used to smack my wrist with a plastic spatula when I didn't chop mushrooms in the approved manner."

"Was that when you were writing *Karin*?"

"Penniless grad students are much too overworked to try to write novels," he said. "No, I tried that later, after I was married. Don't look so sad, Faythe. If you lined up all the academics who'd tried to write a novel and failed, they'd reach from here to Hong Kong. This is not a tragedy. It's a wounding of the ego. A set-back."

"I sometimes think my problem has always been reading too much into things," she said. "People who want to act suffer from this fatal desire to make life work out in an orderly way. It doesn't have to be a happy ending, either. It can be perfectly awful or it can be mediocre, but it always has to conform to some dramatically satisfying structure. In real life, everything is messy. There are loose ends that lead nowhere, and stories that get broken off and never resolved. You can never write *The End* and live happily ever after, or even miserably ever after. It just keeps going on."

He touched her cheek lightly from across the table. "Consider the alternative," he said.

"I know. I do know. It's what I was trying to tell that girl we mentioned last night. It's so much easier to dispense advice than to take it."

"My advice, if you can stand to hear it, is to stop thinking about other people for a while. Give yourself a chance to consider Faythe McBain. What does she want? What doesn't she want? What would make her happy? What is she willing to give up, and what is essential to her well-being?"

"That seems a pretty selfish premise to live a life by," she said. And then, "Oh, excuse me, I've ended a sentence with a preposition."

He grinned ferociously. "See me after class," he said, leering, and then he stood up and pulled her away from the table. He was surprisingly strong, and she let her body relax and go with him as he led her to the living room and the pine-scented fire. They sat on big pillows in front of the fireplace, and his arm was snugly around her shoulder, urging her to rest against him. "You see," he said dreamily, "I think you are three things at once. You're my dream girl and you're also a very nice woman and you're a victim. You're just as much a victim as the girl you told me about."

She pulled away from him. "You're mistaken," she said. "I'm nobody's victim."

"Maybe victim is too strong a word, Faythe, but I can't help hating that man you were married to for so long. He's like some ignorant brute from a fairy tale, a man who finds a precious pearl and uses it for a paperweight because he doesn't know its value."

"Cal's not so bad," she said steadily. "He just never grew up. It's my own fault for not leaving him sooner, but I had these very conventional ideas about Casey needing two parents."

She turned to look at him and saw an expression of such longing on his face that she was instantly aroused.

"Faythe," he whispered, and then he was kissing her, his hands cupping the back of her neck gently, and then not so gently. She felt herself responding to his warm lips and barely held-in passion, and her lips opened to receive his tongue even as she found herself pressing against him.

He tore himself away from her lips and kissed her arched back throat, his hands drawing her closer and closer until her breathing became shallow and urgent. She put her arms around him, feeling his flesh burning through the soft material of his shirt, and her own flesh felt hot and welcomed his hands and lips. She heard herself gasp as he found her breasts and caressed them so gently she sank without volition to the pillow and drew him down beside her.

"I want you so much," he murmured in her ear. "My beautiful Faythe . . ."

And she wanted him with a ferocity that amazed her, but even as she felt the thrill of desire extending from the roots of her hair to her toes, she knew she could not let Tim become her lover. This wild passion she was feeling was not for him and never would be. It was simply the extension of the feeling Ray had started with his kiss at her door. She gave a sob of frustration and despair at having allowed herself to think of Ray. "Forgive me," she said to Tim. "I can't. I just can't."

He propped himself on an elbow and looked at her with disbelieving eyes. "It's right," he said, "and you know it. You want me, too, and God knows no one could adore you more than I do."

Maybe that was the problem. She didn't want to be adored. She wanted to be loved, the way a woman is loved by her equal, and not adored by someone who had fallen in love with her in a movie theater. More than anything she couldn't permit herself to make love to one man while thinking of another.

"I'm so sorry," she said, stroking Tim's hair. "You're a wonderful man, all a man should be. You're handsome and smart and good and witty, Tim. You're decent and sexy and anything a woman could want, but I just can't."

"Is there someone else?" He was looking away from her now, his face still flushed with desire.

"Yes," she said. "There always has been, really. All through my marriage there was someone else. I never touched him, never spoke to him, never knew him when I was married to Cal. He goes back all the way to those movies you saw when you were a kid. He's unreliable and . . . promiscuous, but

I can't seem to shake the habit of wanting him."

"So you're together again," he said harshly. "Why did you let me think—"

"No, Tim. We're not together and we never will be. I came here expecting that we'd make love, you and I. Right up until a minute ago I was anticipating it so . . . eagerly, but it wouldn't be right. Not right to . . ." She didn't know how to say it without offending him.

"Not right to let me think I had a future with you," he said. His voice was almost bitter, although he was trying to keep it ironic. "You do have a point," he conceded, "although you may be the last woman in the late twentieth century to have such fancy principles."

She managed to coax a smile from him when she told him about her ploy, her pretext of wanting to see Tiger Markowitz on the Broadway stage. "No Tiger and no Tim," he mused. "Your trip was in vain."

Five minutes later he put her in a cab on Perry Street. Just before she got in he took her hand and kissed it. "I ought to be furious with you," he said, "but somehow I'm not. It always seemed too good to be true anyway."

As the taxi pulled away she told herself
she was quite possibly the biggest loser in
the world.

Thirteen

Faythe peeled the tangerine carefully, so as not to ruin her manicure, and then regarded it without much satisfaction. Lunch. This was her week of austerity. She'd swum her laps and changed in Juanita's pool house and sat now, eyes focused on the blue water but seeing herself as she'd been a few days ago— walking rapidly toward the Oak Bar in New York, going to meet her lover. Almost-lover, he'd been, and then it turned out as badly as only she could make it.

She popped a section of tangerine into her mouth and let the juice trickle into the back of her throat. *Eat it slowly,* she told herself. *It's all you get until this evening, when you can have a salad dressed with lemon and a piece of skinless, white meat chicken. Yummy.*

Juanita came out onto the patio with her enormous Rolodex and plunked herself down across from Faythe. "That's your lunch?" she said, indicating the tangerine. "You are a caterer's nightmare."

"I was a real pig in New York. You wouldn't believe the amount of crusty bread I shovelled down with this fantastic paella, or the squash soup made with fresh cream."

Juanita looked up with a professional's interest at the mention of food. "I do a killer squash soup," she said. "The secret is, it shouldn't taste like pumpkin pie."

"It didn't," Faythe sighed.

Juanita was updating her Rolodex, ruthlessly ripping up certain names and adding others. Her thick black hair was caught up in a big, sloppy bun today and she was wearing a T-shirt that said *Born to Bake Alaska*. "So, tell me," she said, not looking up from her chore, "did you have any fun in New York? Besides eating, I mean?"

Faythe licked her fingers before eating the last section of fruit. "New York is always fun," she said. "It snowed a little."

Now Juanita did look up. "It snowed a little," she said in a sing-song voice. "That must have been a thrill. What I meant, honey, was did you get laid?"

Faythe looked at her politely, but inwardly she was alarmed. Was she now the kind of woman people supposed went to strange cities in pursuit of secretive sex?

"I'm sorry," Juanita said. "That was too crude for you. What I meant was: do you have a fella in New York with whom you engage in certain tension-releasing practices?"

Faythe laughed, choking a little on some pulp that had gone down the wrong way. She coughed and coughed, tears pouring from her eyes, waving her hands in the air to let Juanita know she wouldn't be requiring the Heimlich Maneuver. When she could speak again, she said, "I thought I had a fella, but it didn't work out."

Juanita lifted an eyebrow. "I can't imagine the man who'd reject you," she said.

"He didn't, Nita. It wasn't that way."

"No, of course not. Nothing is ever simple with you. Let me guess— he turned out to be a sicko who wanted to wrap you in a garment bag and then throw darts at you?"

"Far from it," Faythe said. She seemed to be in such a confiding mood lately, but for years there had been no girlfriend to whom she could tell her secrets and she wasn't sure how to begin.

"Do you have a lover, Juanita?" she blurted out with all the finesse of an adolescent.

Juanita got up and stretched, then strolled over to the pool house and picked up a long-handled tool with a net at one end. She poked the tool out over the water of the pool and carefully raked in a single palmetto leaf.

"I shouldn't have asked," Faythe said, but Juanita brushed the apology away with an impatient toss of her head. "We're about the same age," she said, "and yet I sometimes feel like your mother. For a sophisticated lady, honey, you're awful innocent. Nothing wrong with that, it's just rare. I get the impression that your emotions have been kind of frozen in time, as if you stopped feeling anything after you married Superagent."

She searched Faythe's face to see if her remarks were unwelcome, but Faythe just nodded, her eyes wide with recognition.

"To answer your question," Juanita continued, "I've been with the same man for almost ten years. His name is Frank— you wouldn't know him— and he's married. His wife is a hypochondriac who hasn't left her house since I've known him. She's mentally ill, and he feels he can't leave her. We love each other, whatever that means, and it's enough for me.

"Am I lonely on holidays, when he's with her? Sure. Would I like to be married to him? You bet. But that's not in the cards, and I'm grateful for what I have. I don't feel guilty, because Frank's wife stopped being a wife to him a long time before I met him. Does that answer your question?"

Faythe nodded. "I didn't mean to pry," she said.

"Of course you didn't. You only asked me to avoid asking what you really want to know." Juanita replaced her pool rake and came back to the table, resuming her duties with the Rolodex. "I'm waiting," she said.

Faythe took a deep breath and began to speak, and once she'd started it seemed she couldn't stop. She told her about Tim, about her refusal to go ahead and do what she wanted, and about her conviction that you couldn't sleep with one man when you were in love with another. "Maybe it's not love," she said. "Maybe it's just craziness. All I know is that everything with this man feels like unfinished business. They have this new term now, closure. The relatives of murdered people get to confront the killer in court. Abused kids confront their parents years after the fact. They need that confrontation for closure. I never got it with this man. One minute we were in love and the next I felt that he'd murdered my happiness, but I didn't do anything about it but run away. I wouldn't see him, wouldn't talk to him, I wouldn't even admit that he existed. I erased him from my world, and that was my state of mind when I married Cal."

"Like I said, you're still frozen back in those days, honey. You look like a grown woman, you talk like one and live your life like one, but inside you're still like a kid Casey's age."

Juanita stood up briskly. "I've got to see a man about some fresh swordfish," she said. "You stay here as long as you like, and think about what I've said. I don't pretend to be any authority about the human heart, Faythe, but you don't have to go through life hurting. If that man is still around and available, why don't you give him another chance? A lot of years have passed, and he won't be the same man he was back then. People change, most of them. What do you have to lose?"

"Everything," Faythe said. "My peace of mind, for one thing."

Juanita shook her head in exasperation. "Sweetie," she said, "if you are enjoying peace of mind, then I am the Queen of Rumania."

She blew Faythe a kiss and walked off,

leaving her to contemplate the palmetto leaf, which looked as dried up and useless as her love life.

It was painful to recall the misery she'd felt when Ray revealed his feet of clay. It was unlike any other misery she'd ever known, like a blow to the belly that left her sore and breathless. The very shape of the external world had seemed to change— colors were dulled and sounds exaggerated and ugly. Her eyes burned and her hands felt icy, even on the hottest days. She had been in a state of grief so total that it was as if Ray had died, not simply taken another girl to bed.

A part of her whispered that you had to be very young to feel such soul-shattering sorrow, but another part countered with the theory that a second disillusionment would be much worse. A woman her age couldn't hope to survive it. She had none of the resilience the twenty-two-year-old Faythe had possessed in such abundance. And she had been resilient, despite her pain and sense of loss; she had permitted Cal to make love to her, she'd married him, for God's sake, and by these acts she had forged a new life for herself. Never mind that the new life had been less than ideal . . .

She saw so much now, in retrospect. Cal's

vividness, his larger-than-life quality, even his crudeness had brought her out of that state of grief, had restored the color to her world. She had valued him precisely because he was so unlike Ray. Apart from not being able to keep their pants on, Ray and Cal were polar opposites. Ray was sensitive and Cal was brash, Ray was a dreamer and Cal a doer. Nothing about Cal would ever remind her of Ray, and that's what she had wanted.

But why had she married him? The feminists would say that she had undervalued herself, seen herself only in terms of the men she took up with. They would be partially right, but how many women were courted by a man like Cal, who could offer just about anything and produce it? She blushed to think that she had been so impressed with Cal's power and money, but it wasn't for wealth and position that she'd married him. It was because she'd confused his ability to make things work with an ability to make her happy.

"But why do you want to marry me? You barely know me." That had been her question when Cal proposed to her. He'd known her for two months, taken her out half a dozen times, and there he was, his grapey eyes shimmering with lust and earnest emotion, saying *Marry me. Marry me, Faythe*. To the charge that he barely knew her, Cal had replied that he knew her better than she knew herself, and she had no words to rebut him.

After all, he had every right to his assumptions about her. She had behaved with him like a different Faythe. He wasn't to know that the Faythe he thought he knew was reacting to the loss of Ray, that huge sorrow that gnawed away inside her even as she felt a sneaky delight at getting a prime table at Chasens just because she was with Cal Caruso. It was cold comfort, but comfort nonetheless, to eat so well and drink expensive wines, when so recently she and Ray had thought it a big deal if they had enough to dine on lasagne at Sal's in Venice.

It was also cold comfort to know that the man she was with could command respect— or what she thought was respect— from movie stars she'd worshipped as a child. It was bliss to be driven in a purring Mercedes or to have a limo pick her up— and here she thought of Tara's complaint about getting around Hollywood without a car— and heady to know that her date of the moment could, if he chose, sign any unknown hopeful to a lucrative contract.

It was the gifts that bothered her. On their third date— dinner and a screening— he had given her a pretty pin, shaped like a crescent moon, made of topazes and diamond chips. It was a "fun" piece of jewelry, he told her, and he thought the topaz would compliment her eyes.

"I can't accept this," she'd told him, but even as she said it she knew he'd overpower her objections. In her state of mind, it seemed too much trouble to refuse, just as it seemed pointless to refuse his overtures on their fourth date. Later, she would understand that Cal had been exceptionally patient, for him, and, also, that it was because he wanted to marry her.

She would never forget how out of place he'd seemed in her apartment, a one-bedroom she shared with a roommate in West Hollywood. The roommate, a girl she barely knew, made it possible for her to afford the apartment in a featureless modern building, but Nancy had not been there the night Cal decided to make his move. He stood in the tacky little living room in his Paul Stuart suit and looked around, pretending to admire a Gauguin print of a mother and child, sitting uneasily in a beanbag chair, his desire for her filling the room like static electricity.

When he kissed her she held on to his muscular arms, as if to protect herself from his strength, but Cal was remarkably gentle with her. This tenderness from one who had the potential to be bullying, even brutal, had excited her that first time, and she cried out in astonishment when she felt her body responding. In those days she had still believed that only Ray possessed the magic, and the massive body of Cal Caruso seemed more frightening than erotic.

After their lovemaking, the gifts just kept coming in little boxes from Rodeo Drive shops. When she opened a box to find a pair of diamond earrings, she realized she was in danger of becoming that most shocking of things to a Midwestern girl: a mistress. In the end she'd married Cal because he wanted her so much, and she could find no good reason to refuse him. It was a short leap from grateful affection to the process of making herself believe she was in love with him.

Just before she left Juanita's the phone rang. The machine picked it up and she could hear the low rumble of a male voice speaking urgently. She wondered if it was Frank, her friend's married lover, and envied Juanita her happiness, even if it was flawed.

The new restaurant Patina had doors of brushed steel and a stark look inside. It was supposed to be Faythe's turn to choose a restaurant, but Casey claimed that she'd lost her turn on Thanksgiving week and chose Patina because it was new and she was curious.

Today she was dressed all in black, as if in mourning, but she was cheerful enough when Faythe joined her at a table in the corner.

"Mexico was fabulous," she said, grinning. "I met a great guy there and you'll never believe it— turns out he lives two blocks away from me."

"That's terrific," Faythe said, feeling the familiar panic at the idea of her baby daughter with a man. This time, though, it was tempered by sprigs of relief. Hadn't she worried that Casey cared only for deals and money and prestige? "What's his name?"

"Matt," said Casey with a grin. "Matthew McGregor. Isn't that a solid name? You're really going to love him, Mom. He's incredibly smart and has a wild sense of humor. He's a lawyer, and he knows lots about the business, even though he specializes in tax law."

"Well, that's a bonus." She knew something bad was coming. Whenever Casey had anything to say which she knew would shock her mother, she laid on the good news first.

"He's really great looking, and out of all the women around the pool he picked me to talk to."

"He has good taste, honey." Wait for it. He was married, although of course he and his wife were divorcing soon, or he was bisexual . . . the possibilities were endless.

"How old is Matthew?" she asked.

Casey said she wanted the veal and olives, or would the crab legs be better?

"How old is Matthew?" she repeated, but the waiter had arrived and was reciting the specials. Casey chose the veal and Faythe ordered a salad. The waiter went away and the question of Matt's age hovered over the table.

"The thing is," Casey said, "that Matt is a full partner in his firm. He's everything I always wanted in a guy but could never find. The cute ones were never successful and the successful ones were rarely cute, you know?"

"How old is he?"

"Forty-one," Casey said.

"Honey, he's twenty years older than you!" *Five years younger than me!*

"I can count, Mom. I know. He's really youthful looking. You'd think he was about thirty. He's divorced and has two kids, ten and twelve, but his ex has custody. He only has to see them on vacations, I think. Marcie and Mandy are a pain like all kids, but they're basically nice."

Faythe swallowed half her glass of mineral water, trying to lubricate her suddenly parched throat. "I can't take this in," she said. "I'm sure he's a wonderful man, but I think you'd be making a mistake to get serious about him." Privately, she wondered how nice a man could be who romanced a girl Casey's age.

"There you go," Casey said. "You always make these pronouncements before you even know what the situation is. You haven't even met him."

"You are serious about him? Is it mutual?"

"We haven't set a date or anything, but if I had to bet on it, I'd say you'll have a son-in-law by next year." She looked delighted with herself as she said the words "son-in-law."

Faythe tried to picture her forty-one-year-old, tax lawyer son-in-law and failed. Their food arrived and Casey fell on her veal with exaggerated ecstasy. "This is marvelous," she cried.

"Don't try to divert me," Faythe said, eyeing her salad with no pleasure. "Have you told your father?"

Casey nodded, mouth full. When she could speak she assumed her stern tone. "Dad was happy for me, glad I'd met someone I cared for. He didn't even ask how old Matt was. It didn't even come up."

When Faythe didn't reply, Casey seemed to relax a little. "Look, Mom, it might not work out. Who knows? I just wanted to prepare you in case. There's so much about Matt that's right for me. For example, he has his two kids, which is perfect. He got that out of his system, right? I don't want to have any children, and this way, if we do get married, I won't have to feel I've deprived him of anything."

Faythe felt her head swim. Hungry as she had been, her salad didn't fit the bill. What she wanted, and couldn't have, was a big cheeseburger with lots of lovely fries, or maybe onion rings. Middle American soul food, the kind that made you forget your troubles for a while. She excused herself and went off to the ladies' room to be by herself.

"Faythe!" She heard her name being called in that curious and vivacious way that sometimes passed for friendliness in Hollywood. Seated at a table directly in her path were two older women dawdling over their coffee. The one who had called her name had hair dyed a lusterless black and lips painted with wet-looking scarlet. It was her "trademark shade" and hadn't been changed for twenty years. There was a smeary crescent of red on the rim of her coffee cup, and Faythe could remember red-tipped cigarette butts piled high in Venetian glass ashtrays at the Palisades house.

She appeared to have given up smoking, but in all other particulars Estelle Kraft had remained just as Faythe remembered her.

"I thought that was you," she said, not bothering to introduce her companion. "And is that little Cassie all grown up? How the time flies."

"Hello, Estelle," she said. Now she recalled something else— Estelle Kraft always spoke in clichés. Always. She was famous for it.

"You're looking awfully well, Faythe. Better than you have any right to, as a matter of fact. I suppose it's because you're working again. There's nothing like honest work to keep a woman young." She beamed at Faythe, as if they'd just shared a girlish secret. "I was heartbroken when I heard you and Cal had split up, but it happens to the best of us."

Estelle Kraft was wearing a hot pink Chanel suit and had the latest look in eyes— permanent eyeliner tattooed onto the upper and lower lids. The effect was startling, as if a woman of seventy had ringed her eyes in Cleopatra kohl.

Faythe had nothing to say to her. This very rich wife of a dead producer represented nothing in her own right. She was neither intelligent, kind, nor amusing. Her husband had been a Hollywood legend, and she was still frightening people who had once feared him. Estelle was like an old vulture who picked away at piles of carrion, hoping to come up with a morsel that would satisfy her endless appetite for gossip and intrigue. She loved to see people fail, publicly and with the maximum amount of personal humiliation. Estelle Kraft could no longer harm her in any way; she was yesterday's news and fading away to a richly deserved oblivion.

"So nice to see you again," she said with obvious insincerity and continued on her way to the ladies' room. She ran tepid water over her wrists and then soaked a paper towel and patted it along her neck and throat. Estelle Kraft would be regaling her friend with tales of Cal's monumental infidelities, snickering at the unsophisticated wife he'd married who hadn't been able to play her role successfully.

"Who cares?" she said to the mirror, finger combing her hair and applying a fresh coat of lipstick. Casey's romance with a man old enough to be her father was her main concern, but right now she was almost grateful to Estelle for distracting her.

"I understand men like your husband," Estelle had murmured to her many years ago. They'd been standing in the tiled rotunda that looked out over the ocean, the space where Cal conducted his bi-monthly poker games with industry heavies. There had been a round table covered in green baize, with an ivory box that contained the poker chips. Although it was regularly aired, the rotunda smelled permanently of old cigar smoke. She'd been standing at the window, noting the difference between the stuffy air of Cal's masculine preserve and the wild, clean view of waves breaking against the cliff rocks, when Estelle had oiled her way into the room, glass in hand.

"What do you understand about them?" she had asked.

"A man like Cal gives his wife everything, and he's only too glad to do so. He pampers her, adores her, and all he asks in return is the freedom to play a little. He will always come back to the home, to the wife and children. She has this security for life, Faythe dear. For life. All she must do is turn a blind eye. Who's the loser?"

She wanted to believe she had delivered a retort of devastating wit and moral surety, but to the best of her ability to recall, she thought she'd said: "I'd rather skip the security for life in return for fidelity and trust." Yes, that was probably it.

"Then," Estelle Kraft had whispered, "you're a very silly girl and you ought to go back where you came from."

Estelle had left when Faythe came back from the ladies' room, and a crumpled, lipstick-stained napkin was all that remained of her. The oily lip-print on the pink linen napkin said it all. Estelle was one of those women who gave Hollywood a bad name. The Sherry Brooks's were awful enough, with their anorexic daughters and their marble statues celebrating breast implants, but at least Sherry played at having careers. Estelle Kraft had never done anything but live off her producer husband and give parties and foment trouble.

Casey was drinking coffee and rummaging in her super-large bag for a pen. Her personal diary, as distinct from her Rolodex, lay spread open on the table.

"Let's see," she was saying. "When's a good date for you to have dinner with Matt and me? I know you're shooting on Catalina next week, but how about the week after? How does the 17th look?"

Faythe had no more idea of what she was doing on the seventeenth of December than she had of quantum physics.

"Sure," she said. "Pencil me in."

You ought to go back where you came from. You're a very silly girl, and you ought to go back where you came from.

"Great," said Casey. "Gotta go, Mom."

* * *

The ocean was gray today, with a deep, cruel-looking green underlay to it that made her shiver. She walked along the edge of the shore, a shoe in each hand and her panty hose stuffed into her handbag. It was the first time she'd thought to take O'Connell up on his invitation to use the Malibu house while he was gone.

She'd driven straight from the unsettling lunch with Casey to the Beach Colony, pressed the complicated code into the intercom, and entered the Cammarada house feeling like a thief. She didn't know why she wanted to be there, but it had something to do with a proximity to the Pacific Ocean. She'd skinned out of her hose in the big, stark living room and then— a measure of her shaky state of mind— gone out onto the beach carrying her shoes.

A man jogged past, his dog, a big golden retriever running in his wake. She thought she'd like to try jogging and ran for a few tentative steps, but running in her slim-skirted Karan dress felt silly, and she came to an abrupt halt and continued to stroll, her toes curling into the sand with a delicious sense of freedom. She felt she'd like to walk forever down the coast of California, abandoning her Hollywood life, her sense of angst over Ray once more inhabiting her sphere, the miniseries, and yes, even Casey.

It was a matter of fact that she, who still felt like a girl half the time, was forty-six years old and had no more idea of how to live her life than she ever had. She'd done her best all these years, but it obviously hadn't been enough. Casey was probably going to marry a man like her father and she, Faythe, would be powerless to prevent it. Why not relinquish her responsibility and just disappear, move to New York or London and let everyone make their mistakes thousands of miles from Faythe McBain?

She bent to pick up a rosy shell that was so pretty, so delicate and well formed, it seemed to be winking a message at her from the sand and kelp. She dipped it in the water, watching the rose hue deepen and turn mauve. Life was like the shell, a precious commodity that could all too easily get buried in detritus and exist without anyone noticing it.

She continued on, letting an occasional wave eddy around her bare toes, and when she began to feel tired she turned and headed back. O'Connell's house seemed very far away, a bare pin-prick on the horizon, and she was suddenly exhausted. She longed for an external sign, like the snow in New York, to let her know that the seasons were turning, but it was another perfect day in southern California and the next day would be just the same.

She felt very tired when she climbed up to the deck and let herself in to O'Connell's borrowed house. She lay on one of the couches in the living room and let her body relax as she listened to the sound of the waves. The boom of the surf acted as a sort of lullaby, and she felt her eyelids close as if they'd been magnetized.

She was suddenly in a room as rosy and glowing as the seashell she'd found on the beach. It was beautiful in the heart of the shell, and she knew utter peace. Outside she could hear voices— Casey's was one of them, and there were a number of male voices— and they were raised in a kind of irritable quarrel. *Well, thank God I don't have to take part in that,* she thought, but gradually the voices calmed and were engaged in normal conversation. She heard someone say "Does she want to go home?" and knew they were talking about her. She wanted to tell them that there was no home to go back to. For better or worse, this was her home, but when she tried to put it into words her voice failed her. She became very anxious then and tried to find her way out of the rosy room, but there were no exits. Round and round she went, hands against the smooth walls, trying to find a door or even a chink she might slip through, but the room was seamless.

The other people were so near, but they might as well be thousands of miles away, because nothing she could do would alert them to her presence. She began to weep, it was the only sound she was capable of making, and as she wept she knew she was dreaming. If only she could wake up. Maybe if she cried hard enough she could wake up. A persistent ringing noise was nagging at her, and then a booming voice filled her chest and she woke with a start, her cheeks wet and her heart racing.

"This is Himself," O'Connell's voice was saying on the answering machine. "He's not here, but leave a message and wait to see if he'll get back to you."

A very English voice told Des O'Connell that she'd be coming to California in three days, and wouldn't it be super if they could see each other? "I hope you're being a good boy, darling, but knowing you . . . oh well, mustn't grumble. See you. Byeee."

Faythe thought of all the women hoping against hope that some man would have a change of heart, would miraculously alter the habits of a lifetime all on account of her influence.

"I've been there," she said companionably to the English voice, and then went up the stairs to use the bathroom. She passed through the master bedroom, where the king-sized bed was as neat and squared away as something in a military barracks. On the bedside table were three books and she stopped to see what Des had been reading.

She had to smile because, true to his character, the books gave nothing away about their owner's personality. They might have been the reading material of someone afflicted with multiple personalities. The first was a trashy bestseller about spies and beautiful women, the second was a book of Buddhist meditations, and the third was a slender volume of what looked like poems. She couldn't be sure, because it was printed entirely in Irish.

And then, in the bathroom, she had a small surprise that cheered her and made the day seem better. The tiles perfectly matched the color of the sea, just as Milagros had told her. The maid's bathroom contained no window, so the tiles there were ordinary. To make the magic work sunlight was necessary, and by the light of the seaward-facing windows, the tiles glowed gray with an underlay of green.

Fourteen

She was at Hugo's having a pot of tea and reading the *Hollywood Reporter*, eager for news about the location shooting, but there was nothing but a small mention of a blizzard which had disrupted a day's shooting. She was about to pay for her tea and leave when she realized the woman next to her was reading *Deep Dish* with fascinated concentration. She sneaked a look and saw a headline that made her queasy: STREETWISE STARLET'S BID FOR FAME— THE RUNAWAY'S REVENGE.

"Excuse me," she said to the woman, "where do you get those?"

A pair of dark eyes looked at her in confusion. "Those . . . what?" she asked.

"Oh, sorry, I meant the paper, *Deep Dish*. Where do you buy it?"

Now the eyes were pitying. They belonged to a youngish woman who looked as if she might be an aspiring actress, although she was dressed in ratty jeans and wore old-fashioned, horn-rimmed glasses. "You don't really buy it," she said, as if Faythe had asked where she might buy youth or fame. "It just kind of appears. People pass it around. Sometimes you'll find a stack of them in one of the clubs."

"They're a nonprofit organization," Faythe said drily.

"Well, they, whoever they are, are in it for the fun. You can see the quality is really poor, but the gossip's the best. It's, like, guerrilla journalism. Hollywood terrorists— probably some mailroom clerks, if you want my opinion. They know everything." She took another look at Faythe and said, kindly, "You can have mine when I'm through."

Faythe ordered another pot of tea and waited for the woman to finish. The story about the "streetwise starlet" was on the first page, so she assumed she'd be waiting for some time. She tried not to watch as the woman read about Tara, for it must be Tara the article was about, but the temptation was great. The woman, however, had one of those masklike expressions and gave nothing away.

Hollywood terrorists, she'd called the creators of *Deep Dish*, and Faythe thought that's exactly what they were. People who assassinated characters from deep cover, where there could be no reprisals. Hadn't Casey told her they were careful to avoid outright libel, resorting to the well-worn tactic of phrases like "a source who wishes to remain anonymous says" or "close associates reveal."

The woman turned the page, dipping her napkin in a glass of water and removing ink from the tips of her fingers. Whoever put out *Deep Dish* made it look like some endearing old relic of the counterculture sixties, a publication from before the days of laser printers or desktop publishing.

The woman in the large glasses took a bite of her grilled cheese and sprout sandwich and then turned another page. Faythe sipped her tea, longing for a pot of strong espresso, and tried to be patient. She looked around the room to see if one of Cal's rivals, a superagent who liked to order Cheerios at Hugo's, was present, but there was no one she'd ever seen. Horn-rims continued to peruse *Deep Dish* at her leisure. Faythe knew Casey could get her a copy in a minute, but she didn't want to talk to her daughter about the article, certainly not before she'd read it.

She remembered Casey's promise not to help the rumor surface and hoped with all her heart that Casey had nothing to do with it.

At last horn-rims set the paper aside, looking like a ravaged grad student who'd just finished a particularly complicated nineteenth century novel. She shook her head, as if in disbelief, and then, with a tight smile, handed the paper to Faythe.

"Here you go," she said. "Lotta good reading in this baby."

Faythe paid the check and left Hugo's, getting into her car and spreading the inky paper over the steering wheel. On second thought, much as she wanted to read the article right now, she shoved *Deep Dish* down and out of sight, started the car, and headed for Melrose and home. She didn't want anyone to be able to report that they'd seen her avidly reading hurtful gossip, so intent on ingesting the poison she'd been caught at it on Santa Monica Boulevard.

In the privacy of her kitchen she settled down to the story about the "runaway's revenge." At the beginning she half hoped it would be the kind of harmless pap *People* sometimes ran about celebrities, always careful to present a counterpoint for every unflattering comment, but that was not the style of *Deep Dish*. No, *Deep Dish* was both a clever parody of the old Hedda Hopper-Louella Parsons school of gossip and a mean, gloves-off, 1990s brand of outrageous smear.

A few short years ago," she read, "the runaway was dressed in hot pants and high heels as she plied her aimless way along the Strip, but today she's being outfitted in designer gowns and costly gems in her role as Rosie Madigan in the major new miniseries directed by Ray Parnell. Brand new actress Tara Johanson used to be called Karin, the name her parents gave her when she was born in a farming community in North Dakota. The journey Karin took to become Tara is a seamy one, and *Deep Dish* has interviewed scores of street people who knew the foxy blonde when she was just another runaway. A topless dancer, identified only as 'Brandy,' revealed that she had worked with Tara-Karin and that patrons loved her because she was a 'natural blonde.' In the table dancing, Brandy said, Tara-Karin had really excelled, making a small fortune in tips every time she consented to do a 'private dance' dressed only in g-string and high heels. 'She had that corn-fed look the guys go for,' Brandy said. 'She also had these really large jugs, and you could see they were real, too.'

Next up came Chauncey, a boy prostitute from Portland, Oregon, who said that he and Tara-Karin had often worked the Strip together. She was like a big sister to him, Chauncey said, because she'd been an older woman. She was eighteen to his twelve. "I never saw her turn a trick," Chauncey said, "but she was out there."

'I would have to say,' confided Bobbi, another underage prostitute, 'that her drug of choice was always Demerol. That, or Ecstasy. She never smoked crack that I know. She was always on my ass about smoking crack.'

'She had problems,' remarked an unattributed social worker. 'She was hostile and snapped at you like a wolf when you tried to help her, but she was special. She seemed to know that she was destined for greater things, and that is often fatal in a runaway. I'm glad that she has a chance to realize the self-esteem she deserves.'

"Oh, what bilge," Faythe screamed at the paper, feeling the particular fury that is brought on when an attack comes from an anonymous source. The "social worker" sounded entirely fabricated, and so did the others. Or if the street people were real, by any chance, they'd say anything if they were offered money. Small amounts of money would coax a teenage runaway to make up reminiscences about someone he'd never heard of or seen or a topless dancer to concoct false memories. She could hardly wait to burn *Deep Dish*, but there was more to read. What, Faythe wondered, would the runaway's revenge be, and on whom?

First, though, she had to wade through the musings of someone called Vickianne, described as a former "sex industry worker," who had much to say about Tara. "She could have made a bundle if she only did porno movies, but Tara wasn't into that. She said she was gonna be an actress someday, and it would hurt her image. Really, she wasn't into men at all—they weren't her thing." Vickianne was a recovering alcoholic and said she'd lost track of Tara when she'd been lifted off the streets and put into detox.

Deep Dish has discovered a lot about the beautiful and talented Tara Johanson that she'd rather not have you know, but secrecy is impossible in our town. That's something even a twenty-one-year-old runaway should have been aware of. She seems to have more talent than sense, and she's already earned the enmity of many with her arrogant ways and unstable behavior. On the other hand, she has an industry heavy in her corner in the person of director Ray Parnell who cast this unknown in a starring role in *The Senator's Daughter.* Always a class act, Parnell may have made a major error this time out. The blonde table dancer from North Dakota could exact a juicy revenge by bringing down the career of a respected director. As everyone should know, you can take the girl out of the Hollywood Strip, but you can't take the Strip out of the girl.

The article carried the byline "Jaundiced Eye." With great self-restraint, Faythe prevented herself from burning the paper. She folded it away and put it in her desk. Katherine would have to see it when she returned from Montana.

She sat in her kitchen, thinking about what the foul article would do to Tara, who was due to return from Montana in a few days. She counted off the things that did not seem to show her in a bad light and came up with only two— she didn't turn tricks, although that had been left ambiguous, and she didn't do porn. On the other hand, she was a nude dancer, or had been, and took drugs. Instead of giving her credit for winning a prize role, Jaundiced Eye had insinuated that Tara was doing it just to see how much havoc she could wreak. It didn't make sense, but then *Deep Dish* didn't want to make sense. It wanted to chip away at people and ruin them and amuse all the envious folk by portraying anyone who got a break as sleazy, reprehensible, or pathetic.

Deep Dish also made it seem that Ray had personally picked Tara right off the streets to star in his miniseries. It took only a tiny stretch of the imagination to see Ray sitting in a topless club, bemused by the supple blonde dancer, waving a hundred dollar bill to let her know he wanted her to be his private dancer.

She wasn't getting something here. *Think, Faythe. Think!* Her radar had told her that Ray was not involved with Tara in any way other than in his capacity as director. But how had he known about her in the first place? Who was her agent? How had she come to audition for *The Senator's Daughter?* In her own anxiety over her comeback, she had simply accepted Tara, first as a talented young actress who happened to be difficult, and then as the troubled girl Kate had described. Who the hell was Tara? And why did anyone who might know have to be in some remote and unreachable location in Montana?

She grabbed the phone and stabbed out the number of her husband's agency.

"Caruso Creative," came Georgia's dulcet tones into Faythe's kitchen. She asked for Casey.

"Good afternoon," said the voice of a secretary after Faythe had waited for what seemed like a long time. "How may I help you?"

"Casey, please."

"Ms. Caruso is on another line," said the new voice.

"Then get her off," said Faythe. "This is her mother." She bit her lip, realizing she had sounded like Joan Crawford in *Mommie Dearest* mode, but it must have worked, because the next sound she heard was Casey's voice.

"Hi, Mom. What's the crisis? Are you okay?"

"Who is Tara Johanson's agent?"

"Whooah! I see my mom has read *Deep Dish*. I told you, didn't I? Now will you believe me?"

"I don't believe everything I hear or read. Who is Tara's agent?"

"Why do you want to know?" Casey's voice had turned indolent, as if she were playing for time.

"Never mind. Just answer the question, please."

"You sound so tough. I don't understand why you need to know the name of her agent. Get a grip, Mom. Are you thinking of a lawsuit or something? It's all true, what the Eye says about Tara. She doesn't have a leg to stand on legally."

"I'm not interested in lawsuits, dear. I asked a perfectly simple question, and I'd like an answer."

"Are you going to call the agent and make

some grandstanding speech? All about how one ought to show compassion for unfortunates?"

"What good would that do? Agents are not known for their compassion, Casey, as I'm sure you know."

"Well, in that case. She signed with Linda Corvo, over at Burger, Blank & Whitestone. She was a complete unknown, but she signed about a week before Ray Parnell did the final casting for the miniseries." Casey allowed a tasteful pause before she said, "Linda Corvo is a beast."

"Why is that, Casey?" Faythe tasted the iodine flavor of fear in her throat.

"She's young, from New York, and she thinks she knows how things work here. But she's wrong. She doesn't have a clue, really. She's just flavor of the month."

"In other words," said Faythe, "she's your rival."

"Mom, I just told you. She doesn't have a clue. If she knew what she was doing, she would never have signed Tara, right?"

"Because you can take the girl out of the Strip?" Faythe found she was shaking with anger. Her knees, pressed so decorously against each other, were dancing a flamenco beneath the table. Her daughter's voice seemed to come from very faraway.

"You simplify things," said Casey. "Things are extremely complicated, and you boil them down to their easiest components."

"Would you like to tell me what's complicated about any of this? All I see is a nasty, spiteful article that serves no purpose other than to hurt its subject. What am I missing?"

"How about the public's right to know?" Casey said virtuously.

"That's ridiculous and you know it. If Tara were a justice on the Supreme Court her background might matter, but she's an actress. An actress, Casey. The public doesn't need to know what she may or may not have done to survive when she first came here."

"Fine. Have it your way. You always do. If she's got any sense she'll ignore the whole thing. As I think I said, it's good for her career."

"I think we'd better terminate this conversation," she said. "I don't want to say anything I'll regret."

"Suit yourself, Mom, but before you go I just want to say I had nothing to do with that article. I know you think I'm a jerk and a heartless bitch, but I kept my promise to you."

"Oh, Casey." Her daughter was the only person on earth who could make her rage one minute and dissolve in tenderness the next. "I don't think you're any of those things. I love you and I'm very proud of you. I think we're just . . . temperamentally very different."

"Whatever," Casey said cheerfully, and put down the phone.

Linda Corvo was a few years older than Casey, and she was not nearly as successful. Far from being a beast, she was a slightly overweight young woman with shiny black hair and hazel eyes. She was trying very hard not to show how much Faythe's visit bewildered her.

"The article is a piece of trash," she said indignantly, "but I don't see what anyone can do about it. Most people will just consider the source. That's what I hope."

Linda Corvo had the smallest office in a low-key agency in Beverly Hills. Her desk was littered with scripts and glossy eight-by-ten headshots of actors. The only color in her decorating scheme came from a bright blue bowl containing sugarless mints. Her neatly manicured hand dipped into the bowl and she popped a mint into her mouth with a groan. "I'm trying to keep on this diet," she said, "and it's murder. It wouldn't be so bad if I didn't have to eat out all the time."

"I know," said Faythe. "I know the problem."

"Doesn't look like it, Ms. McBain," she said with a rueful smile. "I appreciate your concern over Tara, but I don't quite see— " She broke off, apparently too polite to ask Faythe what business it was of hers.

"Kate Iverson asked me to keep on eye on Tara. Perhaps I'm overreacting, but I think she'll be so upset about this. Is there any way to keep it from her when she gets back from Montana?"

Linda came from behind her desk and went to a file cabinet. She riffled through and extracted a folder. She withdrew one photo of Tara and passed it to Faythe. Both of them stared at the image of a girl whose natural beauty had a love affair with the camera.

"When a girl looks like she does," Linda said, "people are going to talk about her all the time. Human nature being what it is, most of what they say won't be very nice.

I don't think there's any way she could be back in Hollywood one day without someone mentioning it to her."

Faythe sighed, knowing it was true. If Tara had led the most blameless of lives, someone would find a way to make her seem tarnished.

"Don't look so glum," Linda said "She's tougher than you think. I'm in touch with her every day, practically, and the shoot is going along wonderfully. She's sharing a trailer with Katherine, and she says Montana reminds her of home."

"I shouldn't think that would be very pleasant." Faythe noticed that Linda didn't register her remark, and now it was her turn to feel bewildered.

"I think Tara is going to be a major star," Linda said. "A lot of people are going to wonder why she has an agent like me instead of one like your former husband. Or even," she winked, "like your daughter. I'm going to tell you something, because you deserve to know. I'm not in the Caruso league, but I'm going to be the best possible agent for Tara. I'm going to work very hard for her. She will have all my loyalty and my admiration. Sometimes that counts for more than all the power plays."

No wonder Casey didn't like Linda Corvo. She must sound just like Mom when she spoke her mind. Faythe told Linda she was glad Tara had signed with her and said she'd taken up enough of the agent's time. Just before she left, she asked Linda Corvo how Tara had come to her attention.

Linda stroked her shiny hair and said, "I saw her as a favor to Ray Parnell." Her hand strayed over to the bowl of mints again. "You might say Tara is his protégée."

Faythe went down the wooden stairs and out the circular entrance. Linda's office was in the Writers and Directors Building on Little Santa Monica, and it was possible to believe you were in the Hollywood of forty years ago when you were inside it. Billy Wilder had once had an office there, back when wooden stairs and two-story buildings and no air-conditioning was the norm. Faythe was glad Tara's agent had her quarters there— there was something reassuring about it, just as there was something reassuring about Linda Corvo. Her mind rabbitted along on this subject to avoid thinking about that word— "protégée." Tara was Ray's protégée.

The ground floor of the Writers and Directors housed Boul' Mich, one of her favorite stores. They weren't having a sale, but she went in anyway and browsed the racks. There were quite a few Caseyish outfits, stern little numbers that looked cute on her daughter but would look, on a woman her age, prim and peculiar. She held up a suede vest, looked in the mirror, and put it back. Nothing in Boul' Mich was going to please her today, nothing anywhere was going to please her today, until she addressed the protégée subject.

She bought a cream silk scarf with a border of forget-me-nots and left the store. She got in her car and drove out toward Ventura. Why hadn't she given more attention to the relationship between Ray and Tara? Clearly one had existed before the casting of *The Senator's Daughter.* Ray had hand-picked an agent for Tara, choosing well, and for all she knew he'd taken the project on because he knew how superbly Tara would be able to play Rosie. What did this mean?

She'd told herself for years that Ray was almost as bad as Cal in the fidelity department, but she'd always believed him above cradle robbing. *Deep Dish* had implied, through Vickianne, that Tara didn't like men. They'd stopped short of hinting that she was a lesbian, because it was natural for a runaway to distrust men. It was men who preyed on them, and usually men from whom they were running— fathers.

Tara obviously admired Ray, and that, too, was natural. She had never believed that there was anything sexual in Ray's feelings for Tara, or hers for him, but there was a piece of the puzzle missing.

A deep bass heartbeat invaded her car, and she turned to see two boys in a rusted out Mustang keeping pace with her in the right lane. They were listening to rap, to the sinister, urgent rap of a voice urging men not to take any garbage from bitches. The driver had straggly reddish hair and an open, freckled face— a slightly seedy Hollywood version of Huck Finn— but when he turned to look at Faythe he ran his tongue over his lips and then puckered for her.

Charming. She let them pull ahead and saw that their license plate read: ICE AGE. *Very apt,* she thought, and then, *what if I'd had a son and he was like one of them?* Instead she had a daughter, who was, come to think of it, her father's protégée. One thing she knew, and that was Ray's absolute admiration for talent, for a real gift. He would do anything to encourage a person he thought truly gifted. She knew, she thought sadly, because he had once sensed that gift in her.

The piece of the puzzle that was missing, then, was: how had Ray known Tara was so talented?

She was approaching the graffiti explosion that heralded the vicinity of Dove House, and all she could think of was Tara. Tara lied. She'd told Faythe so. Was it possible that the whole runaway story was something she'd made up herself? Casey had spoken of her with such venom right from the start. But then, Casey had called Linda Corvo a beast. Faythe laughed helplessly at her own confusion, thinking that if the boys in the Mustang could have a license plate that said ICE AGE, she herself could have one made up that said NO CLUE.

She had almost passed Dove House by when she braked abruptly and stopped the car. There was no face at the window, no sign of life. Except for the neatness of the building, it might have been deserted. She walked up to the intercom and pressed the button. After a long silence, the thing crackled at her and she could hear a voice asking her what she wanted.

"Could I see Ms. Kinnock?" she asked.

"Have an appointment?"

"No, but she knows me. Tell her it's Marie Raymond, please."

"She ain't here."

"Oh. Well, did Daisy have her baby?"

"Ain't no Daisy here."

The machine crackled vindictively, and just as she was turning to leave, the face of Tina, the girl with lank hair, appeared at the common room window. She signalled to Faythe to wait, and then came to the door and opened it a crack. "I remember you," she said. "You were here the first day I came."

"That's right," said Faythe. Tina's hair looked cleaner. She was wearing a thin, long sleeved sweater, so her track marks weren't visible, but Faythe remembered them vividly.

"I guess it's okay to tell you," Tina said. "Daisy had a boy. Eight pounds, seven ounces." She spoke proudly, as if the high birth weight of Tina's son spoke well of all of them.

Faythe wished she'd bought a baby present, but offered the bag from Boul' Mich instead. "Would you give that to Daisy?"

"What's in it?" Tina poked a long finger into the bag and withdrew the scarf. "Classy," she said doubtfully, in a tone that implied she'd never wear it herself. "Don't you want to know the baby's name?"

"By all means."

"Orlando." Tina smiled suddenly, and her face became what it had never seemed before: intelligent. "We're not supposed to talk to nobody without an appointment, but I figured you were okay on account of something Ms. Kinnock said."

"What was that, Tina?"

"Well, she said we were getting a new washer and drier, but that ain't all she said."

Faythe waited patiently, sensing that it wasn't often that Tina got to make a witticism.

"She said we got to rename the laundry room. Before it was just the basement, but soon as we get them new machines it'll be called the Marie Raymond Laundry Facility."

"I'm certainly honored," Faythe said as Tina exploded with silent laughter, her shoulders shaking. She had just realized that the girl was from West Virginia or Kentucky, what used to be called a hillbilly. "It isn't every day that a woman has a laundry facility named after her, is it?"

"Whooo!" said Tina. "Sure ain't. We all thank you, really, we surely do."

Then she slipped back inside Dove House, closing the door smartly in Faythe's face.

When she got home she discovered a van from the local TV station parked in front of her house. A man with a minicam was at her door, and even as she was getting out of her car she saw the well-groomed figure of Sally Sample descending from the van. The familiar golden hair and expensive silk blouse were Sally's, but as she came toward Faythe it became clear that she was not Sally at all.

"Hello, Ms. McBain, I'm Patsy, Sally Sample's interviewer. If we could get started right away I'd appreciate it." She saw Faythe's blank look and said, "Didn't your agent tell you? I spoke with him this morning and he said he'd call you right away."

"I'm sorry, I don't know what you're talking about." She felt as if she'd wandered into a farce. She wanted to know how Patsy got her hair to look exactly like Sally Sample's, and why Sally, who was an interviewer herself, needed to have a duplicate of herself.

"Oh, rats," said Patsy. "Your agent said you'd be delighted to give an interview. I'm sorry if there's been a screw up."

Faythe knew the interview could have

nothing to do with *Deep Dish*— one of L.A.'s most popular chat-show hostesses would not concern herself with the ravings of an anonymous gossip sheet— but she was flustered anyway. How dare Barney give his permission without checking with her first? Then she remembered the blinking lights she'd ignored in her haste to meet with Linda Corvo. She knew what his message would say. *If I don't hear back from you I'll assume it's all right.*

"I've been gone for most of the day," she told Patsy. "Is this about *The Senator's Daughter?*" She let the crew in— the photographer and a sound man as well as Patsy— and immediately the men swarmed into her living room and began to rearrange things to their liking.

"In a manner of speaking," Patsy said, standing in her kitchen and looking relieved that she'd gained access. Now Faythe noticed that Patsy was Sally Sample only from the waist up. Beneath the flossy, burgundy blouse she wore jeans and sneakers. "Of course we'll touch on the miniseries in your segment," she said, "but we also want you to tell us what it feels like."

"What what feels like?" From the corner of her eye, she saw the blinking red light on her answering machine. Six people had called, and Barney was only one of them. Then again, maybe all six calls were from Barney.

"The show is called *Late Bloomers,*" Patsy said. "Sally wants to examine women who are embarking on a new career after the age of forty."

"Old broads make good," Faythe said.

"Excuse me?" said Patsy.

"Oh, nothing. Suppose I run upstairs and freshen up a bit while your crew sets things up?"

"That'd be good," agreed Patsy. "Could you put on something glamorous but understated?"

"You bet," said Faythe, taking the stairs two at a time with murder in her heart. How could Barney have agreed to let her appear on something called *Late Bloomers?* It made her sound like some musty old plant that produced a bloom against all expectations.

She stood at her closet, viciously swiping hangers along the rail in search of something Patsy would find glamorous but understated. She selected the silk gabardine coat dress that Casey liked so much, and then went to the bathroom to remove her makeup and start all over again. By the time she was sitting at her dressing table, debating between gold earrings or topaz studs, her anger had dissipated. Wasn't a late bloomer exactly what she was? If, that is, she bloomed and didn't bomb.

Talent she might have had in abundance years ago, but that talent had not been widely showcased in anything but the two movies where she cavorted in a bikini and screamed when the horror at the boardwalk surfaced. How pompous it would sound if she were to tell Patsy that she'd had a career and was now resuming it after a quarter of a century! *Get a grip,* she told herself, coming down the stairs.

"You look gorgeous," Patsy said, surveying her with hard, professional eyes. Faythe's living room was unrecognizable to her. The chair she liked to read in had been pushed aside, and her couch had been placed in front of the fireplace. The small table that had been piled with books now held a cloisonné jar sporting silk flowers she'd never seen before. An ambient light filled the room, and the assistant was holding light meters to her cheekbones.

A kitchen chair had been dragged in for Patsy, who assumed her position on it as interviewer. Faythe understood that Patsy, filmed from behind while the camera focused on its subject, would appear to be Sally Sample. All Patsy's earnest questions would be overdubbed by Sally's voice, and the audience would thrill to an intimate moment between Sally Sample, star interviewer, and Faythe McBain, late bloomer.

"So," Patsy began, "how does it feel to be featured in a major television movie at the age of forty-seven? Is it scary, or the fulfillment of all your dreams?"

"It's scary," said Faythe, "and I'm forty-six."

It was only her imagination that caused Patsy to lean forward and say, with perfect indifference, "Whatever." What she really said was: "You were an actress when you met your former husband, the agent Cal Caruso. What prompted you to give up your career?"

"As a child of the fifties," Faythe said, "I'd been brought up to believe that marriage was a full-time job. By the time my daughter was old enough for me to be comfortable about going back to work, I'd lost interest in acting. I suppose it seems strange now, but I imagine that happened to a lot of women in many fields." Actually, she had thought that acting was related to Ray, and without him she doubted her abilities.

Patsy asked cagey questions, which Faythe fielded in the best way she could. She felt strangely at ease during the interview, as if she could say nothing wrong. She was unprepared when Patsy said:

"You knew the director, Ray Parnell, before you were married. He directed you in the teen horror flicks, which were your only work in film." Here Patsy held up a publicity still from *Horror Boardwalk* that showed a youthful Faythe, dressed in a bikini, eyes unnaturally wide. "What prompted him to cast you in a TV movie after so many years?"

"I've wondered about that myself," Faythe said sweetly. "You'd have to ask him."

Patsy didn't like that answer and tried again. "Ray Parnell is known for creative casting. Do you think he might have outsmarted himself by choosing an unknown actress for the starring role in *Senator's Daughter?*"

"I believe Ray knows what he's doing," Faythe said. "He always has. The actress, Tara Johanson, is so good she won't remain unknown. Everyone has to start somewhere."

The interview was winding down, and

Patsy elicited some inspirational stuff from her about how interesting it was to be starting over. It was interesting, but perhaps not in the ways the audience imagined. Faythe encouraged women everywhere to take a chance if it was offered, and then the interview was over.

"You were fine," Patsy said. "Sorry about that picture from *Horror Boardwalk*, but it was too good to pass up."

"At least you didn't ask me to scream," Faythe said.

The small crew packed up, restored her living room to its natural condition, and disappeared in record time. Patsy's parting words were, "Good luck with everything, Faythe. I really mean it."

People who said "I really mean it" usually didn't.

Faythe pressed the button on her answering machine. Four of the calls were from Barney, the fifth was from Sherry Brooks, who wanted to know if it was true about Tara, and the sixth was from Kate Iverson. "I'm back from Montana, and everything went like a dream," she said. "Tara and Des and the others will be returning in a few days. Call when you have a chance. Oh, and Faythe, I should warn you that the child,

Heather, is absolutely beastly. She's a good little actress, but if I were her mother I'd— how long can I talk on this thing? Suffice it to say that Heather is truly, truly dreadful. She actually says things like— well, I'll tell you in person. You'll be able to handle her better than I could. To give you an idea of her sheer awfulness, she— "

The machine cut her off. *Well, well,* Faythe thought, *the end of a perfect day.*

The phone rang, and just to prove that more unpleasant surprises were yet to come, a woman's voice said, "This is Sylvia Lewison, Heather's mother. We're still in Montana, but I wanted to set a meeting up with you. I think it's important that you spend some time with Heather, don't you? I mean, before the location on Catalina."

"Mrs. Lewison," Faythe said. "I can get to know Heather on the set. There's always plenty of time."

"But it's not quality time, Ms. McBain. I was thinking that the three of us might spend a day together."

The problem, Faythe thought, was that half the time she didn't know whether to laugh or cry.

Fifteen

A big dish of pistachio ice cream, Heather's favorite, was placed in front of the child by her hostess, Faythe McBain, but Heather shook her head. "I can't have ice cream when I'm in the middle of a movie," she said. "My mother says I might break out."

"You're too young to break out," Faythe said, but Heather was firm. "Well, why did your mother tell me how much you liked it if you can't have it? I asked her what your favorite foods were."

They were sitting in her small back garden, eating the lunch Faythe had prepared in an effort to get out of spending "quality time" with Heather. Mrs. Lewison was even now in the bathroom upstairs, and it was the first time she'd been alone with Heather since the Lewisons had arrived.

Heather sat very still in her garden chair, her hands folded on the peach-colored table cloth. "I know what must have happened," she said, looking relieved. "There's the menu of things I can eat, and then there's the food my mother tells people I like— you know, if someone is writing a story about me. She must have got confused when she was talking to you. Going on location to Montana was a big strain on her."

Faythe glanced uneasily around, as if the looming presence of Sylvia Lewison might at any moment step through the French doors and out onto the lawn. "Don't worry," said Heather, "she won't be back for a while. We're supposed to be getting to know each other. She's probably looking through your medicine cabinet right now."

"Heather! I'm sure your mother wouldn't— "

"No you're not. You know she would."

Faythe looked at the small, fineboned face but couldn't read anything into it— neither malice, amusement, nor contempt. Heather's hair had been tinted to match Tara's, but if you didn't know it, she'd appear to be just another ten-year-old girl, dressed in pink leggings and a white T-shirt.

"Tell me," Faythe said, "did you enjoy working in Montana?"

Heather shrugged. "It's a job," she said. "I liked Des O'Connell, but the actress who plays my mother, that Kate, I didn't get along with her at all. I told Lisbet, the makeup girl, to make her look older in her scenes with Tara. I mean, she is old, but she's got that kind of face that doesn't show it. It makes sense, doesn't it? Rosie's mother is older when Tara plays her daughter than when I do."

"Heather," said Faythe softly, "it's not the customary thing on a set for a ten-year-old to call the shots. Kate was probably just protesting such an . . . irregularity."

"I don't know about that, but you'd better get rid of that bowl of ice cream before my mother comes down."

"I can't eat it either," Faythe said. "Let's just watch it melt, shall we?"

Heather gave a small smile. "My mother thinks you're really cheap for asking us here instead of meeting us at a restaurant where everyone would see us."

Faythe regarded the wreckage on her prettily set table. Apparently she'd been given part of the menu before Sylvia Lewison fell prey to stress, because mother and daughter had polished off their shrimp cocktail and spinach salad, but the bowl of melting pistachio ice cream contrasted badly with the jug of yellow roses and Faythe's colorful Mexican plates and bowls. She was determined not to rise to the bait of being thought cheap, but Heather was, after all, a child and deserved an answer to her rude comment.

"What do you think, Heather?"

She plucked at her new, strawberry blond hair and sighed. "I think I'd like to be a thousand miles away and ten years older," she said. "No offense to you— you seem okay— but most people are such buttheads. They're so screwed up. That Tara isn't too tightly wrapped, and all dear, sweet Kate is thinking about is how she looks on camera. Beverly and Dirk are doing it every chance they get just because they're bored. And even Mr. O'Connell— he's really nice, but he's drunk half the time, thinks we don't notice because of that peppermint crap he drinks. My mom is having an affair with Xanax, it makes her feel sooooo in touch with herself."

"If it's any comfort to you," Faythe said, "all she'll find in my medicine cabinet is Oil of Olay and Tylenol."

"Oh, great," said Heather. "Do you want an award?"

"Frankly," Faythe said, "all I want is to think that you and I can do our scene well together. There's a lot more I'd say to you, but I don't think you're in a listening mood."

Heather stood up and took the bowl of ice cream through the French doors and into the house. A moment later the sounds of the disposal could be heard together with the rush of running water and the scraping of a spoon.

Sylvia Lewison chose that moment to re-enter the garden. Her face was tense to the point of madness. "Where's Heather?" she said in a grating tone, as if Faythe might have caused her daughter to disappear.

"She's helping, clearing the table. Do sit down, Sylvia. Would you like some tea or coffee?"

Sylvia sank into a chair and placed her chin on one hand in a combative position. "I wouldn't want you to make a mistake about Heather," she said. "She's flippant and irreverent like any girl her age, but her talent is enormous. Heather is going to be very big, Faythe, very big. She's already demonstrated her ability at Disney. Did you see *My Favorite Otter*?"

Faythe said that she had missed that one.

"Yes, well," Mrs. Lewison's eyes skittered around the backyard as if she knew something was hidden from her. "Well," she said again, losing her train of thought. No wonder Heather was such an unpleasant kid—her mother appeared to be a maniac. She repeated her offer of coffee or tea.

"Tea, thank you." She sat at the table abruptly. Heather reappeared and lifted an eyebrow at Faythe, tossing her head in her mother's direction. "See what I mean?" she murmured.

"Heather, why don't you go in and read or watch TV for a few minutes. I'd like to talk to your mom alone."

"You think I'd rather watch TV than read, don't you? Well, you're wrong. I love to read." She went over to the bookshelf and cocked her head.

"There are more books in the little room upstairs."

"Oh, here's *The Senator's Daughter,*" said Heather, drawing the book out eagerly. "I've already read it, but there's some parts I'd like to read again."

Faythe didn't think it was appropriate reading matter for a child so young, but Heather was already curled up on the couch, nimble fingers scanning for one of the sex scenes, no doubt. Faythe went to make a pot of tea, which she then carried outdoors, shutting the French doors firmly behind her.

Sylvia Lewison seemed not to have moved in her absence.

"Sylvia, you seem distressed. Didn't things go well in Montana?" She poured the tea and watched while the other woman considered her question. "Things went very well. I'm sure Heather has told you. I would say things went unusually well. If I seem nervous, it's because of the Catalina location. Heather should be just fine, but if things went wrong at this late stage I don't know what I would do."

"Why should anything go wrong?"

"Well," she said, and Faythe was afraid she'd get stuck on that word again, but Sylvia rallied. "Heather is afraid of heights. Don't ever let her know I told you, but she's been afraid of them ever since she learned how to walk. You know the scene on the yacht, where the senator keeps jumping into the ocean with Rosie in his arms?"

Faythe nodded, thinking she didn't want to hear what would follow.

"I took Heather to a public pool in the Valley, near our home. They have a high dive there, about fifteen feet. I figure that's about the height of that boat they're renting at Marina del Ray, *The Viking Princess.* I explained it was for her own good—"

"But why? They can use a double. There's no need for Heather— "

"Yes there is. This was before she'd been cast. If I were to say that she'd need a double, that might have tipped the balance in some other girl's favor. I wanted her to be prepared for all eventualities. You should have seen her face when she stood on that diving board. White as a sheet. Now, there was nothing to worry about, you understand. She's an excellent swimmer. All I wanted her to do was jump so she'd conquer her fear.

"I told her how much better she'd feel, but she didn't believe me. In the car going over to the pool she begged me not to make her jump. 'Please, Mommy, don't make me jump'." She imitated her daughter in a squeaky soprano. "She was nearly in tears, and Heather *never* cries."

Faythe felt a profound revulsion as she stared at Sylvia Lewison.

"I just stood there, poolside, looking up at her. She knew how important it was, and there were other people waiting on the ladder, so she was embarrassed at holding them up. Finally, she did it. Jumped. Broke surface and discovered nothing very bad had happened. I made her do it again and again—

just to make sure— and by the sixth or seventh time she was jumping like a trooper. She hates it, but she won't let anyone see. That's the kind of kid Heather is. She needed me to push her, but once she saw it was necessary— " She spread her hands, a reasonable woman who was certain she'd done the right thing.

"So you see," Sylvia said, "I've been under a lot of stress. If I'm nervous, it's because I want so badly for Heather to be perfect in this role."

So this, Faythe thought, was the mythical stage mother. She'd heard of them all her life and never met one before. The mother who would do anything, short of murder, to push her daughter to prominence. Sylvia must have mistaken her look of horror for one of admiration, because she said:

"People think it's easy to be the mother of a star, a child star. They think you just sit back and enjoy that baby's earnings. I'm living proof that it isn't that easy. From the time she was toddling I was preparing her. I even sacrificed my marriage for Heather. Mr. Lewison said I should let her be a kid. 'Let her enjoy her childhood, Sylvia,' was what he said, and I fired back 'If I let her enjoy her childhood, Pete, she'll grow up to be a big, fat zero. A nobody and a nothing, and that isn't what I want for my daughter'." She drank her tea, as if the memory of all that hard work had made her thirsty.

"You're a mother, Faythe, I don't have to tell you. I hear your little girl is doing great things over at her dad's agency. If you don't think ahead, you wake up one day with a teenager who's sniffing paint and getting pregnant."

Faythe had an image of Casey sniffing paint and laughed, but she was appalled at Sylvia's assumptions that they were alike.

"Tell me," she said, "is it true that Heather can't have ice cream because she might get spots? Isn't she awfully young to worry about her skin?"

"That's just one of the tricks in my bag, Faythe. I'm conditioning her now so it'll be easier later. No pizza, no ice cream, no candy, no burgers. This way she won't crave them when she's older. Heather is enrolled in gymnastics, ballet, aerobics, and music therapy. A sound background, a good early system for building the character a star needs to survive."

There was a tapping sound at the French doors, and they turned to see Heather ask-

ing for permission to come out into the garden.

She inched out slowly with a crafty expression on her fox-like face. She held *The
Senator's Daughter* carelessly in one hand
and looked at her mother meaningfully.

"Have you been boring Mrs. McBain?"
she asked. "I think it's probably time to go,
don't you Mom?"

"Goodness, where are my manners,"
Sylvia said. "Heather, thank Faythe for the
lovely lunch."

"Thank you," said Heather, boring ice
blue eyes into her hostess's own. "I bet you
enjoyed it as much as I did."

Faythe felt like all the mothers of the
world rolled into one imperfect mother.
Casey, Tara, Daisy, Tina, and now Heather.
Didn't the mothers of the world understand
what they were doing to their daughters?
Were they all as hapless and misguided as
they had been, at some time, when they
were daughters to their mothers? Didn't it
ever end?

"You're very welcome," she said. "I'm
looking forward to working with you,
Heather."

She saw mother and daughter to the door
and watched while Sylvia eased her large

body into the driver's side of the red Toyota. She imagined their ride back to the San Fernando Valley and thought they'd be safer with Heather at the wheel. At the last moment, before the Toyota backed out, Heather turned round in her seat and waved goodbye. Her face seemed innocent and childlike, the face of a child who obediently thanked her hostess for a nice lunch.

Faythe waved back, knowing that the mother's nervousness had been prompted by a genuine emotion. Sylvia Lewison was laid low by good, old-fashioned guilt.

"Where's Tara?" Ty Gardner asked.

No one seemed to know but all agreed she'd been invited. O'Connell was hosting an impromptu party to celebrate their return from Montana. He'd had succulent barbecue brought in from a new place, Hermosa, and the delicious smell was tormenting Faythe. She promised herself a feast when she'd completed her scene, but for now she was morosely eating coleslaw, lifting the bits of shredded cabbage and shaking off the creamy sauce.

"You're nuts, Faythe," said Bev Redfox.

"You don't have a weight problem. You're not going anorexic, are you?"

"Bev, my dear, any woman over thirty anticipating a close-up thinks she has a weight problem. As soon as this is over, I'll go back to eating like a normal person."

"I'll freeze some of this for you," O'Connell said, dropping a hand on her shoulder and squeezing her affectionately. "Then when we get back from Catalina we'll have another party and stand around watching you eat."

They all looked relaxed and vivid, even glowing, after their successful time in Montana. Bev had that added glow, the one that bathes a woman with a new lover. She and Dirk held hands like kids, and Faythe could hardly bear to look at them. Bev had plaited her thick hair in two braids and wore a beaded headband, and the Englishman couldn't take his eyes off her. Even Kate was looking festive in bright red silk evening pajamas. Apparently she'd forgotten about her encounters with the formidable Heather, because she referred to her as the "poor child" when they recalled a scene in the snow that had required many takes.

Faythe envied them. They'd had ten days of satisfying work and knew it was going well, but every day that brought her closer to Catalina was a day in which she felt agonizing doubt. "I'm getting cold feet," she told O'Connell.

"Nonsense," he said. "You've no reason to be afraid."

Montana had delighted him, and he was dressed like a rancher in jeans, cowboy boots, and even a bolo tie. "This look will go down well in Donegal," he said.

"Do you always get so into your roles?" she asked him.

"Only when I like the clothes." He turned and took the hand of a beautiful woman Faythe didn't know. "This is Jill Chase," he said. "She's visiting me from London. We go way back, don't we Jilly?"

Jill Chase smiled at Faythe, her sapphire eyes taking in everything about her. She was a classic English rose, with pale brown hair and creamy skin that was showcased in her black, off-the-shoulder dress. "I knew Des when he was just a young one," she said, and Faythe realized she was the woman whose voice had awakened her on the recording machine. Of course. A woman who had no doubt once loved O'Connell and given up on him but still couldn't keep away. "I was five years old when I first saw

him," she said, "and I fancied him immediately."

Her voice was light and playful, but she
was stating a matter of fact. Faythe thought
Jill Chase couldn't be more than thirty-five,
which meant she'd been in love with O'Connell for thirty years.

"Jilly is a very good stage designer,"
O'Connell said. "Pity she couldn't have met
Betsy."

"Who's Betsy?" Jill asked.

"Was," said Faythe. "She was Ray Parnell's
wife."

Jill turned to O'Connell. "Parnell? Is he
the other man I fancy? The one with the
soulful eyes?"

"The very same," said Des. "Our esteemed director."

Like something from a drawing room
comedy, Ray came down the stairs just as
the words "esteemed director" were heard.
"I was trying to reach Tara," he told them.
"No one's seen her."

Faythe hadn't known Ray was in the house,
and as always she felt the shock of seeing him
in the pit of her stomach. But she wasn't an
actress for nothing and greeted him as casually as she had the others.

"Maybe she's had enough of us for a while," O'Connell said.

"I'm worried," Ray said. "While we were gone that damn rag *Deep Dish* did a hatchet job on her."

"I saw it." Faythe sounded more solemn than she'd intended. "It was pretty awful."

"Tara is an actress, isn't she?" Jill looked up at Ray appealingly, her blue eyes glittering. "She's probably used to it." She stood up and brushed her hair back with a graceful hand before walking off to get another glass of wine. All eyes followed her, as they were meant to, and took in the feline quality of her supple body.

"Someone has set her little cap for you," O'Connell told Ray, but Ray's mind was still on Tara, even if his eyes had been on Jill.

"Excuse us," he said to the room at large, and taking Faythe's arm, he walked out on the deck with her. He asked her to tell him what the article had said, so she repeated it, leaving nothing out. He ran his hands through his hair in that distracted gesture she remembered so well. "Oh, Jesus," he moaned, "it's worse than I thought."

"It isn't true, is it?"

"More or less," he said. "Does it matter to you?"

"If you mean does it change my feelings for Tara, no."

The material of his blue shirt looked so soft she wanted to reach out and touch it. *Not Ray*, she told herself, *just his shirt*. She was intensely aware of the waves breaking a few yards away and felt suddenly unreal. "I know of a place where she might have gone," she said. "It's the only place where she'd feel safe and protected. It's a long shot, but maybe we could try."

"Do you mean Dove House?" He looked surprised, confused. "How do you know about Dove House?"

"It's a long story." She gave him an abbreviated version, not mentioning the Marie Raymond Laundry Facility.

"I've already called Wilma," he said. "They haven't seen her."

"But she wouldn't tell you, Ray. Everything is confidential there."

"She'd tell me, Faythe. Wilma Kinnock trusts me, particularly regarding Tara." He took her hand and led her to the steps, where they sat side by side, the noise of the party in back of them and the boom of the waves before them. It was like being on an island with Ray, and it felt natural, somehow, but still unreal. She thought he was

going to explain things to her now, tell her
why Wilma trusted him, but he remained
silent. She jerked her hand away.

"Why do you have to be so mysterious?"
she cried. "Why is everything concealed with
you?"

"What do you want to know?" he asked
mildly, seeming almost amused by her outburst.

"Here's my list," she said. "Why does
Wilma trust you? How do you know Tara?
Why did you hand pick Linda Corvo as her
agent?"

"Come for a walk," Ray said. Behind
them someone had changed the music and
the voice of Annie Lennox had got Ty's wife
up on her feet and dancing. She caught a
glimpse of Bev and Dirk moving to the music— he restrained in his movements and
Beverly wild. Faythe felt a little drunk, although she'd had nothing but a Diet Pepsi,
and she allowed Ray to lead her down to
the edge of the water.

They walked, as she had done a few days
before, at the edge of the water, close but
not touching. "To take your questions in order," he said in a mock-pompous voice, "the
answer to number one is that Wilma trusts
me because I've occasionally worked with

Dove House girls. I'll show you tomorrow, if you'll let me. That answers number two. I met Tara in that capacity. Number three is very simple. When I thought Tara was ready for an agent I wanted someone who would really care about her, and Linda fitted the bill. I'm not some sinister Svengali, Faythe. I spotted a talented kid, I worked with her, and naturally I wanted to do all I could for her."

"And *The Senator's Daughter?* Did you agree to direct it for Tara's sake?"

He stopped her, gently taking hold of her shoulders, and forced her to look at him. There was little starlight and only a smudgy, three-quarter, December moon, but she could see him very clearly. His features were distinct and very solemn, as if he had something of immense importance to say to her.

"Tara didn't enter my mind," he said in a low voice. "I agreed to direct because it was a superb script of a wonderful novel. I knew I could bring it to life. I realized later that Tara might be the perfect Rosie, and I arranged for her to test. You saw them, you saw how amazing she was. How right."

"Yes." Tara had been magnificently right. "Why did you ask me to see the tests? You knew. You didn't need me to validate your judgment."

"Oh, but I did, Faythe. On the simplest level I couldn't trust myself to be objective. Do you understand what I'm saying?"

"I think so. You'd trained Tara, I guess? You'd taught her? You needed an outsider to confirm what you thought about her ability."

He bent his head until it nearly touched her, making a small sound of disbelief, a sigh. "That's part of it, of course, but it's not what I meant. How can you call yourself an outsider?" He shook her, not hard, but with enough force to make her eyes widen. "Tara reminded me of you," he said. "Not her physical self, not her history. And not her brand of pain and self-destructiveness."

"What then?" Her voice was faint and rough with emotion. She thought she could live forever and not understand Ray Parnell.

"Her gift," he said simply. "Despite everything, she was so good, so potentially great. You don't see it often, that blind, glorious, rich gift for expression. You see it in painters and writers and musicians, but you don't often see it in actors. Not in our town, anyway. It's all mixed in with power and show and greed, all the usual things, and it gets diluted and debased. I've only seen it in its most rarified form twice."

She squeezed her eyes shut against such lavish praise. She blotted him out, and only the sound of the waves remained, and from far off the voice of Annie Lennox. "Stop, Ray," she pleaded. "I looked good in a bikini and I screamed well. How can you compare me with Tara?"

He put an arm around her and drew her close. She could hear his heart beating beneath the soft material of his shirt. "I knew," he whispered. "I knew from the first time I saw you do that scene in class. It was *Look Back in Anger*, and you were playing Alison. You were this very proper little beauty from the Midwest, with a Midwestern accent you didn't know you had, but you burned right into me like an acetylene torch. You had the right stuff, Faythe— better than the right stuff— the incomparable stuff. Then skip a few decades and here's Tara doing a scene from *Camino Real*, and she's incomparable, too. I thought my heart would burst.

"One of the greatest sadnesses of my life is that I could take you only as far as *Horror Boardwalk*. By the time I had the clout to direct anything real, you were lost to me. My lost lady."

She lay against his breast in a state of agonizing emotion. She wanted so terribly to believe him, but the memory of his betrayal made her feel fragile and hurt all over again. She didn't want ever to relive those days of animal sorrow, like a dog whose master has gone away without a thought for the trusting companion who thought he would always be there.

"What are we going to do about Tara?" she said, both to distract herself and because she had horrid visions of Tara lying dead somewhere, or locked up in a police station for her excessive way of being.

"We're going to wait for Tara to come to her senses," he said. "She'll realize that she's got more ammunition than the people who want to shoot her down."

"It's really that simple, that easy?"

He kissed her closed eyelids, forcing them open. "I hope so," he said. "My lost lady, I do hope so."

The music had changed when they got back and people were slow-dancing to Natalie Cole's duet with her dead father. "Shall we?" said Ray, drawing her into his arms on the deck. "Unforgettable" sang Natalie and her father, and Faythe, not caring that Ray could feel her heart beating so hard against his own, felt herself melting into him as if all the years without him had been erased.

Her precarious happiness was interrupted when O'Connell came out on the deck with an apologetic look and said, "Sorry to bother you, but there's someone who wants to be let in. Her name is Casey, and she says she's your daughter."

She felt as thick-tongued and flustered as if she'd been wakened from a dream. "Yes," she said. "I don't know what she's doing here, but I suppose you'd better let her in."

She and Ray stood apart, the mood shattered, and waited for Casey's red Beamer to make its appearance, but when Casey came into view she was on foot. She was wearing a yellow micro-mini and looking very pleased with herself.

"Where's your car?" Faythe asked.

"I was with some people, friends. They dropped me off. I figured you could give me a ride home." She saw who stood beside her mother and said, "Hey, Ray."

"What are you doing here?" Faythe asked.

"I wanted to meet O'Connell, and I heard all of the cast was here pigging out on barbecue, so I just came. Kind of spur of the moment."

"Great timing," Ray said in an undervoice, and Faythe laughed. She brought Casey in and introduced her to the few people she didn't already know, and then to O'Connell. Casey was looking flushed and very pretty, and Faythe felt proud of her even if she had made her entrance at exactly the wrong time.

"You are your mother's daughter," O'Connell said, turning on his famous and meaningless seductive manner.

"She might disagree," Casey said demurely. It seemed clear that Casey, so used to famous people, felt O'Connell to be in a different league.

"Your daughter looks overwhelmed for once," Kate murmured to Faythe, "and I know why. She's meeting her first real movie star. We have personalities and celebrities here nowadays, but O'Connell is a star in the old sense."

Someone changed the music again and the mood altered instantly. Casey began to dance with Ty Gardner, her long bare legs weaving and pumping energetically, and Jill Chase cornered Ray. Faythe saw him shake his head no, and she knew Jill had asked him to dance. Ray only liked slow-dancing and had confided to her long ago that performing the Funky Chicken made him feel like a fool.

Even though he wouldn't dance with her, he remained talking to her, seemingly unaware when she lay one of her slender hands on his wrist while she was making a point. Faythe felt tired suddenly and wanted to go home, but she sat and talked to a man who turned out to be a member of the crew of *The Viking Princess*, the yacht where she would perform her scene off Catalina.

"The island's very built up," he told her, "but there are stretches that will look good from a distance." It was an unfortunate choice of words and set her thinking that she, too, could look good from a distance, but what about that close-up? She giggled, and then realized he thought she was tipsy.

It was very late when the party broke up. Nobody had a call the next day, and even Casey, who liked to be in bed by eleven so that she could be her competitive best the next day, showed no signs of wearing down. Just before they left, Ray detached himself from Jill Chase and made his way to Faythe. "I'll pick you up at one tomorrow," he said. She'd forgotten that he was going to show her something that would explain his relationship with Tara.

Casey sat beside her in the car, her excitement drained away now that they were alone together. The night had grown cool, and a wind from the desert blew the smell of mesquite into the car. Faythe remembered the night she and Ray had driven so aimlessly around town.

"Beverly told me that nobody knows where Tara is," Casey said. "You're all so protective of that girl, and she's utterly bogus. She's probably sitting somewhere with one of her scuzzy friends and laughing her head off."

"Don't start," Faythe said. "I'm too tired."

"It's all that dancing with Ray Parnell. Honestly, Ma, if you're going to get all romantic with someone, at least get a new guy. This makes it look as if you left Dad to take up with your old lover."

"I haven't taken up with anyone, Casey. Where's Matthew tonight?"

"How should I know?" Casey jammed her feet irritably up against the dashboard. "Damn!" she said. "Someone spilled red wine all over my left shoe. These were brand new. I got them at Thieves' Market just a few days ago, and now they're ruined."

"Can I take it that you and Matthew have had a quarrel?"

"You can take it that he's history." Casey said. "He wasn't at all the man I thought he was."

Faythe looked at her daughter with sympathy, but Casey wasn't having any. She looked defiant and bored at the same time—an expression only Casey could assume.

"Did you find out that he's still married?"

Casey snorted. "No. I found out that he wasn't a partner. He was building himself up to impress me. What can I say, Mom? I make mistakes, too."

When they drew up in front of Casey's condo the streets were deserted. "Shall I walk you to your door?" Faythe asked.

"Please," Casey said.

Faythe kissed her daughter's soft cheek and said goodnight. She knew better than to express relief over the demise of her threatened son-in-law. It was a wonder that Casey had even admitted to making mistakes. She watched until the yellow micro-mini disappeared into the building and her little girl was safe.

Sixteen

Ray came for her at one, driving his Mustang with the top down. He was dressed in jeans and a baseball jacket, and he looked as fresh and relaxed as she felt worn and tired. Her mirror told her that, in fact, she looked fine, but it was as if she had contracted a case of spiritual flu.

She forced herself to ask if there'd been any word of Tara, but he shook his head. They rode along in silence, Faythe listlessly wondering if she looked as funereal as she felt in her straight black pants and quilted black Chinese jacket. Even as she'd dressed in black, like the Chekhov character who says she is in mourning for her life, she'd wondered why, and then, to counter the somber look, she'd put on bright red cowboy boots.

"You're so quiet," Ray said.

"Sorry, don't mean to be. Maybe I'm getting the flu."

He looked at her anxiously.

"Not really," she said. "I wouldn't want you to think of a green-faced Carlotta in Catalina. Carlotta in Catalina— it has a ring to it." They were making good time on the Santa Monica Freeway, but instead of turning north on 405, Ray kept on heading east. "Where are we going?" she asked.

"You'll find out," he said. "Want music?"

"Yes, the High Andes music, please. It's very soothing."

"And you need soothing." It was a statement, not a question. Soon the breathy pipes and reeds filled the car. She'd forgotten how messed up your hair can get in a convertible on a freeway, but it felt good. "What did you think of my daughter?" she asked.

"That's a loaded question. What do you expect me to say?"

"Be honest."

"All right. I've met Casey professionally ever since she went to work for her father. I could never be objective about her because she was your daughter. The parts of her that remind me of you, her mouth especially, touch me, but she seems to expend a lot of effort on not being much like you. Too much effort. In other words, she comes across like a spoiled brat half the time, and she's proud of it."

"In other words, you think she's like her father."

"No. Oddly, no. Casey has to work at being like that. It came naturally to Cal, if you'll forgive me for saying so."

"Really, Ray, you seem to think you can say anything to me. Being with you is like being in the presence of a big emotional grab bag. Reach in and— Pow!— a moment of tenderness. Reach again and— oh, no!— it's brutal truth time!"

"That's me," he said, grinning. "A big emotional grab bag." He exited off the freeway and continued in a southerly direction. It was territory that was unfamiliar to her and she lost track of the turns and twists leading her to God knew what destination. The streets were mean, heavily occupied by liquor stores and small shops still sporting riot gates from the summer of '92. Unlike the Dove House neighborhood, which seemed merely seedy and abandoned, south-central L.A. was full of electric energy, and all of it the wrong kind.

"I think I've guessed," she said to him. "You're taking me to a drive-by shooting."

When he said nothing, she tried again. "I'm going to be inducted into a gang?"

"Relax, Faythe. Don't be a wimp. This isn't so different from where I grew up. It's warmer, that's all."

He maneuvered down a side street that seemed to contain mainly derelict warehouses and slowed to a stop in front of a building that wouldn't have looked out of place in downtown Beirut. The windows on the ground floor were boarded over and heavily graffitied in what she knew were gang tags. Three young men, one hulking and dangerous looking, were congregated in front of the steel doors. The other two were smaller and slighter, but no less ominous in appearance. One had a tattoo that looked like barbed wire around his neck; the other, who had an angelic, caramel-colored face, wore one earring in the shape of a skull.

"Here we are," Ray said, raising the roof on the Mustang.

She got out of the car wondering if Ray had gone crazy, but the part of her that always remained reasonable knew that they were in no danger. Ray took her hand in his and they approached the three young men, who had been deep in conversation.

The big, mean looking one looked up and his face split into a radiant smile.

"Hi, Ray," he said. "You're early, man."

"I've brought a friend today," he said. He raised Faythe's hand, as if she were a prize fighter. "Meet Dexter, Tony, and Silfredo," he said to her. "This is Faythe, a very good actress who's come to observe."

Dexter, Tony, and Silfredo shook her hand in turns and said it was their pleasure to meet her. Ray produced a huge ring of keys from his pocket and did something complicated with a padlock. The steel door swung open, and they all passed into the building. The ground floor was rubble, and it was dark and evil smelling. Faythe thought of rats and moved quickly along, gripping Ray's hand.

They climbed up a staircase that seemed stable enough, but there were sixty-watt bulbs every five feet or so to guide them, and it felt like the approach to a medieval prison. The bulbs were ensconced in wire-mesh cages, and the smell of decay and urine was almost overpowering. Behind her, she could hear Silfredo say to Tony, "Man, I'm getting into Samuel Beckett."

Ray unlocked another door on the landing, and suddenly they were in a cavernous space, completely dark. He hit the switch and lights came on, revealing a large, clean room with a small proscenium stage constructed at one end and a circle of canvas director's chairs at the other. The floor was concrete but broom swept, and the air, although not fragrant, was at least breathable.

"Welcome to my alternate job," said Ray to Faythe. "This is my pro bono work, and I enjoy it like you wouldn't believe."

"I don't quite understand," she said.

He pushed her gently into a chair removed from the others and said, "You will in a few minutes." She sat watching while Ray fiddled with a dimmer switch and Dexter pushed a button that started air circulating. It all seemed amazing to her. Here, in the middle of devastation, was a big loft that had been wired for light and electricity. How? And by whom? There was nothing of value in the room to steal, but the fact that it hadn't been vandalized was surprising.

Another kid came in the door, a girl she judged to be about seventeen. She had her hair in locks and wore cherry red sweats. Her eyes skittered away from Faythe's and hung on Ray, desperately, until he noticed her and came over.

"What is it, Loretta? What's wrong?"

The girl said something to him in an urgent undertone; Faythe could hear the West Indian cadences but not the words. He said something back to her, and her taut shoulders began to loosen and relax, and soon she was smiling. Now a steady stream of young people began to arrive, talking and laughing, all dressed casually and anticipating whatever it was that was going to happen. A girl who looked Vietnamese pulled a script out of her bookbag and sat quietly, reading, and Faythe realized that these were Ray's students and that what was going to happen was a workshop or class of some kind.

At a given signal she didn't see, all of them took seats and quieted down, arranging themselves in a semicircle facing the stage.

"Okay," said Ray, "we're going to start. For the information of our visitor, this is a weekend workshop for anyone who has a serious interest in acting or directing. We meet every Saturday when I'm in town, and when I'm not, as happened last week, students meet informally on their own and rehearse or just get together. This workshop has no name, requires no tuition, and has existed for approximately four years.

"Some of the men and women here are

simply interested in theater and film and want the opportunity to see how things work, while others are very serious about making it their life's work. Both are okay with me— all I want is to work with young people who want to learn and maybe help them a little. Already one of our graduates has found her way into a role in a television miniseries." He stopped while shouts and cries of "Tara— All right!" rang out.

"I don't pretend to hold out the hope that I can cast everyone who comes here. Maybe it'll never happen again, but in Tara's case she was the right actress at the right time for the right project. If the network hadn't accepted her, my word alone wouldn't have meant a damn thing." He looked momentarily flustered, and Faythe realized it was because in his last few sentences he'd been talking to her alone.

"Let's get started. Who's up first? Silfredo, I think, and Luke."

He retreated to her side, behind the students, and then, realizing he had nowhere to sit, crouched down beside her.

"This has been directed by Tran," he whispered to her. "She's the one getting up to speak. It's her first directing effort."

The girl who had been reading so seriously

addressed them in a voice so soft it could barely be heard, nervously poking her silky hair back behind each ear as she spoke.

"This is a scene from *Footpath*, an original play by James Sanford," she said. "Luke and Silfredo play brothers who are at odds with each other and always have been. Luke is Toby, the older brother who has been away for a long time, and Silfredo is Rob, the younger brother who has always been the parents' favorite."

Luke and Silfredo strode to the stage, the house was plunged in darkness, and then the lights came up on them in a passionate brotherly embrace. They broke apart slowly, and at the first line Faythe felt herself sitting forward, totally absorbed. It wasn't that the acting was so good but that both kids were working, really working to discover the bright core of each character, the nugget that would throw light on all that person's actions so that they were completely immaculate. There was none of the grandstanding stuff young would-bes often tried out, but neither was there the painfully inward-directed mumblings the Actor's Studio had once encouraged. It was just two young actors feeling their way, and it was very moving.

Within two minutes she forgot that Silfredo's voice badly needed training and that
Luke looked nothing like the dashing, wayward man he was portraying. The scene
hinged on the brothers' inability to remember that they loved each other for more than
a few moments. The younger one's resent-
ment came from being the dull and loyal
brother who had stayed at home and earned
his parents' love, and the older one was
clearly suffering because he felt he'd never
been loved. (She thought of Cal, briefly, but
Cal had no place here. Cal would no more
come to south-central L.A. to help disadvan-
taged kids than he would go to Hamburger
Hamlet with a client.)

Tran had done her job well, too, posi-
tioning her actors in imaginative ways
and— Faythe suspected— advising Luke to
underplay his character's glamor. The
scene ended with a tragic misunderstand-
ing. Each brother mistook the other's admiration for veiled contempt, and they
parted angrily.

The others applauded, and Luke and Silfredo resumed their seats.

"Good," Ray said. "Very good, Tran and
guys."

She suddenly realized that Ray had the

power to invest the tritest words with real emotion. When he said good he meant good, and when he said excellent or superb he meant that, too. When Ray was disappointed with you, she remembered, he always used to say not *could* be better but *will* be better.

The students made their comments, courteously but with real points of view on display.

"I thought," said a girl called Carmelita, "that there was too much fairness going on. It was like we were supposed to see both sides all the time, but sometimes you only see one side."

"Yes," said Dexter, with his rumbling basso voice. "That occurred to me, too. When Rob is feeling he's been used, there's too much focus on Toby."

"I think Tran did a great job," said Loretta. "I can't criticize a thing she's done."

Ray bounded to his feet and went to confer with Tran, his head bowed toward hers in passionate involvement. She nodded and went to talk to her actors. They ran the scene again, and this time the even-handedness the students had complained of vanished. This time the viewer didn't know which brother deserved more compassion, and that was exactly right. It mirrored life and had the power to remind each member of the audience of a parallel moment in their own lives.

All during that Saturday afternoon, Faythe sat entranced, remembering her own student days, when issues were discussed with an ardent intensity that had vanished from her life. How important it all seemed! How important still. She looked around at the young faces of Ray's students, not a one of whom could have afforded acting classes at U.S.C. or anywhere else, and thought it took a special kind of man to see what Ray had seen: poor kids could have dreams as extravagant as affluent ones, but they rarely had anywhere to go to put them into motion. Other people wrote checks to charity or attended thousand-dollar-a-plate dinners and wrote it off their taxes, but Ray had come to the ghetto itself and set up shop. She was sure it was his money that had wired the place and made it habitable. But best of all, in her view, nobody knew about it. He wasn't doing it so people would admire him or write him up, and she found that the most admirable thing of all.

When Loretta, she of the locks and early jitters, took the stage it was to do two monologues from *Saint Joan*. She was trembling at first, but as soon as she began to speak the shakes left her, and she became the no-nonsense peasant girl who was Shaw's idea of the saint. *Loretta may be a different color than Joan,* Faythe thought, *but she's the right age and understands the role.* When she had finished, there was a thick silence, and then everyone applauded furiously.

Slowly, Loretta began to smile. "I got it?" she called to Ray.

"You sure did," he said.

Later, before the workshop ended, Ray went around to each student and talked privately. Many eyes cut in Faythe's direction, and some smiled shyly at her, but nobody approached her. "Remember," Ray said, "we're filming next week."

When the steel door had been locked and all the students had gone their separate ways, Faythe got into the Mustang and realized her spiritual flu had gone away. She felt wonderful and wanted to tell Ray how terrific she thought he was, but the words wouldn't come.

"Next week I'll be lugging equipment in," he said, sliding behind the wheel. "Even I am not trusting enough to leave cameras here. Funny thing, no one's ever tried to vandalize the place or my car."

"What was Loretta so upset about when she first arrived?" Faythe asked.

"She had cold feet, like you," he said. "I talked her out of it. I told her that was how Tara always felt." He turned to her. "A kid like Loretta is capable of so much, but no one ever taught her anything. When she first did Joan a month or so ago, she was playing her like this brave, badass broad. She thought Joan was invincible, so she must feel invincible. I discovered she'd never read the play, only these monologues from a book of speeches. I told her she wasn't getting it and got her a copy of the play. Do you remember the scene where Joan confronts the inquisitor about torture?"

"Sure," said Faythe. "She says she can't bear to be hurt, and she'd tell them anything they wanted to hear. Then she says as soon as they stop hurting her she'll take it all back."

"That blew Loretta away. 'She's so human,' she said to me. I told her that's what made the character accessible to us—the fact that she was afraid, like anyone else, but still wouldn't save her skin."

When they were back on the freeway, Faythe asked how Tara had appeared at the workshop. "Did she just walk in one day like an apparition from Dakota country?"

"Wilma told her about it. I'm one of many services for the girls at Dove House, but not many choose to come. Wilma lets them know it's serious work, not fun, and kids who wind up there don't generally want to be actresses. Tara was the great exception."

"I think what you're doing is wonderful," she said to him. "I want you to know that."

"Thank you," he said simply. When the Mustang was back on the Santa Monica Freeway she felt herself wishing that the journey home would take longer. Even bumper-to-bumper traffic would be better than another Rayless evening. She felt open to him, chastened for her assumptions about him, and very ready to risk everything again. Everything was timing, she thought painfully, and time was against her again, because Ray would never try to make love to her just before she had to face the cameras. If something should go wrong— *but nothing, oh, please, don't let anything go wrong again*— if he upset her in any way, it could jeopardize the shooting schedule. Ray was a romantic man in many ways, but no director would ever put his project at risk for an amorous interlude.

All too soon they were rolling up to her house in the dusk, and she felt the expected loss when he took her hand formally and said, "Next time I see you we'll be off the coast of Sardinia."

"I'll be a timeless paramour," she said.

His face showed nothing as he backed out of her drive, and then he was gone.

It was little more than a luncheonette, a burger place that smelled of French fries and beer, up beyond Point Dume. Tara had asked her to meet her there, where there was small chance of seeing anyone they knew. The message had been waiting for her when she came home, and Tara's voice had said she'd be there until eight. "I know you're going to Catalina tomorrow, so if you get this message too late to come, don't worry. Mainly, I wanted you to know I'm okay. Don't worry about anything, and break a leg."

Faythe got out of her car and approached the lighted windows with trepidation. She'd passed the place many times but never gone in. She pushed open the door and looked around. It was half full, mainly kids, and then she saw Tara sitting in a booth at the end of a row. She hadn't noticed her at first, and now she saw why. Tara had covered her hair with a scarf, hiding that profusion of strawberry blonde hair beneath a red calico kerchief. In her denim jacket and farmer's kerchief she looked like a farmer's daughter out for a milkshake. Only the beautiful bones of her face proclaimed her as someone soon to be famous, someone already notorious, at least here in Hollywood.

Her face lit up when she saw Faythe. A beer and a plate of onion rings stood untouched before her. "Hey," she said, "I much like those boots: Where have you been?"

"That," said Faythe, sliding into the booth across from her, "is a story in itself. More to the point, though, where have you been? I was so worried— "

"Yeah," said Tara, "I know. It hit me how selfish I was to make you or Ray worry, not to mention Kate. But you, especially. I looked at the shooting schedule and realized it's almost time for Carlotta's big moment."

Faythe had to smile. "Thank you for even thinking about me. With all you had to worry about, I'm gratified that I even entered your mind. Are you really all right, Tara?"

"Absolutely. Don't I look all right? At first I wasn't though. I hadn't been back for ten minutes when I saw that sleazy article. My roommate had it all laid out next to my bed, with a big black arrow pointing to it on the page, in case I missed it. What consideration, huh?"

"What an awful thing to do."

Tara shrugged and picked up an onion ring. She used it more as a prop than an edible commodity. She held it up to the light, twirled it on her finger, and then returned it to the plate. She took a sip of her beer. "She doesn't know any better, really. She thought I'd be excited to see my name in print. What can I say, Mrs. McB? People can be dumb in the most amazing ways.

"The thing is, I came back from Montana feeling great. I was basically on top of the world for the first time in ages, and then I read that thing. Part of me has always expected to get caught, but when it happened I just caved. I rented a car and drove up the coast to see this friend. She lives in a mobile home and asks no questions, you know? I bought a fifth of vodka and drank till I passed out. I knew I just wanted to be unconscious, someplace where nobody would bother me."

"Oh, Tara—"

She held up a hand like a traffic cop. "I'm telling this story. I know you want to lecture me about how I shouldn't abuse myself with booze or drugs, and you'd be right, but that's beside the point right now. I woke up with the worst hangover ever, and I wanted to die. I forced myself to roll out the door of that trailer and go sit under a big old scrubby tree. A kind of calm voice came to me, like it was inside my brain, and it said: 'Are you going to let those bastards end your career before it's even started?' And it said: 'You've come so far— farther than you had a right to think you ever would. What's a silly article in some rag that's put out by envious, untalented people got to do with you? They're the kind of people you always hated in the Midwest. The ones who'll slap you down for ever thinking you could be someone special.' Do you see what I mean?"

"I see your voice was right," said Faythe.

"It was right, but more than that. It was your voice. People have been saying things like that to me for a long time, but it was always in a voice I didn't recognize. It was

Kate's voice, bless her, or this woman Wilma's voice, or Ray's voice. I respected all those people, but what did they have to do with me? One was the voice of an old movie star who couldn't understand because she'd been safe and secure for so long, and another was the voice of authority, which I never trusted, and the last one, Ray, was the voice of a man who couldn't possibly understand where I was coming from."

A waitress appeared and withdrew, seeing the intensity of the conversation. The jukebox played Sinead O'Connor's "Nothing Compares to You."

"Do you get it?" Tara bent forward with agonizing sincerity, her pale eyes gone silver. "The moment I saw you I wished you had been my Mom. I saw how Casey treated you, all flip and full of that generation gap contempt, and I wanted to slap her. I'm sorry, Faythe, but I really wanted to rough up your daughter for not understanding what a good deal she'd been given."

"Casey's father is another matter. All is not gold that glitters, honey."

Tara shrugged again, as if to say she knew it all. One hand stole up to rub her reddened eyes. "The deal is," she said, "my father used to beat me. He hit me because I was kind of good looking and he thought I was the devil's work. I used to laugh at him when he hit me with his fists or whatever came handy, because I wanted him to know he had no authority over me. That was very important. It was important for me to laugh and say it didn't hurt me or touch me in any way. But all the time, while I was the family's scapegoat, while my little brothers looked on, I had this fantasy. It was of my mother, creeping up the stairs with a warm washcloth and a bowl of hot soup. She would come and comfort me while she apologized for him. I was willing to forgive her for not standing up to his violence, as long as she acknowledged it to me.

"But she never did. Never once. She just stood by with her lips compressed in a thin line and nodded her head, as if what my father was doing was the right thing. Afterwards, she would scoot around with spray cans of bleach and mop up my blood. My blood. My mother made me feel that I was nothing more than a housekeeping problem. What product will efficiently erase Karin's inability to impersonate a suitable daughter? How can I scour her out of the Johanson family permanently?"

It was painful to hear, but Faythe thought if Tara could live it she could listen, staying silent and letting Tara get it all out. She gritted her teeth to keep from making a sound.

"The worst thing was," Tara continued, "I never knew what would set him off. There was no logic to it. The very sight of me seemed to offend him. I felt so . . . hated. So loathed. I thought of killing myself, even. I swallowed a bottle of aspirin, once, but I just threw up." Her hands flew to her mouth, seeking the old comforting habit, but as the false nails touched her lips she realized it was unavailable to her now.

"There never was a talent scout, of course. I just made that up. When you lie as often as I do it's hard to keep track."

"You ran away," Faythe said, "as anyone who wanted to stay alive would do."

"I suppose that's true, about wanting to stay alive. A person who'd determined to die can always find a way. My father had guns, but I never once thought of using them. The thing about North Dakota is there's nowhere to run to, nowhere to go. I couldn't go to my pastor, the way advice columnists are always telling you to do. My father and mother were pillars of the church." She smiled ironically. "I used to watch my old man praying on Sunday and think the same hands clasped so reverently were the ones that had given me a black eye and a split lip."

"I don't know what to say. I'm so sorry you had to grow up like that, but I rejoice that you got away."

"I think he might have killed me eventually. Everyone knew. They could see. And nobody did a thing. It was as if I was expendable. Finally I got the brother of a friend to drive me to Fargo one night, and I hitched from there. Clear across the country, and voila, a star is born." She said the last words in her old, self-deprecating way.

"What made you come here, of all places?"

Tara began to fiddle with an onion ring again, then thought better of it and fastidiously wiped her fingers. "I was standing on this two-way street in Fargo, and I told myself whoever stopped first would decide my destination. If they were going east, it was New York. West, Hollywood. To tell you the truth, I would have preferred New York, but the first one that stopped was headed west. He only took me forty miles, but he was real nice. I had a kitchen knife in my back-pack, just in case."

"Let me make a guess," Faythe said. "You acted in a school play, and discovered it made you happy. You could forget who you were for a while, disappear into someone else."

"Only partly true. I got cast in a school play— *The Miracle Worker.* I loved rehearsals so much . . . it was just like you said, I could disappear. I had all this anger to play around with, and that came in handy be-cause little Helen Keller was pissed off, too. Only trouble was one of my brothers ratted on me, and my parents made me drop out of the play."

"Why? Was acting the devil's work?"

"Exactly. Was it that way where you came from, too?"

"No," Faythe said, "not at all. I was very lucky. I guess I never knew how lucky. It makes me feel physically sick to think of you being battered. How can they do it, those awful parents? There are so many of them."

"That's what I found out when I got here, and that was good for me. I used to think I was the only one. At least I discov-ered I wasn't alone. On the street, and later, at this place where I stayed for a while, I heard stories that made mine seem mild by comparison. I found out I had something to be grateful for . . . at least my father didn't, you know, put the move on me."

"Oh, honey, you break my heart. No child should ever have to go through what you did."

It had begun to get crowded. People were waiting for a booth where two women sat ignoring the onion rings and refusing to order. "Let's get out of here," Tara said. "I feel like I'm in a fishbowl suddenly." She slapped money on the table and stood up.

It had grown dark, and they stood in the parking lot, looking at all the winking lights that danced beneath them. Faythe didn't touch Tara, sensing that she didn't want, couldn't bear, too much sympathy just now. "Come back and stay the night with me," she said.

"Thanks, but I won't. I'm headed back to my own place. I've decided to ignore that article. Let people think whatever they want to about me. I'm not ashamed of anything I did to survive." She spoke uncertainly.

"You're not the one who should be ashamed. Did your parents ever try to find you?"

"Not that I know of, and I'm glad. I imagine it was a big relief to them when I split. I've learned a lot about families like mine. Sometimes they'll pick a scapegoat and let all their rage descend on her. Or him. Someone has to do the picking, though. My father picked me and everyone fell into line."

They were leaning against Faythe's car, Tara staring straight ahead now and Faythe looking at the lovely profile of the one-time scapegoat. She knew she was supposed to think that Mr. Johanson was a sick man, mentally ill, deserving of treatment, but she could find no pity for him and others like him. She hated Mr. Johanson and his self-righteous wife and the brother who had ratted on Tara; she thought they were brutal and disgusting people and marveled that Tara could come from them.

As if reading her mind, Tara said, "When I was getting some counselling I was afraid the therapist would tell me I had to forgive my old man, 'reconcile' with him or some such bull, but you know what? She said it was all right to divorce your parents sometimes and make it final. That's what I've done. I don't hate them anymore, but I never want to see them again. Not ever."

Four teenagers roared up in an old Cadillac and piled out of the car in a jumble of long legs and awesome noise. The girls were shrieking with laughter and the boys were horsing around in the goofy, harmless way of sixteen year olds everywhere. One of the girls had long blonde hair and wore skin tight jeans and a Metallica T-shirt. She did a little dance step in the parking lot and then laughed helplessly. Her face was pretty and open, bland and carefree.

Tara stared at her without comment, but Faythe knew what she was thinking. At sixteen there'd been no horsing around, no shrieks of laughter, for her. There had been only fear and pain and self-loathing for her, and then escape to a sordid life on the streets.

"Think of the future," she told her. "You have a brilliant future if you can forget the past." She heard her words. "No," she said, "I didn't mean that. You can never forget the past, and it wouldn't be good for you to try. But you can make the present yours, and if anyone ever had more chance of succeeding, I don't know who she was."

"You're such a cheerleader," Tara said, smiling. "I'm sure gonna try. Promise."

They stood in silence for a while, and then Faythe told her about being at Ray's workshop and how the students had cheered for her.

"You do amaze me," Tara said. "You're plugged into this town everywhere, aren't you?" She turned to face Faythe for the first time. "You know how *Deep Dish* said I wasn't into men? They made it sound like my sexual preference was for women, but that isn't true. I was scared of men for good reasons, you know? The only men I knew either beat on me or wanted to see me dancing naked on a table six inches away from their faces. They wanted other things, too, but I never let myself. It wasn't because I was better, or purer, than any other girl on the Strip. It was because I was so scared. I'm not a virgin, but my experiences have been mostly . . ." she thought of the right word and then pronounced it, "yucky." She laughed out loud, and some of her pallor seemed to drain away.

"Yeah," she said, "yucky. Remember my friend with the Harley? I liked him because he was gay and never tried to touch me in any other way than a friend."

Faythe remembered Graham of college days, and her initial disappointment at their lovemaking. "I know what you mean," she said, "but you must believe me when I say it doesn't have to be yucky."

Tara doubled over, laughing soundlessly from somewhere deep inside. "You just slay me," she said. "I know, Mrs. McB. I know that. Ray Parnell is one of the people who saved my life. I worship that man. And when I got to know him I realized that there were real men out there in the world. Men a person could want and love and respect."

"Ray's a fine man," Faythe said, somewhat stiffly.

"Oh, Faythe, wipe that look off your face. I never aspired to someone as lofty as Ray. I only meant he gave me hope. Everyone knows he's yours."

"They do?"

"Oh, wake up. The man is crazy for you. All you have to do is whistle."

She felt a sense of joy spread through her at Tara's words, and wondered why her own radar wasn't enough— had never been enough— to advise her about the truth of things.

"Hey!" Tara yelled. "I have something to show you. Follow me."

She set off abruptly, her boots echoing in the parking lot. Quite a few cars had come since Faythe's arrival, and Tara wove through columns of Beamers and Mercs, pickup trucks and Land Rovers and rusted out junkers, coming to rest beside a 1966 Mustang convertible. It wasn't restored to its former glory, like Ray's, and had been painted in an uninspiring shade of olive drab.

"Mine," said Tara jubilantly. "I bought her off a kid upstate. The engine's in perfect working order, but I'm gonna have her painted candy apple red and get leather seats and a great sound system. Isn't she the best?"

"Yes," said Faythe, "the best."

"Gotta go," said Tara. "Gotta go and face the musique. I could really use a hug to speed me on my way."

Faythe drew Tara into her arms and hugged her gently, and then, as the pressure was returned, harder and harder until they were practically crushing each other. She felt the bones in Tara's long spine ripple beneath her fingers, felt the girl's frantic fingers clutching at her in desperation and hope. She tried to telegraph her wishes for Tara's happiness and success in her embrace and held on to her for dear life.

Then Tara got into her car and made a show-offy exit from the parking lot, gun-ning the Mustang's powerful engine and spinning out of sight so rapidly that Faythe felt breathless.

Seventeen

She stood in the launch approaching *The Viking Princess*, dressed in a hooded cloak. Like something, she thought, from the Middle Ages. She'd gone from her house in a car that had picked her up at 9:00 and driven her to San Pedro. At San Pedro she boarded the helicopter that would take her to Catalina Island, where another car and driver waited. She was driven to the western edge, where a launch waited to bear her off to the location. *The Viking Princess* was moored half a mile off shore, and its elegant white structure made it look, from a distance, more like a ghostly dream ship than a seventy-foot pleasure boat.

Turning to look at the receding shore, she saw that Santa Catalina Island would indeed look like Sardinia from half a mile away. The scene scouter had discovered a stretch of coast that was relatively undeveloped. The island itself was so built up it resembled a resort one might find anywhere, but just here there were rugged shoulders of land brooding above the sea, and the scrappy vegetation had the gray-green look of Mediterranean seacoasts.

The hooded cloak was to protect her from the elements. She was fully made up by Lisbet, who had been waiting for her at a rented condo on the western coast. This was, Lisbet had explained, because she didn't care to practice her artistry on a moving boat, although she would be available for touch-ups. Under the cloak she wore a one-piece bathing suit, rather sedate, because the time period of the Sardinia shoot was long before thongs or high-cuts had become popular. It was a bronze silk, designed especially for her, which was intended to bring out the gold in her brown eyes and emphasize the creamy whiteness of her skin. Even her skin was not her own, since Lisbet had applied full body makeup.

Lisbet was sitting directly behind her, holding the wig box on her lap and looking distinctly unhappy. All of the irritating characteristics she had displayed at the long-ago party at Kate's had vanished, buried beneath Lisbet's conviction that she would become seasick on *The Viking Princess*.

Faythe was an excellent sailor and harbored no such fears. All of her fear, which made itself felt as a pit of ice in her stomach, was centered on the feeling that she might somehow fail Ray, fail them all. How or why she couldn't say, but it was the normal fear of a person who hadn't faced the camera for many, many years.

Calm yourself, she instructed. She busied her mind by cataloguing the whereabouts and methods of arrival of everyone involved in today's shoot. Ray had been here since last night and was presumably on the yacht now, unless he was in the smaller boat moored alongside the *Princess,* sizing up the shots with his cinematographer; there would be two sets of cameras, one for the action on the yacht and one for the sequences where the senator jumps repeatedly into the sea, his daughter in his arms.

Heather. Heather, who feared heights. She and her mother had come by public boat, choosing a two-hour journey over the twenty-minute one by air for reasons Faythe knew all too well. O'Connell had been here for a day, sailing over with the crew from Marina del Rey. The extras— there were only seven— were presumably milling about on deck, having taken an earlier helicopter. Faythe's Moroccan caftan of gold cloth, which she would wear over her bathing suit in the last scene, was even now hanging somewhere below decks. Having gone over every point of the logistics of it all, she couldn't shake the feeling that she was being borne ever closer to her destiny as they drew close enough to make out actual people. She could see Heather pestering one of the grips, and at the tail of the ship was the unmistakable, charismatic figure of Desmond O'Connell, gesticulating and calling something over to the other boat. And there, the person Des called to, Ray. His head was bent over a camera, and even as she looked he raised his head and lifted a hand to her in greeting. His hair was blowing in the breeze, and he looked vital and very much in command. She raised her own hand in reply and knew her dramatic entrance upon the scene made her seem like a figure of legend.

Figures of legend, however, were not obliged to climb ladders up to the deck of ships dressed in long, billowing cloaks. The hem of the cloak caught on the steps, making her ascent dangerous, so she shrugged out of it and mounted the ladder in her bathing suit, acutely aware of her vulnerable flesh and the eyes on it. Behind her came Lisbet, cursing under her breath as she clutched the wig box to her chest and grasped the handrail with uncertain fingers.

"Ahoy, there!" shouted Heather snottily as Faythe came tottering over the top. She wore an oversized T-shirt over the bathing suit Rosie would be filmed in and was clutching a copy of *Cosmopolitan*.

The deck was vast and very beautiful, with teak floors that demanded bare feet or sailor's shoes. The scene had already been set up: a built-in bar with slim guardrails to keep the bottles of tequila and vodka and scotch from pitching forward in rough weather. Banquettes on two sides of the bar, and anchored tables with graceful captain's chairs strewn around. This was where the extras— the grown-ups behaving hedonistically while little Rosie was ignored— would tinkle the ice in their glasses and personify the rich guests partying with the senator in the late afternoon. It was just noon now, and Faythe reckoned that they'd be there as long as the light held. Sea birds dove and screamed, the yacht rocked soothingly on the swells, and the sun looked like it would hang in for the duration.

Immediately, Lisbet gestured for her to go down below. Touch-ups were necessary, and the adjustment of the wig. The wig was very important, because the breezes off Catalina were not necessarily the breezes conjured up by Angie's wind machine.

Below decks, *The Viking Princess* was the last word in luxury. Faythe found herself in the dining room, where her Moroccan caftan hung on an improvised rail over the door. She had a brief glimpse of the galley, where a chef was preparing seafood salad at a long table. Most shoots were catered, but *The Viking Princess* came complete with its own chef, a part of the deal.

The Princess had once been owned by Gregory Gifford, a movie star of O'Connell's vintage, and after Gifford's death it had been bought by a racecar driver who'd grown sick of the United States and moved back to Australia. The next owner was a Wall Street mover who'd been convicted of insider trading and gone to a country club jail for a few years. His wife had hit on the brilliant idea of renting it out to movie companies and rich thrillseekers, and ever since *The Viking Princess* had never known a dull moment. Moviegoers had seen her again and again, but by tacit consent they saw her fresh each time. She was lavish and beautiful enough to reinvent herself each time she sailed into the public consciousness.

Lisbet pushed her into a chair and began to retouch Faythe's makeup with a small sponge. "You're going to love the look I'm giving you," she said for the third time. "I call it the Luscious But Costly. Anyone who wants to get close to you is going to have to pay big money."

"I don't think Carlotta is a call girl, Lisbet. She's more your basic paramour."

The dining room was a formal one, equipped with a long mahogany table and twelve chairs. It was papered in the palest of green silk brocade and there were six silver candelabra. It seemed a pity that the movie would use nothing of the yacht but its deck. She tried to imagine what it cost to rent *The Viking Princess,* while Lisbet went on about Faythe's excellent bone structure, ruining the compliment by saying that most women her age suffered from "sinking nose syndrome."

Now Lisbet was fitting her wig, making minor adjustments to Angie's artistry. "Wardrobe made a change in the caftan," she said.

"They wanted more leg to show." A long slit had been made on one side of the beautiful garment, which ran all the way up to the hip. Lisbet produced a velvet pouch and told her to open it. A small but exquisite bracelet of emeralds and yellow diamonds spilled into her hand and she looked up for an explanation.

"Boss man told me he wants you to wear it on your ankle." She clasped the vivid band around Faythe's ankle and said: "That's a good paramour touch, don't you think? An ordinary woman would wear it on her wrist, but a paramour is so used to jewels and stuff she just slams it on her ankle. No big deal."

"Ray told you he wanted me to wear this?"

Lisbet nodded. A gofer entered and began to spread a long cloth over the dining room table. The extras had done their own makeup and were coming below to pass muster with Lisbet. She had just slipped into her caftan when they came in, four women and three men, the men in white trousers and polo shirts, the women in long sarong-like skirts and bikini tops, except for one actress who wore green shorts and a halter-neck top.

Green shorts looked at Faythe and said, "You look absolutely gorgeous, dear. I see you don't remember me, do you? I was your daughter's fifth grade art appreciation teacher."

"Well, my goodness," Faythe stammered. "Hello. Nice to see you again."

That was the way it went in Hollywood, she thought, going up above for light meter check. Your former caterer became a household word, and your daughter's art appreciation teacher showed up on location off Catalina, doing a little extra work. The star of your vehicle was a former runaway, and the director your one-time lover.

Ray was back on the deck of *The Princess*, and when she appeared he stopped what he was doing and stared at her with a look that was almost sinful in its intensity. Then he smiled with delight and shook his head like a puppy emerging from the water. She walked toward him, her bare feet warmed by the sun-soaked deck, aware of the slight stricture round her ankle. It would have been a classic moment, but she knew there were no classic moments on a location shoot. Before she'd gone five feet there was a shout from the cinematographer, and Ray bounded over to the rail.

It would be hours before they shot the scene. It was all coming back to her—the hours and hours of waiting to get three minutes on film.

"Hit me," she told O'Connell. He dealt her an eight of diamonds, and she slid it into her hand with a poker face. They were playing seven card stud, she and Des and three crew members, sitting at one of the tables on deck.

Immediately the crew member she'd met in Malibu folded his hand. "Three diamonds showing," he said. "I'm out."

O'Connell dealt himself another card, folded it into his hand and looked pleased. Two jacks were showing, and he wanted everyone to think he'd added another. Crafty old Irishman. "See you and raise you," he told her, shoving five *Viking Princess* coasters into the pile. Since they weren't really playing for money—the crewmen couldn't afford to go up against O'Connell, and neither could she—each coaster represented a mythical thousand dollars.

Faythe had, in fact, been dealt the fifth diamond and had a flush. She had never been very adept at poker and tried now to remember how high a flush ranked. Pretty high, but could it beat three jacks or a possible full house?

While she was pondering and trying to look inscrutable, Heather and her mother strolled over to the table. Sylvia Lewison approached deferentially, but Heather bounced to a position just behind Faythe.

"You have so many diamonds," Heather announced. "Three showing and two in your hand. Is that good?"

Faythe's partners gave out a chorus of groans and O'Connell roared with laughter. "Is that good?" he shouted. "Is that good? That, my darling daughter, is a flush, and I fold."

Faythe turned to look at Heather, whose expression smacked of pure malice. "You've just cost me, oh what . . . five thousand dollars? Loose lips sink ships, Heather."

The child looked gratified but scared. "Really?" she asked. "Did you really lose five thousand dollars?"

Instantly, Faythe's irritation evaporated. Heather was a child, one who was afraid of heights and would be compelled to perform terrifying feats today. "No," she said. "We're just playing for fun, to pass the time. You haven't done anything wrong, Heather."

"Strictly speaking, that's not true," O'Connell said. "Come here, child."

Heather came to him obediently, and Faythe saw that she adored him, even as she noted his faults. It was too close to their fictional relationship, and Faythe felt a stirring of uneasiness. She turned away, looking at the coast of Catalina hovering above the blue-green ocean like something from a dream, and thought of fathers and daughters. Casey and Cal. Tara and her brutal father, a pillar of the community. Heather and the father who had left when his wife's ambition proved too unbendable for him to stand.

But O'Connell was simply giving Heather a lesson in sportsmanship. His soft Irish voice was telling her that games of chance depended on the honor of all the participants. He knew very well that she had known what she was doing, but his tone didn't reveal it. He was giving her a little civics lesson, and Heather was listening.

"I'm hungry," Heather whined. "I haven't had anything to eat since dawn practically."

"Run down below," O'Connell said. "Jules

will give you something. You'll find him in the galley, and tell him I sent you."

Sylvia Lewison became agitated, simpering and obsequious toward O'Connell, but determined to play a lionhearted mother protecting her daughter. "Heather must keep to a special diet," she said. "I'll just go down to supervise things."

"You will not," he said. "Heather will go down and satisfy the normal appetites of a ten year old, and you, Madame, will join us at poker. The game is dealer's choice, and each coaster stands for a thousand clams." He shuffled the cards and passed them along to Faythe, who was the next dealer.

Sylvia Lewison took a seat, smiling with Xanax-induced good will, and prepared to become a player. Her daughter scuttled below decks with a happy smile directed at O'Connell. Escape!

"Is it a good thing to have three kings?" Sylvia asked.

"Action!"

The senator and other guests were at their leisure on a beautiful white yacht moored off the coast of Sardinia. The senator, a drink in his hand, was chatting to two women, but his eyes were elsewhere. One man was dancing by himself, clearly under the influence of illegal substances; another woman was sunning herself, stretched out flat on her stomach, wearing only the bottom of her bikini. Pan in the direction of the senator's gaze, and there is Carlotta, a mysterious woman lying back in a deck chair, neither sunning nor taking part in the festivities. She is apart, aloof, her head arched back and her auburn hair spread over a pillow like a satiny mantle.

Laughter. A few blips of half-heard dialogue. A long shot of the sea and rocky coast. A pretty child comes up from below and clearly wants attention. She wanders about, looking longingly at her father, but the adults are paying no attention. The little girl walks toward Carlotta and sits quietly on a deck chair near the older woman.

Slowly, very slowly, the woman sits up and removes her dark glasses. Extreme close-up. "I'm sorry," the child says. "I didn't mean to disturb you." There is a ghost of a smile on the woman's face as she considers the child. "You feel lonely, don't you?" Carlotta says, and when the child nods she says, "You've come to the right person. I'm an expert on loneliness."

The camera draws back to reveal the whole scene; at the edge of the action the child and the enigmatic woman are revealed to be deep in conversation. A white-jacketed servant appears with fresh drinks, and the man who had been dancing by himself, is now talking frantically to the others. Cut to Carlotta and Rosie. Carlotta says: "You'd like to go in the water, wouldn't you?" When Rosie says she would like to swim, Carlotta says calmly, "Tom, your daughter would like to swim now." Even though she hasn't raised her voice the senator is so alert to it that he gets to his feet immediately.

He throws off his shirt and calls to his daughter. He is obviously proud of his body, still firm and well muscled in middle age. We feel his power as he summons the child and, by some predetermined signal, she leaps into his arms, giggling. Close-up of father and child. Close-up of Carlotta, looking on.

"Cut!"

A wasp or hornet is circling over one of the extras, and she is grimacing as she tries to shoo it away. The extra playing the servant kills the insect with a rolled-up newspaper.

"Take two."

Again Rosie leaps into her father's arms, but this time one of her small, sharp heels catches him in the solar plexus and doubles him over for a moment. When he's caught his breath they do take three, and this time the jumping scene goes flawlessly. Faythe has schooled herself not to appear to notice any expression of terror on Heather's face; in any case, any fearful look might be quite appropriate. The senator, cradling his daughter tenderly, walks to the divide in the railing where the ladder is, and then, instead of descending it, leaps into the Tyrrhenian Sea with her, and the camera crew on the smaller boat records it.

"Cut!"

There has been a technical difficulty, and the scene will have to be shot again. There is a long break while O'Connell and Heather are made to seem dry again. An assistant of Lisbet's has to blow-dry the girl's hair back to its former condition. All in all, the leaping into the sea scene is repeated seven times, with the actors in slightly different positions, since the senator and his little girl indulge in this odd sport for hours.

Ray is careful to be considerate to Heather. Is she cold? Tired? Would she like a longer break? But the child is a real trouper. On the sidelines her mother watches, impassive behind dark glasses.

Most of the scenes are repeated. Faythe sits up from her deck chair again and again. She removes her own dark glasses over and over, aware that the unveiling of her eyes is an all-important moment. After what seems like days, the jumping into the sea scenes have been shot to Ray's approval, and O'Connell and Heather are once more made dry. They must appear to be baked by a fierce Sardinian sun . . .

It was now, in fact, late afternoon, the time Ray wanted for the final scenes on the yacht. Faythe went below to get into her caftan, massaging her stiff neck which hurt from all that arching. Lisbet was arranging Heather's hair for the scene in which the overexcited child would be lost to the world on the deck.

"You were terrific," she said to Heather. "You didn't complain once."

"That's what I'm paid for," Heather said laconically. And then, "Do you really think it went okay?"

"Better than okay."

Heather got out of the chair after Lisbet reapplied strong sun block to the exposed parts of her body. She was wearing a T-shirt over her swimsuit, and Lisbet cut it off to avoid disturbing her hair.

Next Lisbet removed Faythe's wig so she could drop the caftan over her head. The garment settled around her in a whoosh of perfumed movement. She experimented with the slit that revealed her leg, and realized that she and O'Connell would have to experiment in finding the most becoming position in which to dally for the camera. Lisbet retouched her, fiddled with the wig, and then sent her up top.

"Come to my lecherous arms, paramour," he said, reclining on the same deck chair where her character had earlier shown kindness to his character's daughter. He was now wearing a heavy white terry robe and managed to exude an aura of decadence and glamor.

"It's hot," he whispered to her. "We've had a long afternoon, bored out of our skulls while I played with the child. Now she's safely asleep and the others have gone below, and we can safely indulge in our passions."

"If you say so," she said, settling between his knees. It was one of the great secrets of the movie business that actors playing sexy love scenes were usually in a state of mind so far removed from sensuousness that they

were longing for it to be over. Creaky necks
and tired limbs and weary voice boxes had
to be summoned, once again, to go the
mile. She settled back against his chest and
found that her head had no place to go, or
no place where the camera could find her.
She lay her head against his shoulder, and
bits of her wig were caught by the breeze
and splayed against his lips.

Heather was already in place, a small figure sunk in exhausted sleep on the deck,
curled into a fetal position at first. Faythe
and O'Connell were still trying to find a
comfortable position in which to enact fore-
play between a charismatic U.S. senator and
his mistress.

"I think," said Ray, coming over to them,
"if we have Faythe on the deck and you,
Des, on the deck chair, it will be better."

"How do you know?" O'Connell said.
"Old hand at this sort of thing, are you?"

Faythe positioned herself on the deck, sitting at O'Connell's feet, and saw that Ray
was right. Now she could lean her head on
her lover's knees and stretch her leg out,
the one that protruded from the gold caftan. Hands appeared to bare her leg at the
right angle, and she saw the emerald and

yellow diamond ankle bracelet winking at her in the light of the mellowed sun.

"You'll have to hitch up a bit, so I can touch your thigh," O'Connell said apologetically.

Perfect, but uncomfortable. She was half suspended in his arms, one of his hands beneath her breasts and the other stroking her bare thigh.

"We'd better get this in one take," she told him. "Otherwise I'll get a cramp."

"Quiet now," he murmured. "I have to get in the proper frame of mind. No cracking wise, darling."

"Action!"

The camera is on Heather, asleep on the beautiful, teak wood deck. Her small body is seen from a height, the body of a little girl sunk in exhausted sleep after an afternoon she has failed to understand. Aerial view of Rosie, crumpled on the deck, surrounded by the sea and backlit by the harsh coast of Sardinia.

Only a few feet away, Carlotta and the senator are engaging in the preludes to lovemaking. He bends to kiss her hair, her face turns up to him and their lips meet lightly, teasingly. The child stirs in her sleep and moans softly. (She is dreaming of something that happened in Montana, which has already been shot. It will be mixed with a montage of today's jumping scenes.)

The senator's hand presses just under Carlotta's heart; his other hand caresses her warm bare thigh. His eyelids are at half-mast with passion that is slowly building, but Carlotta, while clearly aroused, is wearing an enigmatic look. Her lips are parted, but her eyes are clear. The little girl wakens. Close-up of her face. For a moment she doesn't know where she is. It is very quiet now, because all the guests have gone below it seems. She hears only the ceaseless lap of the waves and the wind.

She half sits up and turns. Have they all abandoned her? But no, Daddy and the woman who had been kind to her are snuggling together. Daddy doesn't see her because his lips are pressed to her shoulder, but the woman, Carlotta, sees her. Daddy's hands are moving on Carlotta's thigh, inside the lovely golden dress. The little girl is staring, unable to look away, and Carlotta meets her gaze. Close-up of Carlotta, who has the saddest eyes the child has ever seen.

Close-up of Rosie, who is flushed now. (Heather really can blush at will.) It's a cut and wrap. They have managed to do it in one take. Everyone is very quiet. Sylvia Lewison moves forward to claim her daughter. O'Connell kisses Faythe's hand and goes off to pour himself a stiff shot. Ray and Faythe look at each other as if they can never stop.

The launch took people away in stages. First Heather and her mother and two extras, then Lisbet and two more extras. Little by little, *The Viking Princess* was being deserted. O'Connell got a ride with the cinematographer, saying he had mysterious business to attend to on Catalina Island.

Faythe felt lightheaded, but she didn't want to eat just now. The sun was setting over the Pacific, suffusing the air with a coppery glow. She allowed Ray to pour her a glass of chilled white wine and sipped gratefully. It was over and she hadn't disgraced herself. It seemed a miracle that the final scene had been accomplished in one take.

They didn't speak, just watched the sun sinking, sitting together where the extras had so recently played at being decadent jet setters. After a while, she rose and went below deck to the deserted dining cabin. She took off her golden caftan and hung it in its place. Then she removed the wig and brushed out her own hair. She wanted Ray's hands to encounter nothing artificial the next time he touched her. The last thing was her bathing suit. She got out of it, but then realized she had no change of clothes. Her clothes were on the island. She stood naked in the dim room, still wearing the ankle bracelet of precious gems, and then put on the full length cloak she'd worn on the way over.

Then she climbed back up to the deck, where Ray had moved to the rail and was staring out to sea.

"I'm not Carlotta," she said. "It's just me."

He turned and looked at her hungrily, his hazel eyes gone dark. "I don't want Carlotta," he said, so softly she could barely hear him. The wind had risen and dark was coming on. "I just want you," he said.

She came to him and stepped within the welcoming circle of his arms. His hands tilted her face up to him and he said, "I love you, Faythe. I've always loved you." Their lips met with a sweetness and urgency that made her grow strong and supple even as she felt the weakness in her legs. She felt his tongue in her mouth and she sucked on it, tasting wine and his sweetness. His hands stroked the length of her back and seemed to burn through her cloak. He picked her up in his arms and carried her to the long deck chair, where she lay back and waited for him impatiently. He parted the cloak and fell on her, kissing her breasts, her belly, her thighs, and she laughed with joy, her fingers in his floppy hair. This was what it was like to feel alive, she thought. She drew him up to her and clasped the beloved body, remembering each of the quivery muscles in his long back, just as he seemed to remember her body, which he had memorized with such love so long ago.

He was murmuring her name, planting little kisses on her eyes and lips, breathing harshly now, and she opened to him with a sharp cry of pleasure. He seemed to fill her entire body with warmth and fire as they moved together ecstatically. Both wanted to prolong their pleasure, but they had been apart too long and it was impossible to wait. She felt the searing pleasure of her climax claim her with an almost frightening fierceness, and felt the warm tears of happiness sliding down her face. She was liquid everywhere, and he kissed the salt from her cheeks, tasting it with his tongue.

She lay wrapped in his arms for a long time, until the first star came out.

"You know," he whispered to her, "there's a very comfortable master cabin on this boat. A place where a guy could make love to his girl the way she deserves to be made love to."

"I'm sure it's lovely," she whispered back, "but I can't let you go just yet. I've missed you so much."

"I want you for keeps, Faythe. I never want to be away from you again."

"You said that a long time ago," she reminded him, "and I believed you."

"I meant it then, and I mean it now. The difference is, I'm a tame old codger this time around, and you won't ever have to doubt me."

"Some codger," she said, pulling at his hair. "I wouldn't exactly describe you as tame, either."

"Domesticated," he said.

Presently they went down to the master cabin on *The Viking Princess*. With its fitted carpets and king-sized bed it seemed like a suite in a five-star hotel, and only the slight rocking motion and portholes reminded her she was at sea. She lay on the big bed while Ray went to the galley, returning with a bottle of champagne and a bowl of fruit. She bit hungrily into a pear while he opened the champagne. She could smell the fragrance of flowers borne on an errant breeze, perhaps all the way from Hawaii.

When she'd eaten another pear and fed Ray a peach, she lay back down and drew him to her. "Now," she said, "you can make good on that boast."

He began.

Eighteen

"So, how did it go?" Casey sounded pre-occupied, as if she weren't really very interested, but Faythe knew different.

She carried the phone out beneath her jacaranda tree and assured her daughter that it had gone very well, perfectly, in fact, and all the while she couldn't stop smiling. She felt so unlike the woman who had gone to Catalina. That stiff and frightened person had become relaxed and looser in her movements; her body actually felt different in the way she inhabited it. She mentioned none of this to Casey, of course. She wasn't sure where she and Ray were going, only that wherever it was they would be together.

"You sound so pleased with yourself," Casey said. "Secretive, almost."

"I am pleased, honey. Why shouldn't I be? The shoot went flawlessly. Well, maybe not flawlessly, they never do, but very, very nicely. Why shouldn't I be pleased?" she repeated, really wondering if her daughter grudged her any joy.

"No reason, I guess. Only, I don't want you to think this is going to turn your life around. Hear what I'm saying? It's only a cameo role in a TV movie, Ma. You're not going to wake up the day after it's released and find a hundred offers to work."

"Let's be realistic, shall we? Forget the hundred offers, but how about a few? Does that seem so unrealistic to you?"

"There just aren't that many parts rolling around for women your age. Back when you so graciously allowed me to be your agent, I tried to impress that fact on you."

"Yes," said Faythe, sipping at her espresso. "You did. Relentlessly. Sometimes almost cruelly, it seemed to me."

For once, silence at the other end.

"My dear, dear daughter, allow me to tell you something. I'm pleased to have done a job of work without slipping up. If there are no offers to work, I'll be disappointed but it won't ruin me. It won't be the end of my life."

"That's good," said Casey tightly, "because I've been worried"

"Worried about me?"

"Why didn't you come home with the

others? Why did you have to stay on that yacht with Ray Parnell? It looks odd, Ma, as if you think you can do whatever you want."

"And why shouldn't I do what I want, within reason?" Instead of the old sensations of guilt mixed with hurt and irritation, she felt a need to know why Casey treated her as she did.

"You have responsibilities," Casey said importantly. "You have responsibilities to this family."

"What family is that, honey? I acknowledge responsibility for you, even though you're an adult, but that's because I love you and you're my daughter. That's forever. We're a family, you and I, and your father and you are a different family. That's the way it is, honey, and all your railing won't change things."

"Fine," said Casey contemptuously. "You're the last person I ever thought would become totally selfish, but I have to say you have. Become selfish. I was really calling to ask you where we'd have lunch today, but forget it."

Faythe had forgotten it was a Wednesday. Her choice of restaurants. "Tell you what," she said. "Instead of going to lunch, why don't you meet me at Century City? We're going to look at the rushes from Catalina. It might be interesting."

Silence again, while Casey figured. Would it be embarrassing? Would Ray be professionally inconvenienced by her presence? Was she, in fact, welcome?

"Okay," she said at last. "What time?"

She sat between Ray and Casey, watching the private screening he'd arranged for her. If he'd been surprised when Casey appeared, he didn't show it. "Whoah!" Casey shouted when Mom/Carlotta sat up on her deck chair and removed her glasses. "You look incredible, Mom." She was silent for the rest of the time, as they saw, each in their separate ways, the power and jaded beauty of the scene that told the tale of the death of innocence.

Faythe felt slightly embarrassed to have her daughter watch the last scene, with O'Connell's hand on her thigh. It was powerfully erotic, much more so than she would have imagined, but Casey said nothing. She was pitched forward in her seat, chin on her hands, looking intently at the screen. As the final image of Carlotta filled the screen, Ray picked up Faythe's hand and planted a kiss on her fingers.

When the lights came up Casey's brow was furrowed. "You were . . . I don't know. You were magic," she said.

"It's only a cameo," Faythe said.

"I had no idea she could be so powerful on screen," Casey said to Ray.

"Your mother is a very powerful woman," he said, smiling at both of them. "Excuse me for a minute. I've got to make a call."

Casey remained in her chair, obviously thinking something over. "This is going to be hard for me," she said. "I find it so difficult to admit to being wrong, and then I just get ten times more stubborn. I'm a little like Dad that way."

"You don't have to apologize—"

"Please, Mom. Just let me say what I have to say. If you interrupt, I'll lose my train of thought. Okay? I've been a real pain in the neck lately. I know it, and you know it. I was a snob about Tara—I could hear it in my voice but I couldn't stop myself. I think I was jealous because you seemed to like her so much, but none of that matters compared to how snotty I've been to you.

"When you divorced Daddy part of me knew you had every right, but the part of me that isn't very mature felt you were leaving me, too."

"Never," said Faythe.

"Shhhhh. I wanted to be your agent so I could keep you safe. That's what I told myself. You'd be safe, playing frumps and dowdy mommies. Really it was all for me, so I'd feel I had my mother back. But I can see that's not what you're about. You were never intended to bake pies on screen or plow the north forty." She sneaked a quick look at Faythe, who was laughing silently but looked slightly tearful, too.

"All that stuff I said about you having a responsibility was just garbage. You have one, all right, but it's to yourself."

Faythe hugged her daughter then, and for the first time in years Casey relaxed against her and hugged back. "I love you, Mom," she murmured.

"I love you, too, Casey." She inhaled her daughter's fragrance: French soap, Patou perfume, and beneath it the sweet, apple-like odor she remembered from Casey's baby years.

Casey broke away first. "Whew, what a love fest," she said.

"That's my girl. A few minutes more of

that sentimental stuff and I wouldn't recognize you."

"Are those Manolo Blahniks?" Casey asked, peering at the slingbacks on her mother's feet.

"Yes."

"I can't believe you're wearing an ankle bracelet."

"A momentary whim," Faythe said.

"No it's not. You were wearing it in the scene." Casey's eyes narrowed, appraising the jewelled band. "You get to keep it?" she asked.

"It's a gift," Faythe said.

"It's not very liberated to wear an ankle bracelet, Mom. It's like you're someone's love slave or something." She made the gesture of zipping up her lips. "Not my business, right?"

Faythe nodded, delighted. With any luck, Casey would remain this understanding and pleasant for at least another day or two.

"Gotta run," Casey said. "I'm having lunch with Felix Bannister at The Grill. He called right after you did, so I arranged a late lunch. Isn't that incredible timing?"

Faythe didn't know who Felix Bannister was, but she didn't say so. "Incredible," she agreed.

* * *

Ray lay beside her in her bedroom, on the bed that now seemed too small. He was selling the house in Bel Air that had been his and Betsy's and came to Faythe rather than forcing her to confront old ghosts. He was reading a script, occasionally out loud when he discovered something she would enjoy. She was making a list of all the people she wanted to invite to a party they were giving at O'Connell's Malibu house. It would be both a farewell party for him, when shooting wrapped, and an opportunity to show people they were a couple.

Ray groaned. "Listen to this," he said, reading from the script. "I didn't know how much I loved you until you left me."

"Sounds like a soap opera," she said.

"Sounds like me," he said, dropping the script and nuzzling at her shoulder. "Except I did know. I've always known. Life is a soap opera part of the time. I don't know how I've lived without you all these years. How's that? I wouldn't accept it in a script, but it's true."

"Me, too. I feel the same."

He pulled her into his arms and stroked her hair. "So much lost time," he lamented, kissing her earlobe. "We'll just have to make up for it."

"Not a bad idea," she said, stroking his shoulders. "Not a bad idea at all."